DAWN

Words and Pictures by URI SHULEVITZ

A Sunburst Book
Farrar, Straus and Giroux

 Library of Congress catalog card number: 74-9761 / Distributed in Canada by Douglas & McIntyre Ltd. Printed in Singapore / First edition, 1974 / Sunburst edition, 1987

9 11 13 15 14 12 10 8

To my parents

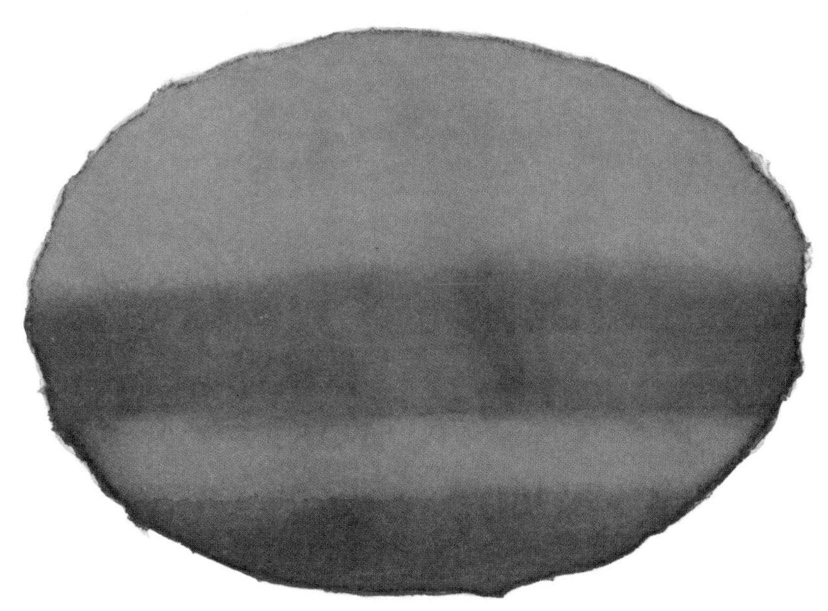

Quiet.

Still.

It is cold and damp.

Under a tree by the lake

an old man and his grandson
curl up in their blankets.

The moon lights a rock, a branch, an occasional leaf.

The mountain stands guard, dark and silent.

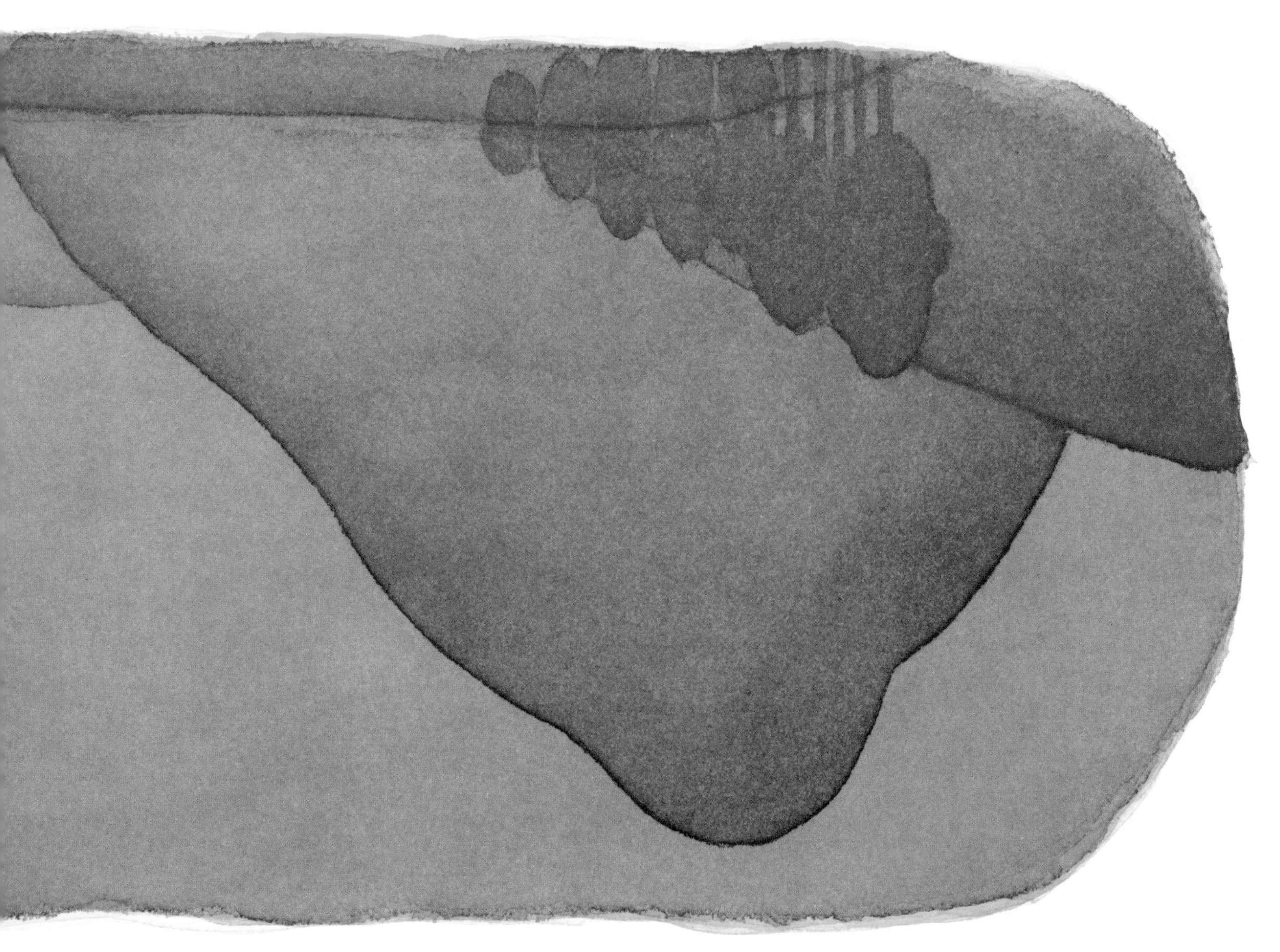

Nothing moves.

Now, a light breeze.

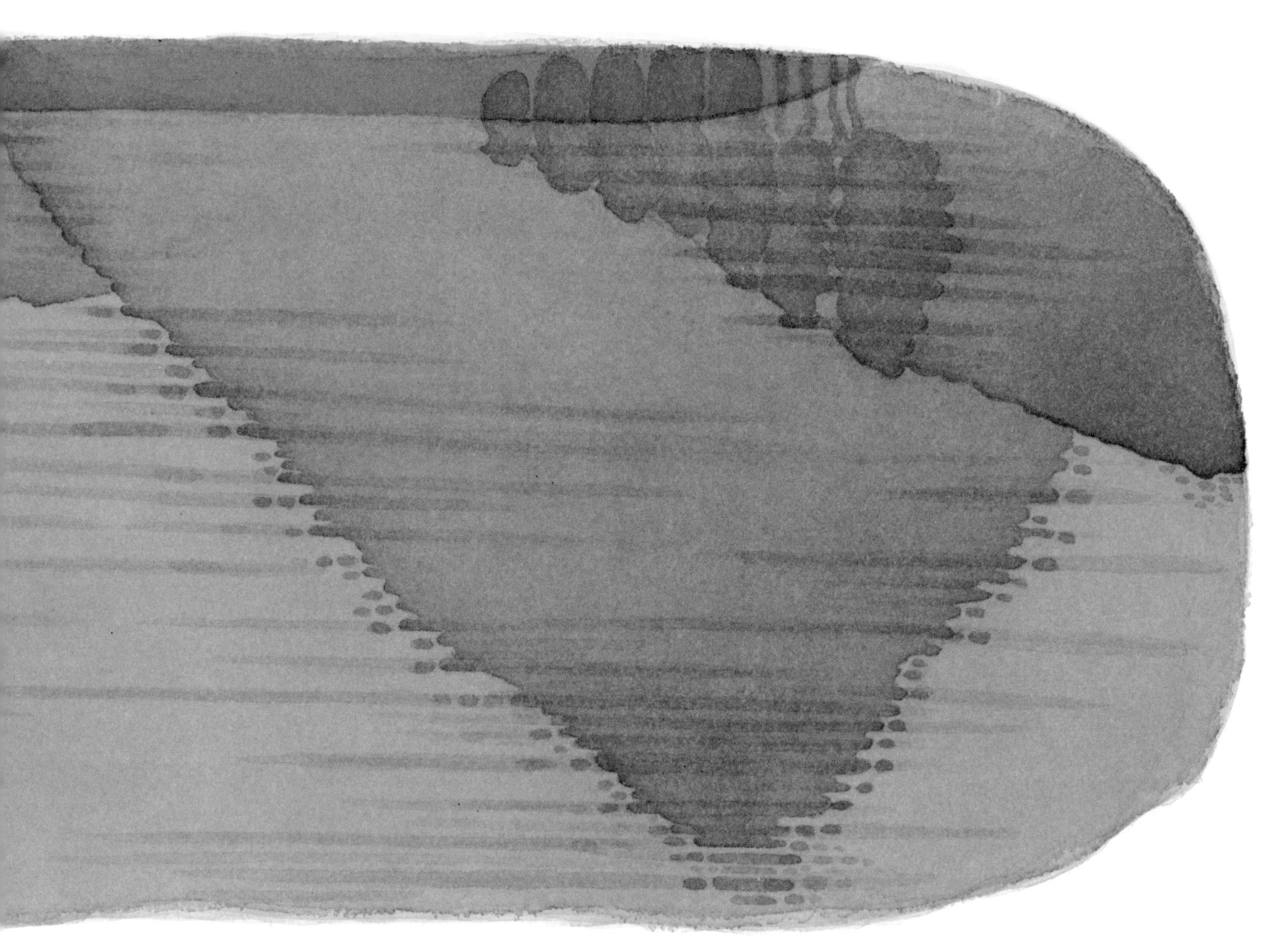

The lake shivers.

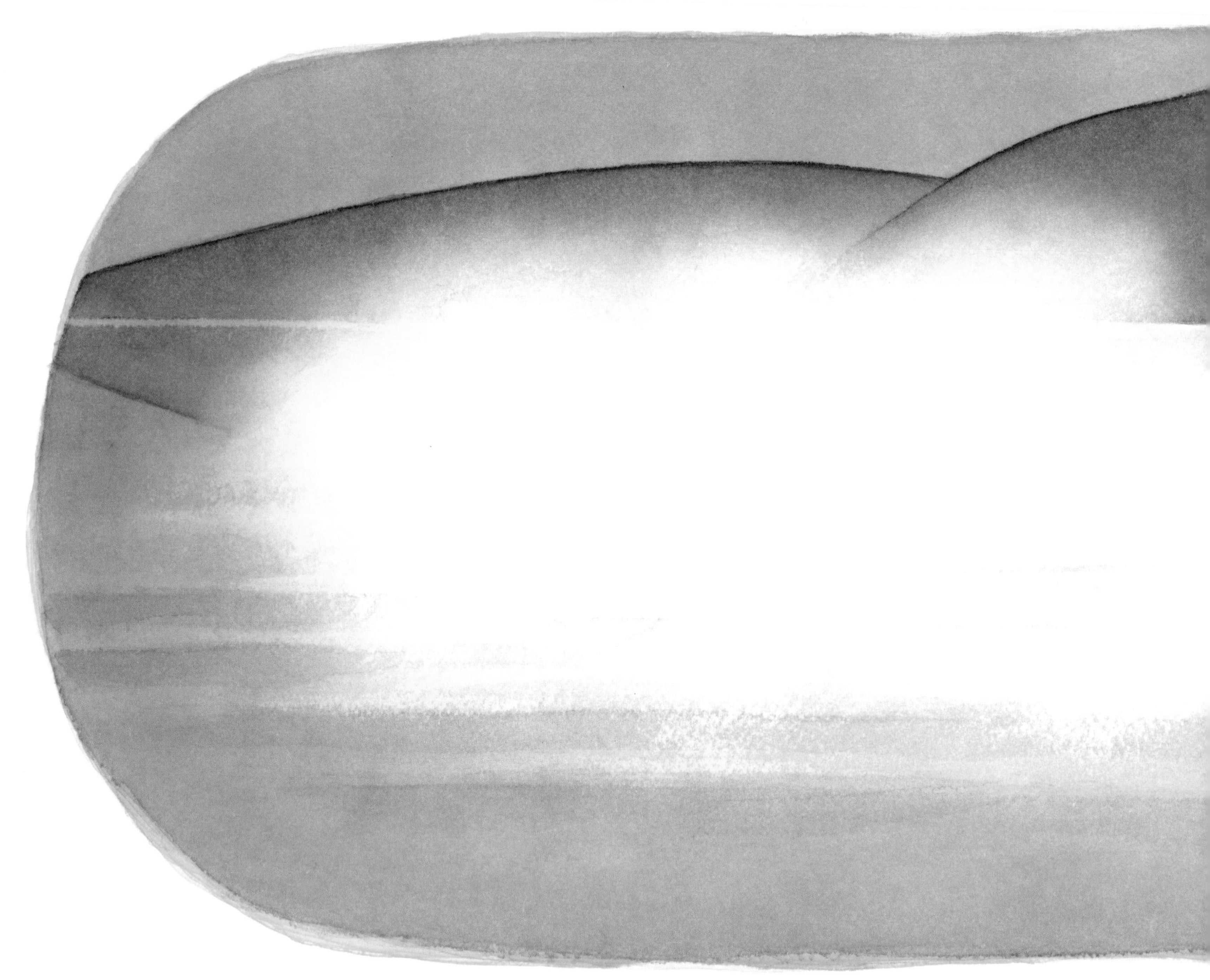

Slowly, lazily, vapors start to rise.

A lonely bat circles in silence.

A frog jumps.

Then another.

A bird calls.

Another answers.

The old man wakes his grandson.

They draw water from the lake

and light a small fire.

They roll up the blankets

and push their old boat into the water.

Alone, they move in the middle of the lake.

The oars screak and rattle,

churning pools of foam.

Suddenly

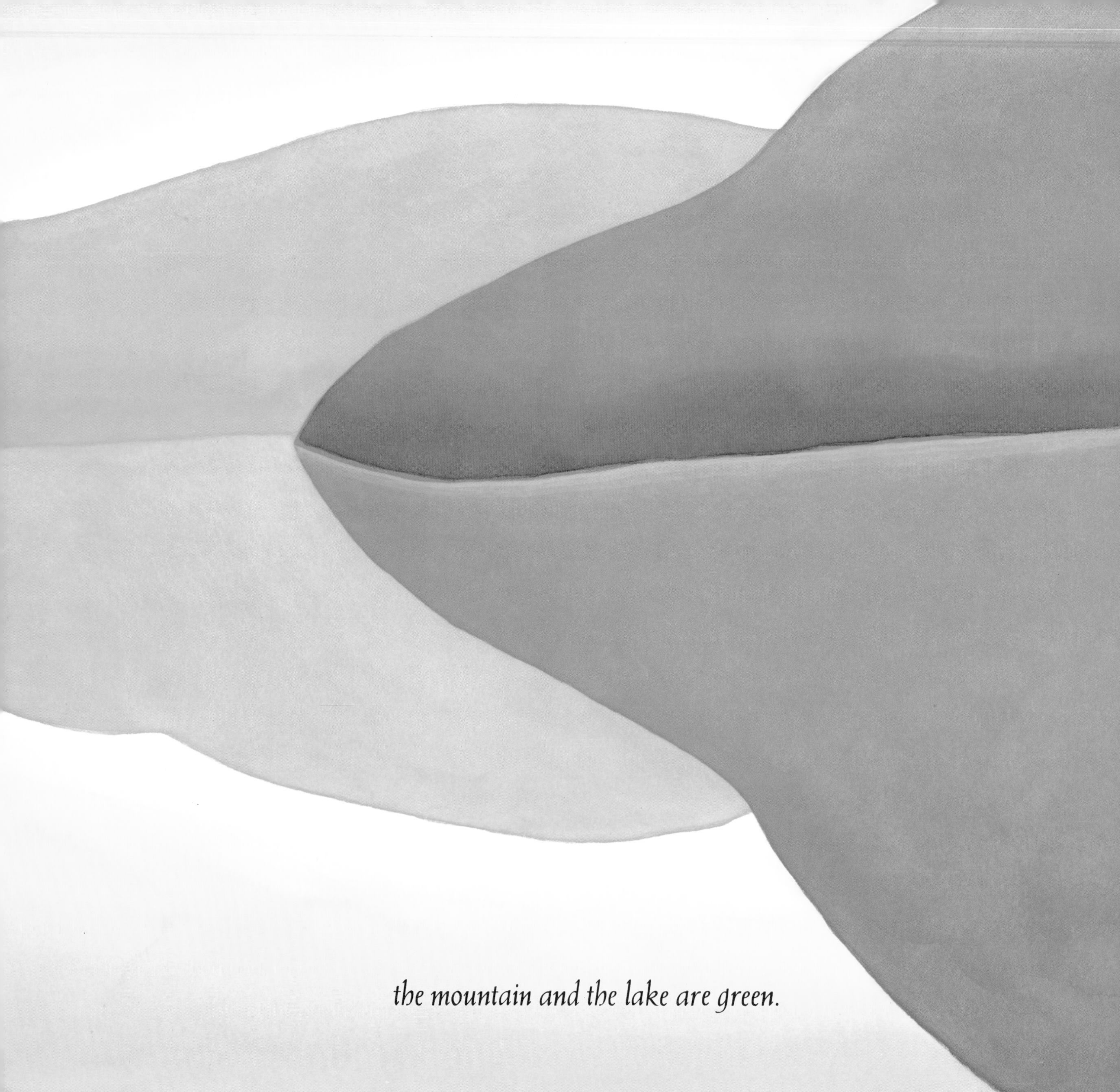

the mountain and the lake are green.

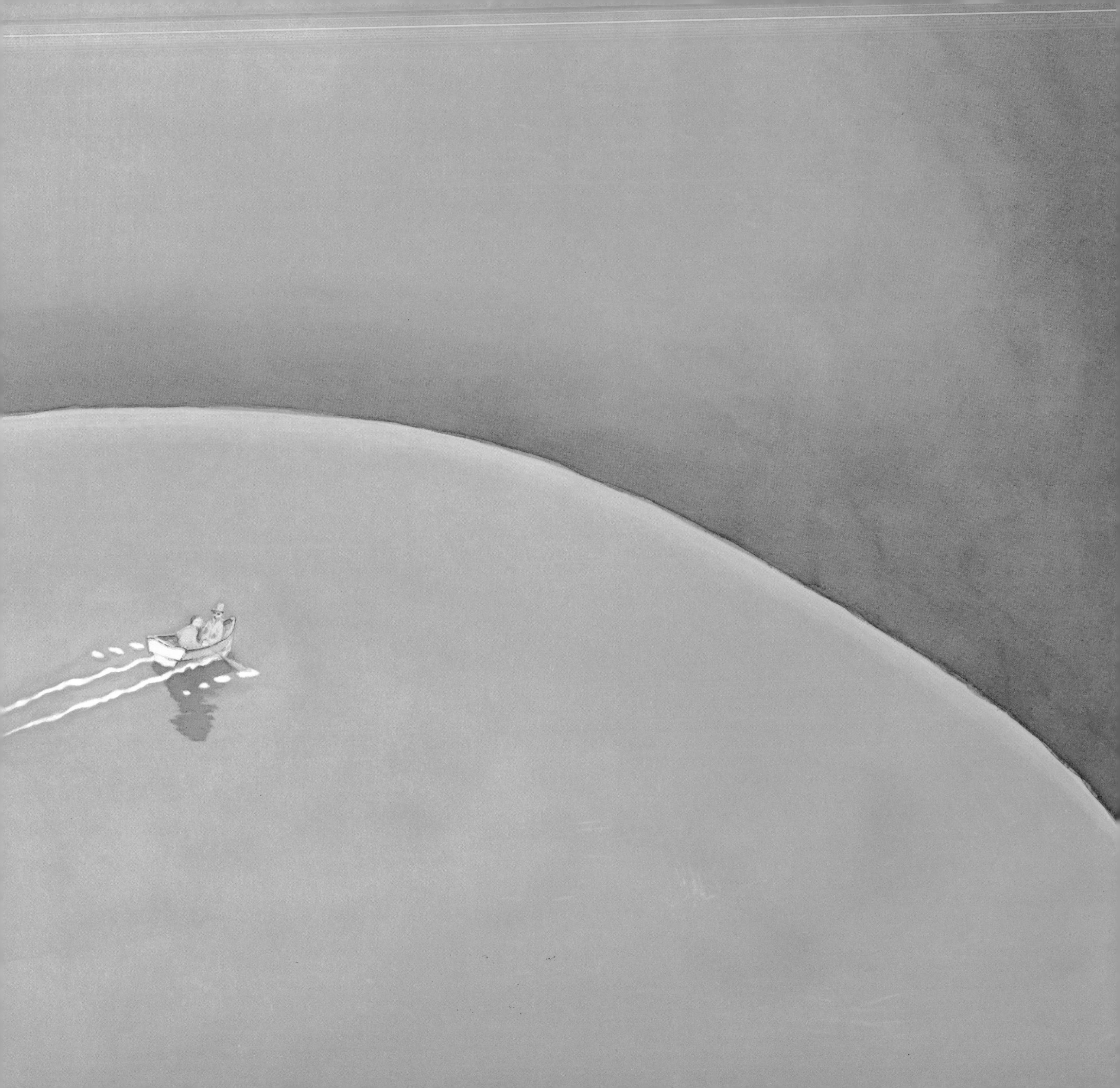

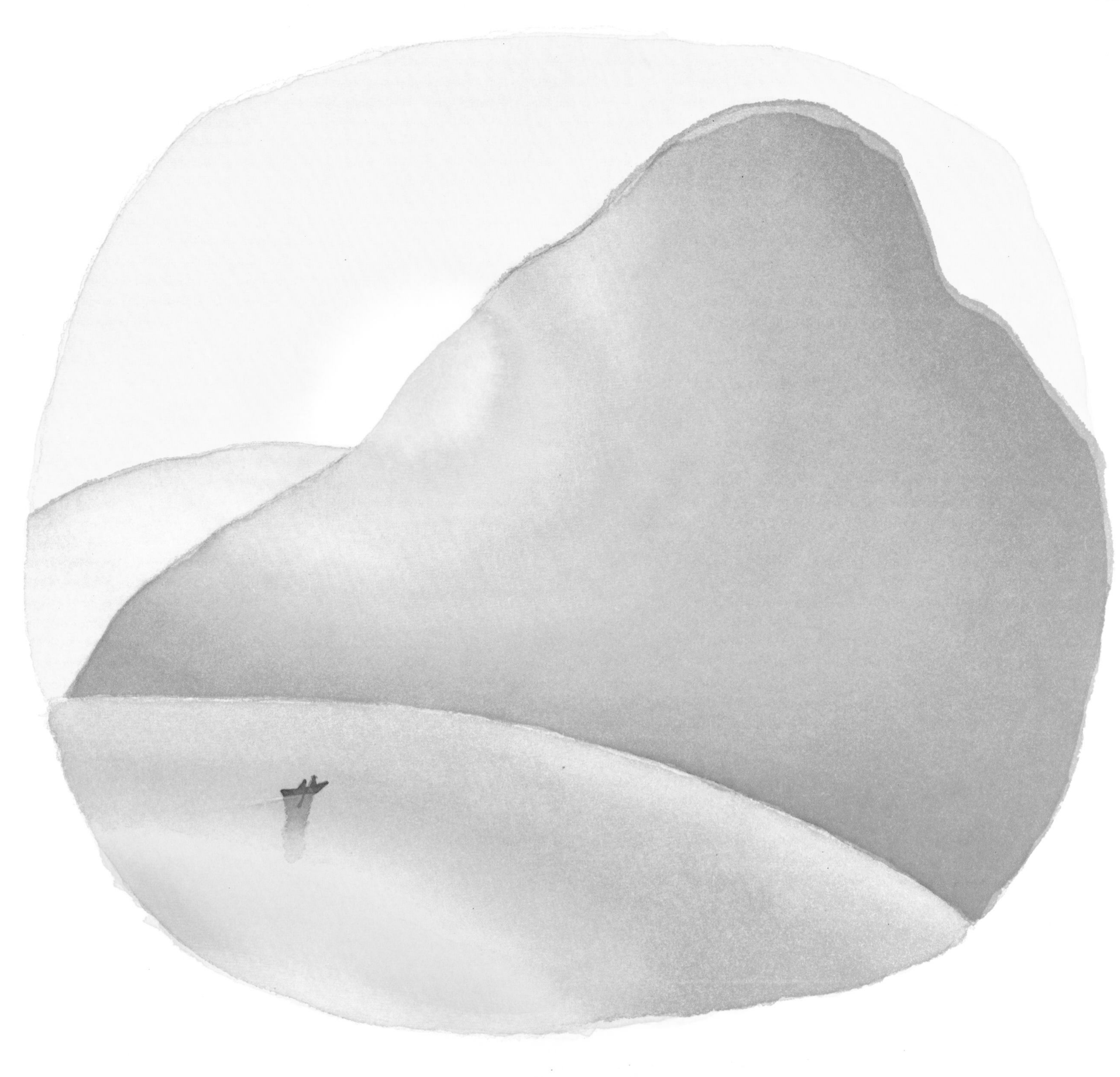

Privateer Press™ Presents

WARMACHINE™

PRIME

CREDITS

Game Design
Matt Wilson

Lead Developer
Jason Soles

Additional Development
Brian Snoddy
Steve Benton

Final Rules
Steve "Bulletproof" Benton

Rules Editor
James Sanders

Fiction
Bryan Steele
J. Michael Kilmartin
Jason Soles
Matt Wilson

Editor in Chief
Joe Martin

Art Direction
Matt Wilson

Illustration
Brian "Dolemita" Snoddy
Matt Wilson
Daren Bader
Scott Fischer
Steve Tappin
Trevor Hairsine
Greg Staples
Rich Wright
Torstein Nordstrand
Sam Wood

Graphic Design
Mike South

Logo Design
Daniel Gelon

Packaging Design
Robert Campbell

Symbols & Cartography
Todd Gamble

Miniatures Direction
Mike McVey

Scenery
Todd Gamble
Jason Soles
Mike McVey

Sculpting
Mike McVey
Chaz Elliott
Jerzy Montwill
John Winter
Paul Muller
Roy Eastland
Jim Warner
Will Hannah
Christian Danckworth

Miniatures Painters
Mike McVey
Allison McVey
Jason Soles
Rob Stoddard
Joe Hill
Matt Parks

Photography
Craig Cudnohufsky

Director of Operations
Sherry Yeary

Special Thanks
Bob Watts
Dave Schwimmer

Playtesters
Scott Hill
Jason Hill
Rob Hinds
Bob Russel
Eric Wilson
Dan Tibbles
Chris Holt
Scott Briggs
Jeremy Mueller
Cody Dupras
Kurtis Trimbo
Jason St. Pierre
Doug Carter
Kayo Blackmoor
Chris Vermeers
Clint "Ogre" Whiteside

For our wives, fiances, and girlfriends,
who knew that we would achieve what we only dreamed we could.

Visit: www.ikwarmachine.com • www.ironkingdoms.com • www.privateerpress.com

Privateer Press
8415 5th Ave, NE, B1 • Seattle, WA 98115 • Tel (425) 562-0259 • Fax (425) 562-0260

For online customer service, email : frontdesk@privateerpress.com

Second printing: August 2003. Printed in the U.S.A.

ISBN: 0-9706970-7-4 PIP01001

TABLE OF CONTENTS

WHERE CREDIT IS DUE...

In your hands, you hold a journey. What began as a small, modest endeavor, has snowballed into a runaway juggernaut. The task of creating a miniatures game is not to be undertaken lightly—something they don't teach you in school. Science has not yet created an instrument that can measure the magnitude of effort that went into creating WARMACHINE. It is a dream achieved through sheer perseverance and tenacity, and is only possible because of the amazing people who saw its potential and mustered in themselves the willpower to put aside any semblance of a normal life...and in some cases, their sanity!

The beginning of this journey is difficult to pinpoint—a trio of creators dedicated to quality, and a mission to make a life at something they enjoyed. Along the way, others were drawn to this mission, and WARMACHINE only exists today because of the incredible individuals who joined the efforts. Some were long time friends while others were nothing more than divine blessings that appeared at the right time to lend their skills to a project that they knew they'd be proud to be part of.

Because I am the last person to see this book before it goes to press, I am fortunate enough to have the unique honor to thank the souls that have bourn us so far and for so long. The only difficulty is finding a place to start...

Brian Snoddy and Mike McVey—their talents are why we are here today. They are masters of their craft and amazing individuals and I can only hope to be working by their side for years to come.

Fortune shined upon us and we acquired Jason Soles. Without him, WARMACHINE might be a scattered ream of paper afloat in the Pacific, flung there in a fit of frustration. What he has brought to the game and to Privateer is something that could not be recounted in a few short lines. His efforts and dedication will continue to ensure the progress of this company.

Out of the blue came a series of individuals that would allow us to realize the true potential of this game. The first was Steve 'Bulletproof' Benton. With his redrafting of the rules, Steve brought WARMACHINE to an unparalleled level of professionalism. It is impossible to praise enough, his contribution to this project. At the same time, James Sanders donated his editing skills in a lapse of blind generosity. His expert touch honed our texts to razor sharp accuracy. Meanwhile, the man with the perfect name to author Iron Kingdoms fiction appeared—Bryan Steele. Reams of background material and flavor packed descriptions sprang from his fingertips to cover the pages before you.

Joe Martin, our editor in chief, brought the text together, polishing our words, managing our continuity, and giving the Privateer touch of quality to everything we do.

Once again, Mike South graced us with a beautiful design for the book, while Rob Campbell provided his expertise with packaging design. Upon these pages, we have the rights to boast some of the industry's most fantastic artists: Daren Bader, Scott Fischer, Steve Tappin, Rich Wright, Greg Staples, Trevor Hairsine, Sam Wood, and newcomer, Torstein Nordstrand. Once again, we must thank their generosity and willingness to contribute to a labor of love for these brilliant illuminations.

Our sculptors: the enchanting Chaz Elliott, Jerzy Montwill, John Winter, Paul Muller, Roy Eastland, Jim Warner and Will Hannah—you have proven that you need not be a massive corporation to achieve the highest quality. And our painters, Allison McVey and Rob Stoddard—you have completed the creative process with the wonderful color these models deserve. Of course, only the talented eye of Craig Cudnohufsky could bring the amazing models of WARMACHINE to full color life in the vivid photographs that adorn these pages and our website.

Dave 'you must get that a lot' Schwimmer, Kelly Yeager, Rob Hinds, and the indomitable spirit of Eric Pulkka are the reason that WARMACHINE is on the shelf today. These men could put machines out of business! And let us not forget our play testers, who are too many to mention—but we are indebted for your time and feedback.

Lastly, I must thank Sherry Yeary, who holds our operation together. Without her, we would be lost at sea; the man himself, Bob Watts, who over many long lunches, imparted the wisdom of his experience and helped us navigate a treacherous path through the creation of a miniatures game producing company; and to Ally Benton and Marnee Evans for givng up their husbands for so many days and nights.

Doubtless, there are many I have forgotten mention of, and I only hope that you have already been thanked at some time. Every step of this journey has been assisted by the benevolence of unbelievable people. And thanks to them, our journey is far from over.

WARNING: NOT SUITABLE FOR WUSSIES!

Sissies. Little girls. Nancy boys…go home. This game is not for you.

If you cry when you lose, get lost—you're going to lose. If it hurts your fragile sensibilities to see your favorite character get pounded unmercifully by a rapid succession of no-holds-barred iron fury, you'd better look the other way. If you've ever whined the words, "That's too powerful," then put the book down slowly and walk away before making eye contact with anyone or they'll realize your voice hasn't changed yet.

This game is about aggression. This is the game of metal on metal combat. This is fuel injected power hopped up on steroids. This is WARMACHINE—the battles game that kicks so much ass we have to use all capital letters.

We didn't set out to reinvent the wheel with this game—we just armor plated it, covered it in spikes, and rolled it over your grandma's house.

WARMACHINE is simple. It's easy to learn, has no reference charts, no heavy arithmetic, and doesn't require constant trips to the rule book. At the same time, WARMACHINE possess deep strategy. The ability to unlock combinations of abilities and spells and maneuvers is practically limitless. For every perfect strategy, there is a foil. For every immovable object, there is an unstoppable force. Just when you think you've got it all worked out, you'll be blindsided by something you never saw before. The more you dig, the more you'll find.

WARMACHINE favors the aggressor. You've got to throw the first punch if you want to land on top! Too many games set players up to be timid. Games drag out with little action because the game favors defensive strategies. Players park their soldiers behind walls like old ladies hiding from a loud noise. Not in WARMACHINE! If you wait for your opponent to come to you, you're going to get steamrolled. You've got to have balls to play this game! You've got to charge your opponent and hang it all out there! You've got to break his formations. You've got to be relentless with your onslaught. You have to go for the jugular and latch on like a rabid dog that hasn't eaten in days. Anything less, and you'll be hamburger.

You're playing with power now. Don't be afraid! Few things are more satisfying than slamming your opponent's warjack into a unit of soldiers and watching them fall like bowling pins! (We call this 'jack bowling.) Try picking up an enemy warcaster (with a warjack, of course) and throwing it across the battlefield! It's almost more fun than you should be allowed to have with a miniatures game.

The miniatures of WARMACHINE deliver on every level that the game does. These warjacks radiate power! We're pouring so much metal into these things that at our current rate, we'll deplete the world of pewter by 2006. And these things were made for modeling. The incredible detail and expert sculpting will create one of the most enjoyable painting experiences you've ever had.

This is a new era in tabletop miniatures wargaming. This is a game made for you, by people like you. It's not a load of sterilized mass market drek designed by a room full of corporate meatplows. This is raw. This is brutal. This is WARMACHINE.

So play like you've got a pair, or put down the metal and go find something made of plastic.

ASHES TO ASHES

A PRELUDE TO BATTLE

"Damn that wind!" Commander Coleman Stryker huffed. The flaps to his war-room tent whipped savagely and he quickly thrust his long dagger through some parchment maps on his wooden table, pinning them before the wind could scatter them about.

The commander looked up as an armored figure entered. "Secure those flaps, Vicky…I concentrate."

"I hate this weather," said Captain Victoria Haley, her breath pluming in wisps of steam. The woman pulled down a heavy woolen scarf from her beautifully sculpted face and peered around the room. Satisfied they were the only two in the tent, she spoke candidly, "'Tis no wonder the Khadorans want our lands. Anywhere would be better than this windswept hellhole."

Though clad head-to-toe in her steam-powered warcaster rune armor, Captain Haley moved with a fluid grace as she bent to strap down the tent flaps. "So why did ye call me here, Coleman?"

Stryker ran his gauntleted hand through his flame-red mop of wind blown hair and sighed heavily. "I need your expertise in dealing with the undying."

Haley reddened past the color of her chapped cheeks. "'Tis simple," she answered as she leaned her spear against the table's edge. "Render them down to bones, burn the remains, scatter the ash to the winds, then go home and spend the crowns for a nice, hot bath." The woman paused, clenching and unclenching her gloved fists to conjure warmth back into her fingers as she looked down at the maps on the table. "But ye already knew all that…what else do ye want?"

"It seems Lord Toruk's making a move. His eyes are set on the Ordic coast. One of his Iron Liches has all but laid a total siege to try and conquer Berck, and is already marching undead forces down the coast looking toward Carre Dova."

"That's not far from Five Fingers!" Haley's eyes went wide with realization. "King Leto's there meeting with Baird the Second…oh, by Morrow." She straightened out Stryker's maps with her hands and leaned over the table, looking at the rough drawn marks of army advances and the like. Haley ran a gloved finger along the blue line that marked her own force's approach, pausing to move her attention to a dark brown splotch in the section of Ord nearby the 'X' of the war camp.

"'Tis the Lich," Stryker explained.

"What's this then?" She pointed at a red dotted line coming up on the Blue Sands coast from the south.

"My garrison. We were stationed in Ceryl. Came as soon as I heard."

Captain Haley cocked her angled brow. "If ye didn't come from the north and yer path obviously didn't bring ye in contact with the Schardes, how do ye know this isn't all just a Khadoran trick…or some Menite ploy?"

Commander Stryker smiled and whistled. "A reliable source."

The rear flap of the tent came halfway open, and Stryker watched as Captain Haley's expression stiffened.

"G'mornin', me ol' muckers!" A well-known gobber approached the table, grinning at both of the warcasters. He was wrapped tightly in a thick woolen cowl clasped with a gaudy gemstone set in the knuckle-rivet of a warjack. A menagerie of trinkets from the countless strange and wonderful places he claimed to have visited jingled and clattered from where they hung from his pockets or suspended from various bandolier belts slung over each shoulder. In addition, the gobber wore an over-large Cygnaran longcoat that dragged the ground and a peculiar, short-brimmed black hat he referred to as a bowler. "Lon' time no see, eh Cappin?"

"Reinholdt," Captain Haley growled the name, her eyes hardening on Stryker as he fought laughter.

The gobber walked over and stood between the two warcasters, putting his hands on their backs like old friends. "So I was bodgin' fer this troll 'n upp'r Ord a few spans north of the Rohannor when the big bloke need'd me t'go pick up some gubbins for the pr'ject, an' that's when me seen 'em. Dirty bonebags, rows 'n rows. I was knowin' me old fr'end King Leto would wan' t'know, so's I…"

The gobber continued telling his lengthy tale on how he met up with Commander Stryker, but the two

Cygnarans walked to the other side of the table, having their own conversation above the gobber's droning. "Ye trust the word of this gobber?" asked Captain Haley.

"He never steered us wrong before. Anyway, even if he were wrong what harm would it do? If there's no invasion force, we call it a holiday."

"What?" Haley's features hardened. "Coleman, we're bloody soldiers. We're not allowed the luxury of normal lives...especially holidays."

"...an' that is how I got C'mand'r Stryk'r here to save 'em!" Reinholdt finished his winding story and nodded his mottled gray-green head in punctuation. As if his nod was some kind of divine signal, the tent shook from a massive impact nearby. The gobber was thrown to the ground, yelping in his native tongue, and both of the warcasters clutched the edge of the table to steady themselves. A brief moment later, another explosion showered the outside of the tent wall with chunks of rocky soil.

"Cannons?" Stryker inquired.

"Cryx doesn't have cannons of that caliber on land!" Captain Haley hissed as her vortex spear leapt into her hand.

In one smooth motion she twirled her weapon and stepped out into the cold through the new opening she'd created in the tent wall. Stryker lowered his goggles over his eyes, checked his scabbard for his blade, and rushed out behind her. Reinholdt kipped to his feet, straightened his wide-brimmed hat, and jogged out behind them.

Outside it was chaos. Two craters smoldered nearby Commander Stryker's tent, the smoke disappearing instantly in the bitter wind. Soldiers and squires clamored out of their tents in various states of disarray.

The two warcasters ran amidst the troops, toward a half dozen warjacks that suddenly lifted their mechanikal heads in response to their approach. Faceplate grills and eye-slots lit up a flickering orange and their heartfires began churning within their furnaces. The metal giants stomped into formations the warcasters mentally assigned to them as a soldier in a thick, fur-lined, hooded coat jogged up to meet them.

"Who in the bloody hell is shelling us?!" Captain Haley demanded of the scout.

"Mercenaries, captain! Lots of them. I don't recognize the standard, but I counted no less than four Khadoran 'jacks. Looked like Juggernaughts." The scout pointed to the dark shapes in the wood's edge. "They've also got one of our old..." he was cut off

as another explosion ripped apart a loosely grouped unit of long gunners nearby. "...one of our old cannons!"

"How did the buggers get so close?"

"That no longer matters," Commander Stryker said. "Captain, prepare to engage."

Stryker motioned to two towering Ironclads behind him and they groaned into motion. A loud *thrum-thrum* started pulsing from the quake hammers in their articulated iron fists, and thick black smoke belched up from their smokestacks. The commander pointed at the woods—more specifically at the shapes within it—and gave his mental orders to the massive machines. With not so much as a nod, the Ironclads stomped past him and toward Stryker's intended targets. A third warjack—a recently repaired Charger—walked up to the warcaster and silently waited for his attention. Stryker nodded to it, and the Charger's hydraulic legs pumped it into a run toward the flank of the wood line. It loaded a pair of shots into its dual-cannon as it moved, a loud *ka-ch-chunk* resounding out from the warjack's arm.

Reinholdt jogged over to a very unhappy looking Captain Haley as she spouted orders to the three long gunner captains. Wisely, the gobber decided to listen instead of interrupt.

"Terrell, ye and yers will pull down those tents and roll them up for cover. If we're to be shelled, I want some protection up front. Braun, put a few dozen volleys into those trees...the Commander's only sending in 'jacks and Storm Blades, so don't worry about aiming." She turned to the third long gunner. "Marlowe, ye have the most important job of all."

"Wut's that?" Reinholdt blurted curiously, shouting over yet another impact a few yards wide of an empty tent, tearing it to canvas shreds. Haley shot him a fierce look, then returned to the gunner.

"Ye're coming with the Commander and me into those woods to provide cover fire."

One of the Ironclads rocked from the impact of a cannon strike, but its thick iron skin withstood the red-hot chunks of lead and iron that showered it. Stryker reached out and commanded his warjacks to push on.

Haley and half a dozen long gunners grouped up with Stryker, Reinholdt trying to keep up behind them. Behind the little gobber, four more warjacks walked over—one heavy Defender chassis, two more of the Chargers, and a single, rare Lancer model. The ground trembled with their collective weight as they moved in front of the group.

Haley turned her will to the metal monsters, and they began slowly marching ahead. The Chargers loaded their dual-cannons, and the Defender cycled a wrought iron ball into the chamber of the heavy barrel replacing one of its fists. The captain ran just behind them, issuing her mental commands, and the entire cadre moved toward the wood line while a volley of rifles cracked out from behind a stack of rolled up tents and bedrolls. Rounds zipped overhead and into the trees and a single man's scream pierced the gloom. An explosion from the trees quickly followed this as another cannonball hummed toward the Cygnarans.

Stryker's Charger was partially struck by the ball and spun like a ten-foot iron top, its hammer and the arm holding it suddenly blasted apart into so much scrap. The impact had caused Stryker to dive for cover but he quickly rose with a curse. He gave his warcaster armor a once-over, making sure everything was intact before the charge. Suddenly, Reinholdt was there, ducking in and tightening one of Stryker's leg straps.

"Dere we go. Wut would ye e'er do wi'out me?" he grinned, showing a gold-capped tooth sparkling in the rising sunlight.

Stryker drew his mechanika sword and it crackled to life with the same magical energy as the arc nodes on the metal brows of various warjacks. The smell of ozone erupted from the softly thrumming blade, and Stryker smiled down at the gobber through the blur of heat-distorted air. "Thanks, friend. Seems they caught us half-cocked with our breeches 'round our ankles, though. Stay here, Reinholdt. This is going to get ugly."

"Ye don' 'ave to tell me twice, me mucker." Despite the chaos, a smile lit the gobber's wide mouth. "Anythin' else?"

"Aye. If we don't make it out of those woods, I want you to go to Five Fingers and tell the kings what happened here." Stryker ground his teeth visibly and looked toward the treeline. "But let's hope that won't be necessary."

"Right," Reinholdt replied. "So go kick their arses, Stryker."

The warcaster nodded, and strode away in the company of his Storm Blades.

Meanwhile, Reinholdt scampered back to the wagons for cover. He leapt into one and settled in behind the canvas covering, then yanked an elaborate

spyglass from one of his pockets and brought it up to one wide eye. "Come on, me boys. Go'n gets dem bonebags."

One of Stryker's Ironclads had already made it to the trees. One powerful swing from its quake hammer turned a forty-foot pine tree into sap and splinters. The warjack carried its swing through into the cloud of debris, the sticky wooden shrapnel clinging to its pocked blue armor. The other Ironclad stepped into the newly made clearing and swept its fiery "eyes" wide, in search of a more satisfying target.

As if in answer, an enormous Khadoran warjack charged from behind some cover and slammed into the sap-covered Cygnaran war machine. The sound was akin to a derailing steamrail car, hitting with enough force to send the enormous metal beast toppling through another tree like it was thatch.

The huge Juggernaught stood defiantly where the Ironclad once stood, dark black smoke trailing up from its smokestacks. It was painted a dark violet—very different from the trademark crimson of the Khadoran 'jacks—and its oversized ax bore the marks of many years' hard use and very little maintenance. The large northfolk-made mechanika vented its excess steam through the grill of its face, and the howl of releasing pressure was like a dragon's roar.

It raised its ax to strike at the fallen warjack, but the other Ironclad intercepted the blow, catching the Juggernaught's arm with its open hand. Steamwork strained against steamwork, and waves of heat immediately rolled out from heartfire furnaces put to the test. When Haley and Stryker entered the scene, the two metal gladiators were at a standstill, which was fine by them.

"Down!" Stryker cried to his troopers, the air split by the unique booming sound of blunderbusses erupting. The commander and his Storm Blades dropped into a roll, a cloud of pellets, scrap bits, and rock salt passing over them and into an unfortunate long gunner. The launched debris cut into the lightly armored Cygnaran like a hundred tiny knives, and he fell backward sucking at breath that was being robbed from him by tiny holes in his neck and chest.

Haley saw her man go down and darted forward, hoping to be faster than the soldiers reloading their blunderbusses. She ducked forward between the stomping legs of her Defender toward the shredded foliage where the hail came from, and pointed her mechanika spear at the hazy manlike shapes in the shade of the tree cover. With less than a whisper from her lips, a streak of white light leapt from the tip of her vortex spear and burned into the shapes. The area exploded immediately in a swirl of arcane flame that sent five Khadoran mercenaries sailing through the air like rag dolls.

Stryker's Storm Blades came to their feet running, and soon they were engulfed in the arcs and sparks of lightning created by their powerful storm glaives. Not wanting to be undone by the captain, Stryker reached out to his damaged Charger and grinned as the plan unfolded both in his mind and in full metal reality a few dozen yards away.

The injured Charger, its right arm severed at the elbow joint and leaking boiling water onto the cold ground from shattered steamwork, turned toward the tree line and broke into a hard sprint. It launched a double shot from its cannon aimlessly into the cover, and followed immediately behind the volley. Stryker watched what the Charger saw through the magic of its cortex, seeing his intended target a few warjack strides away—the cannon and, more importantly, its powder stores. The Charger selflessly wore the mantle of its namesake and pumped its legs harder, straining its surging pistons. It didn't even pause as it smashed into and through enemy axmen, heading straight for the artillery landing. The cannon crew was frantically attempting to reload when the iron warrior broke through.

Stryker pulled his mental connection just as the Charger dove into the powder kegs. Even wearing his goggles, the warcaster sheltered his eyes from the ensuing eruption. Fire, molten iron, and scorched wood shot hundreds of feet above the treetops. The wave of heat knocked the wind from the lungs of the surrounding Khadorans, and an ear-splitting explosion spiraled in a dusty ring from where the cannon once stood. The Charger and the artillery team were disintegrated in an instant; the remarkable iron skin of the Cygnaran warjack had been atomized by the blast, and every Khadoran soldier within fifty feet had been torn apart.

As the booming echoed off the distant foothills, Stryker's Storm Blades were already leaping into the woods to finish the job. Lightning jumped from one storm glaive to the other, and then forked into the enemy with devastating power and a sound not unlike thunder, rendering a pair of mercenaries still, smoking, and lifeless.

Also in the fray, Stryker cut one ax-wielding soldier down with his disruptor blade and then leveled his mechanika pistol at another, but before he could pull the trigger his target went down from a well-placed shot in the head. Not far away, Stryker saw one of Haley's long gunners waving to him. Stryker raised his hand to respond when the gunner abruptly became a spray of red; a violet warjack had suddenly emerged from a settling dust cloud and cleft the man in twain with a single half-swing. There was a sound like creaking metal as the gunner's body froze into two stiffened chunks before hitting the ground, and an

odor similar to mint wafted from the warjack's weapon, a trail of light blue vapor venting from the ax's blade and haft. The blood from the gunner crystallized instantly against the blade of the ice ax, and even the heat from the warjack's vented steam could not so much as soften it.

"Coleman! Move!" Haley shouted over the clanking of steamwork, and Stryker jumped aside just as he felt the impulse from the incoming warjack's cortex.

Haley's prized Lancer charged past him and impaled the Khadoran heavy 'jack on its thick spear. Black fluids from inner workings dripped slowly down the shaft of the weapon and off the hinged knuckles of the Lancer. The spiked warjack brought its ice ax up for a powerful blow, but a surge of arcane power blasted out of the special channeling arc node on the Lancer's shoulder and scoured most of the head right off the larger warjack. It trembled and the ice ax fell from its twitching metal fingers. The Lancer stepped back, yanking its spear out of the torn gash with a grating squeal of metal against metal. Stryker thought twice about waving his thanks, remembering the grisly result of his last attempt just moments before.

In the meantime, the pine-covered Ironclad had regained its feet and was barreling toward the wrestling match between its fellow Ironclad and the violet Juggernaught. The bigger and stronger Juggernaught was stressing the gears and pistons of the Cygnaran 'jack to the limits, and hydraulic fluids and pressure leaks shot from splitting hoses and cracked boilers. A jet of flame shot out from a burst pipe, and the grappled Ironclad buckled to its knee. The Juggernaught took this moment as an advantage, leveling its heavily armored head and the sharpened spike at its apex into the hunched shoulders of the smaller 'jack. The spike punched through the thick armor and ripped the Cygnaran crest that was embossed there into a twisted, jagged wound. Before it could bring another head butt to bear, Stryker focused his mind and energies into the pine-covered Ironclad. With his arcane assistance, it landed an unbelievably powerful blow with its quake hammer onto the shoulder of the Juggernaught and both of the wrestling 'jacks were separated by the wave of mechanikal force.

The Juggernaught's ax-wielding arm hung limp and twisted from its thick shoulder, and Stryker forced more of his power into the Ironclad. A second blow split its hard violet carapace and sent the forty-ton mammoth sliding away along the ground, digging a trench of leaf litter and pine needles two feet deep and forty feet long.

"I have fought Thralls with less skill than these snow-stomping peasants!" Haley laughed over the sound of the metal giants thrashing around the battle. Her spear bit deeply into one of the mercenaries, and another was sent flying with an arcane flip of her wrist. Stryker looked back from the warjack brawl in time to dispatch his own enemy with a deft plunge of his blade.

"These mercs are terribly well equipped for such poor warriors," Stryker replied as he leveled his pistol and unleashed a devastating bolt of energy into an oncoming attacker. "There must be something more to this!"

Somewhere, a horn suddenly sounded, and the mercenaries abruptly withdrew. A few parting shots from rifles, and a volley or two from the Chargers, and they were gone as quickly as they appeared. Stryker took note of their wounded and dead, and Haley jogged over to him.

"Shall we pursue?" she asked eagerly.

"I don't think so. No."

"I don't want to seem daft, but why not?" She sank her spear into the ground with a *schuk*.

"These were not warriors. Some are not even Khadoran." Stryker toed one of the fallen mercenaries, and then gestured to his red hair. "This poor fool looks Cygnaran to me."

"So why would these glorified bandits have a cannon? Or warjacks for that matter?" Haley asked.

"I think we've been played for fools, Vicky" he paused, feeling how sluggish the warjacks around him had become. They were in need of fuel for their heartfire furnaces and some needed reloading. "Our' jacks are spent. It'll take hours for us to pull together and move out now."

"I knew the little gob was crooked," spat Haley. "Where are these undead he was supposed to have seen? Ye should have never—"

Stryker waived her off her soapbox. "Reinholdt isn't deceiving us."

The commander turned toward the hilltop where the gobber was watching from the safety of the wagon and waved to him with great sweeps of his sword. He turned back to Haley and popped his goggles off his eyes, leaving two circles of clean on an otherwise ash and soot-covered face. "I'm sure whatever he saw wasn't this. There's more going on here than one little gobber, Vicky. Trust me."

The captain took up her spear. "I do trust you, Coleman. But I'm still going to be keeping me eye on the gob. Whether it hinges on Reinholdt or not, something bad is in the works."

"Agreed," Stryker nodded, and then looked around at the carnage. "For now, we'd best pull ourselves together. Come along, Captain. Let's move."

⁂

Witnessing the entire battle through his prized and priceless Ordic spyglass, Reinholdt committed every swing and shot to memory for retelling later. This had the makings of a damn fine story, and he was there…*right in the middle of it.* He chuckled as Stryker waved to him.

"Tis funny he be lookin' aft'r me," he laughed to himself. The gobber stood up quickly, and hopped down from the wagon. He stretched his arms and went to snap the spyglass shut, but a twinkle on the ground caught his eye. A single gold crown caught the morning sun and sparkled just right.

"Ooh, col'r me lucky t'day!" Reinholdt ducked down to snatch it up but when he stood he smacked his knobby head hard on the wagon's crossbeam. Stars flew across his field of vision and he stumbled forward, dropping both the coin and the spyglass and throwing his hands over the soon-to-be lump on his brow. The gobber bobbled unsteadily over the horse yoke, causing him to fall forward onto the ground with a loud *whump*.

Reinholdt grunted and rolled over, clutching at his belly, and ended perfectly lined up with the spyglass, albeit upside down. As he opened his eyes, the throbbing was set aside, drowned out by the curiosity of what he suddenly spied through the lens.

"Eh? Wut's this?" On the horizon, framed by the early light, were two barely distinguishable shapes next to each other. The gobber flopped onto his belly and squinted into the glass. He plucked a tattered rag from one of his pockets and wiped the dust from the lens. With a bit better focus, he could make out two vaguely humanoid shapes on the crest of a faraway hill.

"Now, wut do we've 'ere?" he sighed, wincing at the pain in his head as he tried to bring the two shapes into view. "Eav'dropp'rs?"

⁂

"Perfect, Deneghra," hissed Asphyxious, as he dispelled the mystically enhanced image of the ensuing battle with a wave of his mechanikal claw. *"Now our armies are free to siege Carre Dova ahead of schedule. A splendid idea, witch. Our Lord shall be pleased."*

"I live to serve," the war-witch Deneghra answered through pale blue lips. The cold was almost numbing to her in her scantily forged armor, and the wind whistled over her witch-barbs. An armored thrall sprinted up the hill and bowed behind the two mighty necromancers. The Iron Lich, even though primarily composed of thick iron plates and chain-linked hooks and blades, turned silently to acknowledge the lesser undead.

"What news doth thou bring?" The greenish flame wreathing the lich's floating skull blazed with anticipation.

The thrall hushed out eerily, "The mercenaries pitted against the Butcher's force in Volingrad are slaughtered."

The Lich waived him off and turned back to the beautifully wicked witch. *"A loss for them. Now neither King Leto's fools nor Queen Vanar's lackeys will stand in our way. Prepare thine helljacks for immediate transport, my war-witch."* The Iron Lich floated backwards into a slowly opening portal of brimstone and vanished upon its closing.

Deneghra stalked toward where the secret armies of the Cryxian Empire awaited her return. She paused only briefly, looking back to the rapidly closing battle she had orchestrated, angry that she could not be down amongst them. "One day, Cygnarans. One day soon…I will have thee."

The pale-skinned war-witch turned and descended the hill. Arrangements must be seen to for her masters in Cryx. Arrangements for war.

THE IRON KINGDOMS

FORGING A WORLD IN BLOOD AND METAL

From the journals of Arron Furlaine the "Crimson Plume," famed writer and traveling cartographer

Midsummer, 4th Night

Here I be—sitting again in one of the many pubs of western Caspia, the famed and fabled City of Walls. From my view here, dwarfed as I am by these mighty bulwarks, I have to wonder just how many wars have been fought beyond these great gates? How many swords and spears have torn human flesh in order to purchase just another step into the sacred confines where I now sit sipping cider and scribing away? It was right here that the dwarves helped our ancestors forge the enormous Colossals—giant war machines called warjacks originally used to fight off the Orgoth invaders that had held our people captive for so long. It was then that our history truly began, the history of the Iron Kingdoms, and I'm of a mind to undertake my own telling of it.

Man lived in roaming tribes for a very long time, and wherever man gathers, you'll soon find those that take up the mantle of priest. The first of these most likely worshipped Menoth, the Creator, the Lawgiver, the Shaper of Man; his is the oldest human faith in our known history. Throughout the eons, most Menites hold the claim he is the creator of the world itself, but I cannot be so sure. As a pragmatist and a writer of some integrity—some may call this a paradox—I put my faith in fact more so than fiction. I try not to pass on biases, which, if you'll forgive me, I have found often run rampant with religion and clergy. Be that as it may, the Menites helped in forming the early villages and farming communities into towns and cities, many of which subsist even to this day.

In the centuries that followed came the rise of the Twins, the first gods to appear after the birth of man—Morrow, the brother of good and light, and his twin sister Thamar, goddess of sorcery and darkness. They are widely worshipped today, and have been the cause of some of Immoren's greatest conflicts…I'm sure some to come, as well.

It was the Thousand Cities Era, and although we were growing under the tutelage of our gods and their servants in leaps and bounds, we were experiencing some major growing pains in the process. Like a giant stained-glass window, the map of western Immoren at this time was segmented into countless city-states of various sizes; each one lorded over by a different and often short-term warlord. Pub-born treaties and back-alley allegiances lasted only as long as it took to organize the border wars that were the law of the day. Our petty foolishness was not limited to our own people either, as we tried on many occasions to encroach upon the ancient lands ruled by the elder races—the stalwart dwarves of Rhul and the inscrutable elves of Ios. Our foolhardy efforts to attack their borders resulted in bloody defeat after bloody defeat. The dwarves would not be budged from the lines drawn in the rocky soil of Rhul, and every force sent into Ios simply vanished as if it never were. It didn't take too long for us to turn away from the elder lands and rest our kaleidoscopic focus back onto our own. Through a fair bit of self-destruction, things began appearing as if the elder races would soon enough be without men as company in just a few hundred years, until one misty morning when the first fleet of black longboats struck our shores.

The day of the Orgoth had arrived.

The foreign explorers that sullied our shores that day came from a society far from Immoren. They appeared human enough, but more cruel and calculating than our ancestors, and accustomed to a dark and callous way of life. They saw our lands and its puerile citizenry as a pure and untapped resource for the taking. Before long, countless longboats spilled cruel warriors onto the beaches of Immoren. The once-warring tribes and towns of the Thousand Cities fought valiantly alongside one another for the first time, but the disorganized resistance was akin to one man's attempts to stand steadfast in the surf of a Meredian tide; it could not hold forever.

In those days, we were little more than spear and shield against the unfettered arcane might of the Orgoth nation. Their foreign arms and armor, enchanted as it were, resisted our poorly ordered ancestors with their primitive weaponry. We had yet to devise the steamjacks one sees today, and gun foundries were quite unheard of. The land eventually became theirs. We were pacified through great rivers of our own blood, although we resisted them for two centuries by sheer numbers alone. The Orgoth never tried to invade the lands of the elder races, perhaps knowing the elves and dwarves were stronger and more organized in that day than men, and those of Ios and Rhul merely looked on with the belief that these Orgoth were just another

In great long ships, the Orgoth swept upon the shores of Immoren, beginning of a reign that would last six hundred years.

tedious affliction upon the upstart race's otherwise brief existence. *Let them destroy themselves,* was the oft-heard mantra in those days.

But the Orgoth did not wish to destroy the men of Immoren. No, indeed. Much work and toil needed to be done in this raw land, so rather they sought to subjugate us. They needed slaves. Their horrible slave camps pounded out many of the fine roads we still use today; basalt ruins were erected by thousands of bloodied, stone-torn hands, standing as strong today as they did when the final slab was wedged into place ages ago; even the rulers of Khador have long inhabited a mighty stone bastion shaped by countless broken backs and flesh spent under the conqueror's lash. Our forefathers gave their very lives for the world the Orgoth had sculpted out of our chaotic primal clay, and much of that stone and marble foundation yet holds up our world. Perhaps, in the end, it was their subjugation that saved us.

During the Orgoth rule, Thamar played her part by giving the "Gift of Sorcery" to man, for reasons that have been speculated throughout the ages. What sprung from The Gift were things of wonder, such as the fabulous mechanika that quickly evolved into warjacks. Empowered by this new magic, mankind transformed simple steamwork and clockwork toys into magical constructs to work their mines, tend their fields, protect their cities, even fight their wars. The last time I witnessed steam-powered bodies surging into battle—nearly three years ago during a border skirmish near Llael—I was reminded of a ballroom dance, albeit one with giant iron dancers engaged in a Tordoran reel of utter devastation. I can only imagine what those ancient combats must have been like, their numbers a hundredfold what I saw near Llael that day, with the gargantuan Colossals dominating the field with their size and thunder. Those Colossals have passed into oblivion now, but they must have been incredible to behold as towering constructs belching ash into the heavens.

The dwarves of Rhul were so impressed with man's commitment to creativity and resourcefulness that they pledged themselves to our cause. It is said they recognized a stagnation of the Orgoth culture, so they aided the rebellion, making moves toward a peaceful existence between men and dwarves that exists to this day. Indeed, with the Rhulfolk's expertise came the Colossals, mighty tools indeed for pushing the conquerors of Immoren away. Indeed, what those masters of metalworking accomplished alongside Cygnar's technicians heralded a new age of steam and mechanika that has touched nearly every corner of our lives.

It took two hundred years to be fully rid of the tyranny, two hundred years of warfare and strife, but with the advent of the Colossals, the Orgoth were vanished in less than three decades. But they did not go quietly. No, they went with a vengeance. The Orgoth razed scores of cities as they left, poisoning wells, salting fields, and defiling the lands before disappearing on the horizon of vast Meredian. The Scourge, it became called, was the Orgoth's last gesture of rage. Some mudflats in Cygnar and the frozen wastes of Khador yet bear the scars of that harsh leave-taking.

Once the Orgoth departed, we were left without rule. Rather than much-desired peace however, the chaos began anew. Barbarian warlords grabbed as much power as they could, but the leaders of the Iron Alliance felt the strength of the machine they had forged in Immoren and wanted to retain the stability it provided. The warlords were put down quickly. The armies of the Iron Alliance kept the rebel warlords at bay while the founding fathers met in Corvis, the City of Ghosts, in Cygnar. Still under repair from the Scourge, Corvis now had a strong martial presence and was easily reachable by the members of the Alliance. The nexus of the Dragon's Tongue and the Black River filled with steamships ferrying the smiths that had hammered out the Iron Kingdoms on their political anvils.

Within the ash-laden marble chambers of the Corvis City Hall, the Council of Ten lasted for weeks. Harsh debates and sometimes harsher words were parleyed—the Thousand Cities era was long past, but blood is thick and these hard-nosed men were of lineages once longtime enemies. No matter the path they took, eventually the Council of Ten drafted and signed the renowned Corvis Treaties. The negotiations provided for lines drawn that would serve as borders for the newly formed territories. Cygnar, Khador, Ord, and Llael—the original kingdoms—were given shape using much of the same lines that the Orgoth had used to mark provinces governed by their generals; for this, they deemed, would be easiest for their peoples. And so, through the Corvis Treaties, the mighty Iron Kingdoms had been forged.

Winter's End, 17th midmorning

The sun is setting over the Dragonspine Mountains, and from here I can see the beauty of it all. I have walked, ridden, even flew once, across the many stretches of our fine realm. In my studies I have seen just about everything this continent has to offer, and from the warjack graveyards in Thornwood to the birthplace of the dragons on Scharde…I must admit I love it all.

Western Immoren stretches from the sandstorm-ridden Bloodstone Marches and the secret confines of Ios in the east to the long, unending Meredius in the west. The dark lands of the necromantic Cryx—the Scharde Islands—form the southern edge of Immoren and the northern tundra and their savage, snow-covered, glacial plains, inhabited by the territorial winter elves, cap this wondrous realm. Indeed, within these dangerous and sometimes deadly borders, a lot of history has unfolded. Wars have been waged, peace shattered, kings and queens come and gone, old kingdoms devoured, new ones born fresh, borders bending, and crowns ever changing hands—sometimes bloody ones. Aye, the Iron Kingdoms have seen much strife in their time, and I, for one, am sure they've not seen the last of it.

Summershome, 8th Day

The elder races, the elves and dwarves, live in their own kingdoms in general solitude. Even though I have welcomed hospitality from both peoples, I'd not presume to call them friends.

Ios, the ancient home of the elves, crowns the northern mountain ranges of the Bloodstone Marches. The forests there are so thick and beautiful that the very cities the elves call home are a sight—as they bend and twist magically around the ancient trunks of the Iosan whitewood trees. All concerning Ios is greatly rumor, as that the reclusive elves patrol their borders with lethal determination. Humans are forbidden to enter Ios with very few exceptions—myself counted amongst them—and even though the wilderness is beautiful and full of game to be hunted with ease few dare to enter the Iosan fields and forests. Many foolish adventurers have ventured into Ios uninvited never to be heard from again, and I'd wager ten crowns that no one ever will.

Ios is an enigma. For centuries the kings and queens of Immoren have sought to seal treaties and pacts with the elves, but the ambassadors are always turned away at the borders at sword or arrow-point. The Iosans seem burdened with a terrible weight, some great emotional encumbrance. It is said that many of them charge mankind for this mysterious plague of misery. Whatever it might be, a long shadow of superstition is cast from their borders, and some whisper of dark machinations growing within that shadow. Insular and secretive, I'm certain the Iosans will one day surprise us all—I pray relentlessly it will be a pleasant one.

Rhul is the rocky and mountainous home of the dwarves. Honorable, stoic, stocky and robust, they have changed little over the centuries, and neither has their land. Masterwork stone castles and towering fortresses, home for millennia to the numerous clans of the dwarves, have stood here since before man could draw words. Most Rhulfolk can trace their heritage back to the original Thirteen Families who founded the Dwarven nation. They have lived for centuries by the Codex, lengthy clan laws compiled lifetimes ago, and to enter Rhul with thoughts of treachery or malice is to subject one to its harsh edicts.

Unlike the Iosans, the dwarves enjoy the nearby company of mankind. They trade with Khador and

Cygnar in some great amount, giving some of their most mundane trades for source materials they can rarely gather in their own rocky homeland. Lumber, grains, and certain spirits are often traded for dwarf-made armor or weapons made from the impossibly durable ores found deep within the mountainous lairs of the Hundred Houses. They have only recently involved themselves in the travails of mankind, making their insights crucial to the expulsion of the Orgoth. With every generation they get more and more attached to the happenings of the "youthful beardlings," and I expect to see more from the dwarves in the decades to come.

Honor is their code, and should they choose to back one of the kingdoms of man, they will come out of their millennia-old ancestral homes and defend their honor with every dwarf's life. It is passing well for mankind to have established alliances with the denizens of Rhul.

Blight's Day, evening

It isn't often I get to the lesser kingdoms of Llael and Ord. I always seem to skip over them when I am chronicling. But today I shall touch on them in brief, for they have managed to grow within the shadows cast by the larger kingdoms.

Llael is a rather smallish place, positioned at the easternmost corner of Immoren. On the southeastern corner of the coal rich kingdom is the Bloodstone Marches, a terrible place filled with horrifying, savage beasts. The kingdom also borders the powerful Elder Kingdoms, Ios and Rhul. Their western border is in constant flux with the martial Khadorans, and commerce is tightly restricted with the northfolk. The mighty Black River runs through Llael, always dotted with the many packet ships and steamers of the Minister of Trade. Llael has seen many kings come and go, and their last has passed without heir. Governorship has fallen to the Prime Minister these days, and I wonder if we might ever see another king in our lifetime. This is a matter of growing concern amongst both the common folk and the patriciate of Llael, not to mention the other nations of the Iron Kingdoms.

The other smaller kingdom of Ord is a sailor's paradise. The sea is not only the western border of the kingdom of Ord, but also the primary way of life. Every sailor from the Windless Waste to Cape Mercir has likely experienced the nautical might of Ord one way or another. A harsh mistress, the sea is, filled with Cryxian pirates and countless other hazards; the Ordic Royal Navy, undeniably the most powerful in all of Immoren, is often the answer to such perils, and one would be a fool to ply the waters of Berck Harbor or the Bay of Stone without offering due homage.

The capital city of Ord may be Merin, but its most notorious one—and I daresay interesting, as it's one of my favorites—is doubtless Five Fingers. This

The first steamjacks, known as Colossals, drove the Orgoth hordes from the lands of Immoren.

infamous sprawl along the five rivers is a port city on the mouth of the Dragon's Tongue, and home to some of the most disreputable rogues and sailors in the realm. Many a laggard has passed out in the seedy taverns and windy streets of Five Fingers only to awaken in chains within the dark belly of a Cryxian cog, bound for Port Blackwater's infamous slave trade. Pinched on all sides by kingdoms much stronger than their own, one day this seafaring kingdom of rogues and traders will have to make a choice who to side with in order to survive, but to which side their massive navy will sail, I cannot say.

Day of Markus, evening

Khador is a deep-rooted place. Some call it the spine of the body that is Immoren, and it is comprised of a tough people, irascible, choleric, weathered, and proud. They have customs that reach far back into pre-Orgoth times when barbaric horselords roamed and ruled the Khardic Empire. These inclinations remain, and the Khadorans are a very strong folk devoted to their traditions and their Motherland. In point of fact, many queens have governed Khador, and all women are held with higher regard than some would think in such a harsh and masculine land.

During the hard northern winter, which is often five months out of the year, much of Khador is frozen. Strong winds snap trees in half and sudden snows sweep in so fast that entire wagon trains have been flash frozen in mere seconds, many never to be seen again. In such a harsh place, only the strong survive, and this strength is personified by their military, where huge warjacks thunder along next to their ever-enduring men and women.

Conscription is the rule of the Khadoran queen, and every adult male—and any females who wish to—is expected to serve the Motherland for no less than three years. This makes every male citizen of Khador a capable soldier. True, they practice less wizardry than other nations, relying on their strength of arms and massive warjacks to fight their wars, but their mechanika is as strong and durable as any found in Immoren.

Almost as many Khadorans are followers of Menoth as they are of Morrow, and thus have a thick contingent of Menite support. Perhaps partly because of the strict tenets of the Menite faith as well as the militaristic bent of the Morrowans known as the "Sword" faith, the Khadorans have adopted a very aggressive stature concerning their place in the world. They never deny their Motherland's greatness, and have often fought bitter battles with their neighbors to expand her borders.

Cygnar remains their strongest adversary in these skirmishes, known for often coming to the aid of their Llaelese allies and even stubbornly independent Ord, despite no direct involvement. No less than three post-Rebellion wars have occurred between these two nations, the last roughly a century ago, and the Khadorans have never forgotten such transgressions. Indeed, Khadorans often bear grudges against the "meddling Cygnarans." Every soldier is trained to be one swing faster or one step ahead of a Cygnaran soldier and the recent outbreak of border skirmishes may mean another major war is inevitable. While Khador does not have the resources of Cygnar, the magical skills of Cryx, or the spiritual intensity of the Protectorate, they will go to all lengths to secure victory for their Motherland. A military campaign against this mighty nation always proves to be expensive and undoubtedly long, and it should be noted, there is no word in the Khardic tongue for "surrender," but over a dozen that are synonymous for "revenge."

Early Harvest; 3rd afternoon

At the center of the Iron Kingdoms lies Cygnar, and I find myself here for one reason or another more times than I can count. It is upon Cygnaran soil that most of the battles have been, are, and probably will be fought. They have the greatest amounts of natural resources at their disposal, which leads to unparalleled trade with the kingdoms of Ord, Llael, and even Rhul. Cygnar's technology and alchemy is second to none, and improving every day. It is their advances in mechanikal engineering that has given them the greatest edge. The mechanika that stomps along Cygnaran borders are numerous, wielding some of the finest inventions of war that Immoren has ever seen. Recently, I've beheld their advancements using lightning, and their warjacks are some of the most inventive armaments ever to bow to a warcaster's will.

Cygnar's borders touch all of the other true Iron Kingdoms involved in the original Council of Ten—Ord to the northwest, Khador to the north, and Llael in the northeast—and they are ever heedful of their neighbors. The Bloodstone Marches once made up their easternmost border, until the Cygnaran Civil War. After the bloody conflict between the Caspians and the Menites of the south had been resolved, the Menites had been granted a strip of rocky, resource-poor land at the southeast corner of the kingdom, which became what is now the Protectorate of Menoth.

Tensions have risen between these two nations of late, and the Cygnaran king watches his borders carefully for the ever-present threat of invasion. Despite loyal allies in Ord and Llael, he is aware of the bitter hearts of his enemies in Khador and the Protectorate.

In most recent times Cygnar has endured great tragedy, as the current King Leto ousted his older brother, the former King Vinter Raelthorne IV—also called "The Elder"—in a horrible coup. Vinter, a most unpleasant man, managed to escape, and has recently returned from the Bloodstone Marches with strange allies in tow. He attempted unsuccessfully to sack Corvis, but was pushed back into the storm-ridden wastes due to the efforts of some fine heroes. I hear that the Elder has vowed to return, just as so many other neighboring kingdoms have done, and it is said that King Leto sleeps very little these nights. It has never been easy to wear the Cygnaran crown.

Sulonsphar, early morning

From my inn room's balcony, as I overlook the solemn processions in the streets below, I am reminded of the strength of faith. Faith is the tie that binds this place, and it is the strongest faith in the entire realm…even the world I'd wager to guess. It shows in their fervor on the fields of battle.

The youngest of the Iron Kingdoms, the Protectorate of Menoth, was born of the blood and tears shed during the Cygnaran Civil War when Hierarch Sulon fought against the growing faith of Morrow. Caspia was torn apart from within when the amassed Menites of Cygnar took a stand for their faith and fought for their independence. After long negotiations, Cygnar granted them a province of resource-poor lands on the southwestern side of the dangerous Bloodstone Marches, as well as a major prize in eastern Caspia. The city proper, on the west bank, is of course, older, larger, and fashioned much better, and thus kept by the Cygnarans—this was never a question—while the eastern portion of the city had endured the brunt of the fighting. Many of the buildings were little more than rubble-strewn husks. Nevertheless, in due time, a newly fashioned city was pulled up from the ashes and dubbed Sul, after the Hierarch himself.

The Menites say they knew what they were getting when they agreed to the terms—no standing army, high taxes paid to the Cygnaran crown, royal watchmen throughout the newly formed Protectorate; all of this ceded for a strip of rocky land that is home to tribes of gypsies, vagabonds, outlaws, barbarians, and worse. Although this sandy and often barren land has little lumber and even less ore to be found, the wind-blown plains have surprisingly yielded great amounts of diamonds in recent decades, which are perhaps the Protectorate's saving grace. In addition, beneath the rocky soil an abundance of oil has been discovered; oil used in every walk of life—fuel, light, even in the weapons they create in secret for their theocracy. Yes, despite the order of no armies in the Protectorate, it is said the Menites have warjacks and soldiers that selflessly wield a fiery fluid in many forms, from death-vomiting flamethrowers to powerfully experimental rockets. For them, the challenge to survive is more than worth the suffering involved in carving out a life in their new home.

The Protectorates worship a powerful god who punishes harshly in the afterlife if one's life is deemed without value, and so each Menite is prepared to follow the holy orders of the hierarchy without question. The Hierarch's tenets just barely allow for contact with the kingdoms of Ord and Llael, but adheres to Menoth's teachings that man is the true race of Caen, and so thus have very little to do at all with the "lesser" races of Immoren, namely the elves, dwarves, and gobbers. Khador retains a large Menite faith within its borders, and I am told that the northfolk of Khador have found a great ally among the Protectorate's faithful, for it is known that Cygnar places Morrow over Menoth, and that is a great and unforgivable sacrilege in their eyes. I have seen the secret workshops in the Protectorate, and when the word comes down to the people from their Hierarch, I hope Cygnar is ready for what the Menites have in store for them. Faith is a powerful provider, especially faith as strong as theirs. It takes that sort of faith to perform some of the duties required of the Menites, and I do not envy the targets of such bloody deeds. It may be Menoth's will to punish and torture those unworthy who pass into the afterlife, but sometimes it does seem his children are overly eager to send them to him. Very eager, indeed.

Somewhere off the Gulf of Cygnar, date unknown

From here in the crow's nest of a north-bound steamer, I can see the fortress of Hell's Hook, on the tip of the island Scharde, and beyond it the dark clouds that obscure the island kingdom of the Cryx. Very few, myself included, have walked the black soil amidst the undying hordes and necro-mechanikal constructs that call this place home.

The Scharde Islands are known also as the Cryxian Empire, the dark dragon god-king "Toruk's

Roost," and the Pirate Kingdom; all of these are names for the rocky island grouping just off the Broken Coast of southern Cygnar. The kingdom of Cryx spirals out over the Scharde Islands from Skell, the place where the evil Lord Toruk landed thousands of years ago and claimed the islands as his own. He is the oldest dragon in the world, called the Father of All Dragons, and his rule is without question. His blight extends for miles from the ashen city, and if it were not for my enchanted livery, I may very well have succumbed to it by now. Entire towns have been ground to dust under Toruk's ancient talons, and thousands have felt the lash under the command of his generals, the Lich Lords and their sultry war witches.

The Cryx sail out past their island homes in search of raw materials and resources, spilling hundreds of bloodthirsty pirates, warriors, and strange necromantic constructs onto the shores of the mainland. These sought-after resources include ore and lumber, gold and silver, the bodies of the dead for use in their infernal rites and rituals, and slaves to work in the dark obsidian mines on Scharde or else lashed to an oar in the galleys of pirate vessels. Some end up forcibly enlisted in the armies of the Cryx as thralls, part undead creature and part mechanika. What is salvaged of those who are nearly dissolved away by the powerful acidic solvents the Cryx spray, vomit, or hurl at them, are kept for use in the creation of the frighteningly fast and lethal bonejacks and helljacks. Through the necromancy of his warcasters, Lord Toruk wields an eternal army that grows with every victory, even those of the other kingdoms. War and death go hand-in-hand, and in the Cryxian Empire death is only the lubricant for the great war machine itself.

No one truly knows what Lord Toruk is planning, but I have noted an increase in the armies of his undying machinations sailing toward the inland kingdoms these past few years. I fear if the Iron Kingdoms do not settle their own disputes, we may all very well feel the lash of another tyrant rather before long.

Midwinter, 13th day

It was once that I would look out over the storm-laden sands of the Bloodstone Marches and wonder what it would be like to traverse its fierce expanse. Now, I do not wish to look that way ever—except maybe to watch for the unknown, something that I cannot say happens to me often.

Although not a kingdom in its own right, something should be said about the recent happenings in the Bloodstone Marches. Located north of Menoth's theocracy and east of Cygnar, the Bloodstone Marches is a sun scorched, wind swept terrain. It is difficult to survive in such a place where uncharted sand dunes are veritable death traps. Beyond the howling winds, illusive mirages, and indigenous beasts is a vast expanse of storm-blasted deserts called the Storm Lands, which even the bravest adventurer would be mad to enter. This is a withered realm pockmarked by lightning strikes and dust devils and the cries and howls of savage creatures echoing from within its sandy wastes.

The only human settlement I know of anywhere near the Marches is a small mining town called Ternon Crag. The miners of the Crag make a perilous living digging gold and coal from the mountains that ring the Marches, and they have learned but one thing about that treacherous void to the east: stay the hell out. In recent times, however, one man of great note has not followed the miners' advice: Vinter Raelthorne IV, "the Exiled." No one except he knows what happened when he journeyed into the wastelands beyond the great storms, but he came back across those mountains with terrifying allies the likes of which had never been seen before in the west—the Skorne.

I know very little about these Skorne, except that they are powerful warriors that remind me, from my studies, of another race with much the same warlike tendencies: our former conquerors, the Orgoth. The Skorne use a foreign alchemy in their firearms and cannons, and have great beasts to carry them into battle, augmented by powerful wizardry rivaling that of the elder races. When Raelthorne's invasion force attacked Corvis, the beasts and warriors of the Skorne nearly bested Cygnar's soldiers. Even the mighty warjacks were hard pressed against the titanic creatures at the Elder's command, if it were not for help—some claim—through divine intervention. Heroes of some renown were instrumental in handing Vinter and his Skorne a surprising defeat, sending them back across the Storm Lands into the Marches, but it is said the Exiled has vowed to return. Should more of the alien race be waiting to join his campaign, I can only pray Morrow is still watching over us.

Morrowsday, dusk

In the Iron Kingdoms, it seems war is always happening. Mankind is a destructive lot. I hear the echo of a cannon's roar not far from my balcony here in Five Fingers. It is strange that I no longer flinch as I once did in my youth—have I become so accustomed to the sounds of war?

It looks as if we are a people that revel in the bloody soil of the battlefield. Quick and ingenious are the minds of men in learning the most pernicious arts, and where once soldiers wielded sword and spear they now launch cannon shot from massive ordnance and deadly rounds from mastercrafted pistols, while mechaniks put these very elements and more to work in the weapons of the volatile, ash-spewing warjacks. The science of war has evolved, and now there are as many alchemists and wizards employed by today's armies as blacksmiths and fletchers. Indeed, it is such that a single warjack is replacing entire companies of cavalry and the role of commander has turned over to these infamous warcasters.

I fear we stand in the calm before the storm in western Immoren. But I do try to remain hopeful. In spite of everything, our finest hours have often come sprouting from the swirl of our most chaotic times. In my studies and travels I have seen this realm come ever closer to its own end, only to stand hard and fast when the time is right. I have noticed that Immoren's—maybe even Caen's as a whole—heartfire is stoked by the wars and skirmishes around and within it. It seems to keep this great machine stomping ahead on the path of time.

I think it will survive.

After all, these are the Iron Kingdoms…and perhaps we are all cogs…in this everlasting *WARMACHINE*.

THE GAME

RULES BASICS

GENERAL KNOWLEDGE FOR WARMACHINE STEAM-POWERED COMBAT

GAME OVERVIEW

In WARMACHINE, the very earth shakes during fierce confrontations where six-ton iron constructs slam into one another with the destructive force of a locomotive, lead-spewing canon chew through armor plating as easily as flesh, and a tempest of arcane magics sets the battlefield ablaze with such Armageddon-like proportion that the gods themselves fear to tread such tormented ground.

WARMACHINE is a fast-paced and aggressive 30mm tabletop miniatures battle game set in the steam-powered fantasy world of the Iron Kingdoms. Players take on the role of elite soldier-sorcerers known as *warcasters*. While the warcasters are formidable combatants on their own right, their true strength lies in their ability to magically control and coordinate mighty *warjacks*—massive steam-powered combat automatons that are the pinnacle of military might in the Iron Kingdoms. Players collect, assemble, and paint fantastic Rivet Head Studios models that represent the varied men, machines, creatures, and worse in their army. This book provides the rules for using those models in steam-powered miniatures combat. This is Full Metal Fantasy—and your tabletop will never be the same!

A WARMACHINE army is built around a warcaster and his *battlegroup* of warjacks. Squads of soldiers and support teams may be fielded to further bolster a battlegroup's combat capability. Sometimes, huge armies with multiple battlegroups and legions of soldiers take the field to crush their enemies with the combined might of muscle and iron.

Warjacks, called 'jacks for short, are specialized fighting machines—hulking iron behemoths powered by a fusion of steam technology and arcane science and controlled with deadly precision by a warcaster. While generally most deadly in hand-to-hand combat, warjacks can be outfitted with a plethora of wicked melee or ranged weaponry and equipment. Specialized jacks, known as *channelers*, are equipped with a device called an *arc node* that lets the warcaster project a spell through the warjack itself.

A warcaster is in constant telepathic contact with the 'jacks in his battlegroup. During the course of a confrontation, warcasters continually draw on a magical energy called *focus*. A warcaster's focus points may be used to *boost* his own combat abilities or those of his warjacks in his *control area*, or to cast powerful spells.

The caster is the tie that binds the battlegroup as well as its weakest link. If the warcaster falls, his 'jacks become little more than iron shells.

The outcome of a battle depends on your ability to think quickly, use sound tactics, and decisively employ your forces. A crucial component of your strategy will be the management of your warcasters' focus points and how you use it to boost your warjacks' abilities. Focus points can be used to significantly enhance a 'jack's already impressive combat power; properly allocated, they can make an entire battlegroup a nigh-unstoppable instrument of destruction!

Victory favors the bold! So bring it on, if you've got the metal.

In addition to this book and your army of WARMACHINE models, you will also need a few basic items to play:

- A table or playing surface, typically 4' X 4', where you can conduct your battles.
- A tape measure or ruler to measure movement and attack distances.
- A few six-sided dice—four or more will be plenty.
- A handful of tokens to indicate focus points, spell effects, and so on.
- The appropriate stat cards included with each model. We suggest you put them in card sleeves and use a dry erase marker, or make photocopies.
- The markers and templates found in the Templates section at the back of this book. You may photocopy them for personal use.

SUMMARY OF PLAY

Before a battle begins, players agree on an *encounter level* and a *scenario* to be played, then create their armies based on those guidelines. Next, determine the *turn order*, which will not change throughout the game. Players then deploy their forces and prepare for the battle to begin.

Battles are conducted in a series of *game rounds*. Each game round, every player receives one *turn* to command his own army. During his turn, a player may *activate* all the models in his force, one after the other. When activated, a model may move and then perform one of a variety of *actions*, such as attacking, repairing a jack, or even casting spells. Once all players have taken their turns, the current game round ends and a new one begins, starting again with the first player. Game rounds continue until one side wins, either by destroying all opposition, meeting scenario objectives, or accepting its opponent's surrender.

DICE AND ROUNDING

WARMACHINE uses six-sided dice, abbreviated d6, to determine the success of attacks and other actions. Most events, such as attacks, require rolling two dice. Other events typically require rolling from one to four dice.

Some events call for rolling a d3. To do so, roll a d6, divide the result by two, and round up.

Some instances call for a model's stat or a die roll to be divided in half. With the exception of distances, always round a fractional result to the next highest whole number.

GENERAL GUIDELINES

This section covers how WARMACHINE handles game terms, the relationship between standard and special rules, sportsmanship between players, and the procedures for resolving rules disputes.

Game Terms

When these rules introduce a game term in a definitive fashion, its name appears in **bold**. If the rules reference a term from another section, its first appearance in that section will be in *italics*. For ease of reference, all game terms have their complete definitions in the Glossary.

Rule Priority

While WARMACHINE is a complex game that provides a multitude of options, the rules are actually intuitive and easy to learn. The standard rules lay the foundation upon which the game is built and provide all the typical mechanics used in play. Added to these are various *special rules* that usually depend on specific models and modify the standard rules in certain circumstances. When they apply, these special rules take precedence. For example, a situation may call for a model to make a *command check*. However, if that model is a warjack, it does not make the check since warjacks are specifically mentioned as never taking command checks.

Sportsmanship & Sharing Information

Although WARMACHINE simulates violent battles between mammoth forces, you should still strive to be a good sportsman in all aspects of the game. Remember, this is a game meant to provide entertainment and friendly competition. Whether winning or losing, you should still be having lots of fun.

From time to time, your opponent may wish to see your records to verify a model's stats or see how much damage a particular warjack has taken. Always represent this information honestly and share your records and information without hesitation.

Resolving Rules Issues

These rules have been carefully designed to provide as much guidance as possible in all aspects of play. However, you may encounter situations where the proper course of action is not immediately obvious. For instance, players may disagree on whether or not a model has *line of sight* to its intended target.

During a game, try to quickly resolve the issue in the interest of keeping the game flowing. After the game, you will have plenty of time to decide the best answer, which can then be incorporated into later games.

If a situation arises in which all players cannot agree on a solution, quickly discuss the matter and reference this rulebook for an answer, but don't spend so much time doing so that you slow the game. In striving to resolve an issue, common sense and the precedents set by the rules should be your guides.

If the dispute cannot be solved quickly, have one player from each side roll a d6—the highest roller gets to decide the outcome. Reroll any ties. In the interest of fairness, once a ruling has been made for a specific issue, it applies for all similar circumstances for the rest of the game. After the game ends, you can take the time to reference the rules and thoroughly discuss the issue to decide how to best handle that same situation in the future.

WHAT'S A D6? HOW ABOUT A D3?

A six-sided die is referred to as a d6. Two six-sided dice are abbreviated as 2d6, three dice as 3d6, and so on.

A d3 is a quick way to say "roll a d6 and divide by 2, rounding up". Quite a mouthful! Here's how to quickly read the results of a d3 roll:

1 or 2 = 1

3 or 4 = 2

5 or 6 = 3

MODELS—THE DOGS OF WAR

MODEL TYPES, STATS, AND ARMY BUILDING

MODEL TYPES

Each WARMACHINE combatant is represented on the tabletop by a highly detailed and dramatically posed miniature figurine, referred to as a **model**. There are several basic **model types:** *warcasters, warjacks, troops,* and *solos*. Warcasters, troops, and solos are collectively referred to as **warriors**. A warrior is a living model unless otherwise noted.

Warcasters

A **warcaster** is a tremendously powerful sorcerer, warpriest, or battlemage with the ability to telepathically control a group of warjacks. A warcaster is a deadly opponent, highly skilled in both physical combat and arcane spell casting.

During battle, a warcaster commands his *battlegroup* of warjacks in an effort to complete his objectives. A warcaster may use his *focus points* to enhance his combat abilities and cast spells, or he may assign them to individual warjacks to increase their fighting abilities. A warcaster may also channel spells through 'jacks equipped with *arc nodes*, effectively extending the range of his magical powers.

Warcasters are *independent models*.

Warjacks

A **steamjack** is a mechanikal construct given the ability to reason by a magical brain, known as a **cortex**, housed within its hull. A steamjack does not possess high cognitive powers, but can execute simple commands and make logical decisions to complete its assigned tasks. Steamjacks are used throughout the Iron Kingdoms for a variety of heavy or dangerous tasks that would be impossible for a human to perform.

A **warjack** is a steamjack built expressly to wage war. Armed with the most fearsome ranged and close-combat weaponry yet devised, a warjack is more than a match for a dozen men. While able to think and operate independently, a warjack reaches its full destructive potential only when controlled by a warcaster. The warcaster forms a telepathic link to each of the warjacks in his battlegroup. This link lets the warcaster give his warjacks commands and use focus to *boost* their abilities with just a thought. Through focus, a warcaster can make his warjacks' attacks more accurate and powerful. A well-controlled warjack can even perform amazing *power attacks*, such as slamming its opponents into buildings, grappling their weapons, or even throwing them.

The telepathic link binding a warcaster to his warjacks is fragile. If a warjack's cortex is disabled, it can no longer receive focus points. Even worse, should a warcaster become incapacitated, the telepathic links to his 'jacks will sever. The accompanying feedback of uncontrolled magical energies overloads and shorts out his warjacks' cortexes, causing the 'jacks to cease functioning.

A warjack is classified as either a **light warjack** or **heavy warjack**, based on its size and combat abilities. Even though they are assigned to a specific battlegroup, each warjack is an *independent model*.

Troopers

Troopers are models such as soldiers, riflemen, and mechaniks that operate together in groups called **units**. A unit always operates as a single coherent force. All the troopers in a unit share identical attributes and carry the same weapons. Troopers, including *leaders*, cannot receive focus points to boost their abilities.

Some special rules and spells affect entire units. When any trooper in a unit is affected by a special rule such as *terror* or a unit-affecting spell, every member of that unit is affected. Special rules and spells that affect units are noted in their description.

Leaders

Usually, one trooper in a unit is trained as a **leader**, a model with a different stat profile—and possibly different weaponry—that can give its unit *orders*. A leader generally has a higher Command (CMD) stat than the other troopers in his unit. A unit uses its leader's CMD stat for all command checks while its leader is in play.

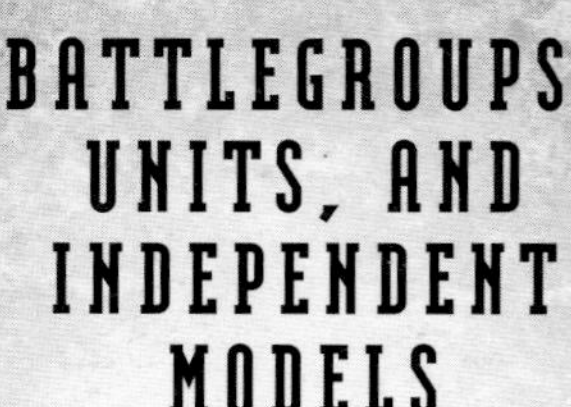

- A **battlegroup** includes a warcaster and the warjacks he controls. A warcaster can allocate focus points to or channel spells through only the warjacks in his battlegroup.

- **Independent models** are those that activate individually. Warcasters, warjacks, and solos are independent models.

- A **unit** is a group of similarly trained and equipped trooper models that operate together as a single force. A unit usually contains one leader and two or more additional troopers.

Solos

Solos are individuals such as assassins and snipers that operate alone. Solos cannot receive focus points to boost their abilities. Solos are *independent models*.

MODEL PROFILES

Every model and unit has a unique profile that translates its combat abilities into game terms. WARMACHINE uses a series of *stats* to quantify and scale the attributes fundamental to game play. In addition, a model may have *special rules* that further enhance its performance. A model's or unit's army list entry provides all the game information required for it to battle across your tabletop.

A model's or unit's **stat card** provides a quick in-game reference for its profile and special rules. The card's front has model and weapon stats, a special rules list, and a damage grid and feat description, if applicable. A model's army creation information, victory points, and summarized special rule and spell descriptions appear on the card's back. Refer to this book for a special rule's or spell's complete rules text, which take precedence over the abridged version on the stat cards.

Model Statistics

Model statistics, or **stats**, provide a numerical representation of a model's basic combat qualities—the higher the number, the better the stat. These stats are used for various die rolls throughout the game. The **stat bar** presents the model statistics in an easy-to-reference format.

SAMPLE STAT BAR

COMMANDER COLEMAN STRYKER

FOCUS 6			CMD 9		
SPD	STR	MAT	RAT	DEF	ARM
6	6	6	6	16	15

The model statistics and their definitions follow:

Speed (SPD) —A model's normal movement rate. A model moves its SPD stat in inches when *advancing*.

Strength (STR) —A model's physical strength. Add a model's STR stat to the *damage roll* of its melee weapons.

MELEE ATTACK (MAT) —A model's skill with melee weapons such as swords and hammers, or natural weapons like fists and teeth. Add a model's MAT stat to its *melee attack* rolls.

RANGED ATTACK (RAT) —A model's accuracy with ranged weapons such as guns and crossbows, or thrown items like grenades and knives. Add a model's RAT stat to its *ranged attack* rolls.

DEFENSE (DEF) —A model's ability to avoid being hit by an attack. A model's size, quickness, skill, and even magical protection can all contribute to its DEF stat . An *attack roll* must be equal to or greater than the target model's DEF stat to score a hit against it.

ARMOR (ARM) —A model's ability to resist being damaged. This resistance may come from natural resilience, worn armor, or even magical benefits. A model takes one *damage point* for every point that a *damage roll* exceeds its ARM stat .

COMMAND (CMD) —A model's willpower, leadership, and self-discipline. To pass a *command check*, a model must roll equal to or less than its CMD stat . **Command also determines a warcaster's** *command range*. Warjacks do not have a CMD stat .

FOCUS (FOC) —A warcaster's arcane power. Add the warcaster's FOC stat to its *magic attack* rolls. Focus also determines a warcaster's *control area* and *focus points*. Warcasters are the only models that have a FOC stat.

Weapon Statistics

Each of a model's weapons has its own stat bar. A sword icon denotes a melee weapon, while a pistol icon denotes a ranged weapon. A warjack's weapon stats also list the weapon's location. A weapon's stat bar only lists the stats that apply to its use.

SAMPLE RANGED WEAPON STAT BAR

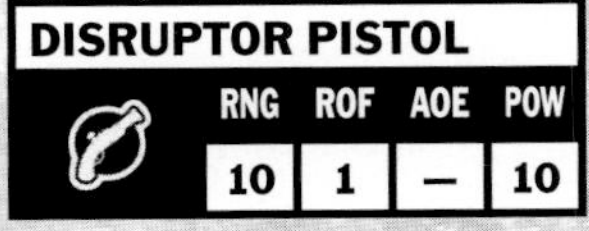

DISRUPTOR PISTOL			
RNG	ROF	AOE	POW
10	1	—	10

SAMPLE MELEE WEAPON STAT BAR

QUICKSILVER		
Special	POW	P+S
Disrupt	7	13

POWER (POW) —The base amount of damage a weapon inflicts. Add the weapon's POW stat to its *damage roll*.

POWER PLUS STRENGTH (P+S) —Melee weapons add both the weapon's POW stat and the model's STR stat to the damage roll. For quick reference, the P+S value provides the sum of these two stats.

RANGE (RNG) —The maximum distance in inches a model can make ranged attacks with this weapon. Measure range from the nearest edge of the attacking model's base to the nearest edge of the target model's base.

RATE OF FIRE (ROF) —The maximum number of times a model can make ranged attacks with this weapon in a turn. Reloading time limits most ranged weapons to only one attack per turn.

AREA OF EFFECT (AOE) —The diameter in inches of the template an *area-of-effect weapon* uses for damage effects. When using an AOE weapon, center the template on the determined *point of impact*. All models covered by the template potentially suffer the attack's effects. See Combat (pg. 39) for detailed rules on AOE weapons. Templates for AOEs can be found on the *templates page*.

SPECIAL RULES—In addition to their normal damage, many weapons have unique advantages or produce extraordinary effects, which their special rules explain. A weapon with more than one such rule lists "Multi," along with a complete effects listing in its card's special rules section.

Special Rules

Most WARMACHINE combatants are highly specialized and trained to fill unique roles on the battlefield. To represent this, certain models have **special rules**, which take precedence over the standard rules. Depending on their use, special rules are categorized as *abilities, feats, special actions, special attacks,* or *orders.*

A model's army list entry and the back of its stat card summarize its special rules. In addition, Combat (pg. 39) and Warcasters and Focus (pg. 54) detail many special rules common to all warjacks and warcasters that do not appear on the stat cards.

ABILITIES—An **ability** typically gives a benefit or capability that modifies how the standard rules apply to the model. Abilities are always in effect and apply every time a game situation warrants their use.

FEATS—Each warcaster has a unique feat that he can use once per game. A warcaster can use this feat freely at any time during his activation, in addition to moving and performing an action.

SPECIAL ACTIONS (★ACTION)—A **special action** lets a model perform an *action* normally unavailable to other models. A model can perform a special action instead of its *combat action* if it meets the specific requirements for its use. Some special actions require a *skill check* to determine their success.

SPECIAL ATTACKS (★ATTACK)—A **special attack** gives a model an attack option normally unavailable to other models. Warjacks can also make a variety of punishing *power attacks*, described in Combat (pg. 39). A model may make one special attack instead of making any normal melee or ranged attacks during its combat action, if it meets the specific requirements.

ORDERS —An **order** lets a model or unit perform a specialized combat maneuver during its activation. A unit may receive an order from a warcaster prior to its activation, or from its *leader* at the beginning of its activation. A *solo* cannot give orders to other models.

Damage Capacity and Damage Grids

A model's **damage capacity** determines how many damage points it can take before being removed from play. Most trooper models do not have a damage capacity—remove them from play as soon as they take one damage point. The army list entry for a more resilient model gives the total amount of damage it can take before being eliminated. Its stat card provides a row of **damage boxes** for tracking the damage it receives. A warjack has a **damage grid** consisting of multiple rows and columns of damage boxes.

Every time one of these models takes damage, mark one damage box for each damage point taken. A model with damage capacity or a damage grid is removed from play once all its damage boxes are marked. However, a model may lose *systems* or become *disabled* before its damage grid fills completely. Warjacks have damage boxes that are also **system boxes**, labeled with a letter denoting what component of the model they represent. When all system boxes for a specific system have been marked, the warjack loses the use of that system. Mark the appropriate **system status box** to show that it is *disabled*. See Combat (pg. 39) for detailed rules on recording damage and its effects.

SAMPLE DAMAGE GRID

DAMAGE GRID	1	2	3	4	5	6
		L			R	
	L	L	M	C	R	R
		M	M	C	C	

SYSTEMS
Left Arm (L)
Rght Arm (R)
Cortex (C)
Movement (M)

Base Size and Facing

The physical model itself has a couple of properties important to game play: *base size* and *facing*.

BASE SIZE

The physical size and mass of a model are reflected by its **base size**. There are three base sizes: **small base** (30mm), **medium base** (40mm), and **large base** (50mm). Most human-sized warrior models have small bases. Larger creatures and light warjacks have medium bases, while very large creatures and heavy warjacks have large bases. A model's army list entry states its base size.

FACING

A model's **facing** is the direction indicated by its head's orientation. The 180° arc centered on the direction its head faces defines the model's **front arc;** the opposite 180° defines its **back arc**. You may want to make two small marks on either side of your models' bases to indicate where the front arc ends and the back arc begins.

A model's front arc determines its perspective of the battlefield. A model typically directs its *actions*, determines *line of sight*, and makes attacks through this arc. Likewise, a model is usually more vulnerable to attacks from its back arc due to a lack of awareness in that direction.

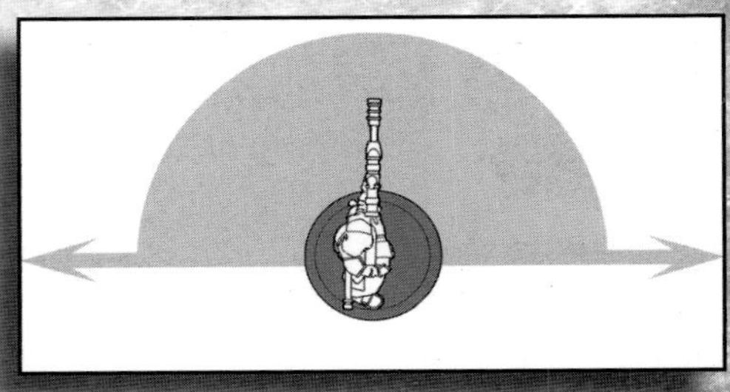

MODEL FACING

PREPARING FOR WAR

BUILDING AN ARMY SUITABLE FOR CRUSHING YOUR OPPONENT

CREATING AN ARMY

A warcaster and his battlegroup form the central fighting group of every WARMACHINE army. Units and solos with a variety of abilities further support the warcaster's battlegroup. In larger battles, you can even field multiple warcaster battlegroups for greater firepower.

To create an army, first decide on an *encounter level,* then spend the allotted *army points* to purchase models and units from the chosen army list. Every army list entry and stat card provides the model's or unit's *point cost* and *field allowance* values, which you must adhere to when designing your force. Specific *scenarios* may modify the standard army creation rules.

Encounter Levels

WARMACHINE battles are played at different **encounter levels** to allow for a diversity of army sizes, strategies, and game experiences. Each encounter level gives the maximum number of **army points** each player can spend when designing an army. You need not spend every point available, but your army cannot exceed the maximum number of army points allowed by the selected level.

Each encounter level also limits the number of warcasters (and therefore battlegroups) available to each player.

DUEL
Max Warcasters: 1 Army Points: 350
Est. Play Time: 30 Minutes

A *duel* occurs when two warcasters cross paths, sometimes on special assignments, other times to settle vicious rivalries. Duels include only individual warcasters and their personal warjacks. Duels are the perfect match for playing with the contents of a Battlegroup Box.

RUMBLE
Max Warcasters: 1 Army Points: 500
Est. Play Time: 60 Minutes

A rumble is an encounter that includes a single warcaster and his battlegroup, supported by a small retinue of units and solos. Rumbles can occur over such things as routine border patrols or elite, surgical missions.

BATTLE ROYALE
Max Warcasters: 2 Army Points: 1000
Est. Play Time: 2 hours

Battles decide the pivotal events in the course of a military campaign. With up to two warcasters in an army, you can fully realize the opportunities for army customization and heavy firepower.

WAR
Max Warcasters: 3 Army Points: 1500
Est. Play Time: 3 hours

When objectives can no longer be achieved by deploying small forces, when both sides refuse to yield, nothing less than *war* can resolve their differences. This huge game, in which each side fields up to three warcasters, allows your forces enough breadth and depth to inflict and recover from staggering blows as the fight seesaws back and forth.

APOCALYPSE
Max Warcasters: 4+ Army Points: 2000+
Est. Play Time: 4+ hours

When a conflict rages so bitterly that war itself cannot resolve it, the final reckoning has arrived, for you have summoned the *apocalypse*. An apocalypse is a massive game, employing four or more warcasters in each force. Although this vast endeavor should never be undertaken lightly, it yields game experiences that can be found in no other arena. Warcasters may be added to a force for every additional increment of 500 pts.

Battlegroups

Each warcaster in an army controls a force of warjacks. A warcaster and his assigned warjacks are collectively referred to as a **battlegroup**. There is no limit to the number of warjacks that may be fielded in each warcaster's battlegroup.

Warcasters can give focus points only to warjacks in their battlegroup. If an army has multiple battlegroups, it is important to distinguish which warjacks are controlled by each warcaster.

Since warcasters and warjacks are *independent models*, each model in a battlegroup can move freely about the battlefield separate from the rest of the group. Although warjacks usually benefit from remaining within their caster's *control area*, they are not required to do so.

Characters

Some models represent unique individuals from the Iron Kingdoms. These personalities receive proper names and are identified as **characters**. Characters follow the rules for their basic model type.

An army may include only one model of each named character. For instance, you can never have two Commander Coleman Strykers in the same army. However, two rival Cygnar players could each field Commander Stryker. How can this be?

In the chaos and tumult that now cloaks the war-torn Iron Kingdoms, pretenders and imposters abound. Thus, you may find yourself fielding one or more warcasters who, impossibly, face their apparent counterparts across the field of battle. Who is the *real* Commander Coleman Stryker or Butcher of Khardov? Victory alone can determine the answer.

Point Costs

A model's **point cost** indicates how many *army points* you must spend to include one of these models, or in the case of units, one basic unit, in your army. Some entries also include options to spend additional points for upgrades, typically in the form of adding more troopers to a unit.

Field Allowance

Field allowance (FA) is the maximum number of models or units of a given type that may be included for each warcaster in an army. For example, Cygnar Trenchers have an FA: 2, indicating that an army may have up to two Trencher units for each warcaster. An army with two warcasters could have up to four Trencher units.

A field allowance of "U" means that an unlimited number of these models or units may be fielded in an army. A field allowance of "C" means that the model is a character; only one of each named character is allowed per army.

SETUP, DEPLOYMENT, AND VICTORY CONDITIONS

WARMACHINE games can be played in a variety of ways. The primary influences on a game's setup are its encounter level, number of players, and victory conditions. Players may also agree to play a specific scenario, or even design one of their own.

Sample Army

We built the following army to illustrate WARMACHINE's army creation concepts. This army is designed for the Battle Royale encounter level, meaning a player can spend a maximum of 1,000 army points and field up to two warcasters.

WARCASTER—COMMANDER STRYKER	64
STRYKER'S BATTLEGROUP	
1 Ironclad Heavy Warjack	103
2 Lancer Light Warjacks	152 (76 ea.)
WARCASTER—CAPTAIN HALEY	58
HALEY'S BATTLEGROUP	
1 Defender Heavy Warjack	122
1 Charger Light Warjack	75
1 Lancer Light Warjack	76
SUPPORT	
1 Long Gunner Squad (FA: 2),	
with one additional trooper	74 (74+10)
3 Storm Blade Squads (FA: 2)	252 (84 ea.)
1 Field Mechanik Unit (FA: 3),	
with 2 additional Bodgers	20 (16+2+2)
Total	996 Points

The chosen warcasters are Commander Stryker and Captain Haley, avoiding duplication since they are named characters. The six warjacks in the army are assigned to specific battlegroups. The unit of Long Rifles has an additional Rifleman, as allowed by the unit options. Three units of Storm Blades are chosen as well. With an FA: 2 and two warcasters, this army could have a total of four such units. Finally, the mechanik unit receives two additional Bodgers as allowed by the options. This brings the total army points spent to 996. Since the Mechanik unit is at maximum size and nothing else is available for 4 points or less, those points remain unspent.

Two-Player Games

In a typical WARMACHINE game, two players match forces across a 4′ by 4′ playing surface. After setting up the battlefield according to Terrain (pg. 59), each player rolls a d6. The highest roller chooses any player, including himself, to be the first player. Once established, the turn order remains the same for the rest of the game.

Players then deploy their armies, starting with the first player. The first player may choose any edge of the playing surface and deploy all his forces up to 10″ in from that edge. Deploy units so that all of their troopers are in *skirmish formation* or closer. The second player then deploys his forces on the opposite side of the playing surface, following the same guidelines.

Multiplayer Games

When playing multiplayer games of WARMACHINE, players can choose to play either a team game or a free-for-all game. After agreeing on the type of game to be played, set up the battlefield, then use the following guidelines to determine the game's turn order.

TEAM GAMES

Before beginning a team game, the players must split into two opposing sides. Decide the composition of the teams. Each team may only include one of any *character* model. To begin, have one player from each team roll a d6 to establish the turn order. The team that rolls highest gets to choose which team goes first; the first team gets to choose which of their players will be the first player. Once the first player is determined, the opposing team chooses which of their players will go next. The first team then nominates one of their players to be third, followed again by the opposing team, continuing until all players have a place in the turn order. This ensures the turn order will alternate between players of opposing teams.

Force deployment should be done in turn order, following the above guidelines, with teammates sharing the same deployment zone opposite the battlefield from their opponents' deployment zone.

FREE-FOR-ALL GAMES

You can also choose to play a multiplayer game in which each player fights independently in a free-for-all game. To establish turn order, each player rolls a d6. Starting with the highest roller and working to the lowest, each player gets to choose any available position in the turn order. Reroll ties as you come to them, with the highest reroller winning his choice of positions, followed by the next highest reroller, and so on. For example, Matt, Jason, Mike, and Steve roll 6, 5, 5, and 3 respectively for turn order. Matt chooses his position first. Then Jason and Mike reroll their tie, getting a 4 and a 2. Jason chooses next, followed by Mike. As the lowest roller, Steve gets the remaining position in the turn order.

Use your best judgment to establish deployment zones based on the number of players and the size and shape of your playing surface. Deployment zones should be spaced so that no player gets a significant advantage or disadvantage—unless mutually agreed upon. As a starting point, for games with three or four players on a 4' by 4' playing surface, consider deploying forces within 10" of any corner of the playing area to ensure adequate separation.

Scenarios

If all players agree, you can set up the game according to a specific scenario. Scenarios add an extra layer of excitement by incorporating special circumstances and unique rules. You win a scenario by achieving its objectives, not necessarily by eliminating your opponent's forces. Certain scenarios have specific guidelines for playing-area size, terrain setup, deployment zones, and turn order. See Scenarios (pg. 63) for the scenario descriptions. If you feel particularly daring, you can randomly determine which scenario to play.

As long as all players agree, you can even design your own scenarios to create a unique battle experience. Just be sure to allow a minimum of 20" between rival deployment zones. Feel free to be creative when setting up your games. For instance, if you have three players, one player could set up in the middle of the table as a defender and the other two could attack from opposite edges. Or you could have a four-player team game, with teammates deploying across from each other on opposite edges of the battlefield, which means everyone will have enemies on either side. Your imagination is the only limit.

Victory Conditions

Establish victory conditions before deploying forces. Typically, victory goes to the player or team who eliminates the opposition or accepts their surrender. A scenario defines specific objectives for each side. You can also use victory points to determine a game's winner.

VICTORY POINTS

Every model and unit is worth a set number of victory points. Award a model's or unit's victory points to the player or team that removes it from play or causes it to flee off the table. If a player accidentally or intentionally removes a friendly model from play, be it his own or a teammate's, award its full victory points to every opposing player or team.

Decide how victory points will be used, if at all, before starting the game. One option is to end the game after a chosen number of game rounds. Victory goes to the player or team that has the most victory points at the end of the last game round. Another option is to end the game once any player or team accumulates a minimum number of victory points. Once a player or team reaches their victory point goal, the game will end at the conclusion of the current game round, with victory going to the player or team that has the most victory points at that time. If you run out of time while playing a game with other victory conditions, you may use victory points to declare a winner.

Starting the Game

After establishing victory conditions and deploying forces, the first game round begins. A warcaster begins the game with his full allotment of focus points. Starting with the first player, each player takes a turn in turn order. Game rounds continue until one side achieves its victory conditions and wins the game.

A WARMACHINE BATTLEFIELD SHOWN WITH FORCES DEPLOYED

GAMEPLAY—THE RULES OF ENGAGEMENT

TURN SEQUENCE, MOVEMENT, AND ACTIONS

THE GAME ROUND

WARMACHINE battles are fought in a series of game rounds. Each game round, every player takes a turn in the order established during setup. Once the last player in the turn order completes his turn, the current game round ends. A new game round then begins, starting again with the first player. Game rounds continue until one side wins the game.

While game rounds organize player turns, rounds handle game effects. A round is measured from the current player's turn to the beginning of that player's next turn, regardless of his location in the turn order. When put in play, a game effect with a duration of one round expires at the beginning of the current player's next turn. This means that every player will take one turn while the effect is in play.

THE PLAYER TURN

A player's turn has three phases: *maintenance*, *control*, and *activation*.

Maintenance Phase

During the maintenance phase, remove markers and effects that expire this turn and resolve any compulsory effects on your models. First, remove markers for unused focus points left over from your previous turn. Then remove any effects that expire at the beginning of your turn. Next, apply continuous effects to any models you control.

Activate fleeing models and units under your control at the end of this phase. A fleeing model or unit may attempt to rally at the end of its activation. See Command (pg. 57) for detailed rules on fleeing and rallying.

Control Phase

During the control phase, each of your warcasters receives a number of focus points equal to his FOC stat. Each warcaster may allocate focus points to his battlegroup's warjacks within his control area and to his spells that require upkeep. If a warcaster does not allocate focus points to one of his spells that requires upkeep, its effects end immediately.

Activation Phase

The activation phase is the major portion of a player's turn. You may activate each model and unit you control once during this phase, except for models that fled in the maintenance phase. Even if the fleeing models rallied, you cannot activate them again this turn. Activate the rest of the models and units under your control in any order. After the active model or unit completes its activation, it cannot activate again this turn.

Typically, an active model first moves, then performs one action. After moving or forfeiting its movement, the model may perform one action allowed by the movement option chosen. See Movement for detailed rules on the different types of movement and the actions they allow. See Actions for detailed rules on action resolution.

ACTIVATING MODELS

Always completely resolve the active model's or unit's movement before it perfoms any actions.

Activating Independent Models

Independent models activate individually. Only one independent model can activate at a time. The formation rules do not constrain an independent model's movement. The active model must complete its movement and resolve its action and attacks before another model or unit can be activated.

Activating Units

Troopers do not activate independently. Instead, an entire unit activates at once. When a unit activates, every member of the unit must complete or forfeit its movement before any member uses an action. After completing the entire unit's movement, resolve each trooper's action and attacks in turn. Every member of the active unit must complete its movement and resolve its action and attacks before another model or unit may be activated.

Units require strong leadership and guidance to be effective on the battlefield. Since a unit operates as one body, it functions best when all members are in formation. A unit must receive an order from its leader or a nearby warcaster to run, charge, or perform a specialized combat maneuver. Additionally, a unit must attempt to end its movement with all members in skirmish formation or closer.

LINE OF SIGHT

Many game situations, such as charging, ranged attacks, and some magical attacks, require a model to have line of sight (LOS) to its intended target. A model has line of sight to a target if you can draw a straight, unobstructed line from the center of its base at head height through its front arc to any part of the target model, including its base. Warrior models present a slight exception to this rule. Unlike warjack models, items held in the hands of warrior models—such as their weapons or a banner pole—do not count as part of the model for determining line of sight. So, a Khadoran Widowmaker does not have line of sight to a Menite Temple Flameguard if all he can see is the tip of its spear poking over a wall.

Simply put, having line of sight means that the model can see its target. If a model's line of sight is questionable, it may be easiest for a player to position himself to see the table from his model's perspective. A laser pointer may also come in handy when determining line of sight.

Intervening Models

A model blocks line of sight to models that have equal- or smaller-sized bases. If any line between two models crosses another model's base, that model is an intervening model. You cannot draw a line of sight across an intervening model's base to models that have equal- or smaller-sized bases. However, you might still have a line of sight to the target if its base is not completely obscured by the intervening model's base.

An intervening model does not block line of sight to models that have larger bases—ignore it when drawing line of sight.

WHAT DOES A MODEL DO WHEN ACTIVATED?

An active model first moves or forfeits its movement. Depending on the movement option chosen, the model may be able to perform either a combat action or a special action. A combat action lets a model make attacks. A special action lets a model perform a unique battlefield function, such as repairing a warjack or creating Scrap Thralls.

Targeting a Ranged or Magic Attack

A ranged or magic attack need not target the nearest enemy model, but intervening models may prevent a model further away from being targeted.

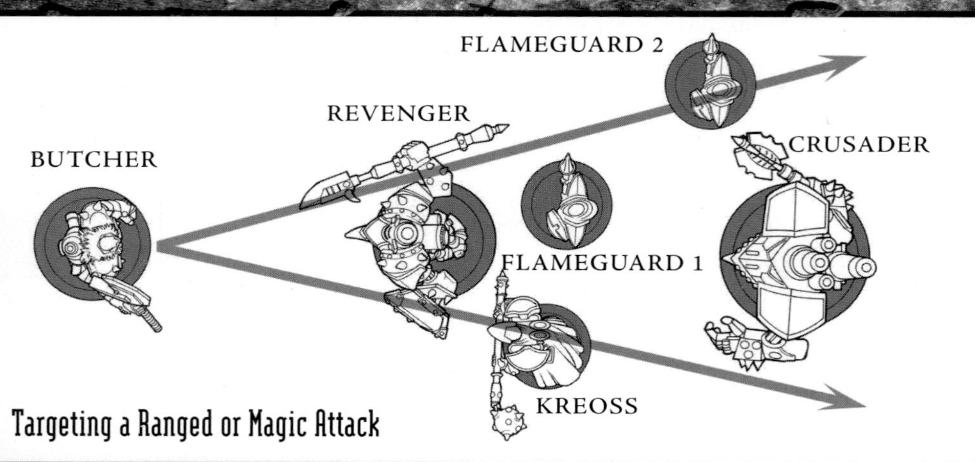

This diagram highlights the LOS rules. The Butcher has LOS to the Revenger. Since the Revenger has a medium base, it is an intervening model for other models with medium and small bases. The Butcher does not have LOS to Flameguard 1 since he cannot draw a line to its base that does not cross the Revenger's base. The Butcher does have LOS to Flameguard 2 since he can draw a line of sight to it that does not cross the Revenger's base.

Since they have smaller bases, the Revenger and the Flameguard are not intervening models for the Crusader—the Butcher can draw a line of sight to the Crusader as if those models were not there.

Kreoss is a special case. The Revenger is an intervening model since it has a larger base, but the Butcher does have LOS to Kreoss since his base is not completely obscured, just like Flameguard 2. The difference is that Kreoss is within 1" of the intervening model, so the Butcher cannot target him with a ranged attack. However, the Butcher can still choose to charge him!

A ranged or magic attack cannot target a model within 1" of an intervening model that has an equal- or larger-sized base, even if the attacker has line of sight. A ranged or magic attack by a model on elevated terrain can target any model on lower terrain and in line of sight, regardless of intervening models. See Combat (pg. 39) for detailed rules on making ranged attacks.

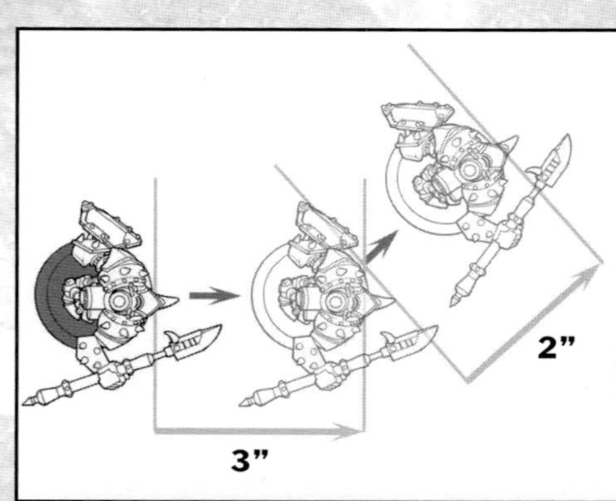

MEASURING MOVEMENT

MOVEMENT

The first part of a model's activation is movement. A model must use or forfeit its movement before performing any action. Make all movement measurements from the front of a model's base. Determine the distance a model moves by measuring how far the front of its base travels. The distance moved is absolute; we suggest using a flexible measuring device to keep accurate track of a model's movement. Terrain, spells, and other effects can reduce a model's movement or prevent it completely. Movement penalties are cumulative, but a model allowed to move can always move at least 1". See Terrain (pg. 59) for full details on terrain features and how they affect movement.

A moving model's base may not pass over another model's base. It can move between models only if enough room exists for its base to pass between the other models' bases without touching them.

A model can voluntarily forfeit its movement by not changing its position or facing. If it does so, the model can perform one action and gains an **aiming** bonus for any ranged attacks made during this activation.

A model unable to move cannot change its position or facing. It may or may not be able to perform an action, depending on the effect preventing its movement. A model that cannot move does not receive the aiming bonus.

There are three different types of movement: advancing, running, and charging.

Advancing

An advancing model may move up to its Speed (SPD) in inches. An advancing model always faces its direction of movement, but may change facing freely while moving and may face any direction after moving. After a model advances, it may perform one action. An advancing model that engages an opponent must end its movement directly facing the target of its first melee attack.

Running

A running model may move up to twice its SPD in inches. Declare that a model or unit will run when you activate it. A running model always faces its direction of movement, but may change facing freely while moving and may face any direction after moving. A model that runs cannot perform an action, cast spells, or use feats this turn. A running model's activation ends at the completion of its movement.

Some models must meet special requirements to run:

- A warcaster or solo may always run instead of advancing.
- A warjack must spend a focus point to run.
- A unit must receive the run order to run.
- An out-of-formation trooper may attempt to regain formation by running.

Charging

A charging model rushes into melee range with an opponent, taking advantage of its momentum to make a more powerful strike. A charge combines a model's movement and combat action. A model denied its full normal movement for any reason cannot charge.

Declare a charge and its target when you activate the model. A model may attempt to charge any enemy model already in line of sight at the beginning of its activation. After declaring a charge, the charging model can turn to face any straight, unobstructed line that will let it move into melee range with its target. The charging model must move its full SPD plus 3" on that line, stopping short only if it engages its target. It cannot move over anything but *open terrain,* cross any *obstacles,* or change its facing while moving. At the completion of its movement, the charging model turns to directly face its target.

A charging model that enters melee range with its intended target performs a combat action. If the charging model moved at least 3", its first attack is a charge attack. A charge attack roll is made normally and may be boosted. If the charge attack hits, add an additional die to the damage roll. This damage roll cannot be boosted. After the charge attack, the charging model makes the rest of its melee attacks normally and may spend focus points to make additional melee attacks. A model may not make ranged attacks after charging.

CHARGING

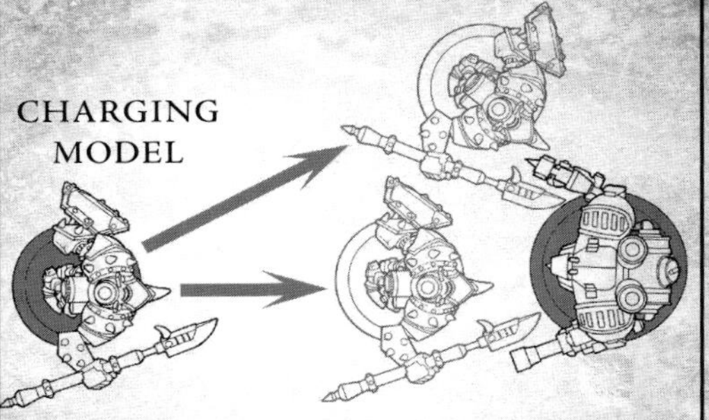

Either of these charge moves are legal for this model. After charging, they must turn to directly face their target.

If a charging model moved less than 3", it performs its combat action and attacks normally, but its first attack is not a charge attack because the model did not move far or fast enough to add sufficient momentum to its strike.

A charging model's activation ends if it touches a terrain feature that obstructs or slows its movement, or if it is not in melee range with its intended target after moving the full charge distance. A model that fails a charge cannot perform an action, cast spells, or use feats for the rest of this turn.

Some models must meet special requirements to charge:

- A warcaster or solo may always charge instead of advancing.
- A warjack must spend a focus point to charge. A warjack cannot make a *power attack* after charging, but it may make a regular *special attack.*
- A unit must receive the *charge order* to charge. Troopers may charge the same target or multiple targets, but the unit must attempt to end its movement with all members in *skirmish formation* or closer. A trooper that receives the charge order but does not have a target to charge, automatically runs and cannot perform an action this turn.

•Ordinarily, a model must have an eligible target in order to declare a charge. However, some game effects can force a model to charge. A model forced to charge cannot forfeit its activation and must make a charge move. In this instance, the model may charge any direction in its front arc. It may charge an eligible target, but it is not required to do so.

Unit Formation

An army's soldiers and support personnel are organized into units. Every member of a unit is similarly equipped and trained to fulfill a certain battlefield role. Some units specialize in melee combat, others excel with ranged weapons, and some provide critical or highly specialized capabilities. Regardless of their duties, one thing is certain—a unit is most effective when all of its members are in formation.

A unit must operate as a single coherent force, but its formation may be of any size or shape. The default and most flexible formation, skirmish formation, lets troopers be up to 3" apart. A unit must begin the game with all of its members in skirmish formation or closer.

Troopers may benefit from formations that group them closer together. For example, to use a special rule, troopers may need to be in open or tight formation. This does not require every trooper in the unit to be in the specified formation, but only those troopers in the listed formation will gain the special rule's benefits.

Troopers up to 1" apart are in open formation. Troopers in open formationare close enough to coordinate attacks and provide each other mutual support.

Troopers that form up shoulder-to-shoulder are in tight formation. These troopers must be in base-to-base contact, or as close as the actual models allow, and all must share the same facing. The tight formation must be at least two troopers wide, and can have any number of additional ranks.

MOVING UNITS

When you activate a unit, you are simulating that its members' movement and actions occur simultaneously, even though each model moves and acts individually. A unit required to make a command check as a result of its movement does not do so until after every trooper completes its movement. Troopers can move

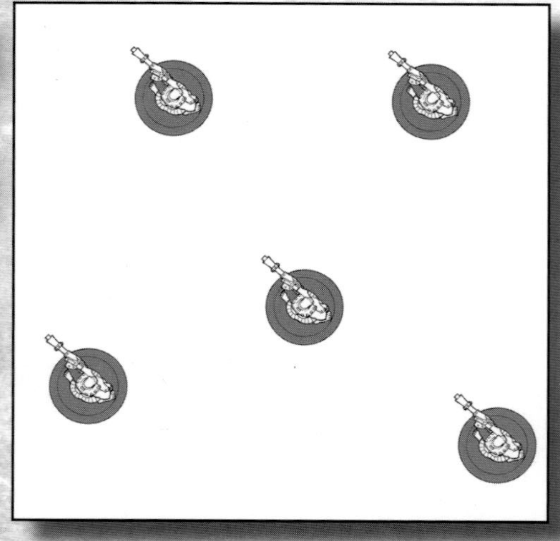

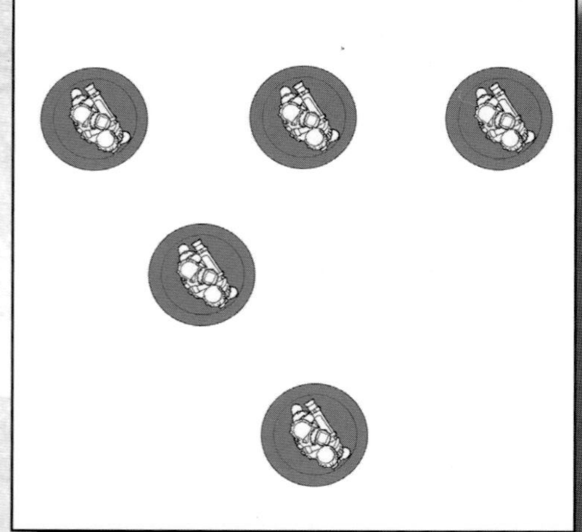

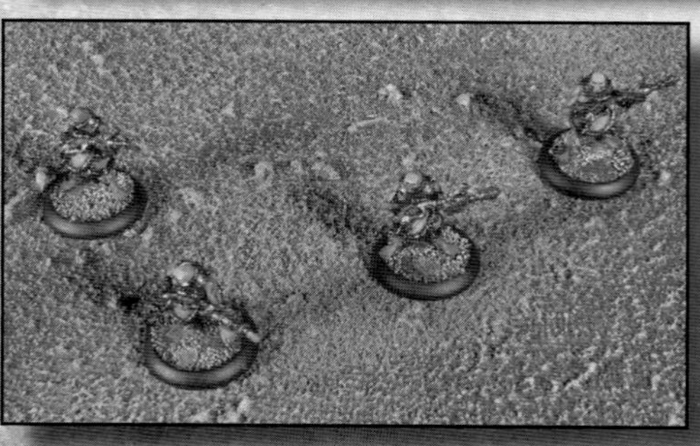

EXAMPLES OF BILE THRALL IN SKIRMISH FORMATION

EXAMPLES OF WINTER GUARD IN OPEN FORMATION

in any order, but you must attempt to have all troopers in skirmish formation or closer at the completion of the entire unit's movement.

After completing the entire unit's movement, determine what formation each trooper is in based on its proximity to the next nearest model in its unit. If a unit is widely scattered, its formation will be centered on the largest coherent grouping of troopers that are 3" or closer to each other. Any troopers more than 3"away from a member of that group will be out of formation.

OUT OF FORMATION

A trooper is out of formation if it is further than 3" from the nearest member of its unit that is in formation. When a unit fails a command check, every trooper in that unit suffers the effects, including those that are out of formation.

At the beginning of a unit's activation, determine if any troopers are currently out of formation. Those who are will not receive any order given to their unit. An out-of-formation trooper must attempt to regain formation, but the desire to stay alive tempers this mandate. The trooper may advance or run in an effort to regain formation, but must move by the most direct route that doesn't take him through a damaging effect or let enemies engage him. If enemy models obstruct a trooper's only path back to his unit, he must engage and attack them, unless he has a ranged weapon. An out-of-formation trooper in this situation can stop moving once in range and make ranged attacks against those opponents. An out-of-formation trooper engaged by an opponent may disengage or stand and fight.

At the end of a unit's activation, every out-of-formation trooper must make a command check or flee. Unlike other command checks made at the unit level, an out-of-formation trooper makes this command check and flees individually. An out-of-formation trooper in a warcaster's command range uses the warcaster's Command (CMD) stat for the check, if it is higher than the trooper's. See Command (pg;. 57) for detailed rules on command checks and fleeing.

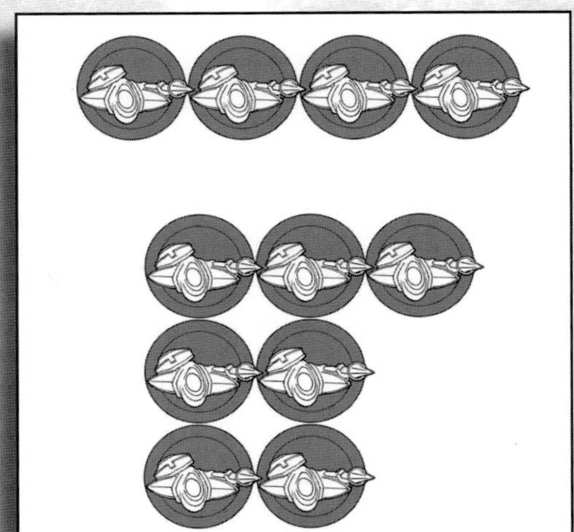

EXAMPLES OF FLAMEGUARD IN TIGHT FORMATION

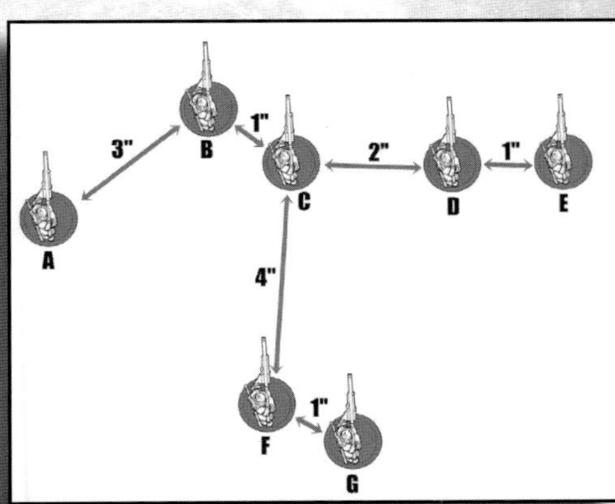

MODELS OUT OF FORMATION

Long Gunner A is in skirmish formation with B. Band C are in open formation which each other, which lets them use the combined ranged attack special rule. D is within 3" of C, so is in skirmish formation. E is within 1"of D, so those two troopers are in open formation with each other. F and G are close enough to be in skirmish formation with each other. However, since neither of them are within 3" of a model in the largest coherent group of the unit, they are both out-of-formation.

ACTIONS

An active model may be entitled to perform one action, depending on the type of movement it made. There are two broad action types: combat and special. A *combat action* lets a model make one or more *attacks*. A *special action* lets a model use a skill or perform a specialized function. A model forfeits its action if it does not use it during its activation. A model cannot move after performing any action or attack unless a special rule specifically allows it to.

Combat Actions

A model can perform a **combat action** after advancing, charging, or forfeiting its movement. A combat action lets a model make *attacks*. A model performing a combat action can choose one of the following attack combinations:

- A model *in melee* can make one *melee attack* with each of its *melee weapons* in *melee range*.
- A model not in melee can make one *ranged attack* with each of its *ranged weapons*.
- A model can make one *special attack*, allowed by its special rules instead of making any other attacks.
- A warjack that did not charge can spend a focus point to make one *power attack* instead of making any other attack.

A model making more than one attack may divide them among any eligible targets. A warcaster or warjack may spend focus points to make additional melee or ranged attacks after the initial ones allowed by the combat action. These additional attacks must be the same type as the first—a model must make either all melee attacks or all ranged attacks. Each additional attack may be made with any of the model's weapons of the appropriate type, but a ranged weapon making additional attacks cannot exceed its rate of fire (ROF). Focus points may be spent to make additional attacks after a special attack or power attack, but they can only be normal melee or ranged attacks, and must correspond to the nature of the special attack made.

See Combat (pg. 39) for detailed rules on making attacks and determining their results.

Special Actions

Some models can perform a **special action** instead of a combat action. Unless otherwise noted, a model can perform a special action only after advancing or forfeiting its movement. A special action's description details its requirements and results.

SKILL CHECKS

Some special actions appear with a **skill value** following their names. When the model performs one of these special actions, make a **skill check** to determine its success. Roll 2d6—if the result is equal to or less than the skill value, the model passes its skill check and its results are applied immediately. If the roll is greater than the model's skill value, the special action fails. Typically, nothing happens if a model fails a skill check. However, some special actions may impose negative consequences for a failed skill check.

As an example, the Cygnar Field Mechanik has the special action ***Repair[9]***. The Mechanik's repair special action will succeed on a 2d6 roll of 9 or less.

COMBAT—THROWING DOWN

MELEE ATTACKS, RANGED ATTACKS, AND DAMAGE

COMBAT OVERVIEW

A model's combat action allows it to make attacks. An *attack roll* determines if an attack successfully hits its target. After a successful attack, a *damage roll* determines how much damage, if any, the target receives.

Unless stated otherwise, an attack can be made against any model, friendly or enemy, and against certain terrain features. However, only the most despicable and ruthless commanders would intentionally slaughter their own soldiers. A player who does so can claim no pride or glory in his victory, and is beneath his opponent's contempt.

There are two broad categories of combat, **melee combat** and **ranged combat**. A model can only make attacks of the same type during its combat action. A model cannot make a ranged attack after making a melee attack, and it cannot make a melee attack after making a ranged attack.

MELEE COMBAT

Weapons locked against each other, the smell of blood, sweat, and iron...this is close combat—the melee. It's violent, personal, and the cauldron from which the stuff of legends flow.

A model using its combat action for *melee attacks* can make one attack with each of its *melee weapons*. Some models have *special rules* that allow additional melee attacks. Warcasters and warjacks may use focus points to make additional melee attacks. Each additional melee attack may be made with any melee weapon the model possesses, with no limit to the number of attacks made per weapon other than available focus points.

A **melee attack** can be made against any target in *melee range* of the weapon being used. A model cannot make a melee attack through an *intervening model* (pg. 33). A model making more than one melee attack may divide its attacks among any eligible targets.

Melee Weapons

Melee weapons include such implements as swords, hammers, flails, claws, saws, and axes. Some warjacks have an open fist or a shield that can be used as a melee weapon. A warjack can also use its body as a melee weapon for attacks such as a *bash*, *head-butt*, or *slam*.

A melee weapon's damage roll is 2d6+POW+STR.

Melee Range

A model can make melee attacks against any target in **melee range.** A model's melee range extends 1/2" beyond its front arc for any type of melee attack. A model with a **reach weapon** has a melee range of 2" for attacks with that weapon. A model that possesses a reach weapon and another melee weapon can *engage* and attack an opponent up to 2" away with its reach weapon, but its other weapons can only be used to attack models within its normal 1/2" melee range.

Engaged Models and Models in Melee

When a model is within an opponent's melee range, it is **engaged** in combat and primarily concerned with fighting its nearest threat. Both the engaged and engaging models are considered to be **in melee** and cannot make ranged attacks. An engaged model can move freely as long as it stays inside its opponent's melee range.

A model can **disengage** from melee by moving out of its opponent's melee range, but doing so is risky. A model disengaging from melee combat is subject to a *free strike* by its opponent.

Melee Range, Engaged Models, and Reach Weapons

If a model is in melee range, it has engaged its opponent in melee combat. These appear to go hand-in-hand—when opposing models are in each other's melee range, they are both engaged. However, a model with a reach weapon can take advantage of its greater melee range to engage an opponent with only normal melee range weapons without becoming engaged itself. While both models are considered to be in melee, a model is engaged only if it is in its opponent's melee range!

FREE STRIKES

When a model moves out of an enemy's melee range, its opponent may immediately make a **free strike.** The model makes one melee attack with any melee weapon in melee range and gains a +2 bonus to its melee attack roll. If the attack succeeds, add an additional die to its damage roll. *Focus points* may not be spent to further *boost* a free strike's attack or damage rolls or to allow any additional attacks.

A free strike is made out of turn but does not affect the model's next activation. A model engaged with several opponents may make a free strike against every opponent that moves to disengage from melee.

Melee Attack Rolls

Determine a melee attack's success by making a **melee attack roll.** Roll 2d6 and add the attacking model's Melee Attack (MAT). A *boosted* attack roll adds an additional die to this roll. Special rules and certain circumstances may modify the attack roll as well.

Melee Attack Roll = 2d6+MAT

An attack hits if the attack roll equals or exceeds the target's Defense (DEF). If the attack roll is less than the target's DEF, the attack misses. A roll of all 1s on the dice causes an automatic miss and a roll of all 6s causes an automatic hit, regardless of the attacker's MAT or his opponent's DEF.

Completely resolve a melee attack's damage roll and *special effects* before applying any special rules from the target. The target model's special rules apply only if they are still usable. For instance, if a Cygnar Lancer's shock shield is grabbed by an armlock or disabled by heavy damage, the shield's shock field will not take effect.

MELEE ATTACK MODIFIERS

The most common modifiers affecting a model's melee attack roll are summarized here for easy reference. Where necessary, additional detail can be found on the pages listed.

·*Back strike* (pg. 48): A melee attack against an *unaware model's* back arc gains a +2 bonus to the attack roll.

·*Charge Attack* (pg. 35.): A model's first attack after charging adds an additional die to its damage roll.

·*Free strike* (above): A melee attack against a disengaging model gains a +2 bonus to the attack roll and adds an additional die to the damage roll.

·*Intervening Terrain*: A model with any portion of its base obscured from its attacker by an obstacle or an obstruction gains +2 DEF against melee attacks from that opponent.

·*Stationary Target* (pg. 49): A melee attack against a stationary target hits automatically.

Warjack Melee Attack Options

Warjacks have melee attack options unavailable to all other model types. Unless otherwise noted, a warjack can use any of these attack options that its equipment and damage state allow.

BASH ATTACKS

A warjack may use its body as a weapon to bash its opponent. This is not an optimum attack, but may be the last resort for a warjack whose melee weapons have all been *disabled*. A bash attack suffers a –2 penalty to the attack roll. A warjack's bash damage roll is 2d6+STR.

A warjack that makes a bash attack can do nothing else during its combat action. Only one bash attack can be made and focus points cannot be used for additional attacks afterward. A warjack held by an *armlock/headlock* or otherwise unable to move cannot make a bash attack.

FIST ATTACKS

Some warjacks have an open fist that can be used to manipulate objects. A warjack can use its open fist as a melee weapon. Open fists follow all the normal rules for melee attacks. An open fist does not have a Power (POW) stat, so a warjack's open fist damage roll is 2d6+STR.

A warjack with an open fist may make the *armlock/headlock* and *throw* power attacks.

SHIELDS

A warjack with a shield has two Armor (ARM) stats. While its shield arm is functioning, it uses the ARM stat indicated by the shield icon against any attacks coming from its front arc. If its shield arm is disabled, the warjack's ARM reverts to the stat listed in its stat bar.

A warjack can use its shield as a melee weapon. Shields follow all the normal rules for melee attacks.

Power Attacks

Power attacks are a specialized subset of *special attacks* usable by warjacks. A warjack can use its combat action to make one power attack instead of making any other attacks, if the specific requirements for its use are met. Unlike other special attacks, a warjack cannot make a power attack after charging.

A warjack must spend a focus point to make a power attack. Focus points may be used to boost the attack and damage rolls as well. A warjack can make additional attacks after a power attack, but must spend focus points to do so.

HEAD-BUTT

As its combat action, a warjack may spend a focus point to head-butt an enemy model and drive it to the ground. A head-butt attack roll suffers a –2 penalty against a target with an equal- or smaller-sized base, or a –4 penalty against a target with a larger base. A successful hit causes damage and knocks the target down. A warjack's head-butt damage roll is 2d6+STR. An attacker that also has tusks, spikes, or horns adds their POW to the damage roll.

A warjack cannot make a head-butt if held in a headlock or if a weapon system located in its head is disabled.

After making a head-butt, a warjack may spend focus points to make additional melee attacks against any models in melee range.

SLAM

As as its combat action, a warjack may spend a focus point to slam an enemy model by ramming it with the full force of its armored hull, sending it flying backward and knocking it to the ground. A slam combines a model's movement and *combat action*. A warjack denied its full normal movement for any reason cannot attempt a slam.

Declare a slam and its target when you activate the warjack. A warjack may attempt to slam an enemy model already in line of sight at the beginning of its activation. A slam may not be attempted against a knocked-down model. After declaring a slam, the warjack must turn to directly face the center of its target. The warjack moves its full SPD plus 3" directly toward its target, stopping short only when within 1/2" of its opponent. It cannot move over anything but *open terrain*, cross any *obstacles*, or change its facing during or after its movement.

A warjack that attempts a slam and enters 1/2" melee range with its intended target performs a combat action. If the warjack moved at least 3", it makes a **slam attack**. A slam attack roll suffers a –2 penalty against a target with an equal- or smaller-sized base, or a –4 penalty against a target with a larger base. If the slam attack hits, the target gets propelled directly away from its attacker, knocked down, and takes damage as detailed under Slam Damage.

After making a slam attack, a warjack may spend focus points to make additional melee attacks against any models in melee range.

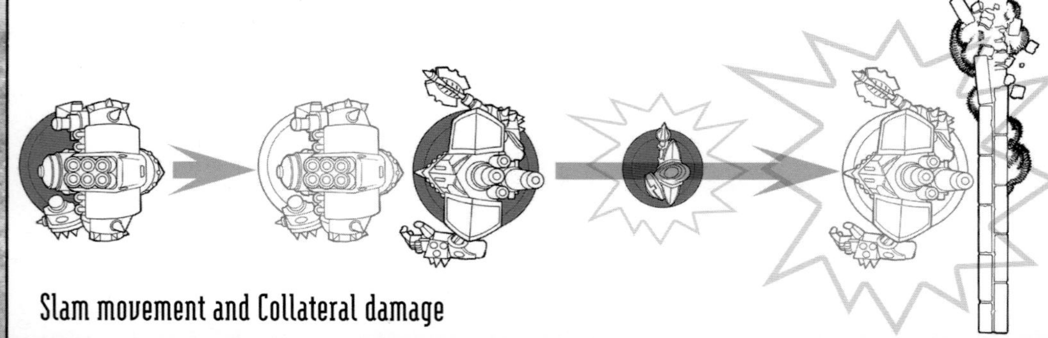

Slam movement and Collateral damage

If a warjack attempting a slam attack moved less than 3", it has not moved fast enough to get its full weight and power into the blow, so it makes a *bash attack* instead. A warjack attempting a slam ends its activation if it touches a terrain feature that obstructs or slows its movement, or if it is not in 1/2" melee range with its intended target after moving.

SUPER SLAM!!!

A warjack that slams its target into a solid terrain feature or a model with an equal- or larger-sized base adds an additional die to its damage roll, for a total of three dice. The warjack may spend a focus point to *boost* this damage roll and add another die, for a total of four dice!

BEING SLAMMED

A model slammed by a warjack moves d6 inches directly away from its attacker. Halve the slam distance if the target has a larger base than the attacker. Terrain affects this movement as normal. A slammed model moves at half rate through rough terrain, suffers any damaging effects it passes through, and stops if it collides with a terrain feature or a model with an equal- or larger-sized base. A slammed model is not subject to free strikes during this movement.

A slammed model moves over a model with a smaller base. If its slam movement ends up on top of a smaller model, push the smaller model back to make room for the slammed model.

SLAM DAMAGE

Determine **slam damage** after the target's slam movement finishes. A slam's damage roll is 2d6 plus the attacking warjack's STR. Add an additional die to the damage roll if the model collides with a solid terrain feature or with a model that has an equal- or larger-sized base. Slam damage can be *boosted*. The slammed model is also knocked down.

COLLATERAL DAMAGE

If a slammed model collides into another model with an equal- or smaller-sized base, that model is knocked down and suffers a **collateral damage** roll of 2d6 plus the STR of the warjack that initiated the slam. Collateral damage cannot be *boosted*. A model that has a larger-sized base than the slammed model does not take collateral damage.

ARMLOCK/HEADLOCK

As its combat action, a warjack with an open fist may spend a focus point to seize another warjack's weapon arm or head and prevent its use. Declare which component the warjack is attempting to lock before making a melee attack roll with its open fist. A warjack can attempt an armlock on any one weapon system with an arm location. A headlock can be used against any

Who Takes Collateral Damage?

SLAMMED OR THROWN MODEL BASE (CD=COLLATERAL DAMAGE)	BASE SIZE COLLIDED INTO: SMALL	MEDIUM	LARGE
SMALL	STOP, CD	STOP	STOP
MEDIUM	MOVE OVER, CD	STOP, CD	STOP
LARGE	MOVE OVER, CD	MOVE OVER, CD	STOP, CD

warjack, even one without a weapon system located in its head. Locks can be attempted and maintained against a disabled system. A successful hit locks the targeted component, but does not cause any damage.

After making an armlock or headlock attack, a warjack may spend focus points to make additional melee attacks against any models in melee range.

Once involved in a lock, the attacker cannot use its open fist and the defender cannot use the locked component or make a bash attack. Being held by a headlock prevents a warjack from making a head-butt warjack special attack._The attacker and the defender are free to attack with any of their other melee weapons.

Instead of making a melee attack with its locked component, the defender automatically attempts to break the lock as part of its combat action. Both models roll a d6 and add their STR. If the defender's total exceeds the attacker's, its arm or head comes free. Focus points may be spent to make repeated attempts to break a lock. Once a weapon is freed, focus points may be spent to make attacks with it.

The attacker may release a lock at any time during its own activation. Neither model may voluntarily move while involved in a lock. Any effect that forces either model to move, knocks a model down, disables the attacker's open fist, or causes the attacker to become a *stationary target* automatically breaks the lock.

THROW

As its combat action, a warjack with an open fist may pick up and throw a model with an equal- or smaller-sized base. Make a melee attack roll with the open fist at a –2 penalty. If the attack hits, both models roll a d6 and add their STR. If the defender's total is greater, it breaks free without taking any damage and avoids being thrown. If the attacker's total equals or exceeds the defender's, the defender gets thrown, knocked down, and takes damage as detailed in Throw Damage.

After making a throw attack, a warjack may spend focus points to make additional melee attacks against any models in melee range. A warjack may not make *ranged attacks* after attempting a throw.

BEING THROWN

After a successful throw attack, the attacker throws its opponent any direction within its front arc. Measure a distance from the thrown model equal to half the throwing model's STR in the chosen direction. A heavy warjack throwing a model with a small base adds 1" to this distance. From that point, determine where the thrown model actually lands by rolling deviation. Referencing the deviation diagram, roll a d6 for direction and a d3 for distance in inches. The thrown model moves directly from its current location in a straight line to the determined point of impact, ending its movement centered on that point.

Rough terrain and obstacles do not affect this movement, but the thrown model stops if it collides with an obstruction or a model with an equal- or larger-sized base. A thrown model is not subject to free strikes during this movement.

A thrown model moves over a model with a smaller base. If its impact point ends up on top of a smaller model, push the smaller model back to make room for the thrown model.

THROW DAMAGE

Determine **throw damage** after resolving where the thrown model lands. A throw's damage roll is 2d6 plus the STR of the attacking warjack. Add an additional die to the damage roll if the model collides into an obstruction or a model with an equal- or larger-sized base. Throw damage can be *boosted*. The thrown model is also knocked down.

COLLATERAL DAMAGE

If a thrown model collides with another model with an equal- or smaller-sized base, that model is knocked down and suffers a collateral damage roll of 2d6 plus the STR of the throwing warjack. Collateral damage cannot be *boosted*. A model with a larger-sized base than the thrown model does not take collateral damage.

Example of a Throw

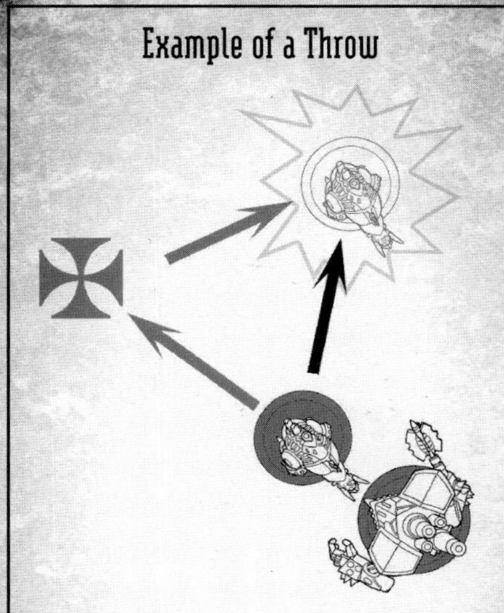

A Crusader throws a bonejack. Since the Crusader has a STR of 11, measure 5 1/2" from the thrown model and determine deviation from that point. The Crusader rolls a 3 for direction and a 2 for distance. Measuring 2" in the direction indicated by the deviation diagram gives the point of impact. The Bonejack moves from its current position directly toward the point of impact, ending its movement centered on that point.

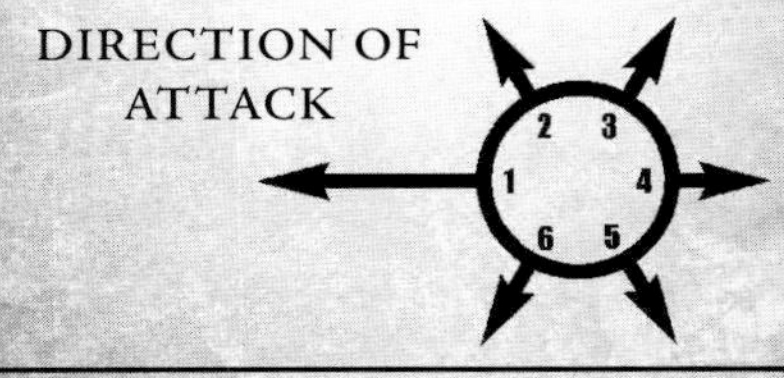

PUSH

As its combat action, a warjack may spend a focus point to push another model instead of making the attacks its combat action normally allows. Both models roll a d6 and add their STR. If the defender's total is greater, it resists being pushed. If the attacker's total equals or exceeds the defender's, the defending model takes no damage but is moved directly away from the attacker one full inch.

Terrain affects this movement as normal. A pushed model moves only 1/2" if in rough terrain, suffers the effects of any hazards, and stops if it collides with an obstacle, obstruction, or into a model with an equal- or larger-sized base. A pushed model cannot make free strikes and is not subject to free strikes during this movement.

A pushed model falls off elevated terrain if it ends its push movement with less than 1" of ground under its base. See ***Falling*** for detailed rules on determining damage from a fall.

After a successful push, a warjack may immediately make a follow-up move to remain in normal melee range with the pushed model, or it may hold its position. The warjack is subject to free strikes during a follow-up move.

After a push attempt, a warjack may spend focus points to make additional melee attacks against any models in melee range.

RANGED COMBAT

Many would argue that there is no honor in defeating an enemy unless you've been close enough to look him in the eyes. But when a soul-burning helljack with two fists full of iron-shredding claws bears down on you faster than a charging destrier, it's a good time to keep your distance and consider your ranged attack options.

A model using its combat action for *ranged attacks* makes one attack with each of its *ranged weapons*. Some models have *special rules* that allow additional ranged attacks. Warcasters and warjacks may spend focus points to make additional ranged attacks. Each additional attack may be made with any ranged weapon the model possesses, but a ranged weapon can never make more attacks in one turn than its *rate-of-fire (ROF)*.

A **ranged attack** can be declared against any target in *line of sight*, subject to the *targeting* rules. A model making more than one ranged attack may divide its attacks among any eligible targets. A model *in melee*, either engaged or engaging, cannot make ranged attacks.

Some spells and special rules let certain models make *magic attacks*. Magic attacks are similar to ranged attacks and follow most of the same rules. However, magic attacks are not affected by a rule that only effects ranged attacks. See Warcasters and Focus (pg. 53) for full details on magic attacks.

Ranged Weapons

Ranged weapons include rifles, flamethrowers, crossbows, harpoon guns, and mortars. A warjack's ranged weapons are generally mounted in place of an arm.

A ranged weapon's *damage roll* is 2d6+POW.

Declaring a Target

A ranged or magic attack can be declared against any target in the attacker's *line of sight*, subject to the *targeting* rules. The attack must be declared before measuring the range to the intended target. Unless a model's special rules say otherwise, it can make ranged and magic attacks only through its *front arc*.

TARGETING

A ranged or magic attack must be declared against a model or an object on the battlefield that can be damaged. Neither attack type can target open ground or a permanent terrain feature.

A ranged or magic attack need not target the nearest enemy model, but *intervening models* may prevent a model further away from being targeted. Neither attack type can target a model within 1" of an intervening model with an equal- or larger-sized base, even if the attacker has line of sight. Intervening models with smaller bases than the target do not affect targeting.

A ranged or magic attack by a model on elevated terrain can target any model on lower terrain and in line of sight, regardless of intervening models.

Certain rules and effects create situations that specifically prevent a model from being targeted. A model that cannot be targeted by an attack still suffers its effects if inside its area-of-effect.

MEASURING RANGE

A ranged or magic attack must be declared against a legal target prior to measuring range. After declaring the attack, use a measuring device to see if the target is within Range (RNG) of the attack. Range is measured from the nearest edge of the attacking model's base to the nearest edge of the target model's base. If the target is in range, make a *ranged attack roll* or *magic attack roll*, as applicable. If the target is beyond maximum range, the attack automatically misses. If an *area-of-effect (AOE) attack's* target is out of range, it automatically misses and its *point of impact* will *deviate* from a point on the line to its target equal to its RNG. See Area-of-Effect Attacks for full details on these attacks and deviation.

Rate of Fire

A weapon's rate of fire (ROF) indicates the maximum number of ranged attacks it may make in a turn. Reloading time prevents most ranged weapons from being used more than once per turn. Some ranged weapons reload faster and may make multiple attacks if a model is able to make additional attacks. However, a ranged weapon may not make more attacks per turn than its rate of fire, regardless of the number of additional attacks a model is entitled to make.

Ranged Attack Rolls

Determine a ranged attack's success by making a **ranged attack roll**. Roll 2d6 and add the attacking model's Ranged Attack (RAT). A *boosted* attack roll adds an additional die to this roll. Special rules and certain circumstances may modify the attack roll as well.

Ranged Attack Roll = 2d6+RAT

An attack hits if the attack roll equals or exceeds the target's Defense (DEF). If the attack roll is less than the target's DEF, the attack misses. A roll of all 1s on the dice causes an automatic miss and a roll of all 6s causes an automatic hit, regardless of the attacker's RAT or his opponent's DEF.

Completely resolve a ranged attack's damage roll and *special effects* before applying any special rules from the target. The target model's special rules apply only if they are still usable.

RANGED ATTACK MODIFIERS

The most common modifiers affecting a model's ranged attack roll are summarized here for easy reference. Where necessary, additional detail can be found on the pages listed.

•*Aiming*: A model that voluntarily forfeits its movement by not changing its position or facing gains a +2 bonus to every ranged attack roll it makes as part of its combat action. A *magic attack* does not get the aiming bonus.

•*Back Strike* (pg. 48): A ranged or magic attack against an *unaware model's* back arc gains a +2 bonus to the attack roll.

•*Cloud Effect* (pg. 52): A model inside a cloud effect gains +2 DEF against all ranged and magic attacks.

•*Concealment* (pg. 46): A model with concealment in relation to its attacker gains +2 DEF against ranged and magic attacks from that opponent.

•*Cover* (pg. 46): A model with cover in relation to its attacker gains +4 DEF against ranged and magic attacks from that opponent.

•*Elevated Target*: A model on higher ground than its attacker gains +2 DEF against ranged and magic attacks from that opponent.

•*Elevated Attacker*: A ranged or magic attack by an attacker on elevated terrain can target any model on lower terrrain and in line of sight, regardless of intervening models.

•*Stationary Target* (pg. 49): A stationary target has a base DEF of 5 against all ranged and magic attacks.

•*Target in Melee* (pg. 46): A ranged or magic attack against a target *in melee* suffers a –4 penalty to the attack roll. If the attack misses its target, it may hit a nearby model.

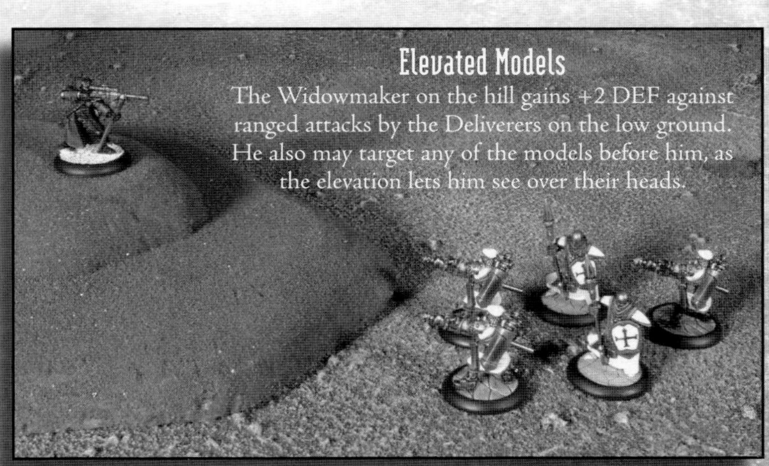

Elevated Models

The Widowmaker on the hill gains +2 DEF against ranged attacks by the Deliverers on the low ground. He also may target any of the models before him, as the elevation lets him see over their heads.

Concealment and Cover

Terrain features, spells, and other effects may make it more difficult to hit a model with a ranged or magic attack. A model within 1" of a terrain feature that obscures any portion of its base from an attacker gains either a *concealment* or *cover bonus* to its Defense (DEF) against ranged or magic attacks from that opponent. Concealment and cover bonuses are not cumulative. However, concealment and cover bonuses do stack with other effects that modify a model's DEF. See Terrain (pg. 59) for full details on terrain features and how they provide concealment or cover.

A model benefiting from concealment or cover may make ranged and magic attacks against targets in line of sight normally.

Some terrain features special effects grant a model **concealment** by making it more difficult to be seen, though they are not dense enough to actually block an attack. Examples include a low hedge or a mesh fence. A model within 1" of a concealing terrain feature that obscures any portion of its base from an attacker gains +2 DEF against ranged and magic attacks from that opponent. Concealment provides no benefit against a *spray attack*.

Other terrain features and some special effects grant a model cover by being physically solid enough to block an attack against it. Examples include a stone wall, a giant boulder, or a building. A model within 1" of a covering terrain feature that obscures any portion of its base from an attacker gains +4 DEF against ranged and magic attacks from that opponent. Cover provides no benefit against a *spray attack*.

Targeting a Model in Melee

A model making a ranged or magic attack against a target *in melee*, either engaged or engaging, risks hitting any model participating in the combat, including friendly models. A ranged or magic attack against a target in melee suffers a –4 penalty to the attack roll. If the attack misses its intended target, roll a d6—on a result of 1 or 2, the attack automatically hits a model in the melee other than its intended target; on a 3 or higher, the attack completely misses.

If there are two or more other models in the melee, roll another d6 to randomly determine which model is hit. For example, if there are two other

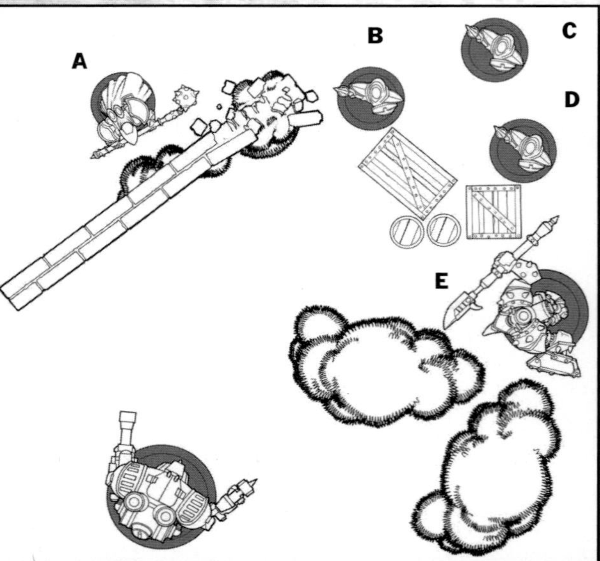

CONCEALMENT AND COVER IN ACTION

It might appear that the defender in the lower left corner has several targets to choose from, but many of them are actually quite well defended. Kreoss (A) is completely behind a wall that obscures him from the line of sight of the Defender, so he cannot be targeted. Flameguard B has cover, due to the large crate blocking a portion of his base. Likewise, Flameguard D is completely behind the crates, gaining the benefits of cover, while the Revenger, hidden in the brush is gaining concealment. Only Flameguard C is left completely open. While the crates are certainly between Flameguard C and the Defender, the Flameguard is not within an inch of the cover, so he cannot gain the cover bonus.

models in the melee, the player whose model made the ranged attack names one to be the first target and the other to be the second, then rolls a d6: the first will be hit on a 1 through 3, the second on a 4 through 6. If there are three other models, the player who made the ranged attack determines which will be first, second, and third, then rolls 1d6: the first will be hit on a 1 or 2, the second on a 3 or 4, and the third on a 5 or 6.

An *area-of-effect attack* that misses a target in melee *deviates* normally instead of following these rules.

Area-of-Effect Attacks

An **area-of-effect attack**, such as from an exploding rocket or a gas cloud, affects every model in an area centered on its *point of impact*. The attack covers an area with a diameter equal to its *area of effect* (AOE). Templates for AOEs can be found on the Templates page.

Target an AOE attack just like a normal ranged or magic attack. A successful attack roll indicates a **direct hit** on the intended target, which takes a **direct hit damage** roll of 2d6+POW. Center the AOE template over the **point of impact**—in this case, the center of the targeted model. Every other model with any part of its base covered by the AOE template is automatically hit by the attack and takes a **blast damage** roll of 2d6+1/2POW. Make separate damage rolls against each model in the area of effect; you can choose to *boost* each roll individually. Every model caught in an attack's area-of-effect is subject to its *special effects*.

An AOE attack that misses its target deviates a random direction and distance. An area-of-effect attack declared against a target out of Range (RNG) automatically misses and its point of impact *deviates* from a point on the line to its target equal to its RNG. An area-of-effect attack that misses a target in range deviates from the point directly over its intended target.

DEVIATION

When an AOE attack misses its target, determine its actual point of impact by rolling **deviation**. Referencing the Deviation Diagram, roll a d6 to determine the direction the attack deviates. For example, a roll of 1 means the attack goes long and a roll of 4 means the attack lands short. Roll another d6 to determine the deviation distance in inches. Determine the missed attack's point of impact by measuring the rolled distance from the center of the original target in the direction determined by the deviation roll. If the intended target is beyond the weapon's RNG, determine deviation from a point on the line to the target equal to its RNG.

An attack will not deviate further than half the distance from the attacker to its intended target. For instance, an attack made at a target 4" away from the attacker will deviate a maximum of 2", even if you roll a 3, 4, 5, or 6 for deviation distance.

Terrain features, models, or other effects do not block deviating AOE attacks—they always take effect at the determined point of impact.

Center the AOE template over the point of impact. Every model with any part of its base covered by the AOE template is automatically hit by the attack and takes a **blast damage** roll of 2d6+1/2POW. Make separate damage rolls against each model in the area of effect; you can choose to *boost* each roll individually. Every model caught in an attack's area of effect is subject to its *special effects*.

Deviating area-of-effect attacks never cause *direct hits*, even if the point of impact is on top of a model.

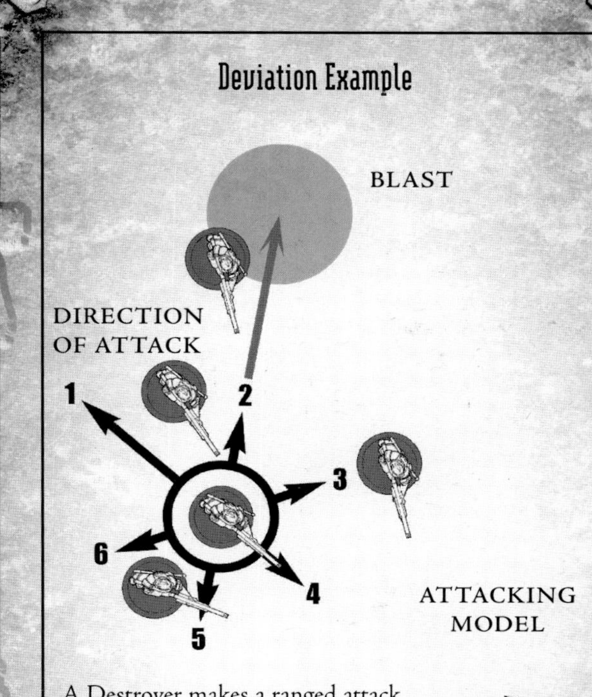

A Destroyer makes a ranged attack with its Bombard. Its ranged attack roll is unsuccessful and since the Bombard is an area-of-effect weapon, it must roll deviation to determine the attack's point of impact. It rolls a 2 for direction, followed by a 4 for 4" of deviation. Measure this distance in the deviation direction from the center of its original target—this point is the point of impact. Center the appropriate AOE template on that point. All models under the template take blast damage and are subject to the attack's special effects.

Spray Attacks

Some weapons, such as flamethrowers and bile cannons, make spray attacks. This devastating short-ranged attack can potentially hit several models. A spray attack has a RNG of "SP" and uses the spray template. The spray template can be found on the Templates page.

When making a spray attack, center the spray template laterally over an eligible target in the attacker's front arc with the narrow end of the template touching the attacker's base. The targeting rules apply when selecting the attack's primary target. Every model with any part of its base covered by the spray template may be hit by the attack.

Make separate ranged attack rolls against each target; you can choose to *boost* each roll individually. A model under the spray template does not receive any benefit from concealment, cover, or intervening models because the attack comes over, around, or—in some cases—through its protection.

A spray attack against a model in melee suffers a –4 penalty to its attack roll against those models. An attack that misses has the potential to hit another model in the melee, including those already affected by the spray. See Targeting a Model in Melee for full details on resolving this situation.

Every model hit by a spray attack suffers the full effects of the attack. Make separate damage rolls against each model hit; you can choose to *boost* each roll individually. Every model hit by the spray is subject to its *special effects*.

Example of a Spray Attack

A Bile Thrall makes a spray attack against a group of Winterguard. Its player centers the spray template laterally over an eligible target. The player chooses the centermost Winterguard because that trooper's comrades are too far away to be intervening models. Targeting that trooper also lets the player cover the greatest number of Winterguard without covering his own nearby Bonejacks. He rolls a ranged attack against each of the four Winterguard in the spray. Per the "Targeting a Model in Melee" rules, if the attack against the Winterguard in melee with the Bonejacks misses, it will randomly hit one of the Bonejacks instead, even though they are not actually under the spray template!

SPECIAL COMBAT SITUATIONS

The battlefield is a chaotic environment, constantly changing, and producing the unexpected. Although several situations can arise as a result of unique circumstances or a model's special rules, these rules should enable a smooth resolution. Savvy players will use these rules to their best advantage.

Special Attacks

Certain models have special rules that let them make a *special attack*. A model may make one special attack instead of making any normal melee or ranged attacks during its combat action, if it meets the specific requirements for its use. Resolve the special attack following the rules for *melee combat* or *ranged combat*, as applicable. Focus points may be spent to make additional attacks after a special attack, but they can only be normal melee or ranged attacks and must correspond to the nature of the special attack made.

Power attacks are a unique type of special attack. Unlike other special attacks, power attacks cannot be made after charging.

Back Strikes

A **back strike** gives a +2 bonus to the attack roll of any melee, ranged, or magic attack made against an **unaware model** from its *back arc*. To receive the back strike bonus, the attacking model must be in its target's back arc for its entire activation. If any portion of the attacking model enters the target's front arc while activated, the target becomes aware of its opponent. Attacks made at an aware model's back arc receive no bonus.

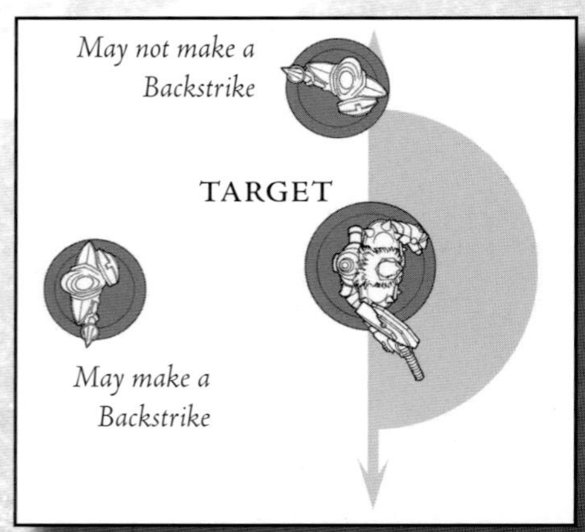

BACKSTRIKES

Falling

A model slammed, pushed or that otherwise moves off of an elevated surface greater than 1" high is *knocked down* and takes a damage roll. A fall of up to

3" causes a POW 10 damage roll. Add an additional d6 to the damage roll for every additional increment of three inches the model falls, rounded up.

For example, a model falling 7" takes a damage roll of 4d6+10!

Stationary Targets

A stationary target is a model that has been *knocked down* or immobilized, or an inanimate object. A stationary target cannot move or perform actions, cast spells, use feats, or give orders. A stationary target cannot engage other models or make attacks. A stationary warcaster can allocate focus points to his warjacks and upkeep spells. A stationary warjack can receive focus points and a stationary *channeler* can be used to channel spells.

A melee attack against a stationary target automatically hits. An attack roll may be made in an effort to score a critical hit, but the attacking model risks automatically missing if it rolls all 1s. A stationary target has a base Defense (DEF) of 5 against all ranged and magic attacks.

Knockdown

Some attacks and special rules cause a model to be **knocked down**. Place a knocked-down model on its back. A knocked-down model is a *stationary target* and obeys those rules until it stands up. Unlike other stationary targets, a knocked-down *channeler* cannot channel spells. A knocked down model does not block line of sight, nor does it provide concealment or cover. It may be ignored for targeting purposes. All attacks against a knocked down model are to its front arc.

A knocked-down model can stand up during its next activation. However, if a model is knocked down during its owning player's turn, it may not stand up until that player's next turn, even if it has not been activated this turn.

To stand up, a model must forfeit either its movement or its action for that turn. A model may face any direction when it rises. A model that forfeits its movement to stand can perform an action as if it advanced, but may not make attacks involving movement, such as a slam. A model that forfeits its combat action to stand can advance but may not run or charge. Standing up does not provoke free strikes.

Combined Melee Attacks

Troopers with this ability and in melee range of the same target may combine their attacks. The trooper with the highest MAT in the attacking group makes one melee attack roll for the group, adding +1 to the attack and damage rolls for each model, including itself, participating in the attack. If multiple troopers participating in the attack have the same MAT, declare which model is the primary attacker.

A unit's melee attacks may be grouped in any manner, including multiple combined melee attacks. Troopers capable of multiple melee attacks can divide them among eligible targets and participate in multiple combined melee attacks.

Example: Four members of a Menoth Temple Flameguard unit, including their Captain, make a combined melee attack against a Cygnar Defender. The Captain makes one melee attack for the group, adding +4 to his attack and damage rolls since there are four models participating in the attack. Two other troopers in the same Flameguard unit make a combined melee attack against a nearby Sentinel. The trooper declared as the primary attacker makes one melee attack, adding +2 to its attack and damage rolls.

Combined Ranged Attacks

Troopers with this ability may combine their ranged attacks against the same target. In order to participate in a combined ranged attack, a trooper must be in open formation with another participant, able to declare a ranged attack against the intended target, and be in range. The trooper with the highest RAT in the attacking group makes one ranged attack roll for the group, adding +1 to the attack and damage rolls for each model, including itself, participating in the attack. If multiple troopers participating in the attack have the same RAT, declare which model is the primary attacker.

A unit's ranged attacks may be grouped in any manner, including multiple combined ranged attacks. Troopers capable of multiple ranged attacks can divide them among eligible targets and participate in multiple combined ranged attacks.

Example: Four members of a Cygnar Long Gunners unit, including its Sergeant, are in open formation and declare a combined ranged attack against a Khador Juggernaut. When measuring range, the player discovers one Long Gunner is out of range and cannot participate in the attack. The Sergeant makes one ranged attack for the group, adding +3 to its attack and damage rolls since there are three models participating in the attack. Two other troopers in the same Long Gunner unit could not participate in the combined attack because they are not in open formation. They declare individual ranged attacks against two Iron Fang Pikemen nearby.

Orders

Orders require additional guidance since they are very specific in the requirements for use and method of execution.

DISABLING SYSTEMS AND WARJACKS

When all the system boxes for a specific system are marked, that system is disabled. A warjack with three disabled systems, or a destroyed hull and two disabled systems, is completely disabled and can no longer function—replace it with a *disabled wreck marker*. Although a disabled warjack can be attacked and will take damage from other effects, it may also be repaired and become operational again.

DESTROYING A WARJACK

A warjack is destroyed when all of its damage boxes are marked. Replace a destroyed warjack with a *totaled wreck marker*—it cannot be repaired!

ARCANE INFERNO
When issued this order, every model in the unit combines its fire at the same target. This attack requires at least three eligible models, which must be in open formation with another participant, able to declare a ranged attack against the intended target, and be in range. The leader makes one attack roll for the group, adding +1 to the attack roll for every model participating in the attack, including itself. This attack is POW 14 with a 3" AOE.

BAYONET CHARGE
When issued this order, a model must charge an eligible target, firing its ranged weapon as it closes. As part of the charge, after moving, the model makes a ranged attack followed by a charge attack with its bayonet. The model cannot attack with its other melee weapons after a bayonet charge.

A model performing a bayonet charge makes a ranged attack even if it is in melee after moving—this simulates the model firing its weapon while charging. If the model is not in melee after moving, its ranged attack must target the model it attempted to charge.

SHIELD WALL
When issued this order, every trooper already in formation moves into tight formation and gains +4 ARM for one round. Once the shield wall is established, each trooper forming it receives its benefits until they are next activated, regardless of casualties that remove models from the formation. Troopers in tight formation can perform combat actions as normal.

Troopers who cannot move into tight formation do not gain the benefit of the shield wall. A trooper that is out of formation when this order is issued can move no closer than 1" to any model forming the shield wall.

Souls

A living model has a soul. Certain models can claim a model's soul, represented by a soul token, when it is removed from play. If more than one model is eligible to claim its soul, the model nearest the destroyed model receives the soul token. A model only has one soul—if more than one model is eligible to claim its soul, the model nearest the destroyed model receives the soul token. Refer to a model's special rules for how it utilizes soul tokens.

DAMAGE

Warcasters, warjacks, and some other models can take a tremendous amount of damage before they fall in combat. What may be an incapacitating or mortal wound to a regular trooper will just dent a 'jacks hull or be deflected by a warcaster's arcane protections.

Damage Rolls

Determine how much damage a successful attack causes by making a **damage roll**. Roll 2d6 and add the attack's Power (POW). Melee attacks also add the attacker's Strength (STR.) A *boosted* damage roll adds an additional die to this roll. Special rules and certain circumstances may modify the damage roll as well.

Damage Roll = 2d6+POW (+STR, if applicable)

Compare this total against the target's Armor (ARM.) The target takes one *damage point* for every point that the damage roll exceeds its ARM.

Completely resolve an attack's damage roll and *special effects* before applying any special rules from the target. The target model's special rules apply only if they are still usable.

Recording Damage

Remove a model without damage capacity from play as soon as it takes one *damage point*.

The army list entry for a more resilient model gives the total amount of damage it can take before being eliminated. Its stat card provides a row of **damage boxes** for tracking the damage it receives. Record its damage from left to right, marking one damage box for each damage point taken. Remove the model from play once all its damage boxes are marked. Grey boxes are provided on every fifth box for quick reference of remaining damage.

A warjack has a **damage grid** consisting of six columns of damage boxes, labeled with the numbers 1through 6. Different warjack's damage grids may be slightly different in shape and number of damage boxes, but they function the same. When a warjack takes damage, the attacking player rolls a d6 to determine which column takes the damage. Starting with the uppermost empty box in that column and working down, mark one damage box per damage point taken. Once a column is full, continue recording damage in the next column to the right that contains unmarked damage boxes. Damage wraps, so if all the damage boxes in column 6 are marked, continue recording damage in column 1 or the next column that contains unmarked damage boxes. Continue shifting columns as required until every damage point taken has been recorded.

Disabling Systems

When a warjack takes damage, individual systems critical to its combat performance may be damaged and disabled. A warjack's blank damage boxes represent its **hull**. Beneath the hull are the model's vital systems, indicated by *system boxes*. Each system uses a different letter to label its system boxes. When recording damage, mark system boxes as normal damage boxes. A system becomes **disabled** when all its system boxes are marked. Mark the appropriate system status box to show this. The effects of disabled systems are as follows:

Disabled Arc Node: A warcaster cannot channel spells through a warjack with a disabled arc node.

Disabled Cortex: A warjack with a disabled cortex loses any unused focus points and cannot receive any more focus points.

Disabled Hull: Disabling a warjack's hull has no direct effect, so no system status box is provided. However, a disabled hull counts toward the disabled systems limit for disabling the entire warjack.

Disabled Movement: A warjack with disabled movement has its Speed (SPD) reduced to 1" and its Defense (DEF) reduced to 7. Disabled movement prevents a warjack from charging or making a slam attack.

Disabled Arm or Weapon System: A disabled arm or weapon system cannot be used to make attacks. The warjack cannot use special rules that require the use of this system. When a warjack's shield arm is disabled, the warjack loses the use of its shield and its Armor (ARM) reverts to the value listed in its stat bar.

Disabling a Warjack

A warjack is completely disabled and can no longer function once three of its systems are disabled. While not technically a system, a warjack's hull counts as such for purposes of disabling it. Thus, a warjack will be disabled if all its hull damage boxes are marked and it already has two other disabled systems.

Replace a disabled warjack model with a **disabled wreck marker** corresponding to its base size. A disabled warjack wreck provides *cover* and counts as *rough terrain* for movement. A disabled warjack may be attacked as a stationary target and *continuous effects* and spells on it remain in play, so it may continue to take damage. A disabled warjack may return to operation if enough of its damage is repaired.

Be sure to keep track of exactly which model a marker represents. We suggest numbering your wreck markers or even making a specific wreck marker for each warjack in your army.

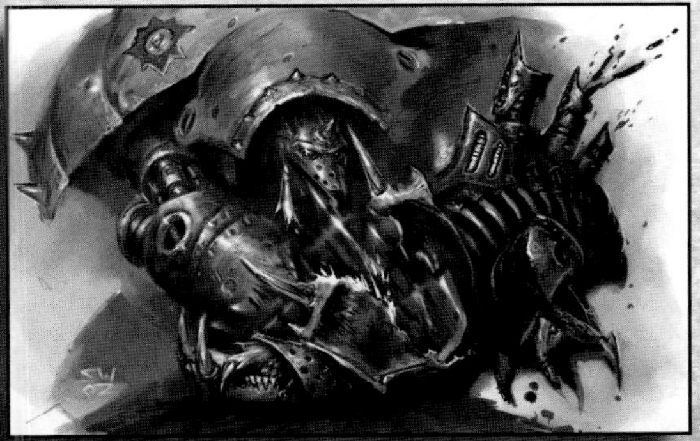

Destroying a Warjack

A warjack is destroyed or **totaled** when all of its damage boxes are marked. Remove a totaled warjack from play and replace it with a **totaled wreck marker** corresponding to its base size. A warjack wreck provides *cover* and counts as *rough terrain* for movement. Any continuous effects or spells on a warjack instantly expire when it is totaled. A totaled warjack cannot be repaired.

Death of a Warcaster

Should a warcaster be unfortunate enough to fall in combat, his entire army will suffer from this harsh blow. Every warjack in the warcaster's battlegroup instantly becomes **inert** and suffers the penalties of being a *stationary target*. Immediately remove from play any upkeep spells cast by this warcaster.

In many cases, the death of a warcaster heralds the end of the battle. However, if an army contains multiple warcasters, they may *reactivate* the inert warjacks and add them to their respective battlegroups.

REACTIVATING WARJACKS

A warcaster in base-to-base contact with an inert warjack may **reactivate** it. To reactivate the jack, the warcaster must forfeit its action this turn, but may still cast spells and use special abilities. A warjack can do nothing the turn it reactivates, but it functions normally next turn.

A warcaster can only reactivate one warjack per turn. Warjacks from other armies cannot be reactivated by your warcasters, be they enemies or allies.

Special Effects

Many attacks cause **special effects** in addition to causing damage. Each special effect is unique in its applica-

tion. There are four categories of special effects: *automatic effects, critical effects, continuous effects, and cloud effects.* A special effect may belong to more than one category, and its category may change depending on the weapon. For instance, a Bile Thrall's bile cannon causes *corrosion* as an automatic effect, but a Slayer Helljack's death claws cause corrosion as a critical effect.

Pay close attention to the exact wording for each model's special effects. Even though the effect may be the same for different models with the same weapon or ability, it may require different conditions to function. Some model's special effects function if the target is hit, others require the target to take damage, and critical effects require a *critical hit* on the attack roll.

AUTOMATIC EFFECTS

Apply an automatic effect every time it meets the conditions required to function.

CRITICAL EFFECTS

Apply a critical effect if any two dice in the attack roll show the same number and the attack successfully hits—this is a critical hit. The target model suffers the special effect even if it takes no damage from the damage roll, unless the specific effect requires that it do so. An *area-of-effect attack's* critical effect only functions with a *direct hit*, and every model under the template will suffer the critical effect.

A weapon with a critical effect has the label "Critical" to distinguish it from an automatic damage effect.

CONTINUOUS EFFECTS

Continuous effects remain on a model and have the potential to damage it on subsequent turns. A model can have multiple continuous effects on it at once, although it can have only one of each continuous-effect type on it at a time.

Resolve continuous effects on models you control during the maintenance phase of your turn. Roll a d6—if the result is a 1 or 2, remove the effect immediately without causing further damage. On a 3 through 6, it remains in play and the model immediately suffers its effects.

Continuous damage effects do not require focus for *upkeep* and cannot be removed from play voluntarily. Remove a continuous effect only when it expires, a special situation causes it to end, or the affected model is removed from play. Continuous effects continue to affect *disabled* warjacks.

CLOUD EFFECTS

A cloud effect produces an area of dense smoke or gas that remains in play at its *point of impact*. Use an area-of-effect template of the appropriate diameter to represent the cloud. Consider every model with any part of its base covered by the cloud's template to be inside the cloud and susceptible to its effects.

In addition to being affected by a cloud's special rules, a model inside a cloud effect gains +2 DEF against ranged and magic attacks, which is cumulative with *concealment* or *cover*. A model in a cloud effect may target models outside of it normally. For a model outside of it, the cloud effect completely obstructs line of sight to anything beyond it. Thus, a model can see into or out of a cloud effect, but not through one. A cloud effect provides no protection from melee attacks.

A model that enters an existing cloud effect suffers its effects immediately. A model that begins its activation inside an existing cloud effect and does not move out of it suffers its effects at the end of its activation.

Remove a cloud effect when it expires or if a special situation causes it to end.

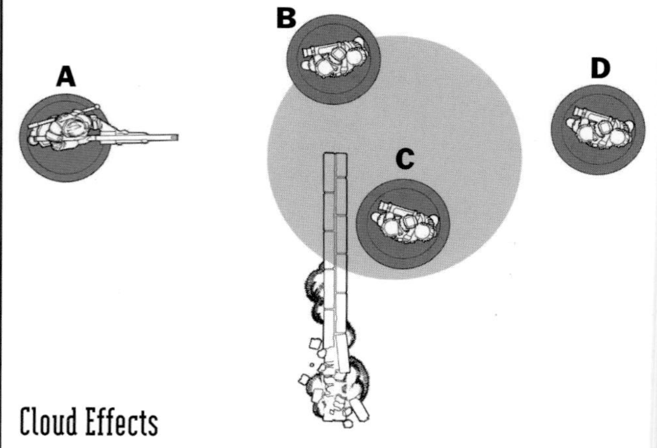

Cloud Effects

Model A has LOS to models B and C, but they both gain +2 DEF against any ranged or magic attack from A. Model A's LOS to model C crosses a solid terrain feature, so model C also gains +4 DEF from cover, giving it a total +6 DEF against model A's attacks. Models A and D do not have LOS to each other since LOS cannot be drawn through a cloud effect.

Models B and C can make ranged or magic attacks against model A at no penalty. However models B and C do gain +2 DEF against those attacks from each other.

WARCASTERS AND FOCUS–TRUE POWER

SPECIAL RULES, MANAGING FOCUS POINTS, AND CASTING SPELLS

The warcaster is the single most important model in a player's army. In large enough games, you can employ multiple warcasters, but each one should be considered significant and essential to the success of any battle.

Warcasters are the Iron Kingdoms' ultimate heroes. Highly trained combat wizards, they are as effective in martial combat as they are wielding arcane forces. However, a warcaster's greatest function on the battlefield is controlling his warjacks, whether he's ordering them to attack or defend, head for an objective, or channel a spell.

Battles are won or lost purely by how well a warcaster manages his *focus*—the magical energy that lets him control warjacks and cast spells. Often, a warcaster must decide between casting a spell and *boosting* a warjack's attack—and choosing well or poorly usually means the difference between victory and defeat.

WARCASTER SPECIAL RULES

Being the most powerful individuals in the Iron Kingdoms, warcasters have many special rules:

FEARLESS

A warcaster has the *fearless* special ability.

FEATS

Each warcaster has a unique feat that can turn the tide of battle if used at the right time. A feat can be freely used anytime during a warcaster's activation, in addition to its movement and action. A warcaster can use its feat only once per game.

FOCUS MANIPULATION

Warcasters are the only models that have Focus (FOC) stats. Every turn, a warcaster receives *focus points*. Focus points can be used for spell casting or to *boost* the combat abilities of the warcaster and his warjacks.

INSPIRING PRESENCE

A model or unit in a warcaster's *command range* may use the warcaster's Command (CMD) stat for any *command checks*. A warcaster can attempt to *rally* any *fleeing* units within his command range. A warcaster can *give orders* to one unactivated unit within his command range during his activation. See Command (pg. 57) for full details on command checks, fleeing, and giving orders.

POWER FIELD

Warcaster Armor is perhaps the most sophisticated blend of magic and mechanika to be found anywhere. Besides its seemingly impossible strength, this armor creates a magical field that surrounds and protects the warcaster from damage that would rend a normal man to pieces.

A warcaster's damage capacity actually represents the power field's protection. The warcaster can use focus points to regenerate damage done to the power field. A warcaster's unspent focus points *overboost* his power field, giving him increased protection.

SPELL CASTER

A warcaster can use focus points to cast spells anytime during his activation, in addition to his movement and action.

FOCUS POINTS

A warcaster's greatest resource is the magical energy known as *focus*. Each of your warcasters receives a number of **focus points** equal to his Focus (FOC) stat during your control phase. A warcaster may allocate focus points to eligible warjacks in his *control area* and to his spells that require upkeep, or he can keep them to enhance his own abilities and cast spells.

Remove unused focus points from your previous round during your maintenance phase.

Control Area

A warcaster's **control area** extends out from the caster in all directions for a distance of twice his Focus (FOC) in inches. Some spells or special rules may change a warcaster's focus area. Some spells and feats use the warcaster's control area as their *area of effect*.

FOCUS? WHY HE DON'T EVEN KNOW US!

Players should use coins, colored beads, or tokens to represent focus points. During a player's control phase, place a number of tokens equal to the warcaster's FOC next to the model. These tokens may be allocated to eligible warjacks in that warcaster's battlegroup by moving them next to those models. Remove focus point tokens from the table as they are used. Each unspent focus point token next to a warcaster gives him a +1 ARM bonus until your next maintenance phase.

A warjack must be within its warcaster's control area to receive focus points or *channel* spells, but it does not have to be in line of sight. A warjack outside of its caster's control area retains any focus points it received this turn and can spend them freely.

CONTROL AREA

A warcaster's control area is a circular area centered on the warcaster with a radius equal to twice his Focus (FOC), measured from the edge of his base.

THE RULE OF THREE

A warjack can receive up to three focus points per turn. A warjack cannot receive more than this unless a special rule specifically allows it.

Allocating Focus Points

During your control phase, each warcaster in your army may allocate his focus points to warjacks in his own battlegroup. Take care to remember which warjacks belong to which battlegroup. A warcaster cannot allocate focus points to warjacks in another warcaster's battlegroup even if they are both part of the same faction.

To receive focus points, a warjack must be within its warcaster's control area, but it need not be in line of sight. A warcaster can divide his focus points between himself and as many of his warjacks as desired. However, a warjack may not receive more than three focus points per turn, unless a special rule specifically allows more.

Using Focus Points

Focus points have many powerful uses. The real trick is knowing which use is best, depending on what dire circumstances your army faces. Some of these uses are available to any model with focus points, while others can only be used by specific model types.

A warjack can only spend the focus points it has received and a warcaster can only spend the focus points it did not allocate to other models. A model's unused focus points cannot be reallocated or spent by other models. Unless otherwise stated, focus points may only be spent on the controlling player's turn.

A focus point can be spent anytime during a model's activation for any one of the following effects:

ADDITIONAL ATTACK

A warcaster or warjack can spend a focus point to make an additional melee or ranged attack as part of its combat action. The model can make an additional attack for every focus point spent this way. A model spending focus points to make additional ranged attacks cannot exceed a weapon's rate of fire (ROF). Focus points cannot be spent to make additional special attacks.

BOOSTING ATTACK AND DAMAGE ROLLS

A warcaster or warjack can spend a focus point to add one additional die to any attack roll or damage roll. The model must spend the focus point and declare it is boosting the roll before rolling any dice. Each attack or damage roll can only be boosted once, but a model can boost multiple rolls during its turn. When an attack or damage affects several models, the die rolls against each individual model must be boosted separately.

CAST SPELL

In addition to his movement and actions, a warcaster can cast a spell anytime during his activation by simply spending the appropriate number of focus points and immediately resolving its effects. A warcaster can cast any number of spells per activation as long as he has enough focus points to do so. See Casting Spells below.

OVERBOOST POWER FIELD

Each of a warcaster's unspent focus points gives him +1 Armor (ARM) against all attacks. This stays in effect until the focus points are spent or until the beginning of hisnext maintenance phase.

REGENERATE POWER FIELD

A warcaster can spend a focus point to regenerate his power field. Each focus point spent in this manner removes one damage point.

RUN, CHARGE, POWER ATTACKS

A warjack must spend a focus point to run, charge, or make a power attack. A special attack granted by a warjack's special rules does not require spending a focus point.

Casting Spells

Warcasters have the ability to cast spells. Each warcaster knows a number of spells equal to his Focus (FOC). A warcaster's army list entry and stat card lists the spells he can cast.

A warcaster can cast a spell anytime during his activation by spending a number of focus points equal to the spell's *focus cost*. Any spell, including ranged spells, can be cast while the warcaster is *in melee*. Resolve the spell's effects immediately. A warcaster can cast as many spells during his activation as he can pay the focus cost for. The same spell can be cast multiple times in a turn. For example, a warcaster could move, cast a spell, use his combat action to make a ranged attack, then cast two more spells.

A warcaster can cast spells before movement, or after movement, but not during movement.

OFFENSIVE SPELLS

An *offensive spell* requires that a warcaster make a magic attack to put its effects in play. Magic attacks are similar to *ranged attacks* and follow most of the same rules. Unless stated otherwise, a warcaster making a magic attack must obey the *targeting* rules when declaring a target. A magic attack's target may benefit from *concealment* or *cover*. However, magic attacks are not affected by rules that only affect ranged attacks. A warcaster does not benefit from *aiming* when making a magic attack, but he can make magic attacks while in melee.

A warcaster making a magic attack against a model he is engaged with, does not suffer from the "target in melee" attack roll penalty. If such an attack (with an non-AOE spell) misses, and there are multiple models in the melee, the attack may hit a random model in the melee, excluding the original target or the warcaster—resolve this per the randomization rules on p.46. An AOE spell that misses in this situation will deviate normally.

MAGIC ATTACKS

Determine a magic attack's success by making a **magic attack roll**. Roll 2d6 and add the attacking warcaster's Focus (FOC). A *boosted* attack roll adds an additional die to this roll. Special rules and certain circumstances may modify the attack roll as well.

Magic Attack Roll = 2d6+FOC

An attack hits if the attack roll equals or exceeds the target's Defense (DEF). If the attack roll is less than the target's DEF, the attack misses. A roll of all 1s on the dice causes an automatic miss and a roll of all 6s causes an automatic hit, regardless of the attacker's FOC or his opponent's DEF.

Completely resolve a magic attack's damage roll and *special effects* before applying any special rules from the target. The target model's special rules apply only if they are still usable.

Magic attacks follow all the rules for ranged attacks, including targeting, concealment and cover, and all other applicable rules. A warcaster can cast spells, including ranged spells, while in melee.

UPKEEP SPELLS

Upkeep spells can be maintained for more than one turn. During your control phase, your warcasters may allocate a focus point to any of their upkeep spells to keep them in play. A warcaster can allocate a focus point to keep an upkeep spell in play even if its effects are outside his control area. If a focus point is not allocated to an upkeep spell, its effects end immediately.

A warcaster may only have one of each specific upkeep spell in play at a time, although he can maintain any number of different upkeep spells simultaneously if he has the focus points to allocate to them. A model or unit may only have one friendly and one enemy upkeep spell cast on it at any time. If another upkeep spell is cast on a model that already has one from the same side—friendly or enemy—remove the old upkeep spell from play and replace it with the newly cast one.

A warcaster can recast any of his upkeep spells already in play. When a warcaster does so, immediately remove the effects of that spell's previous casting from play.

For example, a unit of Khador Iron Fangs currently has the Ironflesh spell cast on them. The Khador player decides that it would be more beneficial to have the Fury spell cast on the unit instead, which immediately removes the Ironflesh spell once cast. During the Cryx player's turn, Deneghra casts the Blight spell on the Iron Fangs, which does not remove the Fury spell because an enemy spell does not replace a friendly one.

CHANNELING

Specialized warjacks known as **channelers** are equipped with devices called **arc nodes** that act as passive relays for a warcaster's spells, extending the warcaster's effective spell range. A warcaster may cast spells through any channeler in his battlegroup that is also within his control area. The warcaster is still the attacker but the channeler becomes the spell's point of origin—determine eligible targets and measure the spell's range from the channeling warjack. Channeling a spell does not require the warcaster to have line of sight to either the channeler or the spell's target. However, the channeling warjack must have line of sight to the spell's target. There is no additional focus cost for channeling a spell.

A channeler *in melee* cannot channel spells. A *stationary* channeler can channel spells, but one that is knocked-down, cannot. A channeler can be the target of a spell it channels, but a spell with a Range (RNG) of "Caster" cannot be channeled.

Make a magic attack for a channeled offensive spell normally. The warcaster may spend focus points to boost die rolls or otherwise enhance the spell as allowed.

Remember, the channeler is just a relay. Channeling a spell is a passive effect that occurs during a warcaster's activation and has no impact on the channeling model's own activation. Focus points allocated to a channeler may not be used to affect the channeled spell in any way.

Spell Statistics

A spell is defined by the following six statistics:

•**Faction:** Only members of the listed faction can use this spell.

•**Focus (FOC):** The number of focus points that must be spent to cast the spell.

•**Range (RNG):** The maximum distance in inches that a spell can be used against a target. Range is measured from the nearest edge of the attacking model's base to the nearest edge of the target model's base. A spell with a RNG of "Caster" can only be cast on the warcaster. It cannot be channeled or cast on another model.

•**Power (POW):** The base amount of damage a spell inflicts. Add a spell's POW stat to its *damage roll*.

•**Area of Effect (AOE):** The diameter in inches of the template an *area-of-effect spell* uses for damage effects. When using an AOE spell, center the template on the determined *point of impact*. All models covered by the template potentially suffer the spell's effects. See Combat ([g. 39) for detailed rules on AOE attacks. Templates for AOEs can be found on the Templates page. A spell with an AOE of "CTRL," is centered on the warcaster and affects every model in his control area.

Channeling

With a FOC of 7, High Exemplar Kreoss has a 14" control area. Kreoss (A) may channel spells through his Revenger (B) warjack, as long as the Revenger touches his control area.

A warjack must have line of sight to a target to be able to channel spells at it. So, the Revenger can channels spells at Bonejack C, but it may not channel spells at Bonejack D, even though Kreoss himself has line of sight to it.

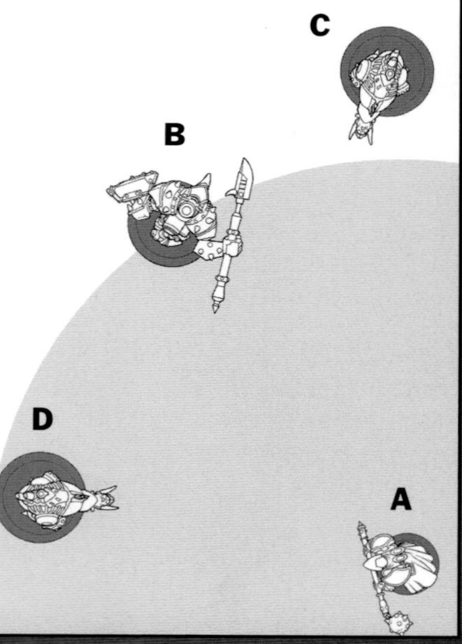

•**Upkeep**: An upkeep spell remains in play if the warcaster who cast it allocates a focus point to it during his control phase.

•**Offensive**: An offensive spell requires a successful magic attack roll to take effect. If the attack roll fails, the attack misses. A failed attack roll for a spell with an area of effect deviates according to those rules.

COMMAND—OF MICE AND MEN

COMMAND CHECKS, FLEEING, AND ORDERS

Regardless of a soldier's skill at arms, his real worth is measured by his will to fight. Warriors may break and flee after suffering massive casualties or when confronted by terrifying entities, while manipulative spells can warp the minds of the weak-willed, causing them to attack their allies. The inspiring presence of a nearby warcaster or a unit's leader can steel the nerves of warriors faced with these mental assaults and even rally them before their panic becomes a full-blown rout. *Command checks* determine the outcome these game situations and effects that test a combatant's discipline or mental resolve.

COMMAND CHECKS

There are several different circumstances that require a model to make a command check: *massive casualties*, *terrifying entities*, and a spell's or other attack's special rules.

MASSIVE CASUALTIES

A unit suffers massive casualties when it loses 50% or more of its current numbers in any player's turn. The unit must immediately pass a command check or *flee*.

TERRIFYING ENTITY

A terrifying entity is one with either the *terror* or *abomination* special ability. A model *in melee* with an enemy that causes terror, or within 3" of an abomination—friendly or enemy—must pass a command check or flee. Make this command check after the active model or unit completes it movement, before it performs any actions.

For instance, if the Iron Lich Asphyxious moves into melee with a Temple Flameguard, the Flameguard unit makes a command check as soon as Asphyxious ends his movement. However, if a Flameguard trooper moves into melee with Apshyxious, make a command check for his unit after every trooper in the unit finishes moving. In either case, make the command check before any model performs an action.

SPECIAL RULES

Some spells and other attacks cause an individual model or an entire unit to make a command check. Reference the specific description to determine the attack's eligible targets and effects. While fleeing is the most common outcome of a failed command check, some spells and effects have more sinister effects.

When one of these situations requires a model or unit to make a **command check**, roll 2d6—if the result is equal to or less its Command (CMD) stat, it passes the check. In most cases, this means the model or unit continues to function normally or rallies if it was fleeing. If the roll is greater than its CMD, the check fails and the model or unit suffers the consequences.

For example, a Khadoran Manhunter has a CMD of 9. The Manhunter passes a command check on a 2d6 roll of 9 or less.

A model that fails a command check against massive casualties or terrifying entities immediately *flees*; one that fails a command check against a spell suffers the associated effect.

An independent model makes a command check on an individual basis, using his own CMD. Warjacks do not have a CMD stat and never make command checks.

In most cases, troopers make command checks at the unit level. Make one command check for the entire unit, using the unit leader's CMD if he is still in play, and apply its results to every trooper in that unit, unless stated otherwise. Some exceptions include a trooper that ends his activation *out of formation* and spells that specifically target single models. A trooper making an individual command check may use his leader's CMD if he is in formation or a warcaster's CMD if he is within the warcaster's command range.

Command Range

A warcaster has a **command range** equal to his CMD in inches. A model or unit in a warcaster's command range may use the warcaster's CMD when making a command check, but is not required to do so.

A unit leader can *rally* and *give orders* to his troopers in formation, while a warcaster can rally any model or unit and give orders to any unit in his command range. A trooper that is out of formation

cannot rally or receive any orders. A trooper making an individual command check may use his leader's CMD if he is in formation, or a warcaster's CMD if he is within the warcaster's command range.

FLEEING

A model or unit that fails a command check against fleeing immediately turns to face directly away from the threat that caused the command check. If this occurs during the model's or unit's activation, its activation immediately ends. Other than changing facing, the fleeing model does not move until its next activation.

A fleeing model activates during his controlling player's maintenance phases. A fleeing model automatically runs away from its nearest threat toward its army's deployment edge, using the most direct route that doesn't take it through a damaging effect or let enemies engage it. A fleeing model cannot perform any actions or use any of its special rules.

A fleeing model that leaves the battlefield is removed from play and cannot return. A fleeing model with no escape route will cower in its current position and do nothing unless rallied.

After its mandatory movement, a fleeing model can attempt to *rally* if it is within its leader's or a warcaster's command range.

Rallying

A fleeing model or unit can make a command check after its mandatory movement if in formation with its leader or in a warcaster's command range. If it passes the command check, the model or unit rallies and turns to face its nearest opponents—this ends its activation, but it may function normally next turn. If the fleeing model fails the command check, it continues to flee during its controlling player's next maintenance phase.

Fearless Models

A model with the *fearless* special ability never flees. However, the model is still subject to a command check that has a penalty other than fleeing. For instance, a Cygnaran Stormblade may succumb to Deneghra's Dark Seduction.

ISSUING ORDERS

An **order** lets a model make a specialized combat maneuver during its activation. Unlike other warrior models, troopers cannot automatically choose to run or charge—they must receive an order to do so. A unit may receive an order from a warcaster prior to its activation, or from its leader at the beginning of its activation. Alternatively, the unit's leader may issue an order granted by his special rules, such as a Trencher Sergeant giving a *bayonet charge* order. A unit whose leader has been removed from play cannot use its leader's unique orders.

A unit can receive only one order per activation. Every trooper in formation receives the order and must obey it. An out-of-formation trooper cannot receive an order and does not perform the task or gain its benefits. A unit not given a specific order can advance and perform its actions as normal.

A warcaster can give a run or charge order to one unit in his command range anytime during his activation, but can only give orders to a unit that has not yet activated this turn.

Certain solo models have orders in their special rules. A solo cannot give orders to any other model or unit—only the individual solo model benefits from it. Declare a solo is using an order at the beginning of its activation. For example, when you activate Eiryss, you can declare that she is using her order to make a bayonet charge instead of a normal charge.

TERRAIN—YOUR BEST FRIEND

THE BATTLEFIELD, HAZARDS, AND STRUCTURES

The lay of the land has a tremendous impact on an army's ability to maneuver. The most cunning commanders use the terrain conditions to their best advantage. These terrain rules provide guidelines for establishing the effects and restrictions that a battlefield's objects and environment can have on a game. Players should discuss the terrain prior to a game and agree on the characteristics for different *terrain features*. Covering the rules for every possible terrain type would be an endless task, so players themselves must determine the exact nature of each terrain feature on the battlefield before the game begins.

BATTLEFIELD SETUP

Use the amount of terrain that suits the type of game you wish to play. A table with few terrain features favors ranged attacks and swift movement, while having more terrain features shifts the emphasis toward melee combat.

Give consideration to model base sizes when placing terrain features close together, as a model can move between terrain features only if its base will fit between them. With careful placement, you can create narrow passages that can be accessed only by models with smaller bases.

All players should agree upon terrain setup. When placing terrain, strive for a visually appealing and tactically challenging battlefield. These qualities provide the most exciting and memorable games. Battlefield setup and terrain placement is not a competitive portion of the game—players should not strategically place terrain features in a manner that unfairly aids or penalizes a specific army. However, a published or homemade scenario might dictate doing so to represent, for example, an overmatched army defending a village or mountain pass. In such a scenario, giving the defending army a strong defensive position would be one way to make up for being outclassed by its opponent.

If all players are involved with the battlefield setup, or if an impartial third party sets up the terrain, establish turn order and deploy forces normally. If only one player or team sets up the battlefield, then the opposing player or team chooses which table edge to deploy his forces on before determining turn order.

Before the game begins, all players should agree on each terrain feature's game effects.

TERRAIN

A model's movement can be penalized depending on the type of ground it moves over. In WARMACHINE, traversable **terrain** falls into one of three categories: *open*, *rough*, and *impassable*.

Open terrain is mostly smooth, even ground. Examples include grassy plains, barren fields, dirt roads, and paved surfaces. A model moves across open terrain without penalty.

Rough terrain can be traversed, but at a significantly slower pace than open terrain. Examples include thick brush, rocky areas, murky bogs, shallow water, and deep snow. So long as any part of its base is in rough terrain, a model moves at 1/2 normal movement rate. Therefore, a model in rough terrain actually moves only 1/2" for every 1" of its movement used.

Impassable terrain is natural terrain that completely prohibits movement. This includes cliff faces, lava, and deep water. A model cannot move across impassable terrain.

Terrain Features

Natural and man-made objects on the battlefield are **terrain features**. Each terrain feature is unique, so you must decide its exact qualities before staring the game. Terrain features are virtually limitless in their variety, but you can quantify each one by how it affects movement, the type of protection it affords, and any adverse effects it causes. Terrain features are either *obstacles* or *obstructions*.

In addition to hindering movement, terrain features can also provide protection against ranged and magic attacks. A terrain feature such as a hedge or a mesh fence, grants a model *concealment* by making it more difficult to be seen, though it is not dense enough to actually block an attack. A terrain feature such as a stone wall, a giant boulder, or a building, grants a model *cover* by being physically solid enough to block an attack against it.

OBSTACLES & OBSTRUCTIONS

Obstacles and *obstructions* are terrain features that affect a model's movement, provide protection from ranged attacks, and serve as *intervening terrain* during melee combat.

An **obstacle** is any terrain feature up to 1" tall. Obstacles are low enough that they can be climbed upon, or in some cases, easily crossed. A model can climb atop and stand on an obstacle that is at least 1" thick, such as a raised platform or the sides of a ziggurat.

An advancing or running model can climb atop an obstacle by using 2" of its movement. A model cannot climb an obstacle if it does not have at least 2" of movement remaining. Place a model that climbs an obstacle atop it, with the front of the model's base making only 1" of forward progress. Once atop an obstacle, the model may continue with the remainder of its movement.

Realize that a model on a medium or large base may have trouble balancing atop an obstacle if it does not continue moving after initially climbing it. With only 1" of forward progress, the back of the model's base will hang off the back end of the obstacle. This is fine—just prop up the model with some extra dice until it can move again.

An advancing or running model can descend an obstacle without any penalty to its forward progress.

A **linear obstacle** is an obstacle up to 1" tall but less than 1" thick, such as a wall or hedge. An advancing model can cross a linear obstacle at no penalty, as long as the model has enough movement remaining to end its move with its base completely clear of the obstacle. If it does not, the model must stop short of the linear obstacle. A model cannot partially cross or stand atop a linear obstacle. A running or charging model cannot cross a linear obstacle.

In some rare cases, a model may be posed with its head so low that it has no line of sight over an obstacle. If this model's base touches an obstacle, or if it is as close as its pose allows, assume the model is standing in a manner that lets it see and attack over the obstacle. When this occurs, determine the model's *line of sight* from a point directly over the center of its base at the height of the wall. However, enemy models that have *line of sight* to that point may attack this model as well.

An **obstruction** is a terrain feature greater than 1" tall, such as a high wall, a building, or a gigantic boulder. Treat obstructions as *impassable terrain.*

FOREST

A typical **forest** has many trees and dense underbrush, but any terrain feature that hinders movement and makes a model inside it difficult to see can also follow these guidelines. A forest is considered *rough terrain*, but also provides *concealment* to a model with any part of its base inside its perimeter.

A model can draw *line of sight* through up to 3" of forest, but anything more obstructs line of sight. For a model outside of it, the forest completely obstructs line of sight to anything beyond it. Thus, a model can see into or out of a forest, but not completely through one, no matter how thick. A forest provides no protection from melee attacks.

HILLS

A terrain feature that represents a gentle rise or drop in elevation is a hill. Since many terrain pieces use stepped sides instead of gradual slopes to represent a hill's elevations, be sure to declare whether the terrain feature is a hill or an obstacle for movement purposes.

A hill may be open or rough terrain, depending on the ground's nature. Unlike obstacles, hills do not impose any additional movement penalties. A model can charge up or down a hill in open terrain at no penalty.

ELEVATION

Hills, platforms, and some obstacles provide elevations above table level for models to take advantage of. A model on a higher elevation can target a ranged or magic attack against any model on lower terrain and in *line of sight*, regardless of intervening models. A model on higher elevation than its attacker gains +2 Defense (DEF) against ranged and magic attacks from that opponent.

HAZARDS

Many things on a battlefield can kill a man just as quickly as an opponent can. These **hazards** include water, flowing magma, and mine fields. Immediately apply a hazard's effects to a model as soon as any portion of its base enters the hazard's perimeter.

WATER

Depending on its nature, **water** can be hazardous to both warriors and warjacks. When placing a water terrain feature, declare whether it is deep or shallow.

Deep water is impassable terrain that cannot be entered voluntarily. However, a model may be slammed, thrown, or otherwise forced to move into deep water. A warjack that enters deep water has its furnace extinguished and is instantly disabled and removed from play. Although otherwise intact, a warjack in deep water cannot be repaired or restarted for the remainder of the game.

A warrior in deep water can advance at half its normal movement rate, but cannot run or charge. It cannot perform actions, cast spells, use feats, or give orders until it is completely out of the deep water. A warrior in deep water cannot engage other models or make attacks. A warcaster in deep water can allocate focus points and use them to maintain upkeep spells.

A warrior in deep water has a base DEF of 7 against all attacks. A warrior that ends his activation in deep water automatically takes one damage point.

Shallow water is rough terrain that can be crossed by any model. Other than hindering movement, shallow water poses no threat—except to warjacks.

A warjack knocked down in shallow water has its furnace extinguished and is instantly disabled. Any friendly model can restart a warjack knocked down in shallow water. To restart a warjack's furnace, the model must be in base-to-base contact with the warjack and forfeit its action. A warjack can do nothing the turn it restarts, but it functions normally next turn. Even if a warcaster other than its controller restarts it, the warjack remains part of its original battlegroup. A model can only restart one warjack per turn.

Structures

Structures present unique opportunities for terrain arrangement and tactical play. A structure is any large terrain feature that can be damaged and destroyed. The most common structures are *buildings*, but you can use these guidelines for fortress walls, bridges, and similar constructions as well. A single house in a field or a bridge over a chasm can be a scenario's major objective, and a series of buildings can be arranged to create a completely urban environment, with warjacks fighting house-to-house in the streets of the Iron Kingdoms' great cities.

All structures are *solid obstructions*. A warrior can enter a structure through any entryway, such as a door or window, regardless of the model's base size. A warjack can enter a building only through an opening big enough for its base to pass through unobstructed.

PLAYING IN ENCLOSED STRUCTURES

Models function normally inside a structure, but how you represent this may change depending upon the nature of the terrain. If the terrain piece is open-topped or has a removable roof, move models about the interior of the structure to their actual positions. All normal rules apply. A model partially obscured by a door or window benefits from cover.

If the terrain piece representing the structure has a closed top or is otherwise unsuitable for moving models inside it, a more abstract method must be used. If a model enters such a structure, remove the model from the table and place a marker outside the building where the model entered.

When using these abstract rules, declare a model's position inside the structure at the end of its movement. When a model first enters a building, declare whether it is staying clear of all openings or using its entryway as cover. On subsequent activations, the model can move up or down one level and can either stay clear of entryways or choose to occupy a specific one. Instead of changing levels, a model can exit a structure through any entryway on the same level.

A model staying clear of openings does not have *line of sight* to anything outside the structure, but models outside cannot target it either. A model standing at a specific opening can draw line of sight out of it to make attacks, but may be attacked in turn by any model with line of sight to its location. The model benefits from cover against attacks from outside the building.

When using this abstract method of interior movement, a model can engage an opponent in a structure simply by entering that building on the same level. Area-of-effect attacks and spray attacks against any model in a closed structure affect every model on that level of the building.

Realize that these abstract rules take a very liberal approach. If you have very large structures, you may wish to divide them into several sectors to maintain some balance. If this doesn't provide you an acceptable level of precision, we suggest you place a properly scaled floor plan for each structure near the playing area and place the models on them in their actual locations once they enter a building. If you choose this latter method, play according to the normal rules.

DAMAGING AND DESTROYING STRUCTURES

A model that would rather blast its way through the side of a structure than use an entryway will need to inflict substantial damage to it. An attack against a structure in range automatically hits. Not all weapons are effective against structures, so a model must have a weapon that will do the job if it intends to punch through one. Ranged weapons, such as handguns, rifles, and crossbows are all but useless. A ranged weapon must have a POW of at least 14 to damage a structure. However, melee and magic attacks, area-of-effect attacks, and attacks that cause fire or corrosion all do full damage against structures.

Every structure has an Armor (ARM) stat corresponding to its composition. See the "Bringing Down the House" callout on this page for the ARM assigned to the most common forms of construction.

A structure can only take so much damage before being destroyed. Determine a structure's damage capacity based on its composition and thickness. For instance, a wooden gate is destroyed when it takes 5 damage points and a small stone obelisk is destroyed when it takes 10 damage points. Damage taken by a structure is cumulative.

Large structures such as buildings, walls, and bridges can be destroyed in segments. A typical building wall can take 5 damage points per inch of width. Fortifed or very thick walls could take 20 or more damage points or more per inch of width, depending on its composition. When a specific segment of a structure takes its total damage capacity, that portion of it is destroyed. If a single attack causes massive damage, it destroys an appropriate amount of the structure. We suggest having some graph paper handy to quickly diagram a structure and record the damage it takes. For example, a wooden wall with ARM 14 takes 18 damage points from a damage roll of 32, so the attack destroys 3" of the wall.

BRINGING DOWN THE HOUSE

Different materials have different ARM stats:

Wood—ARM 12

Reinforced Wood—ARM 14

Brick—ARM 16

Stone— ARM 18

Iron—ARM 20

Steel—ARM 22

A model with a small base can move through a 1" wide hole and a model with a medium or large base can move through a hole at least 2" wide.

Undamaged portions of a wall or other freestanding structure remain intact as the structure takes damage. However, complex structures such as buildings and bridges rely on the support of all segments to remain standing. A building collapses when half of its total wall length is destroyed, regardless of the proximity of the destroyed segments. For instance, a 3" x 6" building collapses as soon as 9" of its walls are destroyed. Remove the building from play and replace it with an equal-sized ruin. A model inside a building when it collapses takes a damage roll with Power (POW) equal to the building's ARM and is knocked down. A ruined building is rough terrain and provides cover to a model with any portion of its base inside the ruin's perimeter.

These guidelines should be tailored to each individual structure. For instance, a rope bridge could be destroyed by any successful melee attack. A small wooden bridge should take damage and have segments destroyed as if it were a wall. Each support of a large stone bridge could take 20 damage points before being destroyed, with the entire bridge collapsing once two supports are gone.

SCENARIOS—WHY WE CAN'T ALL BE FRIENDS

SIX VARIATIONS OF GAME PLAY

There are as many reasons for war as there are wars themselves. Sides seldom clash with only the intent to eliminate one another. It could be a skirmish over boundaries, a fight over resources, or an attempt to hold important, strategic ground. Conceiving a reason for your conflicts can greatly enhance your WARMACHINE gaming experiences.

Here you will find six scenarios, ready to play. Each occurs on a balanced playing field, conveying no specific advantage to any one player. You can agree with your opponent on which scenario to play, or prior to building your army, roll a d6 and play out the scenario indicated below.

1—TREASURE HUNT
2—CAPTURE THE FLAG
3—CROSSED LINES
4—DOMINATION
5—KING OF THE HILL
6—MANGLED METAL

Each scenario provides you with special rules that describe how to handle the unique circumstances of the scenario. Certain scenarios will also have restrictions on army composition as well as how the game table should be set up. Most scenarios can be played on any scale you choose, from a small duel to all out war. Experiment with different combinations, and feel free to create variations or unique scenarios of your own!

TREASURE HUNT

"I hear those Cryx think they've claim to the secrets within that old chamber, sir. I say they're dead wrong—er, heh-heh, dead wrong—er, right then—but we'll beat 'em to it, sir, or else die tryin'! This, I swear!"

—An unnamed trencher lieutenant, now possibly a thrall lieutenant

Description

It's a race for riches, raw materials, or secret lore as rival factions compete to unearth and retrieve hidden treasures.

Special Rules

The object of the game is to attain the treasure and return it to your deployment area. Once the terrain is set up, place a marker in the center of the table to represent the treasure.

When a model first reaches the location of the treasure, it must unearth it. A model must stand on the exact location of the treasure, and forfeit two activations to discover it.

Once the treasure is found, any heavy warjack touching it may forfeit its action to pick it up. The warjack must have the use of both arms but is not required to have an open fist. A warjack carrying the treasure cannot run or make attacks.

If the model carrying the treasure is knocked down or removed from play, the treasure falls to the ground 1d6 inches away. Use the deviation template to determine where it lands.

Army Selection

Players agree on a size of the battle as normal.

Set Up

Treasure Hunt may be played on any size table. Players should agree on the amount of terrain to use and take turns placing it. Once terrain is placed, the location of the buried treasure is marked at the center of the table.

Beginning

At the start of the game, each player rolls 1d6 and the high roller chooses who goes first. The first player gets his choice of deployment zones and takes the first turn. Players are allowed to place their forces up to 10" from the table's edge.

Victory Conditions

The game ends when one player gets the treasure into their deployment zone.

Multiplayer Game

Treasure Hunt makes a great multiplayer game—the addition of extra players makes for more chaotic action. Make sure all players have deployment areas of equal size, and that the buried treasure marker is placed equidistant from all players.

CAPTURE THE FLAG

"We have one. The Cygnarans have one. What say you, comrade? Shall we go take theirs?"

— Man-O-War Kapitan Sergei Dalinski

Description

This time-honored tradition is played out on the fields of the Iron Kingdoms as you make your way to your opponent's flag, seize it, and take it back to your deployment zone.

Special Rules

Players begin the game with their flag marker in the center of their deployment zone. A model touching the flag may forfeit its action to pick it up and cannot run while carrying it. Warjacks that have lost both arms cannot carry the flag.

If the model carrying the flag is knocked down or removed from play, the flag falls to the ground 1d6 inches away. Use the deviation template to determine the direction in which it falls. A model cannot pick up or carry its own army's flag.

Army Selection

Players agree on a size of the battle as normal.

Set Up

Capture the Flag may be played on any size table. Players should choose sides and then agree on the amount of terrain to place. Once the terrain is placed, players mark the location of their flag in the center of their deployment zone.

Beginning

At the start of the game, each player rolls 1d6 and the high roller chooses who goes first. The first player gets his choice of deploymnet zones and takes the firt turn. Players are allowed to place their forces up to 10" from the table's edge.

Victory Conditions

The first player to carry his opponent's flag back to his own deployment zone wins the game.

Multiplayer Game

In multiplayer Capture the Flag, the game ends when one player manages to get all enemy flags into his deployment zone. Obviously this is tough to accomplish and the winner may have to crush all enemy forces beforehand. It is important to make sure that all players begin the game equidistant from one another and that each has a deployment area of the same size. For more than two players, this is best played on a square table.

CROSSED LINES

"Bugger! Are those Menites? What are they doing here? Bleedin' hell, they've got 'jacks and they're headed straight for us! Get Commander Stryker, mate, and step lively!"

—Rodger "the Rake" Digby, Cygnaran long gunner

Description

Sometimes rival forces inadvertently stumble across one another. These clashes quickly become disorganized brawls rather than the orchestrated battles preferred by most commanders, and they typically involve close-quarters fighting in urban settings where battles might be taken structure-to-structure, or in dense forests where one never knows what lies beyond the next copse of trees.

Special Rules

No models from either side are allowed to use the *advance deployment* special ability.

Army Selection

Players agree on the size of the battle as normal.

Set Up

The table should be thick with terrain. Players take turns placing terrain until one player wishes to stop placing terrain. The other player is then allowed to place one additional piece. Each player must place a minimum of four (4) terrain features.

Beginning

Players roll to determine who chooses their deployment point first, and then alternate choosing deployment points anywhere on the table. Each player chooses three deployment points, and players may not choose a point within 12" of a point selected by their opponent.

Players then alternate arranging one unit or battle group at a time anywhere within 6" of one of their deployment points. A player may choose to deploy all of their solos instead of setting up a unit or battle group. Players arrange their units or groups in the same order they chose deployment points. After all forces are deployed, the players roll again, and the high roller chooses who goes first.

Victory Conditions
The game ends when one side loses all its warcasters.

Multiplayer Game
Crossed Lines is a truly chaotic multiplayer game. It is also very easy to adapt to multiplayer play because there are no deployment zones to worry about. Players should simply follow the rules detailed above.

DOMINATION

"The Battle of the Tongue was about land control. The Khadorans gobbled it up all the way to the river, and the Cygnarans let them have it, for they knew the mighty Dragon's Tongue was where they could make their stand and wear the northerners down."

—From *'The Thornwood War'* by Lethyl Harke

Description
Often in battle the goal is to gain control over the majority of the land, resulting in a lot of back and forth conflict. This is often the case on the borderlands between Khador and Cygnar. Domination pits rival forces against each other in a struggle to capture and hold as much of the battlefield as possible.

Special Rules
Domination lasts for eight game rounds. Players rush to capture specific coordinates on the table, capturing them when a model stands directly on top of the coordinate. If a model leaves the coordinate, it remains under his army's control until an enemy model moves on top of it. Only one model may be on top of a coordinate at any time.

Army Selection
Players agree on a size of the battle as normal.

Set Up
Domination is best played on a 4'x4' table. Players decide how much terrain to use and then take turns placing the terrain.

Divide the table into 1 foot squares, placing coordinates at the vertices of each inersection according to the diagram.

Beginning
At the start of the game, each player rolls 1d6 and the high roller chooses who goes first. The first player gets his choice of deploymnet zones and takes the firt turn.

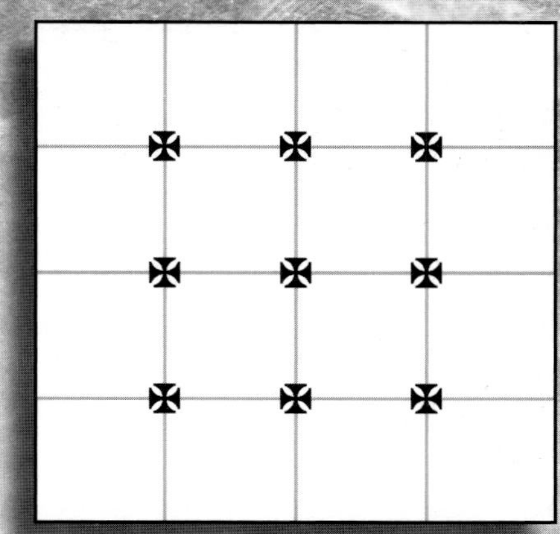

DOMINATION SETUP DIAGRAM

Players are allowed to place their force up to 10" from the table's edge.

Victory Conditions
The game ends at the completion of the eighth game round. The player that controls the most coordinates wins the game. In case of a tie, the player that accumulated the most victory points wins.

Multiplayer Game
Domination requires some care in set up for multiplayer scenarios. All players must be equidistant from each other, and each must have the same size deployment zone.

KING OF THE HILL

"Get three Defenders on that hill. Back them up with three more squads of long gunners. With the elevation and our guns, we shall be as untouchable as any Khadoran fortress."

—Commander Coleman Stryker at Zerkova's Hill

Description
Many battles are fought over strategic locations of uncertain value, but military strategists know the benefit in taking a monumental hill before securing ancillary vantage points. King of the Hill is one such battle. In this scenario, both forces scrabble over land and rush up the hillside to claim the spot for their faction.

Special Rules
The obvious objective of King of the Hill is to take the hill. Any time one player has more models on the hill than their opponent they score a victory point. Units count as one model for the purposes of calculating who

has more troops on the hill. The first player to reach five points wins the game.

Army Selection

Players agree on a size of the battle as normal.

Set Up

Place a hill in the center of the table. Players take turns placing terrain until one player wishes to stop. The other player is then allowed to place one additional piece. Each player must place a minimum of two terrain features.

Beginning

At the start of the game, each player rolls 1d6 and the high roller chooses who goes first. The first player gets his choice of deploymnet zones and takes the firt turn. Players are allowed to place their forces up to 10" from the table's edge.

Victory Conditions

The game ends when one player accumulates five points.

Multiplayer Game

In multiplayer King of the Hill, all players should be equidistant from each other and have the same-sized deployment zone.

MANGLED METAL

"There's nothing like the clatter and clamor of warjacks crashing together, their hulls ringing, their furnaces spewing ash with gouts of sparks and flame, and then the deafening screech of metal as one rends the other apart. What a grand, pernicious thing man has made to fight his wars."

—Casner Feist, ex-warcaster and leader of the Daggermoor Rovers

Description

Mangled Metal is a brutal contest between warjacks. This scenario is an all-out, unrestrained slugfest where the only goal is to survive.

Special Rules

None.

Army Selection

Players agree on a point limit and then purchase their forces as normal, except each player is only allowed a single warcaster regardless of the size of the game. Points may only be spent on the warcaster and his warjacks, as units and solos have no place in Mangled Metal.

Set Up

Mangled Metal may be played on any size table, though a smaller table works better. Each player is allowed to place two obstructions on the table.

Beginning

At the start of the game, each player rolls 1d6 and the high roller chooses who goes first. The first player gets his choice of deploymnet zones and takes the firt turn. Players are allowed to place their force up to 10" from the table's edge.

Victory Conditions

The game ends with either the death of a warcaster or when all warjacks on either side are totaled.

Multiplayer Game

In multiplayer Mangled Metal, all players should be equidistant from each other and have comparable deployment zones.

CYGNAR

OF CROWN AND KINGDOM

A BRIEF HISTORY OF CYGNAR

"The history of Cygnar is as rich as the people of whom it is made up, and may no mortal man forget its significance."

—King Leto Raelthorne

The following is a transcription of the words of Professor Gabriel Parrish, professor of Cygnaran History at the Corvis University and a retired officer of the Corvis Watch. These words were spoken three days prior to his death during Raelthorne the Elder's siege of Corvis in 603 A.R.:

Sit down, lads, sit down. Now, where did we leave off? Oh right, the Occupation Era, aye. Let's see now...the Occupation lasted for several generations. History teaches us, however, that all empires eventually crumble and fall, and it was the Orgoth's supremacist disposition and rigorous segregation of the native races that made this inevitable. The people of western Immoren eventually united against the long-term oppression. It was a long, bloody time to send them off, but ultimately they retreated to their ships and sailed back to the faraway lands from whence they'd come.

It was the Iron Fellowship that declared the rebellion, which 153 years afterward inspired the Iron Alliance, which as you all know evolved into the momentous Council of Ten. Though the founders of the Fellowship fell, their martyrdom was chiefly responsible for giving life to a concentrated rebellion effort. Uprisings came and went, but the brotherhood that had formed in the very heart of Caen inspired an ongoing, open resistance that ultimately secured our freedom, and it is this thing alone, if not any other, that justifies Cygnar's position as the finest kingdom in all of Immoren. For it was on Cygnaran soil that the rival forces of wizardly orders and even the priests of Morrow and Menoth fought as brothers against their common foe. This would never happen again. Cygnar is the home of that ancient alliance—and I daresay it shall one day be the throne of a new and peaceful Immoren.

But back to history. In 202 A.R., the borders of Cygnar were established at the signing of the renowned Corvis Treaties, which took place just down the avenue from here. Our ancestors separated the kingdoms using similar boundaries to the provinces the Orgoth had laid down, but it was the "Iron Kingdoms" that were born that year and, most importantly, the crown jewel called Cygnar. The world was growing in leaps and bounds, and noble Cygnar was the heart of it all.

This inspiration of the Iron Fellowship does not stand alone as Cygnar's sole novelty. Far from it. There are numerous other strong suits worn by the peoples of this country throughout its distinguished history. Tomes of ancient lore claim that Cygnarans were the first to organize the Circle of the Oath, those who wielded "The Gift"—that of magic. And we were the first to entice the Rhulfolk from their mountains, to work alongside our mechaniks and create the Colossals, which were paramount in repelling the Orgoth. Cygnarans are the most industrious and determined people in the entire realm, and it is plain to see why Cygnar is hailed as the birthplace of "the new world," always a step and a half ahead of everyone else.

The kings of Cygnar, as with any kingdom, have been both warriors and sages, and one of the most notable of these to occupy the throne was the legendary King Woldred the Diligent, a man who filled both roles in his time. Many of you know I have devoted much study to Woldred's rule, and rightly so. He is worthy of note, for his was a long rule that saw much conflict and change. The significance of his reign was manifold.

Although his personal demeanor was sometimes grave—a result from his princely years of campaigning against trollkin and in the Colossal War—Woldred was a genuine and rightly good king for Cygnar. As a prince, he was ever eager to lead his troops into the field. The Colossal War was Woldred's proving ground. Tales of his valor won him the support of his people, though he showed he was more than purely a military man. He was also a shrewd negotiator, an accomplished statesman, and lawmaker.

In addition to his part in driving out the invading Khadorans and their Colossals, King Woldred became determined to quash the north's ambitions to invade his kingdoms. As part of his terms to the Khadorans, Woldred convened the Disarmament Conferences of 257 A.R., which saw the dismantling of the north's mighty constructs and the establishment of the Colossal Guard. This significantly hindered Khador's capabilities to wage an effective war, and there was peace in Immoren for nigh forty years.

This gave Woldred time to focus on other matters. He became the first ruler of the Reconstruction Era to set aside personal desire and enmity to encourage not just the rebuilding of the structures the Orgoth had destroyed during the Scourge, but growth as a kingdom on practically every level. He concentrated on the technological and organizational aspects of reform. His reign saw road building, canal digging, shipbuilding, a reorganization of the Cygnaran army and administration, and the minting of money to meet the demands of a growing economy.

He was justifiably wary of the ambitions of his erstwhile enemies, but he was tolerant enough to personally venture into the trollkin warrens at Hadriel Fens in 267 A.R. and negotiate a lasting peace, ending years of bloody and needless conflict. Also among his accomplishments were the orders and planning for the creation of the smaller utility steamjacks, expediting industrialization and trade along Cygnar's various water routes. And it was the Diligent King who, near the end of his reign, declared the hidden followers of Cyriss an official cult, thereby criminalizing (but also verifying) this seditious religion.

King Woldred was never one to allow good deeds—especially his own—go unrecognized by his people and he constructed many monuments to the achievements of the Cygnaran people during the tenure of his prodigious rule. Countless memorials erected during this period remain standing today in various states, some well maintained, others as weathered testaments dotting the aged roads of the kingdom.

In his last few years, Woldred became renowned for two major deeds; one being the retirement of the Colossals in 286 A.R. due to heinous tax burdens, a move that he enforced despite heavy opposition by his court indicating this would renew the Khadoran threat, and the other being the infamous "Woldred's Covenant," also in 286. He decreed that the people of Cygnar would not fall prey to the vicious backstabbing of other monarchic kingdoms, "diminishing into a stagnant pattern of brother betraying brother and father fearing son." Like the iron in which the kingdom was quite literally forged, the crown would be unbending. He drafted his Accord-By-Hand Covenant, which stated that each king shall impart the throne on his own terms and not allow it to be helplessly handed over to "kin of bad quality." With the possibility to gain favor of the kingship, the Temple of Menoth supported the contract wholeheartedly; under the condition the successor be of noble birth and they had sovereign right to exclusively hold and bear witness to each king's passing terms. The Menites were a greater force in Cygnar in those days, and Woldred's council was pressured to accept the offer in order to pass the decree. It wasn't long before this resolution was put to the test.

When Woldred the Diligent died in 289 A.R., the majority of the kingdom recoiled from his sudden death—some crying treachery—but the Temple of Menoth (viciously) quelled such talk and claimed that after the traditional period of mourning, they would unveil the terms of succession. The Church of Morrow, anxious and silent, looked to their Primarch for counsel, expecting much conflict if the Menites gained absolute access to the throne. This never happened.

Woldred's terms had mysteriously disappeared and within a fortnight his nephew, Malagant—called the Grim—entered the palace in Caspia with a force of soldiers five hundred strong and claimed the throne as his own. In light of its absence, by rights, Woldred's Covenant could not be enforced. At the same time, the Temple of Menoth refuted Malagant's right to rule, and secret conflicts raged beneath the surface. Some of the more vocal Menite priests were accused of sedition, dubbing Malagant as a "self-appointed king de facto" and a usurper. Between 290 and 294 A.R., the Grim King had over two hundred Menite clergy arrested and hung. Church and State were at vicious odds, and in 293 A.R., Malagant hailed the Church of Morrow as Cygnar's official religion. Cygnar was in turmoil and headed for civil war. But it was not to be. No, not yet.

Like a wolf on a blood-scent, the Khadoran Queen Cherize initiated a border war with Cygnar in 293 A.R. that lasted until 295 A.R. when Cherize suddenly went missing after the conflict referred to in history books as The Lost Day. Cherize was claimed lost and unrecoverable in less than two months, and King Malagant died shortly thereafter.

A new ruler was inducted in Khador, Queen Ayn Vanar V, a mere girl of five winters and incapable of rule. Her foster, a Lord Regent Velibor, took control of Khador and gathered his most loyal chieftains from the barbarian tribes of the north. Lord Velibor saw possibilities in turning away from the battles with Cygnar and ordering his barbarians-turned-soldiers to extend Khador's borders into her neighbors', Ord and Llael, instead. With Cygnar's attentions turned inward toward a sudden Menite uprising and the quest for a new king, the Lord Regent believed the smaller kingdoms' borders were ripe for the picking.

Bitter conflicts ensued, raging unchecked for more than a decade, until the young queen matured enough to one day countermand Velibor's orders. It was said that the teenage Queen Vanar, who had become quite a beautiful young lady (even by our fine Cygnaran standards), had tired of so much death and strife. In 304 A.R., she ordered the assaults to stop, against the Lord Regent's wishes. Some fighting did cease, but Velibor's promises of wealth and power to the barbarian chiefs made them too eager for war. They refused to recognize Vanar as their queen and the battles continued without her consent. In the Siege of Midfast the following year, the majority of the invaders were destroyed; the great Markus led both Cygnarans and Ordfolk on the very field of his Ascension, and if it weren't for the grace of Morrow we would all likely be standing in the ruins of their wake. The treachery of Lord Velibor and the barbarians of the northlands sparked much disdain and animosity that remains to this day, and relations between Khador and her neighbors has not been pleasant since.

The sixteen-year religious conflict and the Khadoran Border Wars transformed the Cygnaran era into a dark period of confusion and paranoia. The Temple of Menoth, once so strong, struggled desperately to realize their theocratic plans. More and more people, looking for positivism in such dark times, turned to the benevolent preaching of the Morrowan faithful, and over the next couple hundred years, Cygnar became a powder keg waiting to explode. In spite of some good moments during these centuries, such as an alliance with Llael that helped the country get back to its feet after Khador had taken so much of its lands, and the rise of the Church of Morrow, the Menites were collectively aggravated. They sowed unrest through pocket societies, often violently in the very city streets. These circles were condemned and outlawed by the Cygnaran court but the Menites took their operations underground. They continued to vilify the Church of Morrow, denouncing them as dabblers, heretics, and criminals, and what had once been heated debates outside of the churches or in the marketplaces, worsened. Over the course of many years, much blood—most of it innocent—had been spilled.

In 482 A.R., during the Longest Night festival, it came to a head. Organized followers of Menoth—soldiers, in fact, disguised as pilgrims—took control of eastern Caspia, divided as it was by the River Black. Thinking these pilgrims might possibly riot, the Caspian Watch moved to disperse the enormous crowds, but they didn't know the Menites' intentions were much more deadly, organized as they were under the direction of their visgoth, a man named Sulon. Crying Menoth's name, the thousands of pilgrims rose against the Cygnaran militia and slew over three hundred guards. Nearly two hundred years of aggression and resentment suddenly had a name—the Cygnaran Civil War.

The City of Walls was nearly razed from within. The fighting, fueled by the clash of faiths and looting, continued mainly as a result of the dreadful lack of watch guards. At the same time, the Coin Wars on the Khadoran/Llaelese borderlands drew actual provisions and wartime efforts very thin. The armies of mercenaries warring upon each other were a constant worry, but Cygnar was too busy trying to keep its capital standing to aid their neighbor at any great length. This country was in a bad way, and it took the wise words of the Church of Morrow to stave off this downward spiral.

As head of the entire Church Treasury, High Prelate Shevann had great sway with the Cygnaran people and its governing forces. Knowing the Menites would never accept the words of a follower of Morrow, she worked her plans through a Cygnaran official. In this way, Shevann entreated the their appointed leader, Visgoth Ozeall (their Hierarch had fallen in combat some weeks earlier), to negotiate peace. He agreed to hear the terms and after days of arguing, chest-beating, and eventual concession, the newly dubbed Protectorate of Menoth was granted to the Menites.

The Menites were ceded an expanse of land and eastern Caspia—which they immediately renamed Sul, after the Hierarch Sulon, once a visgoth and the innovator of their jihad—became their central point of commerce and travel. In order to steer the zealots further away from Cygnar, Shevann also suggested the Protectorate have the right to create their own government without outside influence. It was understood that the Protectorate would still nominally be part of Cygnar, though the two nations would have no political sway over the other. Many Cygnaran diplomats believed the Menites would reject Shevann's choice of land for them, as it angled the Protectorate to rest against the barbarous domain of the heathen Idrians, but the Menites were eager to bring their faith to the Imer and excitedly took up the challenge. It may have destined the Idrians to become Menites, but it spared Cygnar years of bloody conflict. As such a devout servant of Morrow, High Prelate Shevann ascended after her demise in 500 A.R. and assumed the mantle of Patron of Merchants.

A BRIEF HISTORY OF CYGNAR

A decade before however, shortly after the Cygnaran Civil War ended, King Grigor Malfast acceded the throne in 489 A.R. and led the nation into an era of growth not seen since Woldred the Diligent. For over two decades we knew peace. Cygnar excelled in every way. Steamjacks became more and more common as the Fraternal Order of Wizardry perfected their creation process, and the once-depleted Cygnaran coffers filled quickly with gold and silver. Malfast was very intelligent, but had his most trusted of colleagues by his side, Vinter Raelthorne II, to temper his grandiose schemes. The Raelthorne bloodline had been deeply ingrained in the Cygnaran courts for centuries, a few of their kind having been kings themselves. Indeed, the name Raelthorne had been a mainstay in the Cygnaran throne room in one manner or another for centuries.

The Raelthorne of the era, Vinter II, was in charge of keeping Malfast's fantastic and idealistic plans mortal in execution, where he knew they were accomplishable by Cygnaran hands. While this Vinter II was a hard man, he was quite practical, and knew the best way to handle things behind the crown. Without him, King Malfast would have wasted much of his treasury in short time, leaving Cygnar penniless when tragedy strikes, as it's so apt to do.

In these days, the Khadoran king, Ruslan Vygor, was a right misanthrope with a dark heart, and Cygnar's prosperity as a kingdom over the past decades had stoked his heartfires into a jealous inferno. He mobilized his forces into much larger war hosts, full with powerful Khadoran cavalry, to the borders of Llael, knowing that Cygnar would be moved to action. Indeed, King Malfast sent a great force of warjacks and riflemen to Llael to beat back the impending invasion, but he was duped. If it weren't for the scouts of Fellig that had made it past King Vygor's deadly hunters, Cygnar would have felt the full brunt of a secret Khadoran force carving its way through the "impassable" Thornwood. Small forces from Corvis and Rivercleft met the Khadorans at the Dragon's Tongue, while the forces dispatched to Llael turned back and made an attempt to stop the steamjack-assisted Thornwood advance.

The Battle of the Tongue in 511 A.R. remains one of the bloodiest in recent history. Cygnar was greatly outnumbered. It took all of our superior training, and the aid of nearby mercenary forces—the Shields of Durant and the Ironbears—to hold the river. Centuries-old bridgework was destroyed in order to stop the crossing; tons of Warlord Era stonework was lost to the deep waters of the Dragon's Tongue. This conflict saw the loss of more steamjacks in any conflict in the history of western Immoren. Although we were able to halt the Khadorans at the river, keeping them from sweeping inland, we suffered great losses. It took decades to replace and repair the steamjacks used in the comparatively short four-month Thornwood War, which ended with Vygor's demise in the field at the hands of Vinter Raelthorne II.

During the reconstruction, Malfast had a towering fortress erected at the northernmost end of the "Warjack Road," that which Vygor's army carved through Thornwood. The twisted forest has since reclaimed the fortress. Dark spirits, it is said, has cast the Cygnaran forces out and the dark and resilient Thornwood has enveloped the hold entire. On the sloping banks of the Dragon's Tongue below the wood and throughout the old battle site, bits and pieces of the warjacks used in the war are still unearthed, but only the most impetuous travel that historically bleak area. You're more likely to find the undying minions of Thamar than any treasure or artifice mechanika. Even Khador has, to this day, left the area to the shades of their past failure.

A few short years later, King Malfast fell very ill. He knew his time on Caen was coming to a close. With no heir-apparent, from his deathbed Malfast drafted his terms according to Woldred's Covenant and handed his crown to his courtly advisor, Vinter Raelthorne II. Vinter accepted the burden with a heavy heart, knowing that even with the blood of kings in his veins, sitting upon the Cygnaran throne was the greatest responsibility in Immoren. Soon after the announcement of the coronation, Grigor Malfast passed away in the night before his fifty-sixth birthday. In 515 A.R., Vinter Raelthorne II, now in his forties, was crowned king, and Cygnar entered the most recent era of our history, the Raelthorne Era.

The rule of the Raelthornes has been long—eighty-seven years to this very day. Vinter II ruled with the same approach he had adopted with his predecessor, priding his decisions as utilitarian over frivolous, and for the good of Cygnar overall. Nearly always found deep in thought over matters of state, he became known as the Stone-Faced King. During his rule, he survived two assassination attempts and developed a reputation as a committed Cygnaran nationalist, as well as a strong opponent of unregulated sorcery and Cyrissist cults. He also played an important behind-the-scenes role in the founding of the Mercarian League, a confederacy of merchant cities throughout the kingdom. On the whole, Vinter II was a remarkable and lucrative leader for the people.

In 539 A.R., the crown passed to his son of the same name. Vinter Raelthorne III ascended the throne, and here was a man who had learned much from his father's rule, although he had translated Vinter II's heavy hand to more of an iron fist. Vinter III filled the kingdom's coffers through burdensome taxes, in order to expedite progress and fund privateers to secure the western sea-lanes, which were rife with pirate vessels. Many people hated him for such rigid demands, despite his success against the raiders of The Broken Coast, and he earned a nickname that played off of his father's; he was called the Stoneheart, a title he initially despised but eventually embraced.

He was a stern and harsh king who brooked little nonsense. Often he claimed to be surrounded by deceit and the self-interest of bureaucrats and sycophants, concluding that in this life he could trust very few people. He dismissed most of his courtly advisors, looking to "the counsel of his own soul and conscience…or lack thereof" for making nearly all of the kingdom's weighty decisions. In spite of the mixed feelings of his subjects, nearly every choice Vinter III made moved Cygnar further toward the greatness of today's kingdom. His taxes might have been harsh, but looking back, he was not as tight-fisted as we've been led to believe. He was a pragmatist, and his collected monies often went back to the people in some fashion, usually for the kingdom's defense. If debtors could not pay, rather than letting them rot in prison, he put them on board ships or into quarries to work off what they owed. True, some died under these hard circumstances, but their toil was not in vain as they brought the kingdom ever closer to the Cygnar of today.

Vinter III had two sons; the eldest was also named Vinter, and "the younger" is our current good king, Leto. Nursemaids and midwives raised the boys in their father's absence, as his life was too preoccupied with refining the jewel of the Iron Kingdoms. Perhaps he was never the most gregarious of men, but he did a lot for our kingdom. When he died suddenly (and suspiciously, I might add) in 576 A.R., the kingdom fell to his eldest son, Vinter IV.

So begins our next chapter.

King Vinter Raelthorne IV, the Elder. Most of you know of him, though you were children when his reign came to a sudden end. The Elder's irrational fear of the Church of Morrow drove him to seclude himself from their influence—a good reason he turned out as nasty as he did, I daresay. His father and grandfather may have been called the Stone Kings, but this Vinter was of a different make. Woe for us, I say, that the Stoneheart had no time for Woldred's Covenant.

Vinter IV was known as an insatiably greedy and power-lusty king. Many of your fathers feared he would eventually call them to arms in some expansionist effort. He was a paranoid king, suspecting enemies everywhere he looked, often contravening matters in open court by drawing his blade to intimidate officials and "sway" dignitaries to his position. It was this paranoia that brought about the utter corruption of the Inquisition—a network of spies developed by his father for reasons of national security—turning them into perfidious judges and rapacious executioners. Until that time, the Inquisition was a secret host of discreet information gatherers, but Vinter IV culled them into his own feared guild of cloaked assassins. By his order, the Inquisition had impunity for their actions, no matter how vile or seemingly uncalled for. The Elder ruled with terror and murder, though he termed it justice and royal privilege. Those who opposed him were dragged off in the middle of the night, most of them never seen again.

Also heinous was the Elder's stand against Morrow. In the latter years of his rule, the king completely gave himself over to the inner darkness; accepting advisors from what was later unveiled as Thamar's vile clergy. There were instances recorded regarding priests of Morrow corrupted from their faith with gifts and promises from the royal coffers—some of them even inducted into the ranks of the Inquisition. So deep did Vinter's evil run that he even managed to turn some goodly wizards of the Fraternal Order and the Golden Crucible to his side.

All this time, during his brother's rule, Prince Leto was appalled. It is said he would lay awake at night, sleepless from his brother's torments and fearful of Vinter's spies, who knew that Leto had a close relationship with Primarch Arius and a special affinity for the Church of Morrow. Although they deny their taking part in what was soon to happen, it is assumed the church's concession of action against Vinter is what primarily moved Leto's hand. A palace revolution erupted suddenly in the winter of 594 A.R.. Nine years ago—it seems like yesterday.

Leto and a band of tenacious fighters, including the High Magus Calster, attacked Vinter IV in the great receiving hall. Calster's wizards were pitted against Vinter's Inquisitors throughout the east wing of the palace in a foundation-shaking display of sorcery. To this day, the marks burned into the marble

and stone can be seen. Meanwhile, Leto and his vanguard of knights and paladins battered their way into Vinter's chambers and attacked the king and his personal guards. It is said Leto wept as he cut through his fellow Cygnarans to get to his brother.

It was a bloody day. Vinter IV slew two score of Leto's men with single strokes. He waded through the cleft armor and flesh like an armored galleon sailing in a sea of Cygnaran blood. We have heard that when the Elder stood enraged before his weeping brother, Leto beseeched one last time for him to end his madness. Vinter simply cackled like a man possessed and went for his brother's head, raining down blows onto his sibling in unrelenting fury. Leto deflected the titanic swipes, praying loudly to Morrow over the shouts and howls of his brother. Suddenly, Vinter landed a massive strike that sent Leto reeling—a wide gash across the chest, of which the scar remains to this day. Leto was at his brother's merciless sword point.

Now, you may ask, "Then what happened? Why is Leto our king if his brother defeated him in combat?"

There are many rumors and far-fetched tales of godly intervention, but despite the witnesses in the chamber, nobody truly remembers what happened. It can only be said that one moment, Leto was down and defeated, and in the next, he stood over his brother, the Elder cringing and furious. I wasn't there, lads—would that I were—but I'd wager a hundred crowns on the Primarch Arius. Nothing short of a miracle could have stopped the Elder from slaying his kin, and if anyone short of Morrow himself could conjure up a miracle, it would be that fine man.

Vinter had been subdued and was cast into the royal dungeons. Leto declared the coup at an end, but the Elder had many allies, and they moved immediately. Operatives of that wretched Inquisition took Leto's wife hostage and demanded Vinter's immediate release. Leto loved his bride and felt he had little choice. His council—who also loved the princess—still urged him to refuse the Elder's release, but Leto denied them and gave the command. He watched as his brother fled the palace and the city of Caspia. The Inquisitors never furnished the princess and Leto set trackers and hunters on his brother's trail, but Vinter lost them with a flying contraption. He drifted on the clouds into the east, out over the Bloodstone Marches. Leto's bride was never seen again—Morrow keep her soul.

So there was great sorrow in the hearts of many for a long time, but it was also known that Cygnar had a new sovereign. King Leto Raelthorne "the Younger" was crowned in a solemn ceremony, while noblemen still whispered of the grim circumstances leading to his coronation. The Elder was given a full trial in absentia and was formally stripped of all his Cygnaran rights for his multitude of crimes and dark alliances. He was officially convicted of treason against the crown, and his life deemed forfeit. Execution was left to the perilous Bloodstone Marches.

As I said, that was nine years ago. And so it comes to now. You lads are fortunate to live in a new and prosperous era, with a good king who stands vigilant against the dangers to our country. Leto has negotiated many treaties with the Khadorans, but he'll not forget their treachery at the Thornwood, and he'll also gratify the Protectorate as amiably as he can, though they look at us with villainy in their eyes. King Leto is a just and honorable ruler, and you would all do well to give him your support. We owe much of our way of life to his first decade of rule, and our success as a kingdom lies wholly with him now. As long as he wears the crown, we can rest easy in our beds at night, knowing evil is gone from this land. Offer your prayers to blessed Morrow for King Leto's continued health, my lads…class is over for today. We'll continue next session with an in-depth look at the Ascendants. Don't be late.

WARCASTER–LT. ALLISTER CAINE

"I saw Caine in action once. Five or six years ago. He'd accused a man of treason, called him out to duel in the scrap yards of the industrial 'bourg. Didn't know whom he was dealing with—the poor sod chose pistols. So they walked their ten paces and there was a three count. Caine vanished on two-and-a-half and reappeared an arm's length behind his opponent. Twin streaks of sunlight flashed from his guns. Caine twirled and holstered 'em before the dead man hit the ground…then he just turned toward us and grinned. Some of the brutes applauded him. I was disgusted. No man should be shot from behind. If I'd been Watch captain then, I'd have put him up in the pillory right there."

—Corvis Watch Commander, Julian Helstrom

The Militant Order of the Arcane Tempest teaches its followers to focus their arcane abilities through their specially crafted magelock pistols, and has done so with great diligence for roughly twenty years. Their ideology and practices require a great degree of control over their students, and when they inducted an intense and somewhat troubled youth by the name of Allister Caine into their fold, they had no idea what they were getting. Caine was destined to test the Academe's standards. Not only was he an inherent sorcerer, but he was also an untapped warcaster of superior ability who pioneered a new realm of gun-casting.

In spite of constant behavioral problems—especially concerning his fellow students—Caine excelled in his tutelage. Purely by instinct he learned how to channel his power into his pistol shots, and the ability to place them with unerring accuracy. He claimed his firearms "spoke to him in ways these other buffoons would never understand." Soon, Caine was performing trick-shots and goofing off whenever he could escape the scrutiny of his teachers. His skills became legendary among his peers, and even talked about by the graduates of the Order.

His warcasting capabilities were revealed one day when an instructor happened upon him willing a steamjack to perform his assigned chores as he rehearsed sophisticated drawing and re-holstering techniques. After this, Caine sped through the order. He was granted the title of Gun Mage in little over one year. News of his abilities reached Leto's court, and upon his graduation he was summoned to the king for a display. Caine did not disappoint. He was personally urged to enlist as a warcaster by King Leto himself.

It is said that shortly after Caine graduated the Tempest Academe, he was incarcerated briefly for the murder of a gangster of no small status in his hometown of Bainsmarket. Apparently there had been a long-standing feud between the two and Caine had fulfilled some kind of vendetta. Because the victim was obviously a criminal, and because no one had any idea how to contain Caine, the magistrates chose to cover up this little misdeed. But Caine's practices were not about to change for the better.

Over the next several years, Caine gained the reputation of a loner, a grifter, and a scoundrel. He became a frequenter of seedy spots all along the borders of Cygnar and Ord. Indeed, he often enjoys

"slumming" in the guise of a common drunk just to show off his nearly unmatched skills for a moment's thrill or a handful of crowns. He has spent many a night sleeping off his nocturnal habits in the stocks and cells of many towns, tapping into his mystic abilities once his head clears through the alcohol-induced fog. His firewater binges, his improprieties with countless women (often of rank or title), his unrelenting swagger and utter audacity in the face of his superiors, have all precluded him from attaining commander status. He is the only warcaster in the Cygnaran army who ranks below a captain, and were it not for his great skills, it's doubtful the man would be allowed within a league of the highly valued 'jacks, much less be enlisted in the army at all. His vices notwithstanding, Allister Caine remains a gun mage of the highest regard in the ranks of the Cygnaran army. When pressed about his officer's behavior, Commander Stryker dismisses Caine's indiscretions as "the last vestiges of a chaotic youth."

On the field of battle, Lieutenant Caine sometimes employs his infamous "flash-fry" maneuver, magically blinking from place-to-place to gain the element of surprise. This strange ability to make short-ranged leaps in time and space is unique to Caine and Caine alone. Other gun mages call this a dishonorable practice, but he scoffs whenever he hears this. Caine was once heard to remark, "Don't let 'em trick you, friend. They'll take whatever edge they can get. Be fools not to. If they could do it, believe me, they would."

Feat: MAELSTROM

In an awesome display of speed and skill, Allister Caine launches himself into the air and spins about, firing his brace of Spellstorm pistols in rapid succession like a fiery tornado of death.

Caine makes a Spellstorm Pistol attack against every enemy model that is an eligible target within his control area. Rolls maybe boosted.

FOCUS	6	CMD	8		
SPD	STR	MAT	RAT	DEF	ARM
7	5	4	8	17	13

SPELLSTORM PISTOL

RNG	ROF	AOE	POW
12	2	–	12

SPELLSTORM PISTOL

RNG	ROF	AOE	POW
12	2	–	12

SWORD

Special	POW	P+S
–	3	8

Damage	15
Point Cost	67
Field Allowance	C
Victory Points	5

Base Size: Small

SPECIAL RULES

CAINE

•Crack Shot—Caine can make ranged attacks against any target in line of sight, regardless of intervening models. Targets still benefit from concealment and cover.

SPELLSTORM PISTOLS

•Range Amplifier—Caine's Spellstorm Pistols add 5" to the range of all spells cast directly from him. Channeled spells do not benefit from the Range Amplifier.

Spells	Cost	RNG	AOE	POW	UP	OFF
ARCANE BLAST	3	10	3	13		✓
A magical energy blast radiates from a single point to strike all models in the AOE.						
FLASH	2	Caster	–	–		
Caine instantly moves to any location within his control area with a surface no higher than 5", then ends his activation.						
BLUR	2	6	–	–	✓	
Target model/unit gains +3 DEF against ranged attacks.						
DEADEYE	2	6	–	–		
Target model/unit adds an additional die to its first ranged attack roll this turn.						
SNIPE	Spec	6	–	–	✓	
Increase target model/unit's ranged weapon's RNG by 1" per focus point spent.						
THUNDER STRIKE	4	8	–	14		✓
Target model hit by Thunder Strike is slammed d6" directly away from Caine with the same effects as a Slam Power Attack.						

WARCASTER–CAPTAIN VICTORIA HALEY

"Burn the dead. Consecrate the bones. Render them to ashes. Lest they return to haunt us."

—Captain Haley after a decisive victory over a Cryxian invasion force

A calculating woman capable of both harshness and heroism, the grim Victoria Haley was born in a small fishing village on the north-western coast of Cygnar, a once thriving community north of Frog's Bight called Ingrane. Her parents were simple fishing folk, living a hard life to provide for Victoria and her twin sister. Their lives were seemingly normal, and would have stayed that way, if it were not for the dreaded Cryx.

The girls were toddlers, just five summers old, when, in late spring of 584 A.R., raiders from Scharde landed during the night onto the wooden docks of Ingrane. They charged into the peaceful village meeting little resistance. During the raid, Haley's father ran to confront the pillagers only to be cut down, while her mother thought to hide Victoria and her sister in the clay-carved fruit cellar of their villa. She barely had enough time to push Victoria down the trap door before the Cryx battered their way inside. The door slammed shut and Victoria watched through the gaping floorboards as her mother was murdered and her sister was snatched up and spirited away into the night.

Today, no one lives in the ruins of Ingrane but dark memories and restless spirits. The violence that took place during that raid has somehow refused to be forgotten, and now it is a place of shadowy things where icy winds howl down from those high bluffs above the bight, across the necks of travelers and sailors that venture too near.

The survivors of that night gathered together and made the leaden voyage through moors and woods to Ramarck. Victoria Haley was one of those sullen few. An elderly woman bore the girl the distance to the city, but could not care for the youth, though she tried. A Morrowan seminary eventually took the girl in. She was given education and not treated unkindly, but it was not a life for her. At 13 summers, Victoria fled the school and made her way to New Larkholm, finding employ as a fishmonger's assistant on the docks.

One afternoon, in the marketplace with her employer, a laboring steamjack went haywire and ran amuck. It careened through dockside pier-houses, a giant metal berserker, but as its shadow fell over Victoria, she screamed out in terror for the 'jack to stop…and it did. It froze mid-swing, its riveted fist a mere foot away from her blonde head. She wiped away her tears of shock, brushed her apron flat, and quietly whispered for the

steamjack to return to its owner; this, too, it did. Walking alongside the metal giant, the two of them a paradox of frailty and strength, Victoria never felt so in control of her world. Two years later, in 599 A.R., at the age of 20, she was among the ranks of the Cygnaran army as a powerful warrior, and a very determined warcaster.

Captain Victoria Haley has a furious loathing for anything Cryxian. Where the pirate armies assemble, she is soon found throwing everything at her disposal toward the undying hordes. It isn't hard for her to find targets for her vengeance. She has in some way attracted the attention of a particular warwitch that goes by the name Deneghra. This Cryxian minion seems bent on destroying Captain Haley as much as the reverse is true. Deneghra moves to block her every move, and their forces have collided more than once in bloody conflict.

Given the recent aspirations of the warwitch to directly confront Haley, the captain has had a special piece of mechanikal weaponry added to her personal arsenal—the vortex spear. In her hands it is a blindingly fast weapon, engraved with ancient runes of protection that merge with those of her armor, making her impervious to the ravaging magics of her enemies. Though their forces have clashed more than once, never have Haley and Deneghra met face-to-face in battle. It is safe to assume only one of them would walk away from such a meeting. Captain Haley's motives are clear: there will never be enough blood shed for what the minions of Lord Toruk took from her on the bluffs of Ingrane years ago, when she was a happy girl, just five summers old.

Feat: BLITZ

While she generally prefers a regimented and conservative approach to battle, Captain Haley is capable of launching a massive unified assault with a single command. Carefully conserving the energy and resources of her forces, Haley will trigger a deadly offense at precisely the right moment.

All friendly Cygnaran models within Haley's control area may make one additional attack on this turn, regardless of a weapon's ROF, with no additional focus required.

FOCUS	7	CMD	8		
SPD	STR	MAT	RAT	DEF	ARM
6	5	6	5	16	14

HAND CANNON	RNG	ROF	AOE	POW
	12	1	–	12

VORTEX SPEAR	Special	POW	P+S
	Multi	6	11

Damage	15
Point Cost	58
Field Allowance	C
Victory Points	5
Base Size: Small	

SPECIAL RULES

VORTEX SPEAR

- Arcane Vortex—Haley can negate any spell that targets a model within 3", including herself, as it is being cast by spending one focus point. The negated spell does not take effect, but its focus cost is still spent. Haley can use the Vortex at any time as long as she has focus points to spend.
- Reach—2" melee range
- Set Defense—Haley gains +2 DEF against Charge and Slam attacks.

Spells	Cost	RNG	AOE	POW	UP	OFF
ARCANE BOLT	2	12	–	11		✓
Target model is struck by magical bolts of energy flying from Haley's hands.						
ARCANE SHIELD	2	8	–	–	✓	
Surrounded by a magical barrier, target model/unit gains +3 ARM.						
CHAIN LIGHTNING	3	10	–	10		✓
Lightning arcs from target model to d6 additional models. The lightning arcs, automatically hitting the nearest model within 4" of the last model hit, but cannot strike the same model twice. Each model hit suffers a POW 10 damage roll.						
DEADEYE	2	6	–	–		
Target model/unit adds an additional die to its first ranged attack roll this turn.						
DISRUPTOR	3	8	–	–		✓
Target Warjack loses any unused focus points and cannot be allocated focus points or channel spells for one round.						
SCRAMBLE	3	10	–	–		✓
At the beginning of its next turn, target Warjack activates and runs in a random direction, knocking down any warrior models in its path. The scrambled Warjack is knocked down if it hits an obstruction or another Warjack. Scrambled Warjack cannot activate again this turn.						
TEMPORAL BARRIER	4	Caster	CTRL	–		
While in Haley's control area, all models move at half rate and suffer -3 DEF. Enemy models beginning their activation in the AOE cannot charge or slam. Temporal Barrier lasts one round.						

UNIT–ARCANE TEMPEST GUN MAGES

"If they ever move up to rifles, we'll be out of work, chaps."

—A drunken long gunner captain to his men, referring to a group of gun mages two tables away

LIEUTENANT				CMD	8
SPD	STR	MAT	RAT	DEF	ARM
6	4	5	7	15	12
MAGELOCK PISTOL					
		RNG	ROF	AOE	POW
		12	1	—	10
SWORD					
		Special		POW	P+S
		—		3	7
Base Size: Small					

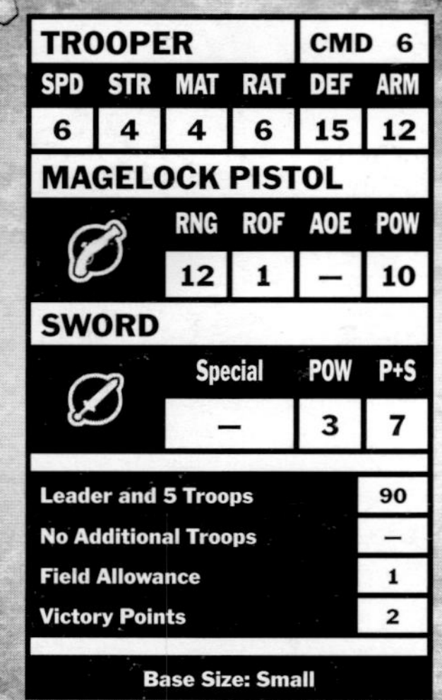

TROOPER				CMD	6
SPD	STR	MAT	RAT	DEF	ARM
6	4	4	6	15	12
MAGELOCK PISTOL					
		RNG	ROF	AOE	POW
		12	1	—	10
SWORD					
		Special		POW	P+S
		—		3	7
Leader and 5 Troops					90
No Additional Troops					—
Field Allowance					1
Victory Points					2
Base Size: Small					

SPECIAL RULES

LIEUTENANT
- •Arcane Inferno (Order)
- •Leader

MAGELOCK PISTOL
- •Arcane Effect
  - •Shocker
  - •Thunder Bolt
  - •Detonator

For nearly two decades now, the Militant Order of the Arcane Tempest has trained sorcerers and apprentice wizards to harness their spells in a different way. The Tempest teaches its members to focus their energies into special rune-cast bullets for their special mage-lock pistols, using the same techniques alchemists use to imbue blasting powders with their own arcane properties. These magelock pistols are cast from very expensive and rare Rhulic metals that the dwarves claim have a "special affinity for the haphazard sorceries of manfolk." So expensive is this metal that the crown limits the number of gun mages the Order may recruit to a minimum, making admittance a lifelong career. A refined gun mage can weave a spell into one of their pistol shots, making even the most fearless foe take care when dealing with a "spell-slinger."

Gun mage instructors know these talents are rare, and also know exactly what the other kingdoms of western Immoren would pay to possess them, so most gun mages are selected not just because of their an aptitude for wielding The Gift, but for their patriotism and loyalty to the Crown. To say most gun mages take their vows to the Tempest quite seriously is hardly an understatement.

Still, some succumb to the gold of foreign kingdoms, and less scrupulous gun mages have recently escaped the Order and enlisted with the highest bidder. These rogues are marked as traitors, and the law demands that a rogue gun mage should be executed with extreme prejudice. Some loyalists have taken to simply taking these rogues by surprise, often slitting their throats or shooting them from behind, but the more honorable among them often challenge rogues to an unsanctioned duel. No matter how justice is dealt out, an honorable gun mage never tolerates a traitor to the Crown, or the Tempest.

GUNMAGE SPECIAL RULES

LIEUTENANT

•Arcane Inferno (Order)—When issued this order, every Gun Mage combines their fire at the same target. Make one attack roll using the Lieutenant's RAT, adding +1 to the attack roll for each Gun Mage, including the Lieutenant. The Arcane Inferno attack is POW 14 with AOE 3, and may not include an Arcane Effect. Arcane Inferno requires at least 3 Gun Mages.

•Leader

MAGELOCK PISTOL

Arcane Effect—Each time Magelock Pistol is used to make a ranged attack, choose one of the following effects:

•Shocker—Target Warjack hit by this attack automatically takes one point of damage to its first available cortex system box. Mark this damage before making the damage roll.

•Thunder Bolt—Target model hit by this attack is pushed back d3". On a critical hit, target model is also knocked down.

•Detonator—On a critical hit, the Detonator explodes inside its target. Roll damage normally, then make a second POW 10 damage roll, adding an additional die to the roll (total 3 dice).

SOLO-JOURNEYMAN WARCASTER

"When you can caress a flower with the same hand that you can render stone to dust…only then are you ready."

—Famous ideal given to apprentice warcasters by their mentors

Not all warcasters begin their careers by accident. Since the advent of these unique folk, some young hopefuls begin training with veterans of the warcaster discipline, in hopes to unlock their potential. Nine out of ten students are immediately turned away, but some potential adepts are accepted as apprentices, usually beginning by learning to control labor-exclusive steamjacks, moving on to disarmed warjacks when ready, and eventually earning a (typically old or battered) 'jack of their own.

The Cygnaran king has mandated that all warcasters-in-training must spend a full tour of duty under the tutelage of a master warcaster before they can graduate. Most commanders dread these journeymen warcasters assigned to them. After all, nobody in the unit wants a rookie driving a six-ton powerhouse when lives are on the line. They may be a necessity, but commanders often eschew any responsibility for a journeyman's failure—which is often inevitable at some point or another. On one hand, another warjack or two has arrived to bolster the unit. On the other, a spirited young patriot comes with it, and most of the time these journeymen are slain in the first month or two, and that's if things go somewhat well—usually they take half the company with them. Still, there's a pressing need for more adepts, and very few commanders can honestly say which hand really outweighs the other.

FOCUS	3	CMD	7		
SPD	STR	MAT	RAT	DEF	ARM
6	5	5	4	14	14

HAND CANNON

RNG	ROF	AOE	POW
12	1	–	12

MAGE BLADE

Special	POW	P+S
–	5	10

Damage	5
Point Cost	25
Field Allowance	1
Victory Points	1

Base Size: Small

SPECIAL RULES

JOURNEYMAN
- Battlegroup Commander
- Fearless
- Focus Manipulation
- Power Field
- Spellcaster

JOURNEYMAN SPECIAL RULES

- Battlegroup Commander—Journeyman may control a battlegroup of Warjacks just like a Warcaster.
- Fearless—Journeyman Spellcaster never flees.
- Focus Manipulation—Each turn the Journeyman receives focus points, which can be used just like a Warcaster.
- Powerfield—The Journeyman possesses a powerfield like a Warcaster.
- Spellcaster—A Journeyman Warcaster may cast spells just like a Warcaster.

Spells	Cost	RNG	AOE	POW	UP	OFF
ARCANE BOLT	2	12	–	11		✓
Target model is struck by magical bolts of energy flying from the Journeyman's hands.						
ARCANE SHIELD	2	8	–	–	✓	
Surrounded by a magical barrier, target model/unit gains +3 ARM.						
DISRUPTOR	3	8	–	–		✓
Target Warjack loses any unused focus points and cannot be allocated focus points or channel spells for one round.						

UNIT–LONG GUNNERS

"I heared they wuz gonna start takin' missed shots outta our wage."
"Well... I reckon we don't miss then."

—One long gunner to another at the Falling Star tavern

SERGEANT				CMD	8
SPD	STR	MAT	RAT	DEF	ARM
5	4	4	5	13	12
REPEATING LONG GUN					
	RNG	ROF	AOE	POW	
	14	2	–	10	
SWORD					
	Special		POW	P+S	
	–		3	7	
Base Size: Small					

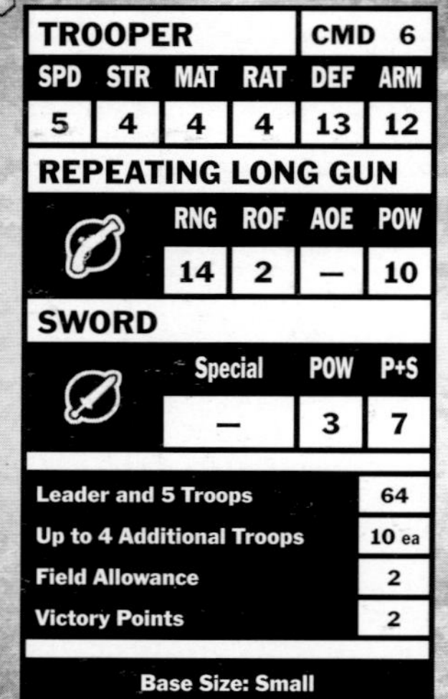

TROOPER				CMD	6
SPD	STR	MAT	RAT	DEF	ARM
5	4	4	4	13	12
REPEATING LONG GUN					
	RNG	ROF	AOE	POW	
	14	2	–	10	
SWORD					
	Special		POW	P+S	
	–		3	7	
Leader and 5 Troops					64
Up to 4 Additional Troops					10 ea
Field Allowance					2
Victory Points					2
Base Size: Small					

SPECIAL RULES

SERGEANT
- •Leader

UNIT
- •Combined Ranged Attack
- •Dual Shot

Since the advent of the long gun, Cygnar has assembled skilled riflemen to support their vast armies. Originally, these were muzzleloaders, and gunners had to load each ball down the barrel by hand, lining up in pairs with one gunner shooting while the other reloads. In time, gunsmiths introduced the breechloader, vastly improving the rate of fire and eliminating the need for firing in pairs. In modern times, the ammo wheel has come into use, and a single gunner can cycle up to six preloaded shots into firing position with the turn of a simple wheel mechanism mounted near the rifle's trigger. Cleaning and reloading a spent wheel requires time, but if a whole squad of Cygnaran long gunners has fired more than six shots apiece, something has gone terribly wrong.

Cygnar is renowned for its long gunner squads, noted as being the finest riflemen in all western Immoren. "The King's Hailstorm," a famous garrison of long gunners in Caspia, once put a decisive end to a city uprising led by the local criminal gang. The long gunners manned the city walls and aimed at the rioters while the commander of the watch announced that each long gunner had a different agitator in his sights and unless the crowd dispersed immediately, they'd be ordered to open fire. By the commander's second count, every gang member threw their hands up and came forward to surrender. The riot was immediately over. Not a shot fired. Such is the reputation of the Cygnaran long gunners.

LONG GUNNER SPECIAL RULES

SERGEANT

•Leader

UNIT

•Combined Ranged Attack—Instead of making ranged attacks seperately, Long Gunners in open formation may combine their attacks against the same target. The Long Gunner with the highest RAT in the attacking group makes one ranged attack roll for the group, adding +1 to the attack and damage rolls for each Long Gunner, including itself, participating in the attack.

•Dual Shot—A Long Gunner may voluntarily forfeit its movement to make one additional ranged attack. These attacks receive the aiming bonus.

UNIT–FIELD MECHANIKS

"As me see it, as long as dey keeps breakin' t'ings, weez ne'er be out'a jobs..."

—Kazza, seasoned gobber bodger

Armor gets cleaved through. Firearms are misfired. Warjacks break down.

All of these things could spell potential doom to a warring commander, if it weren't for the mechaniks that brave the battlefield. Mechaniks bring with them little in the way of personal armor, choosing to keep themselves occupied with staying alive and getting to the necessary position to repair what's broke. They perform miraculous repairs on non-functioning mechanika, and many battles have been turned around at the moment of defeat by a returning warjack that was believed destroyed just moments earlier.

Mechaniks are pretty much unarmed in the field. Their pockets, pouches, and satchels are overflowing with extra parts and tools—any self-respecting field mechanik can never have enough extra gear—for not having a single specific piece might mean disaster for hundreds of men. That's why they keep company with the ever-present and ever-willing gobber bodgers.

A gobber loves to tinker, no matter what, where, or how. Bodgers earn a pittance in comparison to the dangers they endure to carry extra parts and tools for their mechanik employers. To them, however, the adventure and excitement is at least half the pay—although the buggers are often known for tossing equipment and diving for cover until danger is passed.

FIELD MECHANIK SPECIAL RULES

CREW CHIEF

- Leader
- Repair[9] (★Action)—A Mechanik can attempt repairs on any friendly Cygnaran Warjack that has been damaged or disabled. To attempt repairs, the mechanik must be in base-to-base contact with the damaged Warjack or disabled wreck marker and make a skill check. If successful, roll a d6 and remove that number of damage points from anywhere on the Warjack's damage grid. The Warjack being repaired must forfeit its activation and cannot channel spells on the turn repairs are attempted.

GOBLIN BODGERS

- Assist Repair[+2] (★Action)—Every Bodger assisting the Chief with a repair adds +2 to the Chief's Repair skill, up to a maximum of 11. A Bodger must be in base-to-base contact with the Warjack that is being repaired by the Chief.
- Repair[5] (★Action)—Same as Chief, above.

CREW CHIEF				CMD	7
SPD	STR	MAT	RAT	DEF	ARM
5	4	3	4	12	11
RIVET GUN					
		RNG	ROF	AOE	POW
		4	1	—	10
MONKEY WRENCH					
		Special		POW	P+S
		—		2	6
Base Size: Small					

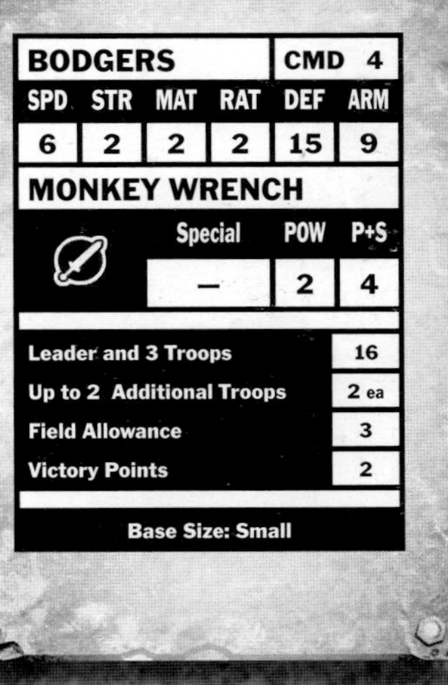

BODGERS				CMD	4
SPD	STR	MAT	RAT	DEF	ARM
6	2	2	2	15	9
MONKEY WRENCH					
		Special		POW	P+S
		—		2	4
Leader and 3 Troops					16
Up to 2 Additional Troops					2 ea
Field Allowance					3
Victory Points					2
Base Size: Small					

SPECIAL RULES

CREW CHIEF
- Leader
- Repair [9] (★Action)

GOBLIN BODGERS
- Assist Repairs [+2] (★Action)
- Repair [5] (★Action)

UNIT–STORMBLADES

"Gods use lightning to wage war on their enemies! Now... Leto can, too!"

—Chief Mechanik Garrison Grohl's words immediately after firing the first storm glaive

SERGEANT				CMD	8
SPD	STR	MAT	RAT	DEF	ARM
5	6	8	5	13	15
STORM ROD BLAST					
		RNG	ROF	AOE	POW
		6	1	–	14
STORM ROD					
		Special		POW	P+S
		–		9	15
Base Size: Small					

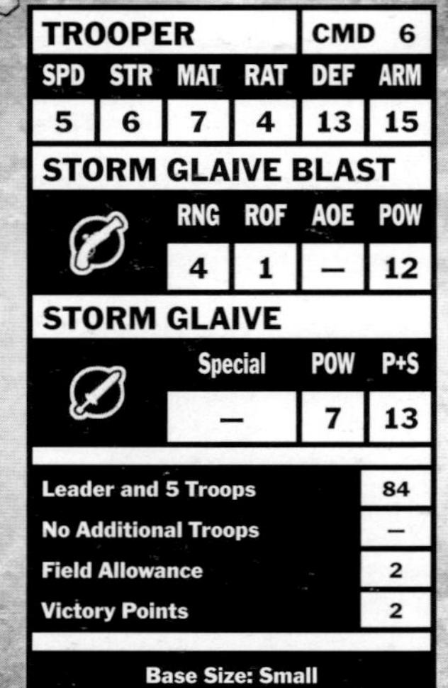

TROOPER				CMD	6
SPD	STR	MAT	RAT	DEF	ARM
5	6	7	4	13	15
STORM GLAIVE BLAST					
		RNG	ROF	AOE	POW
		4	1	–	12
STORM GLAIVE					
		Special		POW	P+S
		–		7	13
Leader and 5 Troops					84
No Additional Troops					–
Field Allowance					2
Victory Points					2
Base Size: Small					

SPECIAL RULES

SERGEANT
- Leader

Storm Rod
- Electrical Arc

UNIT
- Fearless
- Combined Melee Attack

Imagine a man as hard as tack, ready to face insurmountable odds, and wielding the most advanced mechanika Cygnar has to offer. Wrap that package in a powerfully built suit of alchemically tempered armor, give them the King's royal blessing, and you've just conjured up a Stormblade. These heavily armored soldiers have sped through the ranks of the other factions within the army, and each one is a top-quality warrior, highly skilled in the arts of battle.

Upon joining a Stormblade unit, each soldier is bestowed one of the more exceptional weapons in all of western Immoren—a storm glaive. These masterwork quality greatswords have been alchemically altered to withstand and conduct powerful electrical blasts generated from within the oversized hilt and hand guard. Mechanikally-induced lightning arcs throughout the blade and, with practice, can be directed at targets out of melee range. In the hands of a Stormblade, the storm glaive is a fearsome thing indeed, and a devastating glance at the future of Cygnaran warfare.

Each captain is granted a modified version of the glaive, called a storm rod, featuring a longer haft and a set of shorter blades to conduct even more powerful currents than a singular glaive. An astonishing side-effect was discovered during the first field-test when the storm rod automatically arced and channeled its powerful charge through the nearby Stormblade's glaives, amplifying each weapon's charge to create an astronomical blast.

A Stormblade's mechanikal armor is altered to insulate the wearer against strong electric currents and is able to withstand not only the constant contact with their own weapons, but also the dancing arcs of lightning flowing from each member to the next. In combat, the entire Stormblade unit seems to have a nimbus of lightning flashing and surging amongst it, an intimidating sight that so many of their enemies dread seeing.

STORMBLADE SPECIAL RULES

SERGEANT

- Leader

UNIT

- Combined Melee Attack—Instead of making melee attacks seperately, Stormblades in melee range of the same target may combine their attacks. The Stormblade with the highest MAT in the attacking group makes one melee attack roll for the group, adding +1 to the attack and damage rolls for each Stormblade, including itself, participating in the attack.

- Fearless—Stormblade units never flee.

STORM ROD

- Electrical Arc—Storm Rod adds +2 RNG and +2 POW to each of its unit's Storm Glaives whose wielders are in open formation.

UNIT–TRENCHERS

"It saddens me how many of those poor boys are buried out there in my kingdom, but I hate to think where we would be without their noble sacrifice."

—King Leto Raelthorne

Trencher infantry fall into two categories, those who are just too hard to say quit, and those who mouthed off to someone important at the wrong time and ended up in the trenches. Trenchers, also known as "gravediggers," are the first to go into the battlefield, and often the last to leave it, if ever. It's their duty to precede even the van by a few hours, if possible, and prepare a potential battlefield for the main force. With trenches, burrow holes, and farrow spike rows, they attempt to make the conflict area favorable for their comrades.

The trenchers themselves are usually armed with gobber-made smoke pots called *hazers* and bayonet-tipped rifles. The smoke pots, when broken open, emit a thick gray haze of smoke accompanied with a pungent odor that is better left unquestioned as to its origins. Trenchers get out there and make life hell for the enemy, sometimes by throwing themselves out of their holes at them with blades flashing and rifles roaring. They don't go out wanting to be heroes, but they've been honored as such more often than not (usually at burial time).

Soldiers who survive as trenchers for a full year's term receive a shining end to the arduous journey. Nearly all veterans go on to become part of an elite scout team, or into training as marksman. Their survival as a "gravedigger" demonstrates extraordinary skill, personal determination, and just plain dumb luck. Or maybe all those sleepless nights spent just yards away from would-be murderers have driven them mad, and they just don't know anything else.

TRENCHER SPECIAL RULES

SERGEANT

- Bayonet Charge (Order)—When issued this order, each Trencher charges an eligible target, firing its Rifle as it closes. As part of the Charge, after moving, the Trencher makes a ranged attack followed by a charge attack with its bayonet.
- Leader

UNIT

- Advance Deployment—Place Trenchers after normal deployment, up to 12" beyond the established deployment zone.
- Combined Ranged Attack—Instead of making ranged attacks seperately, Trenchers in open formation may combine their attacks at the same target. The Trencher with the highest RAT in the attacking group makes one ranged attack roll for the group, adding +1 to the attack and damage rolls for each Trencher, including itself, participating in the attack.
- Dig In (★Action)—A Trencher can dig a hasty battle position into the ground, gaining cover (+4 DEF) and +4 ARM. The Trencher remains dug in until it moves or is engaged. Trenchers cannot dig in to solid rock or man made constructions. Trenchers may begin the game dug in.
- Smoke Bombs (★Action)—A Trencher may place a Smoke Bomb anywhere within 3" of himself. A Smoke Bomb creates a 3" AOE cloud effect that remains in play for one round.

SERGEANT				CMD	9
SPD	STR	MAT	RAT	DEF	ARM
6	6	7	6	13	13

MILITARY RIFLE	RNG	ROF	AOE	POW
	10	1	–	11

BAYONET	Special	POW	P+S
	–	3	9

Base Size: Small

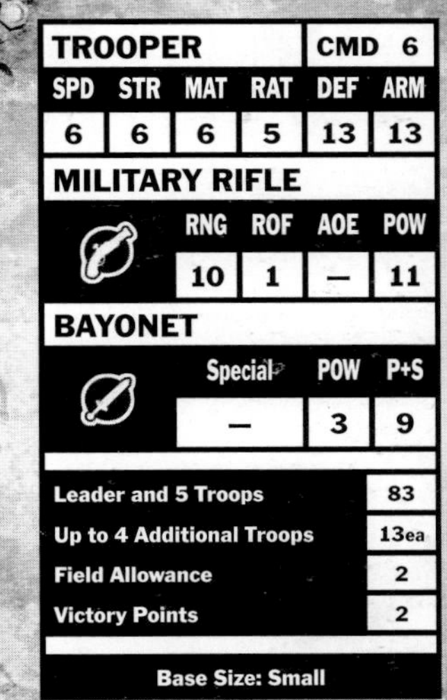

TROOPER				CMD	6
SPD	STR	MAT	RAT	DEF	ARM
6	6	6	5	13	13

MILITARY RIFLE	RNG	ROF	AOE	POW
	10	1	–	11

BAYONET	Special	POW	P+S
	–	3	9

Leader and 5 Troops	83
Up to 4 Additional Troops	13ea
Field Allowance	2
Victory Points	2

Base Size: Small

SPECIAL RULES

SERGEANT

- Bayonet Charge (Order)
- Leader

UNIT

- Advance Deployment
- Combined Ranged Attack
- Dig In (★Action)
- Smoke Bombs (★Action)

LIGHT WARJACK–CHARGER

"I started with just one Charger. That's it. And call me superstitious, if you like, but I don't feel right out there without at least one to keep me honest. I'm keen on the Chargers, I guess."

—Commander Coleman Stryker

SPD	STR	MAT	RAT	DEF	ARM
6	8	5	5	13	16

	DUAL CANNON			
	RNG	ROF	AOE	POW
LEFT	12	2	—	12

	BATTLE HAMMER		
	Special	POW	P+S
RIGHT	—	4	12

DAMAGE GRID	1	2	3	4	5	6
		☐	☐	☐	☐	
	☐	☐	☐	☐	☐	☐
	☐	L	☐	☐	R	☐
	L	L	M	C	R	R
		M	M	C	C	

SYSTEMS
Left Arm (L)
Rght Arm (R)
Cortex (C)
Movement (M)

Point Cost	75
Field Allowance	U
Victory Points	2

Base Size: Medium

One of the original Cygnaran chassis, the Charger is the archetypal vanguard of the army. More of these light warjacks have been produced in the multitudes of mechanik's workshops than any other in the history of using steamjacks in battle. Standing only slightly higher than the average ogrun, the Charger can penetrate lots of spaces that the heavier 'jacks would have to bash down in order to gain access, which isn't always practical—especially when the enemy is dug into some subterranean caverns or below decks in a hole-punched sloop of war.

Without a doubt, the Charger has the highest mobility rate of any Cygnaran 'jack, yet still boasts a respectable level of protection from the tight-fitting interlocked plates composing its shell. Armed with an eight hundred pound hammer forged of the densest iron, the Charger is a very able 'jack in close combat situations. It's also useful in mid-range circumstances, raining lead shells with exceptional accuracy from its dual-cannon assembly. The Charger is a reliable and economical combination of speed, durability, and firepower that Cygnar will continue to exercise as a mainstay in its armies for many years to come, you can count on it.

Height /Weight	8'7" / 3.2 tons
Armament	Dual-Cannon (left arm),Battle Hammer (right arm)
Fuel Load/Burn Usage	135 Kgs/ 5 hrs general, 45 min combat
Initial Service Date	567 AR
Cortex Manufacturer	Fraternal Order of Wizardry
Orig. Chassis Design	Cygnaran Armory

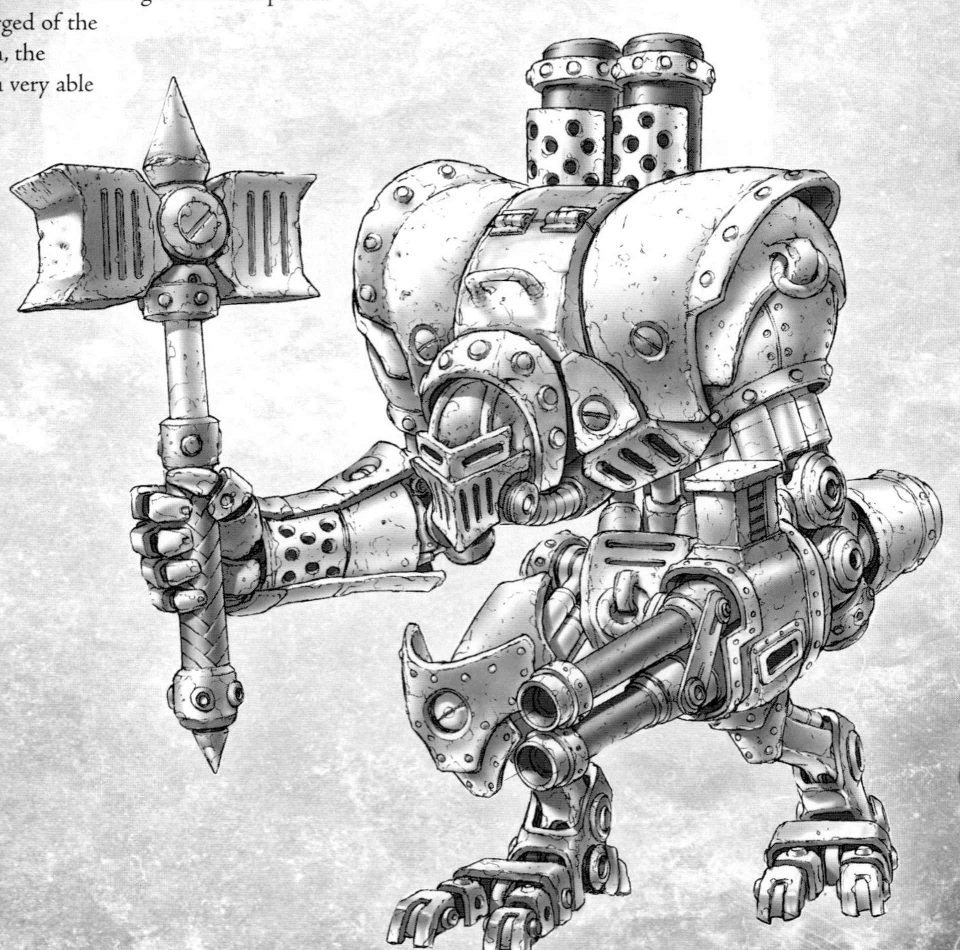

LIGHT WARJACK–LANCER

"I suppose she's respectable enough. A little slow…but a far stretch better than what I had to work with before. Very well. I'll take half-a-dozen. Let's see those Cryxian scum come a'callin' now."

A few short years ago Captain Haley grumbled that her Cryxian rivals' casters seemed to have an infinite amount of minions able to channel wicked spells, while she only had access to "a lightly armored whelp of a node-carrier." She made plain her disgust that the only arc-noded warjack, the Arcane, was too old and out of date to deal with her enemies efficiently. Several decisive Cryxian victories later, the king heard Haley's complaints and agreed that the current 'jack was inferior and in dire need of an upgrade. By the crown's request, chief mechaniks across Cygnar convened in secret at the Royal Cygnaran

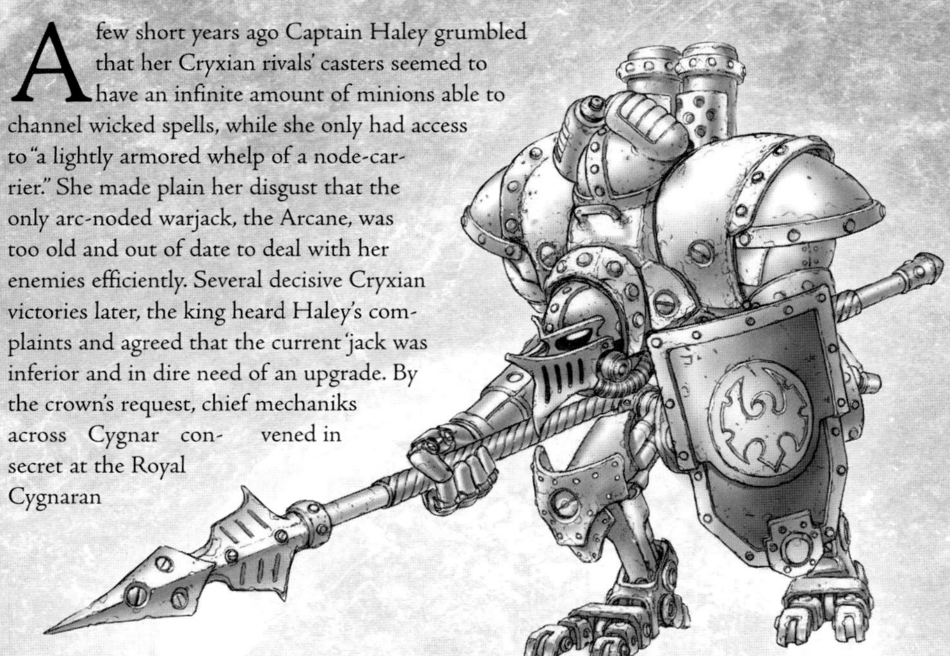

University—Captain Haley was invited as an expert field consultant—and they drafted a solution. Six weeks later, every Arcane in Cygnar was recalled for retrofitting, and the Lancer was born.

The new Lancer is not only faster, but better protected than its predecessor, and the 'jack immediately made strides as a combatant. It channeled magics much better than the Arcane, for greater conduction and improved re-direction. And the Lancer gained ground impressively with its strong spear to keep foes who survived the arcane bombardment at bay. Recent electricity-based technologies added a final touch to the Lancer: a shock shield. This allows the Lancer to protect its arc-node from a diversity of angles, and is employable as a secondary weapon, especially against other warjacks whose cortices are very susceptible to the surge of energy. The discerning Captain Haley, credited with initiating the Lancer, has made it part of her personal regiment. It is the newest of the warjack chassis, but with its continued success it could be the first of many revisions to existing models.

Height /Weight	9'1" / 3.25 tons
Armament	Spear (right arm), Shock Shield (left arm), Grade VII Arc Node
Fuel Load/Burn Usage	75 Kgs/ 9 hrs general, 1.5 hrs combat
Initial Service Date	601 AR
Cortex Manufacturer	Cygnaran Armory
Orig. Chassis Design	Cygnaran Mechaniks Coalition at the Royal Cygnaran University

LANCER SPECIAL RULES

ARC NODE

The Lancer may channel spells.

SHOCK SHIELD

•Shock Field—If the Lancer hits a Warjack with the Shock Shield, or if the Lancer is hit by a Warjack with a melee weapon, its opponent takes one point of damage to its first available cortex system box. Mark this damage before making the damage roll.

WAR SPEAR

•Reach—2" melee range

•Set Defense—Lancer gains +2 DEF against Charge and Slam attacks.

SPD	STR	MAT	RAT	DEF	ARM
6	8	5	5	13	16
				(shield)	18

	SHOCK SHIELD		
	Special	POW	P+S
LEFT	Shock Field	1	9

	WAR SPEAR		
	Special	POW	P+S
RIGHT	Multi	4	12

DAMAGE GRID

1	2	3	4	5	6
		□	□		
	□	□	□	□	
□	□	□	□	□	□
□	L	A	A	R	□
L	L	M	C	R	R
	M	M	C	C	

SYSTEMS: Left Arm (L), Rght Arm (R), Cortex (C), Movement (M), Arc Node (A)

Point Cost	76
Field Allowance	U
Victory Points	2

Base Size: Medium

SPECIAL RULES

ARC NODE

SHOCK SHIELD
•Shock Field

WAR SPEAR
•Reach
•Set Defense

LIGHT WARJACK–SENTINEL

"I'd give my left-most jewel for a pair of those..."

—Lt. Allister Caine

SPD	STR	MAT	RAT	DEF	ARM
6	8	5	5	13	16
				(shield)	18

LEFT	ASSAULT SHIELD		
	Special	POW	P+S
	—	2	10

RIGHT	CHAIN GUN			
	RNG	ROF	AOE	POW
	10	1	—	10

DAMAGE GRID

SYSTEMS: Left Arm (L), Rght Arm (R), Cortex (C), Movement (M)

1	2	3	4	5	6
	☐	☐	☐	☐	
☐	☐	☐	☐	☐	☐
☐	L	☐	☐	R	☐
L	L	M	C	R	R
	M	M	C	C	

Point Cost	72
Field Allowance	U
Victory Points	2

Base Size: Medium

A lbere Gungria, a genius mechanik working currently in the arcane design program of the Royal University of Cygnar, was once locked up in his workshop during a Tharn rampage through the town. The wild men were breaking down doors and ransacking everything. Albere found himself alone, with only a half dozen military rifles he was fixing for the local watch and the broken down wreck of an old semi-functional Charger warjack. He heard a young girl scream outside, and he had an epiphany. A half hour of fevered work later, one of the dodgiest looking warjacks in the kingdoms lumbered out of the heavy wooden doors of Albere's workshop. A long slab of unfinished armor was bolted to one mangled hand, serving as a heavy shield. The other arm was replaced with a tied-on apparatus consisting of a wheel of fine rifles, each one with a fully loaded brace of shot. With a groaning crank of a makeshift firing mechanism, it let out a hail of shot that spun the invaders on their heels and sent them running back to the hills. Immediately after firing, the rifles caught fire and became totally inert, but even so, the first Sentinel had just been field-tested. The original can still be found in the Hall of Lore, many years after its breathtaking debut.

Over a few months, the model was refined and cleaned up, but the original idea remained the same. It hefts the newly designed tornado cannon—named such for the tell-tale howl of its unbelievable rate of fire—faster than a dozen pistoleers at twice the range, while still well protected from most ranged combat by a heavy armored shield. While it lacks sufficient close assault capabilities, its speed and overall sturdiness more than compensated for any deficiencies. The Sentinel is a very role-specific chassis, but one with a history of saving lives and ending conflicts, something that Cygnarans never forget or ignore.

SPECIAL RULES

CHAIN GUN
- Strafe

SENTINEL SPECIAL RULES

CHAIN GUN

•Strafe—A single attack with the Chain Gun may hit its target and several nearby models. First, make a normal ranged attack against an eligible target. If the initial attack hits, roll a d6 to determine the number of additional attacks the initial attack generates, then allocate those hits between the original target and any models within 2" of it. Each model may receive more than one attack, but cannot receive more attacks than allocated to the initial target. Make separate hit and damage rolls for each Strafe attack generated.

Height /Weight	8'6" / 2.45 tons
Armament	Advanced Tornado Cannon (right arm), Assault Shield (left arm)
Fuel Load/Burn Usage	70 Kgs/ 8 hrs general, 1.3 hrs combat
Initial Service Date	573 AR
Cortex Manufacturer	Cygnaran Armory
Orig. Chassis Design	Albere Gungria, arcane mechanik at Royal Cygnaran University

HEAVY WARJACK—DEFENDER

"We cannot remain blindly loyal to the antiquated tactics used by our forefathers against the Orgoth. We must rise above them. Give me two Defenders, a month, and a healthy budget. I'll show you what I mean."

—Freiderick Stulant, Mercirian mechanik responsible for updating the Defender chassis

Cygnar was the first to make the big 'jacks, and the first to make the economical ones. Not that the original Defender was a "poor man's Ironclad" by any stretch, but the heavy 'jack provided the foundation for this slightly more affordable weapon (at the time). Caspian mechaniks essentially stripped down the Ironclad's chassis and replaced the fearsome quake hammer with a smaller and faster shock hammer. The Defender didn't have the overwhelming power of an Ironclad, so the mechs poured a bit more thump into the hammer's spirals. This extra arcane diffusion released massive jolts that effectively stuttered the cortexes of enemy 'jacks, often causing serious delays and misfires.

For a few years, the Defender was semi-effective as-is, but some mechaniks out of Mercir felt it had more potential. Feeling the remaining arm was under-utilized, soon enough the first Defender warjack stepped out of the Mercirian workshops with a powerful, heavy-barreled cannon rather than an empty fist. In its initial combat, the new Defender tore two Khadoran Juggernauts apart with multiple direct hits. Additionally, the Mercirian mechaniks were able to strengthen the chassis, based primarily off of the Ironclad—the original Defenders were notoriously below average in withstanding direct hits—to where the 'jack could take quite a bit of wear and tear in combat and still function. Funds be damned, the crown commissioned retrofits for two score of the 'jacks within the week.

The Defender's durability is now legendary across the kingdoms. Should it lose an arm, it still is quite capable with the weapon mounted on the other, and should it lose its mobility early, the heavy cannon has a more than respectable range to compensate for the loss. The Defender warjack is a fine piece of mechanikal artifice and innovation indeed.

DEFENDER SPECIAL RULES

SHOCK HAMMER

•Critical Cortex Damage—On a Critical Hit, target Warjack automatically takes one point of damage to its first available cortex system box. Mark this damage before marking regular damage.

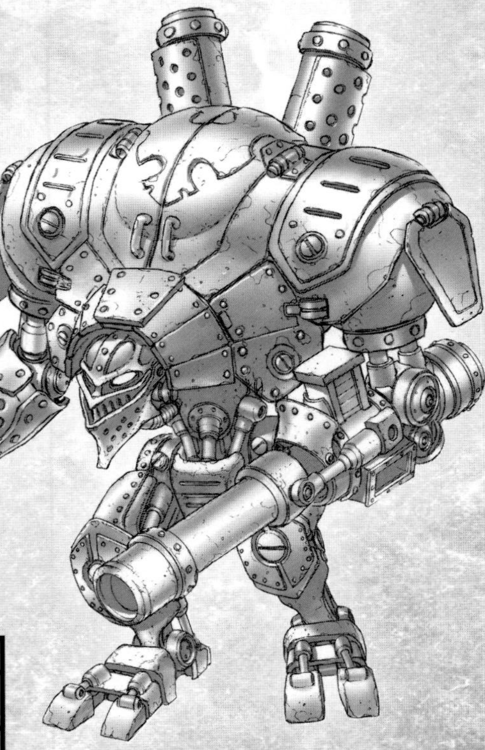

SPD	STR	MAT	RAT	DEF	ARM
5	11	6	5	12	18

HEAVY BARREL	RNG	ROF	AOE	POW
LEFT	16	1	—	14

SHOCK HAMMER	Special	POW	P+S
RIGHT	Critical	5	16

DAMAGE GRID

	1	2	3	4	5	6
			☐	☐		
SYSTEMS	☐	☐	☐	☐	☐	☐
Left Arm (L)	☐	☐	☐	☐	☐	☐
Rght Arm (R)	☐	L	☐	☐	R	☐
Cortex (C)	L	L	M	C	R	R
Movement (M)		M	M	C	C	

Point Cost	122
Field Allowance	U
Victory Points	3

Base Size: Large

SPECIAL RULES

SHOCK HAMMER

•Critical Cortex Damage

Height /Weight	12' 2" / 6.5 tons
Armament	Heavy Cannon (left arm), Shock Hammer (right arm)
Fuel Load/Burn Usage	135 Kgs/ 5 hrs general, 45 min combat
Initial Service Date	564 AR
Cortex Manufacturer	Fraternal Order of Wizardry
Orig. Chassis Design	Cygnaran Armory

HEAVY WARJACK–IRONCLAD

"An Ironclad couldn't break it."

—Cygnaran marketplace phrase when haggling over quality

SPD	STR	MAT	RAT	DEF	ARM
5	11	6	5	12	18

	QUAKE HAMMER		
	Special	POW	P+S
LEFT	Multi	7	18

	OPEN FIST		
	Special	POW	P+S
RIGHT	—	—	11

DAMAGE GRID

SYSTEMS: Left Arm (L), Rght Arm (R), Cortex (C), Movement (M)

1	2	3	4	5	6
		☐	☐		
☐	☐	☐	☐	☐	☐
☐	☐	☐	☐	☐	☐
☐	L	☐	☐	R	☐
L	L	M	C	R	R
	M	M	C	C	

Point Cost	103
Field Allowance	U
Victory Points	3

Base Size: Large

The most recognized heavy 'jack in the Cygnaran arsenal, the Ironclad is a walking behemoth of metal nearly thrice the size of a man. Gigantic smokestacks blow sooty "breath" from its heartfire's furnace, and a bright orange glow emits from its face grill, lending a fiery and fearsome gaze.

Armed with a powerful quake hammer, the Ironclad smashes lesser combatants to shrapnel with its massive blows; sometimes just one strike from this hammer has toppled even another heavy 'jack. The Ironclad's durable armor—smelted from precious ores harvested from the roots of the tallest mountains—provides fantastic protection from all but the heaviest impacts, and because of all these things, the Cygnaran Ironclad is renowned for leading most warjack charges.

Unlike many of the warjack designs that were modified from labor, or commonplace steamjacks used more and more in everyday living, the Ironclad was designed by the conservative mechaniks in Caspia solely as a walking tank. It was made strong, durable, and capable of removing any obstacle from its warcaster's path, be it boulder or building, wall or warjack. Indeed, if an Ironclad cannot break something, it is safe to say it cannot be broken, hence the adage above.

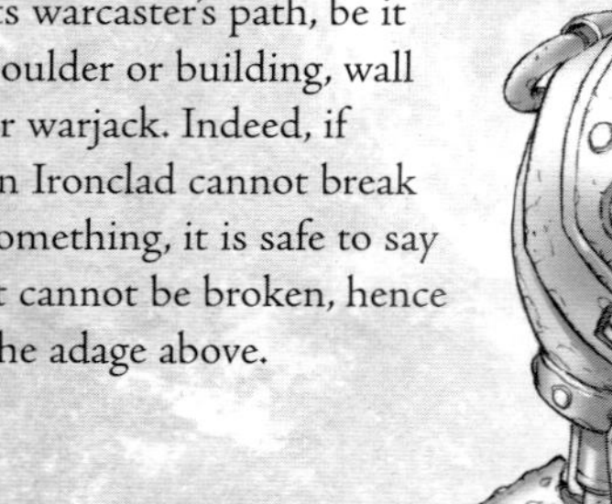

IRONCLAD SPECIAL RULES

QUAKE HAMMER

•Critical Knockdown—On a Critical Hit, target model is knocked down.

•Tremor (★Attack)—Roll 2d6 and add the weapon's POW. Compare the result to the DEF of every model within 2"—these models are knocked down if the total equals or exceeds their DEF. This effect causes no damage and cannot be boosted. A Tremor special attack cannot be made after a charge.

Height /Weight	12' 3" / 6 tons
Armament	Quake Hammer (left arm)
Fuel Load/Burn Usage	120 Kgs/ 6 hrs general, 1 hr combat
Initial Service Date	556 AR
Cortex Manufacturer	Fraternal Order of Wizardry/ Cygnaran Armory
Orig. Chassis Design	Engines East

SPECIAL RULES

QUAKE HAMER
•Critical Knockdown
•Tremor(★Attack)

THE PROTECTORATE OF MENOTH

A MENITE RECOUNTS THE PAST

A BRIEF HISTORY OF THE PROTECTORATE OF MENOTH

"We are justified by faith, and faith is the nexus of our salvation. The road to salvation, however, is long and narrow, and it must be paved with heretic skulls. Those of you with faith are the builders of this road…our road…to salvation!"

—Hierarch Sulon, welcoming pilgrims to Caspia, 481 A.R.

The Temple of Imer, the Holy See, in the year 604 After Rebellion. During the latest induction ceremony, Scrutator Severius addressed the recently ordained Paladins of Menoth. These are his words, recorded for posterity:

As long as man could see the world through mortal eyes, he has worshipped Menoth. And ever since the Creator shaped us from his shadow on the primeval waters of Caen, we have been His chosen. The first men gathered into tribes and wandered for a great many millennia, enduring the elements and toiling to survive. placing them upon the fertile lands on the banks of the mighty Black from the fork of the Tongue to the gulf. He then fashioned two thousand women so that the world might be peopled swiftly with His creation. In the beginning, man was such a trivial thing to his Shaper, but our resilience did not go unmarked. Man had ascended above the beasts. We made structures to show Menoth we knew of Him. Because of this, Menoth came among the tribes. He instructed us and gave us laws by setting down the foundations of the Canon [of the True Law]. He selected our priest-kings, who established the first holy places, where shrines were erected, and then temples. Around these grew villages, and some of these that survived time and the Orgoth's defilement became the cities of today.

Menoth was our Creator and Lawgiver, and because He touched us, we have risen above all other beasts of Caen. Seeing this, He left us once more to our own purpose. Millennia passed. But without guidance, men are akin to children—so easily do they wander astray—and the tribes broke into shards. Man fell to worshipping false idols and worthless gods, some of them becoming Devourer heathens. When Menoth saw this, he was much displeased and man became ill favored. He sent storms to warn us of our defilements, but these were not enough. In spite of his anger, Menoth did not yet wish to destroy His creation. Rather, he sent a greater peril than storms to test us. In 600 B.R., He sent the Orgoth.

It was a hard thing to do, enduring the Occupation, for the invaders were very thorough in quashing signs of the worship of any gods. A small matter, the hardships we bore in those days, for we were being tested. The devout suffered in His name only, and when the time came it was Menoth's will that the Iron Fellowship was forged, to cast off the chains of the Orgoth, who He had sent to hearken us back to Him. Without Menoth's resolution, our bones would lie in the earth, or we would be adrift in a chaotic void of lawlessness. He is the giver of all things, and by serving Him without question we are spared His righteous wrath.

After the Orgoth quit our lands—eight hundred years after they had first come—we re-built our temples and our walls, and erected stone monuments to His glory. We helped all the peoples of Immoren re-build, while spreading His word. There were those who listened and there were those who accepted our aid but would later forsake the Old Faith. It is true, other lesser gods and demigods had arisen into Urcaen, and some of Menoth's children chose to abide by the heretical teachings of other devotions, either uncaring or unknowing of Menoth's judgment when they pass through His hands once more. Our missionaries adamantly taught that all lesser faiths—chiefly that of Morrow—must know their place, and one must acknowledge the life giver, Menoth, as first among the gods of mankind. Despite their strong teachings, the priests were aware of the whispered allegations and obscenities about them.

The faith of Morrow grew over time, especially among the uneducated and lowborn. But those of high blood were more accepting of the True Law, for many of them were descendants of the long ago priest-kings. Among them, Menoth retained a great deal of clout. Indeed, during the rule of Woldred the Diligent in the 280s, we were even granted the right to sanction the passing of the Cygnaran crown to the next would-be king. Years later, when Woldred—who was already an aged king by such time—became ill and died, our priests ushered his soul back to the Creator, but the heretics of Morrow started sowing bad seeds at once. Fingers were pointed at the Menite order and they were blamed for his demise. Morrowans have ever been opportunists, and this was their first true chance to drive a stake into the Old Faith.

Their deceit had the desired effect. Menoth's patience was tried. Only those who knew Truth remained steadfast. The rest, those who were indolent, those who were decadent, began to slip away from his divinity. Our priests could not be faulted for trying. They fought in the Cygnaran courts for a generation and more, but the kings of Cygnar have ever been far too materialistic, preoccupied with their politics and their economies, rather than heeding advice concerning their immortal souls. They turned from their Creator. Locked in their fleshly cages, they had been perverted by the Morrowans, thrown into confusion with adoptions of lies and coin and earthly power.

The greatest affronters were those who dabbled with the so-called Gift—immoral witches obviously touched by the wickedness of the Twins. In an effort to illustrate truth, the Menite clergy established Menoth's Will, a league of priests devoted to stamping out users of dark Thamarite magic. The Will began to seize sorcerers and reveal their evil to the world. The Cygnaran court spoke out against the Menites and demanded an end to the witch-hunts, but Menoth's Will would not be undone. "Truth Above All" was the call, and under the veil of secrecy, Menoth's priests continued putting the black magicians to the holy fire. The blasphemous orders united to resist the Will, and a conflict beneath the surface was born with Thamar's dark agents throwing themselves as a tide against the jagged rocks of Menoth's True Law.

Their numbers could not be determined and they fought like cowards. In the late 300s and through the 400s, a volatile air inundated Cygnar proper. Mysterious explosions in the temples slew priests and innocents. Retaliation often took the form of secret raids, mass executions, and sudden ambushes in the very streets and marketplaces, erupting as swiftly as they died. The Morrowans condemned the violence, ignorant to the fact that it was they who were part of it. They disparaged the Menites, solely blaming them for the conflict by citing a wont for violence and intolerance, yet refusing to recognize it was the dark half of their own religion responsible for such atrocities! The unrest was often burgeoned by the deployment of Cygnaran troops to watch the Menite faithful during holy events and days of festivity. The heavens rumbled with Menoth's discontent. Faith and perseverance might have won the day, but the Cygnarans had turned away. They were like sheep after the shepherd, and that shepherd was their Morrowan king.

Things could not have been bleaker for the Menite faithful when the Creator sent us Sulon, an exceptional visionary and our first great mortal leader. Sulon had been granted the holy sight, and he quickly rose to power among the Menites of northern Cygnar. He began to mark the way for our destiny, and declared a pilgrimage to all the Menites of Cygnar to go to Caspia. From there, the newly appointed Visgoth Sulon ordered a vast increase of the training of scrutators, and began to train warriors, knights and war priests. Knights Exemplar were recalled from their posts and temples throughout the north to join the visgoth at the new era's birthplace. He called his pilgrimage the rebirth of Menoth's Will, and a vast number journeyed to the site of our new beginning, the City of Walls, Caspia, for it was fitting that Menoth's worldly throne would be atop the ashes of the Cygnarans' mortal one.

In 475 A.R., when Visgoth Sulon took control of the massive Temple of Menoth in eastern Caspia, his vision became a reality. He stood atop the altar, looking out over a sea of tents and wagons that filled the city's streets and open spaces, and he saw every faithful soul that could make the journey. Eastern Caspia had become the largest temple to Menoth in the world. Tens of thousands, possibly more, of our holy brothers and sisters joined him in prayer on an early spring day. On the holy day we now call the Birth of Sulon, the visgoth donned the vestments and became the first to take on the title of Hierarch in many centuries, since the days before the Orgoth. Those amassed wept in His glory. Menoth was pleased, and through Hierarch Sulon, His will was made manifest. Though the visgoths of Khador sent their refusal to acknowledge Sulon's claim, he was embraced as the uncontested patron of all Cygnaran Menites.

The Hierarch decreed that all faithful of Caspia move east of the bridge, and by 481 A.R., eastern Caspia was tremendously overcrowded. They lived in squalor in streets, empty lots, and a tent city outside the city walls. The Cygnaran crown refused the Hierarch's petition for expansion of the east and Sulon became incensed. He gave the order to demolish some of the older buildings and construct new ones to make more room for the constant flow of journeymen and pilgrims.

The jealous Morrowan puppets of the Cygnaran court and their Primarch master sent armed soldiers to the borders and bridges of Caspia in preparation to attack the holy patronage. Hierarch Sulon, knowing this would come to pass, implored the Menites to "Send them to Urcaen!" With that, the faithful fell into the Cygnarans with holy fury, their powerful faith overcoming the heretics. Hierarch Sulon gave the holy order, and our forces flooded across the Black River into western Caspia, to initiate the fires from which a new kingdom would soon be forged. We destroyed the bridges and blocked all roads that joined the two halves of the city. Caspia was a city besieged from within. We declared our independence, dubbing the eastern half of the city as Sul, in honor of the first Hierarch of the new age. We were Caspians no longer. Through our faith, we had become Sulese.

For two years the Sulese fought. It was an uphill battle to test one's faith. Hierarch Sulon decreed that the Sancteum of Morrow, the stonework home to the pagan faith, must be torn apart and consecrated with fire and blood. That was his intent, but on the first full moon of 484 A.R., reinforcements from the north entered Caspia and Sulon fell in battle to the infidels under the shadow of the Sancteum. Sulon had done enough and it was Menoth's will his Hierarch should join him. Every year on the first full moon, our tongues remain still and our hands idle for the entire day to commemorate the prophet on Sulonsphar, or Sulon's Suffering.

Three months after the Hierarch's defeat, King Malfast (the Wretched) agreed to a conference with our appointed leader, a visgoth named Ozeall, and the conflict was soon declared over. Negotiations were not long, and a long stretch of land on the southeastern corner of Cygnar became ours to rule as we would. The crown agreed not to impose its political will upon us. We would be free to work in the faith as we wanted, without the binds of Cygnaran law. We knew the land so close to the Bloodstone Marches was bitter and hot, but Hierarch Sulon had once said, "hardship is the coin of Urcaen." Menoth would be proud of His children should they survive in such a place, and was this not a victory? Sulon wanted to expand city walls and was willing to die for it, for his people, so Menoth did more than gives us new walls, He deigned to give us a kingdom of our own. Within the borders of this new protectorate, we could mold the vision that Sulon had sacrificed himself for—a Sulese theocracy to, for, and of Menoth the Creator!

There were, of course, terms, as exist with any agreement. This new Protectorate would remain part of Malfast's Cygnar in title and taxes, if not in law or religion. A percentage of coin, Ozeall stated, was a small cost to pay for religious freedom. Another term disallows us a standing army, only allowing such forces as are required to police our borders on the Marches and protect ourselves from horrors even the Cygnarans acknowledge as evil. These terms were minor hardships, and Ozeall accepted them. A leagues-long stream of humanity trekked into the new lands of the Protectorate of Menoth, the Inherited Lands.

It proved to be a difficult place but, in His name, millions of Menites found their way through dust and desert thorn. Something must be said of the Bloodstone Marches. At first glance, it is a miserable place of but two seasons: very hot and very cold. Though remote and arid, the western strip yields many habitats—salt flats, sand dunes, sparse lowland valleys, semiarid forests of willow and thorn, lava fields clearly as stark as the surface of red Laris. It is an environment reflective of Menoth. The journey was a trying time in that first decade and thousands perished. The people questioned if they had wandered into the Wilds of the Devourer rather than some promised ground. This parched earth, seemingly devoid of precious ores and minerals, provided very little.

But then, something wholly better than unearthed stone arose—the Idrian people. While carving our homes from the red sandstone the Marches are known for, and while erecting our temples amidst the brambles and the dust, the Idrian tribes emerged from the dust and descended, howling, upon us, time and again. Menite and Idrian blood slaked the desert's thirst for several years through repeated raids, but we remained unwavering. Emboldened by our visgoths and sovereigns, we retaliated in kind, putting them to the sword wherever we could find them. If they could not accept our holy expansion, if they did not know the name of our lord, they would perish into the earth.

For years, the Idrian tribes made attempts to force us from our new lands, but never before had they seen such iron resolve. Menoth's followers kept coming. It must have seemed to them whenever one of us fell, five more arrived to replace them. Two forces clashed for the final time in 504 A.R., and a great quake shook the earth, toppling the Idrian raiders while the pious remained standing. When this happened, many Idrians saw this as a sign, and numerous tribes embraced Menoth. In time, the two races lived in tolerance of each other, as evidenced by the Sulese settling of Imer, a dusty, backwater clutter of sand-baked huts and canvas lean-tos that in a short time became the spired and turreted city of red walls that is the capital of our nation today. Separated by blood they may be, but these two cultures became united in faith, and the Idrians became more loyal to their Sulese brothers than any Cygnaran ever was.

It was the Idrians who led us to the diamonds beneath the Marches, a dangerous place but well worth it. We have little weakness for precious jewels, but the heretics of the west crave them madly, so the harvested gems trickle moderately to this day into the hands of the Cygnaran tax collectors. We have also discovered the Blood of Menoth—pure oil that is abundant under the cracked soil. The black fluid is removed from the depths and used to fuel our forge fires, to keep the hearths blazing in the temples, and to cook our meals. With it, we are able to chase the darkness of night and the horrors it hides from our sacred walls. Most importantly, our holy artificers discovered an important use for the sticky fuel. If mixed liberally with the ground rock salts harvested from the shores of our creeks and rivers, a viscous liquid rightly dubbed"Menoth's Fury" forms. This burns hotter and longer than ordinary oil, and adheres to anything not alchemically treated to be proof against it. A great tool to use against our foes was bestowed upon us in this "resource poor" land. Menoth be praised.

Fifty years after our independence, King Vinter Raelthorne III ascended in Cygnar, a man who would tax and harass us mercilessly. This stonehearted reprobate near drained us to the cobwebs in our coffers. Tensions arose and our people starved. Rumors of another imoending war reverberated, but Vinter III died in 576 A.R., and the crown passed to his oldest son. Raelthorne the Elder was the embodiment of Cygnar's evil ways, personified in his treatment of his own people. He used many of the same tactics and regulations as our scrutators, but without the holy sanction of a proper god. He found solace in darkness and evil, putting so much of his efforts into strangling the life from his own people and we wondered on whose side did he fall. During his rule, there was less pinch from his tax collectors and our coffers slowly recovered. While the Elder persecuted his own, we grew.

In 588 A.R., at the height of Raelthorne's rule, High Scrutator Garrick Voyle earned the rights of the Hierarch. Those who opposed his new role found themselves in the interrogation chambers, for to question him was a sure sign of infidelity of the soul. Menoth had chosen Voyle as Hierarch, and it was sacrilege to say otherwise. Our latest successes have been due to him, and I daresay he is the most impressive and powerful scrutator to ever walk our lands. Without his guidance, many of the finest accomplishments of this modern era would not exist. It was he who created the Fist of Menoth, the unarmed experts who walk the world inconspicuously, ready to strike at Menoth's foes with a speed and skill unknown to other kingdoms. It was he who made arrangements with our brothers and sisters across Immoren to work to bring us the mighty steamjacks and other mechanika from the far away kingdoms. They smuggled in parts and experts under the noses of the Cygnaran watchdogs, properly blessing and refitting them into Menoth's holy orders. It is true, before Hierarch Voyle took command of the Protectorate, we would have never used such things, though our enemies had them in abundance. It is clear he is changing our ancient ways, but if we are to succeed where others have failed, we must be willing to adapt our faith in order to strengthen it.

Like a portent discovered in the tortured cries of the heathen, our gaze has turned to Cygnar yet again. Menoth's fist buffeted Raelthorne the Elder in 594 A.R. by inciting his own brother to take arms against him. The City of Walls teeters toward a new civil war—one more example of how Morrow's Sancteum, like lodestone to magnet, draws conflict and hostility to Cygnar. The Elder has been overthrown and cast into exile.

If they but knew these mortal games mean nothing. They are false purposes and denials of Menoth's authority. This prompts serious consequences. In their pettiness, they deny their Creator, to whom all things belong. Because of this, our esteemed Hierarch has made a momentous decision. We shall finish what Hierarch Sulon began so many generations before. We will convert or conquer the lesser faiths, beginning with Morrow. Every faithful member of the congregation, even some of our estranged brothers in Khador, answers the call. Never before have we come together so quickly, and with such great purpose. Hierarch Voyle will lead us to greater glory. He is the Lawgiver's Hand. Menoth be praised!

WARCASTER–GRAND SCRUTATOR SEVERIUS

"Hear the Word of Menoth and tremble! Send them to Urcaen! All of them!"

—Hierarch Sulon, Caspia, 482 A.R., the phrase noted to have started the Cygnaran Civil War

Scrutators have to be of powerful character, full of charisma and social grace, and possess a commanding presence that demands attention. They must snap the minds of the undecided, encompassing them with feelings of piety and servitude. Scrutators cannot show the slightest sign of weakness, for Menoth is ever vigilant, and his wrath is terrible. Scrutator Severius, hand picked by High Scrutator Garrick Voyle, is a pillar fixed to the foundation holding up the grand Temple of Menoth.

The younger patrons and followers have called Severius, who many years ago cast aside his original Cygnaran name in disgust, "the Voice of Menoth." He would no doubt punish those who use the term loosely, but the meaning is close to the truth. The man has single-handedly converted thousands of heathens and infidels to the True Law. He has dozens of servants who work meticulously to discipline the unworthy with Menoth's Flame, while always searching out more supporters of the Old Faith. He expects his scrutators to be industrious, for he cannot personally direct them at all times. His role—and his passion—lies on the battlefield.

In a role that parallels Menoth's ancient war with the Devourer, Severius lives to make war on the enemies of his faith. He has a powerful thirst for the blood of blasphemers, and through his divine magics has little problem slaking it. His warjacks come alive with the same fervor as his converts. His tactics are thought out well in advance, for he has a brilliant tactical mind. His stratagem is often too complex for his peers to follow, but they unfurl on the battlefield as easily as if he were plotting on his war room maps. Indeed, Severius has a plan in motion that will not come to fruition until far past his own lifetime, knowing full well that it will fall into place exactly as Menoth has ordained.

Severius keeps at least one of his favored warjacks—the Revenger—nearby, for physically he is beyond his prime. He is an aged man, callow and gray, and not as fit as the Protectorate's younger commanders. But what he lacks in bodily prowess, Severius makes up in divine power. His ability to harness energy through his faith, and that of the faithful around him, allows him to do marvelous things his other commanders only dream about. He is the blaze of Menoth's wrath, breaching the minds of non-believers with but a single word. Severius is the eye of the hurricane upon the field of battle. So potent is his righteousness, he wades through otherwise deadly spell effects as if they were no more than illusory. So strong is his divine nature, if he so chooses, his voice thunders the Litany of Menoth, declaring Menoth's glory and greatness. This divine rite, like lightning, purges all foreign magics from those within earshot, denying enemy warcasters their connections to their own mechanika. This Litany proves that all things are Menoth's, pagan sorcery and heathen witchcraft notwithstanding. Through Scrutator Severius, Menoth's glory is unmistakable and his voice shall be heard abroad.

FOCUS 8			CMD 9		
SPD	STR	MAT	RAT	DEF	ARM
5	5	4	3	14	14

STAFF OF JUDGMENT	Special	POW	P+S
	Multi	8	13

Damage	16
Point Cost	66
Field Allowance	C
Victory Points	5
Base Size: Small	

Feat: DIVINE MIGHT

Endowed with the power to pass judgement on his fellow man, Grand Scrutator Severius may call upon the grandeur of Menoth to deny arcane magic-users their abilities.

No spells may be cast or channeled within Severius's control area except by other friendly Protectorate models, for one round. All non-Protectorate warcasters within Severius's control area do not receive focus points next turn.

SPECIAL RULES

STAFF OF JUDGMENT

- Reach—2" melee range
- Sacred Ward—Severius cannot be targeted by enemy spells.

Spells	Cost	RNG	AOE	POW	UP	OFF
ASHES TO ASHES	4	8	Spec	10		✓
If target model is hit, d6 nearest enemies within 5" take POW 10 damage roll.						
BLESSING OF MENOTH	2	6	–	–	✓	
Target model may reroll all dice for any one die roll, then the spell expires.						
CONVERT	4	6	–	–		
Target living trooper model must pass a command check or permanently become part of the Protectorate army. Converted model may not activate this turn. Cannot be cast on Characters or Solos.						
DEATH SENTENCE	5	6	–	–		✓
All legal attacks against a model under Death Sentence automatically hit this turn.						
EYE OF MENOTH	3	Caster	CTRL	–	✓	
All friendly Protectorate models within AOE gain a +1 bonus to attack/damage rolls.						
HOLY VIGIL	3	6	–	–	✓	
Target model/unit gains +4 DEF until it moves or is knocked down.						
IMMOLATION	2	8	–	12		✓
Target model is engulfed in flame, suffering Fire on a Critical Hit.						
VISION	3	Caster	–	–	✓	
Severius suffers no damage or effects from the next hit against him, after which the spell expires.						

WARCASTER–HIGH EXEMPLAR KREOSS

"If you didn't believe in the Creator before, you will today."

—Terschel Bannock, Cygnaran conscript during the Cygnaran Civil War

While Menoth does not make room for petty ascendants and scions like the lesser gods of the new age, He does well to make his followers ready for the wars of Urcaen. Mikael Kreoss, High Exemplar of the Knights Exemplar, is a prime example of Menoth's worldly influence on mortal man.

Raised in the Temple as a paladin, born and trained in the harshness of Khador, Kreoss has never known anything but Menoth's Word and the cold truth of his purpose. Mikael's grandfather perished in the Thornwood War on the banks of the Dragon's Tongue and his death left the Kreoss family in poverty. Debtors forced Mikael's father into a hard life, with very little except his arduous labors to occupy his time. When he became a father in his own right, his troubles continued. The mother died in childbirth, leaving him to raise the child on his own. Having little choice, he gave the boy over to the Menite clergy with the hopes of a proper upbringing for his only son.

Priests of the Protectorate raised Mikael Kreoss. He was told only that his family had fallen on hard times due to the Cygnarans. He turned any resentment he may have fostered into a quest for perfection, and the news of his faith and focus spread quickly. As a questing acolyte, Kreoss came upon a small band of crypt-robbing heathens and assailed them with no more than his fists and faith, cracking bones with his bare hands. It is said he was strengthened by the teachings of Menoth. Immediately after the scuffle, dripping with the blood and sweat of his foes, Kreoss hurried to the temple and prayed to Menoth for direction. A visiting exemplar observed the acolyte in prayer and was impressed. When Kreoss left the temple, he left in the company of that paladin, and his training began.

Mikael Kreoss rose in Menoth's grace—and the opinion of the visgoths—very quickly. His crusades were effective in stamping out heretics and blasphemers wherever they were rooted. His quest became to "reclaim Menoth's gift, which they have spurned." It is surmised that Kreoss means their very being, for he has sent many a dissenting soul back to the Creator. In time, he achieved the position of High Exemplar, and within the Protectorate, Kreoss has become a living legend. His flowing robes and ancient runic armor enhances his already impressive physique, and his unwavering faith makes him a pillar of the theocracy. When the decision was made to go back to war with the Cygnarans, thousands gathered to listen to him pray to Menoth for victory.

The High Exemplar is a living warjack when he takes up arms in the name of his Lord. His concentration is unmatched, his prayers never ending, as he directs numerous legions of troops, steers warjacks under his personal control, invokes the wrath of Menoth, and smashes his mortal enemies with his mace, Spellbreaker. So strong is his faith that a mere touch from this blessed weapon can revoke the precious "Gift" of sorcery that the lesser gods granted foolishly to mortals.

A legend he may be, but Kreoss is a nightmare in the minds of the rest of western Immoren's people, especially those dedicated to Morrow. They fear that when Menoth plays the last move against them, High Exemplar Kreoss will no doubt be the piece that topples the King.

Feat: Menoth's Wrath

Few members of the Temple's clergy can command the force of the Old God to greater effect than High Exemplar Kreoss. With but a few chanted words from an ancient littany, Kreoss may unleash the anger of man's creator, smiting all who oppose him to their knees.

All enemy models within the High Exemplar's control area are knocked down.

FOCUS	7	CMD	8		
SPD	STR	MAT	RAT	DEF	ARM
5	6	7	4	14	15

SPELLBREAKER

Special	POW	P+S
Multi	8	14

Damage	18
Point Cost	64
Field Allowance	C
Victory Points	5

Base Size: Small

Special Rules

SPELLBREAKER

- Dispel—All upkeep spells on the target model expire when hit by Spellbreaker.
- Reach—2" melee range

Spells	Cost	RNG	AOE	POW	UP	OFF
ANTI-MAGIC PULSE	2	Caster	CTRL	—		
All Upkeep spells in AOE expire.						
CLEANSING FIRE	4	8	4	14		✓
A massive blast of flames erupts, causing Fire to all models in the AOE on a Critical Hit.						
IMMOLATION	2	8	—	12		✓
Target model is engulfed in flame, suffering Fire on a Critical Hit.						
LAMENTATION	2	Caster	CTRL	—	✓	
Enemy Warcasters in AOE pay double to cast or upkeep spells.						
PROTECTION OF MENOTH	2	8	—	—	✓	
Target model/unit gains +2 DEF and +2 ARM.						
RETRIBUTION	2	8	—	—	✓	
If target Warjack is damaged, its attacker suffers an equal damage roll, then the spell expires.						
WARD	2	6	—	—	✓	
Target Warjack cannot be targeted by enemy spells.						

WARCASTER–THE HIGH RECLAIMER

"He is nameless. Without identity. Without mercy. He is the High Reclaimer. Heretics who learn of his propinquity flee in fear, but a soul does not escape one who sees it fulminating like a beacon in the pitch."

—High Exemplar Mikael Kreoss, regarding the High Reclaimer

Menoth creates, and He destroys. It is the job of the Reclaimers to assist in the latter. Some wayward souls are best returned to the Creator, for they are life and energy wasted on this world. The Reclaimers are an extension of Menoth's Will, returning these rebellious souls to the Creator. But to walk the Path of the Reclaimer, one must be eager and unyielding. A mask of iron is placed over the devotee's head and bolted shut, not to be removed 'til death. The traditional black armor and subfusc raiment become the Reclaimer's last and only attire. They take the Oath, vowing that the only words they will speak are restricted to prayer. Henceforth, only Menoth heeds their utterances, and He marks those strong enough to walk the Path. Their aid in the visiting judgment in this life upon the unworthy will spare them His judgment in the next.

One man who recently took the Oath of the Reclaimer's Last Breath has risen above his peerage. This man has shown a propensity for old magics and displayed his control over the mystical warjacks, the first sign being the firing of rocket salvos by two Redeemer models at his behest. Since then, the High Exemplar took the Reclaimer in and instructed him in the rigors of warjack control. High Exemplar Kreoss dubbed him the High Reclaimer, and promoted him above all other Reclaimers and assigned him a company complete with a dozen 'jacks.

The High Reclaimer's sole weapon, besides his fearsome physique and terrifying appearance, is a modification of the fiery ceremonial torches wielded by other Reclaimers. This huge mace is called Cremator. It is a large spiked fireball at the end of the long haft, the flames made possible by a reservoir of Menoth's

Fury that burns with the sticky oil. One crushing blow from the High Reclaimer's weapon smashes limbs and collapses torsos, even rending warjack armor on occasion. What the mace does not maul, the flaming oil consumes. Though the Reclaimers do engage in personal combat when need be, the High Reclaimer shines in the turmoil of battle. To prepare, he spends countless hours in meditation or silently training with weapons, constantly forging and tempering his body into a bastion of corded muscle and sinew akin to iron. He is feared as a warrior and as a powerful warcaster.

Because of these things, no one is safe from the High Reclaimer. If it is not good enough to castigate heretics for their sacrilege, the High Reclaimer comes forthwith. It is said that Menoth whispers to him during his prayers, naming those who are to be returned to Him. Enemies, allies, even so-called innocent bystanders are oft reclaimed with as much foreknowledge as Cremator's hiss as it delivers a killing blow or the sudden pressure of a Crusader's grip. But these matters are not to be questioned, for all Reclaimers are trained to know Menoth's signs, interpreting even the subtlest suggestions as His divine command—every twitch, every gesture, every deep breath, has meaning to a Reclaimer, and they know they must not fail in their duties or their interpretations, for failure means reclamation, often by the High Reclaimer himself.

FOCUS	5		CMD	8	
SPD	STR	MAT	RAT	DEF	ARM
5	7	6	4	14	15

CREMATOR	Special	POW	P+S
	Fire	7	14

Damage	18
Point Cost	52
Field Allowance	C
Victory Points	5

Base Size: Small

Feat: RESURRECTION

Though the High Reclaimer's purpose is to usher souls into the next existence, he has been given the authority to return them from death in order to carry out Menoth's will.

Return 2d6 dead Menoth troopers to play, placing them anywhere within the Reclaimer's control area. The controlling player chooses which models are returned, and models may be returned to old units or formed into new units of the same type. Ressurected models cannot activate the turn they return to play.

SPECIAL RULES

HIGH RECLAIMER

- Oath of Silence—The High Reclaimer cannot give orders. A model cannot use the High Reclaimer's CMD stat when making command checks.
- Reclaim—The High Reclaimer gains a Soul Token for every living Protectorate model destroyed within his control area. Next control phase, replace each soul token with a focus point.
- Terror—An enemy models/units in melee range must pass a command check or flee.

CREMATOR

- Fire—Target model hit by the Cremator suffers Fire.

Spells	Cost	RNG	AOE	POW	UP	OFF
ASHES TO ASHES	4	8	Spec	10		✓
If target model is hit, d6 nearest enemies within 5" take a POW 10 damage roll.						
BURNING ASH	1*	8	3	—		
Create a 3" cloud effect for each focus point spent. All models inside a cloud effect suffers -2 MAT and -2 RAT. Burning Ash clouds last for one round.						
IMMOLATION	2	8	—	12		✓
Target model is engulfed in flame, suffering Fire on a Critical Hit.						
RITUAL SACRIFICE	1	Caster	CTRL	—		
Remove a friendly living model from play. All warjacks in the High Reclaimer's battlegroup and within his control area receive one additional focus point, not to exceed the Warjack's normal linit. A warjack may only receive one focus per turn from this spell.						
SOULSTORM	3	Caster	Spec	—	✓	
An enemy model that moves within 4" of the High Reclaimer immediately takes one damage point. An enemy model that begins its activation within 4" of the High Reclaimer and does not move at least 4" away from him takes one damage point at the end of its activation.						

UNIT—CHOIR OF MENOTH

"I'll be damned. If them 'jacks start dancing, I quit."

—Lieutenant Allister Caine, Cygnaran gun mage, commenting on the mystic powers of the Choir

WARPRIEST				CMD	8
SPD	STR	MAT	RAT	DEF	ARM
5	5	6	4	12	13
BATTLE STAFF					
		Special		POW	P+S
		—		2	7
Base Size: Small					

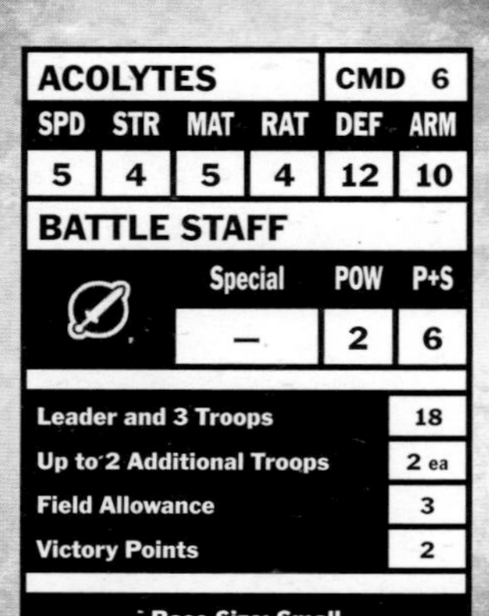

ACOLYTES				CMD	6
SPD	STR	MAT	RAT	DEF	ARM
5	4	5	4	12	10
BATTLE STAFF					
		Special		POW	P+S
		—		2	6
Leader and 3 Troops					18
Up to 2 Additional Troops					2 ea
Field Allowance					3
Victory Points					2
Base Size: Small					

SPECIAL RULES

WARPRIEST
- Leader

BATTLEHYMN (WARPRIEST ONLY)
- Infuse (★Action)
- Safe Passage (★Action)
- Shielding Ward (★Action)

ACOLYTES
- Chant (★Action)

The power of faith is neverending and oft surprising. It took the Menites years to perfect their divine magics in order to drive and augment warjacks, for it requires time to perfect such skills, and they are not as easily applied or harnessed as the witchcraft of the Cygnarans or the devilry of the Cryx. But Menoth rewards those with great perseverance, and the divine war priests that learned to command their 'jacks are gifted indeed. The energies used to warcast with sorcery are very personal, almost private in their connection to a warjack. With divine warcasting, it is more of a shared consciousness, as if the warcaster is leading the warjack hand-in-hand rather than on a leash. Because of this unique connection, sometimes other priests who are not warcasters can lend their aid by focusing their prayers into a 'jack as if it were his or her own.

While acolytes are learning to warcast, they are grouped into schools with devout war priests and led onto the field of battle with their sacred scrolls in hand. The war priest chants the ancient hymns, leading the would-be warcasters in a powerful canticle. It is called Menoth's Choir. This divine chorus invigorates the souls of their followers with their song, not to mention serving as quite the distraction to their enemy. Most importantly, it carries the divine wishes of the warcaster acolytes into the already woven bonds between the warjacks and their warcasting masters. These prayers frequently imbue the 'jacks with boundless strength and energy; the construct's armor takes on a magical sheen, deflecting incoming projectiles and shielding them from the powerful spellcrafts of the enemy's wizards and warcasters. It takes an entire choir to achieve such marvelous effects, which leaves them helpless to perform other acts on the field. Often it is the duty of the Flameguard to stand at the ready and defend the chorus if combatants dare to approach them during their canticle.

Indeed, the results of the choir are a testament to the power of the divine magics of Menoth. They have attained a level of warcasting that the wizards of Cygnar have yet to dream of, and it is no doubt a great concern of all Menoth's foes. If they can incite the Protectorate's warjacks, what happens if these burgeoning casters' hymns one day somehow reach *their* 'jacks?

CHOIR SPECIAL RULES

WARPRIEST

- Leader

BATTLE HYMNS

As a Special Action, the Warpriest may recite one of the following Battle Hymns, affecting all friendly Protectorate Warjacks within a 3" radius of him. A Warjack may only be under the effect of one Battle Hymn at a time. All Battle Hymns last for one round.

- Infuse (★Action)—All Protectorate Warjacks in affected area gain a +2 bonus to attack and damage rolls.
- Safe Passage (★Action)—Warjacks in affected area cannot be targeted by ranged attacks.
- Shielding Ward (★Action)—Warjacks in affected area cannot be targeted by any spells.

ACOLYTES

- Chant (★Action)—Each Acolyte in the Choir adds 1" to the radius of the Warpriest's hymn effects. Acolytes cannot recite the Battle Hymns without the Warpriest.

UNIT–DELIVERERS

"Right, well, inaccurate they may be, it still takes one boxy bastard to stand in the path of a Menite rocket."

— Cygnaran Chief Mechanik Garrick Haige

Thedeliverers are instruments of the Hierarch's invention. Voyle realized the relatively expensive Redeemer warjack employs a cheap and easy to make ammunition—fiery rockets. The Hierarch decided to order a less expensive (and more expendable) method of launching the lethal payloads, for more rockets could be easily made, but more Redeemer 'jacks could not. Hierarch Voyle believed that men could successfully deliver the rockets as easily as the 'jacks, and so the first "deliverers" were soon unleashed.

Moderately armored and having little need for foot speed, the Deliverers lurk in the rear ranks of their army. Originally they lit the dangerous, self-propelled explosives by hand, holding onto a length of wood cautiously until the fuse took hold and the rocket spiraled up into the air, aimed by their prayers alone. Sometimes the rockets landed amongst the enemy lines before exploding in a shower of deadly and painful shrapnel; sometimes they did not. After some spectacular mishaps resulting in deaths by friendly fire, as well as several lost fingers and hands due to short fuse accidents, Voyle ordered a more stable way to launch the rockets. Eventually, reinforced cylindrical tubes were developed. The deliverers drop a lit rocket into the tube, and point the end toward the enemy. As long as they point fast enough, accidents are less common than the old methods. Voyle is satisfied for now, but only the most devoted, or those in need of attrition, are placed into the deliverer units. It's a dangerous gamble lighting those fuses, and though there is rarely a misfire, the possibility is never far away.

DELIVERER SPECIAL RULES

ARMS MASTER

•Leader

SKYHAMMER

•Inaccurate—A Deliverer suffers a -4 penalty to its attack rolls with the Skyhammer.

•Misfire—A Skyhammer rocket prematurely detonates on an attack roll of all 1s, causing a direct hit to the attacking model and blast damage to every model in the AOE.

ARMS MASTER				CMD	7
SPD	STR	MAT	RAT	DEF	ARM
5	4	5	6	12	11
SKYHAMMER					
	RNG	ROF	AOE	POW	
	16	1	3	12	
SWORD					
	Special		POW	P+S	
	—		3	7	

Base Size: Small

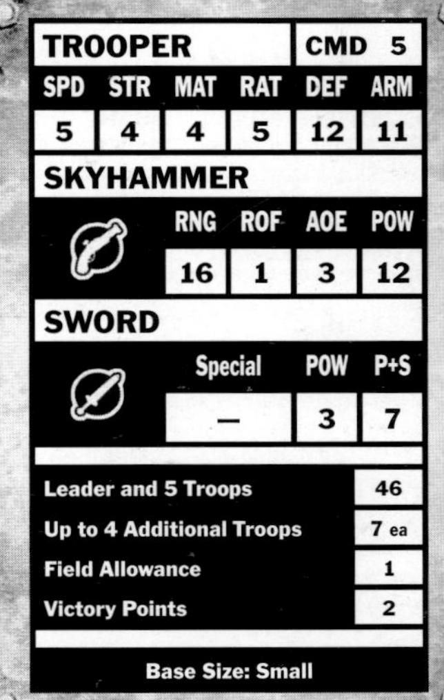

TROOPER				CMD	5
SPD	STR	MAT	RAT	DEF	ARM
5	4	4	5	12	11
SKYHAMMER					
	RNG	ROF	AOE	POW	
	16	1	3	12	
SWORD					
	Special		POW	P+S	
	—		3	7	

Leader and 5 Troops	46
Up to 4 Additional Troops	7 ea
Field Allowance	1
Victory Points	2

Base Size: Small

SPECIAL RULES

ARMS MASTER

•Leader

SKYHAMMER

•Inaccurate

•Misfire

UNIT—KNIGHTS EXEMPLAR

"May Menoth guide us to strike quickly and at the hearts of His foes."

—High Exemplar Kreoss to the Knights Exemplar before a battle

WARDER				CMD	9
SPD	STR	MAT	RAT	DEF	ARM
5	6	8	4	12	15
RELIC BLADE					
		Special		POW	P+S
		—		5	11
Base Size: Small					

KNIGHT				CMD	7
SPD	STR	MAT	RAT	DEF	ARM
5	6	7	4	12	15
RELIC BLADE					
		Special		POW	P+S
		—		5	11
Leader and 5 Troops					69
No Additional Troops					—
Field Allowance					1
Victory Points					2
Base Size: Small					

SPECIAL RULES

WARDER
- Leader

UNIT
- Bond of Brotherhood
- Fearless
- Weapon Master

Many scholars have compared the Protectorate to the body of Menoth. The Hierarch is the head. The scrutators, the mouth. The warjacks are the bones, while the countless zealots are the blood. If this is true, then the Knights Exemplar are the tools of war in His hands.

Heavily armored in blessed suits of full plate engraved with rites of protection and wards, these powerful swordsmen cry out in righteous fury as blows deflect off their armor in tones akin to a hammer striking a chime. Exemplar armor is a prized piece of work combined with a lifetime's worth of divine prayer. The scrutators will spare no amount of servants and zealots to retrieve a suit, and never will a living exemplar part with one.

In their gauntleted hands are the equally blessed "relic blades," holy swords of flawless quality that seemingly burn with the words of Menoth stamped into them. Even in the hands of an amateur these weapons are lethal, but in the grasp of Knights Exemplar, they are capable of legendary effects. The blades pass through the armor and flesh of those out of Menoth's grace as if they were made of water. Knights Exemplar are formidable, and with the divine gifts they receive from the hierarchy of the Protectorate, they seem nigh unstoppable. Should one fall in combat, his loss is the gain of his battle brothers. Seeing one of their number pass on into Menoth's hands fuels their faith. Should they die in His service, the Knights Exemplar become awash in His glory.

The first time the Knights Exemplar raised arms against Cygnar was within the City of Walls during the Cygnaran Civil War. At that time, there were only a few dozen of the holy warriors. Now, with so much time to train and prepare, there is no telling how many of the divine knights will hear the dying cries of the unworthy in days to come.

EXEMPLAR SPECIAL RULES

WARDER
- Leader

UNIT
- Bond of Brotherhood—A Knight Exemplar gains +1 STR and +1 ARM for every member of its unit removed from play. These bonuses are lost if the model is returned to play in this army.
- Fearless—A Knight Exemplar never flees.
- Weapon Master—A Knight Exemplar adds an additional die to its melee damage rolls.

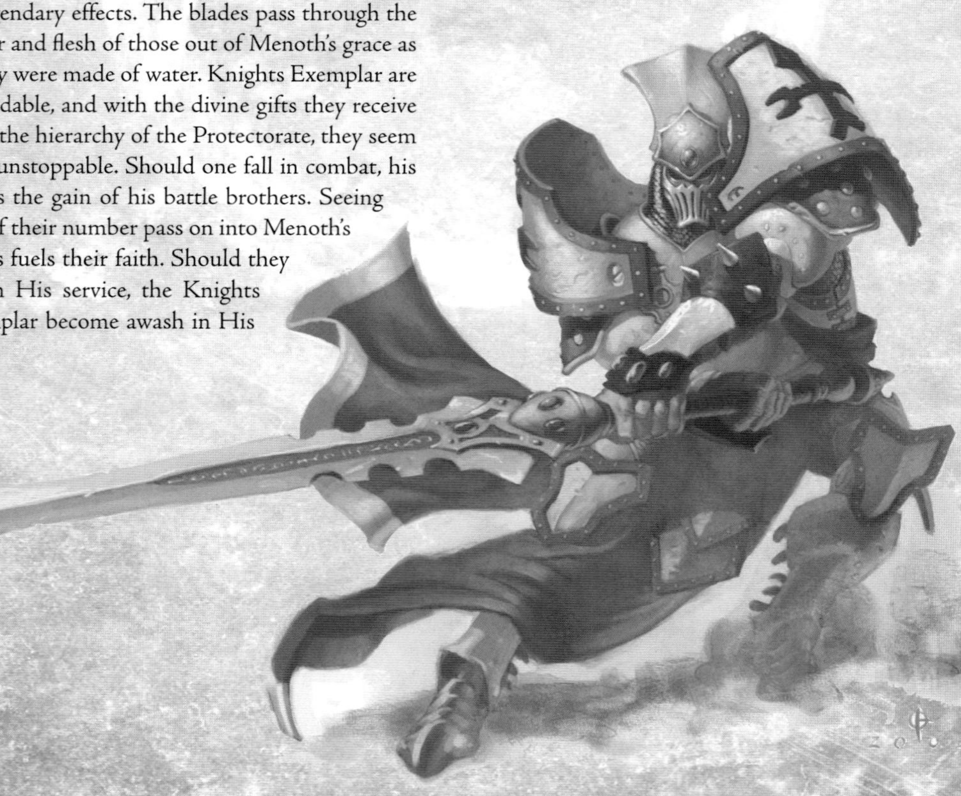

SOLO–PALADIN OF THE ORDER OF THE WALL

"There's no way we just missed him! He's right there! Fire again!"

—Cygnaran long gunner captain to his men after firing at a Paladin of the Wall

The Order of the Wall is growing smaller in these new times; its remaining members are reminders of a lost power. Hierarch Voyle perceives the deeds of the paladins as futile, and it is said that one day soon he plans to disband this heroic order. For now, the paladins are forced to walk alone, mistrusted to perform the necessary things such as the dispatching of heathen foes. They are in fact loath to sully their swords with such dishonor. They prefer to protect His flock rather than drown them in rivers of blood, even if they be wayward.

The Paladins of the Order of the Wall are armed much the same way as the Knights Exemplar. Their ancient armor was crafted and blessed by priests of the Wall generations ago. When donned by a capable warrior, they are a magnificent sight. When a paladin wishes it, he becomes akin to the cornerstone of a fortress, unbreakable and unmoving. Even powerful blows from the likes of warjacks glance harmlessly off the mystic wards, while the paladin's massive holy sword returns strikes capable of shearing mechanikal limbs. It takes a great deal of concentration on the part of the Paladin to sustain this "stone-and-mortar" stance, but when the paladin strikes, his divine sword erupts in holy fire, a sliver of the sun itself. The blade melts through armor and flesh, and few who have witnessed the flame brand in combat argue against the holy nature of the paladin. Even fewer can stand against it.

The Order of the Wall may be diminishing each generation, but its tradition is still felt through the actions of the paladins. For every soul saved by their actions, two more are lost to the racks and thumbscrews of the scrutators. Changes are taking place within the Protectorate, changes the remaining Paladins of the Wall do not care for. These paladins may be the only mercy left in the new theocracy. If Hierarch Voyle has his way, they will soon be gone, and perhaps the last bit of hope for a peaceful future in the Protectorate will be gone with them.

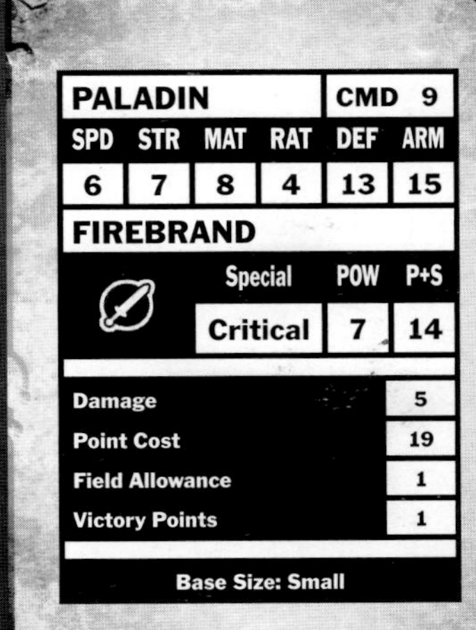

PALADIN				CMD	9
SPD	STR	MAT	RAT	DEF	ARM
6	7	8	4	13	15

FIREBRAND	Special	POW	P+S
	Critical	7	14

Damage	5
Point Cost	19
Field Allowance	1
Victory Points	1

Base Size: Small

PALADIN SPECIAL RULES

PALADIN

•Stone-and-Mortar Stance—A Paladin that voluntarily forfeits its movement gains +5 DEF and +5 ARM for one round. While in the Stone-and-Mortar stance, the Paladin may only attack a model that has attacked him in their previous turn. A Paladin cannot make free strikes while in the Stone-and-Mortar Stance.

•Fearless—A Paladin never flees.

•Weapon Master—A Paladin adds an additional die to its melee damage rolls.

FIREBRAND

•Critical Fire—On a Critical Hit, target model suffers Fire. Fire is a continuous effect that sets the target ablaze. A model on fire takes a POW 12 damage roll each turn during its maintenance until the Fire expires on a d6 roll of 1 or 2. Fire effects are alchemical substances or magical in nature and are not affected by water.

SPECIAL RULES

PALADIN

- •Fearless
- •Stone-and-Mortar Stance
- •Weapon Master

FIREBRAND

- •Critical Fire

UNIT–TEMPLE FLAMEGUARD

"Such dedication must be rewarded. They are wasted watching over these buildings and relics. Let us give them the chance to test themselves. Let us give them the chance to meet the Creator in glory. Let us give them the honor of battle!"

—The Hierarch Garrick Voyle

CAPTAIN				CMD 8	
SPD	STR	MAT	RAT	DEF	ARM
6	5	7	4	13	14

FLAME SPEAR	Special	POW	P+S
	Multi	5	10

Base Size: Small

TROOPER				CMD 6	
SPD	STR	MAT	RAT	DEF	ARM
6	5	6	4	13	14

FLAME SPEAR	Special	POW	P+S
	Multi	5	10

Leader and 5 Troops	53
Up to 4 Additional Troops	8 ea
Field Allowance	3
Victory Points	2

Base Size: Small

SPECIAL RULES

CAPTAIN
- Leader
- Shield Wall (Order)

UNIT
- Combined Melee Attack

FLAME SPEAR
- Reach
- Set Defense

Outside the temples of Menoth, the Flameguard stand ever vigilant. Important scrolls, divine relics, and esteemed personages are within most of them, and they must be protected from those who seek to destroy or spirit them away. The great Hierarch Sulon created the Flameguard, conscripting able-bodied Menites in the days prior to the Cygnaran Civil War. They were garbed in flowing white with heavy tabards and a glimmering helm and trained to use the spear and shield to great effect. Their purpose: to keep the temples and holy sites under guard at all times, and in return for making themselves useful to Menoth, they were granted indulgences by order of Sulon for their past transgressions.

As war with the foes of Menoth draws near, the Flameguard's spears have been fitted with reservoirs of Menoth's Fury. They grip their fiery-tipped flame spears with a new determination. Having begun as bodyguards, now they have become elite watchmen over the warcasters and battle priests. The Flameguard are prized as the last line of defense, and no important official or clergyman can be attacked without first getting through their ranks.

When the time comes for them to be called to the battlefield, unlike the normal zealots of the Protectorate, they display great skill with their flame spears. Each one is roughly seven feet in length, and made of durable alloys, blessed by a visgoth's hand. Inside the haft is a tube of Menoth's Fury, piped up to surface vents drilled into the barbed spear tip, ignited by flint clackers at the blade's base. When used, the spear drips the oily fire from these vents, inflicting excruciating wounds. Their trademark maneuver, called "Menoth's Howl," is to spin the spear like a quarterstaff when the fuel is low. The remaining oil is forced to the business end of the weapon and the nearly empty reservoir whistles hauntingly as the weapon is spun. This is an eerie maneuver that visibly shakes their foes.

All things considered, the Temple Flameguard is an effective use of Protectorate manpower and yet another resource willing to lay down its life for the holy causes as dictated by the Creator. The Flameguard is living proof that the Menites and their faith is just as strong, if not stronger, than any potent firearm or deadly warjack.

FLAMEGUARD SPECIAL RULES

CAPTAIN

- Leader
- Shield Wall (Order)—When this order is given, every Temple Flameguards moves into tight formation and gains +4 ARM for one round. Unit members who cannot move into tight formation do not gain the benefit of the Shield Wall.

UNIT

- Combined Melee Attack—Instead of making melee attacks seperately, Flameguards in melee range of the same target may combine their attacks. The Flameguard with the highest MAT in the attacking group makes one melee attack roll for the group, adding +1 to the attack and damage rolls for each Flameguard, including itself, participating in the attack.

FLAME SPEAR

- Reach—2" melee range
- Set Defense—A Flameguard gains +2 DEF against Charge and Slam attacks.

"…Why even the locals took up arms against us! It was bloody obvious they were no strangers to a weapon, either. Dodgy churchies—beg pardon—had been prepping 'em all along, I daresay."

—Captain Burkett Milburne, Cygnaran Storm Blade commenting on the Menite riots of 596 A.R.

One of the Protectorate of Menoth's concessions in signing the treaties with Cygnar was that they were not permitted to retain a standing army without the sanction of the Cygnaran king, which would likely be never. However, Visgoth Ozeall must have smirked as he penned his name to those papers, knowing full well that should any leader of the Protectorate call for arms, every able Menite in the Protectorate would, without hesitation, answer the call. Followers of Menoth are so deeply absorbed in their devotion that they willingly and ardently fight in His name. They believe in Menoth. They love Menoth. They are willing to die for Menoth.

The Cygnarans are not total fools, however. They are quite aware of the fanatical devotion of the Menites, thus decreeing it is also unlawful for the zealots of the Protectorate to bear martial weapons. Yet, each devotee of the Creator is trained by the faithful of their order to defend their homes and to serve as guardians of their sacred sites. These trained individuals understand that if there is a call to arms, they are to rush to one of the Menite's many hidden weapon caches. These are equipped with basic weapons, but the storehouses also stow censers of Menoth's Fury, in which the weapons may be dipped and coated.

To bolster the faith of their people—and to remind them of the just torments of a coward's death in Menoth's eyes—the Menite priests walk amongst the zealots offering prayer and sermonizing against heathen practices. In recent times, these priests have become so persuasive that entire villages have engaged in bloody uprisings against the Cygnaran soldiers patrolling the fringes of their land. It seems that even one fanatic is a dangerous thing…and a hundred thousand promises to be utterly apocalyptic.

ZEALOT SPECIAL RULES

PRIEST

•Leader

PRAYERS OF MENOTH

As a special action, the Priest may recite one of the Prayers, affecting all troopers in his unit:

•Prayer of Fervor(★Action): All models in the unit gain a +2 bonus to attack and damage rolls.

•Prayer of Protection(★Action): All models in the unit gain +2 ARM.

•Prayer of Warding(★Action): Models in the unit cannot be targeted by any spells.

FIE BOMB

•Critical Fire—On a Critical Hit, target model suffers Fire. Fire is a continuos effect that sets the target ablaze. A model on fire takes a POW 12 damage roll each turn during its maintenance until the Fire expires on a d6 roll of 1 or 2. Fire effects are alchemical substances or magical in nature and are not affected by water.

PRIEST				CMD	8
SPD	STR	MAT	RAT	DEF	ARM
6	5	5	4	13	13

HEAVY MACE	Special	POW	P+S
	–	4	9

Base Size: Small

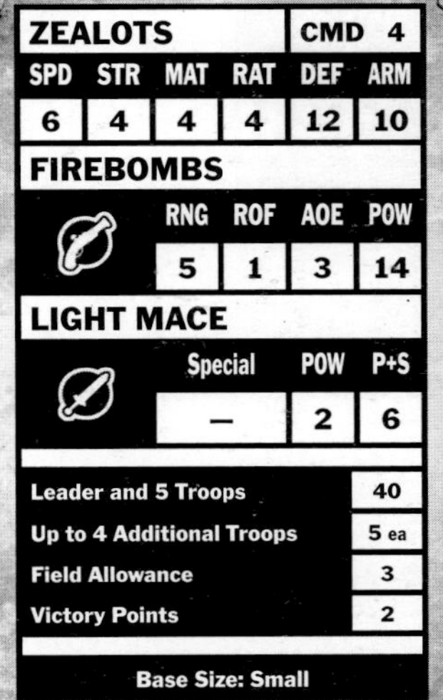

ZEALOTS				CMD	4
SPD	STR	MAT	RAT	DEF	ARM
6	4	4	4	12	10

FIREBOMBS	RNG	ROF	AOE	POW
	5	1	3	14

LIGHT MACE	Special	POW	P+S
	–	2	6

Leader and 5 Troops	40
Up to 4 Additional Troops	5 ea
Field Allowance	3
Victory Points	2

Base Size: Small

SPECIAL RULES

PRIEST
- •Leader

PRAYERS OF MENOTH (Priest Only)
- •Prayer of Fervor(★Action)
- •Prayer of Protection(★Action)
- •Prayer of Warding(★Action)

FIREBOMBS
- •Critical Fire

LIGHT WARJACK—REDEEMER

"Do not fire again, brothers. Rather, let the curs bleed for their failings."

—Senior Scrutator Vorn, advising a novice warcaster controlling an artillery unit of Redeemer warjacks

SPD	STR	MAT	RAT	DEF	ARM
5	9	5	4	12	17

	SKYHAMMER			
	RNG	ROF	AOE	POW
LEFT	16	3	3	12

	BATTLE MACE		
	Special	POW	P+S
RIGHT	—	4	13

DAMAGE GRID

1	2	3	4	5	6
	L			R	
L	L	M	C	R	R
	M	M	C	C	

SYSTEMS
Left Arm (L)
Rght Arm (R)
Cortex (C)
Movement (M)

Point Cost	81
Field Allowance	U
Victory Points	2

Base Size: Medium

SPECIAL RULES

SKYHAMMER
•Inaccurate

Forced to rely on stolen parts and frames, and having to hide their assemblies from prying Cygnaran eyes, the Protectorate leaned toward lighter warjacks to fill the roles of the iron behemoths of the other kingdoms. Lacking the ability to produce such giants, the Menites improvised often. One such improvisation is the infamous Redeemer.

The Redeemer, an altered model of the Repenter chassis, was designed not to charge forward into the enemy like others of its breed, but rather to deliver firey judgment from afar. Although it comes equipped with a heavy mace for smashing those who draw too near, this is considered a last defense. Its main armament is its rockets. The Redeemer carries a great deal of Menite-made explosives, and a mechanika rig to launch them toward the enemy. Similar to the Repenter's ignition system, the Redeemer uses vented heartfire to light the propellants. These simple tubes of shrapnel-to-be are spirited recklessly into the enemy, Menoth willing, and explode in a cascade of deadly debris. Although the explosion rarely affects the mighty mechanika mammoths of the infidel kingdoms, they leave infantry with horrible lacerations and punctures that are notoriously difficult to heal.

The Redeemer is capable of launching multiple shot salvos with a little concentration on the warcaster's part. A single rocket can take entire units out of commission, while a salvo will make them impossible to identify after the battle. Many Cygnaran women are still looking or waiting for their long lost husbands or brothers, their bodies never to be found in the bloody trenches of faraway lands. Likely these are losses attributed to yet another Menite convention of war.

REDEEMER SPECIAL RULES

SKYHAMMER

•Inaccurate—The Redeemer suffers a –4 penalty to its attack rolls with the Skyhammer.

Height /Weight	**9'10" / 4.85 tons**
Armament	**Battle Mace (right arm), Skyhammer Rocket Pod (left arm)**
Fuel Load/Burn Usage	**70 Kgs/ 5.5 hrs general, 1.2 hrs combat**
Initial Service Date	**545 AR**
Cortex Manufacturer	**Fraternal Order of Wizardry/ Greylords Covenent (stolen)**
Orig. Chassis Design	**Cygnaran Armory/Khadoran Mechaniks Assembly**

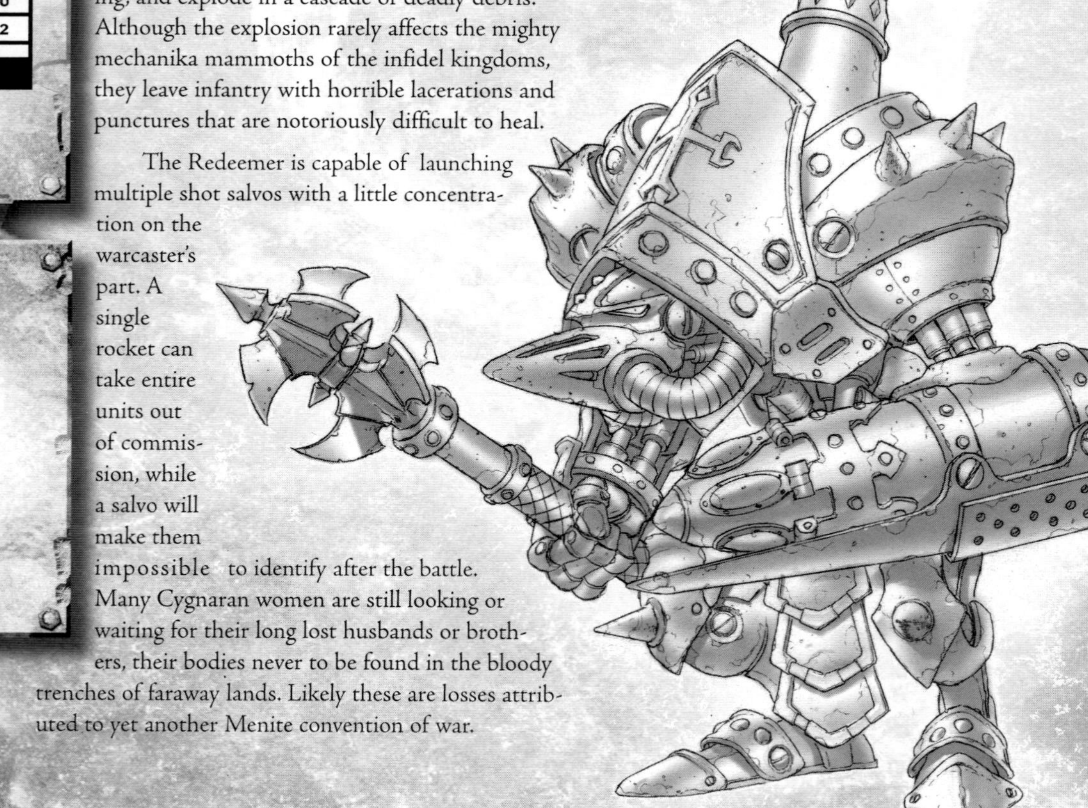

LIGHT WARJACK—REPENTER

"Fire is a relentless enemy, and damned if it's not our enemy's greatest ally."

—Commander Coleman Stryker

The Protectorate of Menoth uses the sticky flame oil they call "Menoth's Fury" in great abundance, for it is far easier for them to attain than the more expensive blasting powders for cannons and other arms. The flame-based weaponry of the Protectorate serves as a wicked reminder of the faith's burning wrath, and the simple effectiveness lends an old standard that the Menites are hard-pressed to alter. Old warjacks like the Repenter, originally designed from stolen and bartered parts from Khador and Cygnar, use some of the oldest versions of the fiery weapons. It was first used to police the borders of the Protectorate, being easy to repair or rebuild. Even if captured or stolen, the Menites were satisfied that nothing of any secrecy or importance could be gained from the simple mechanika from which they are made.

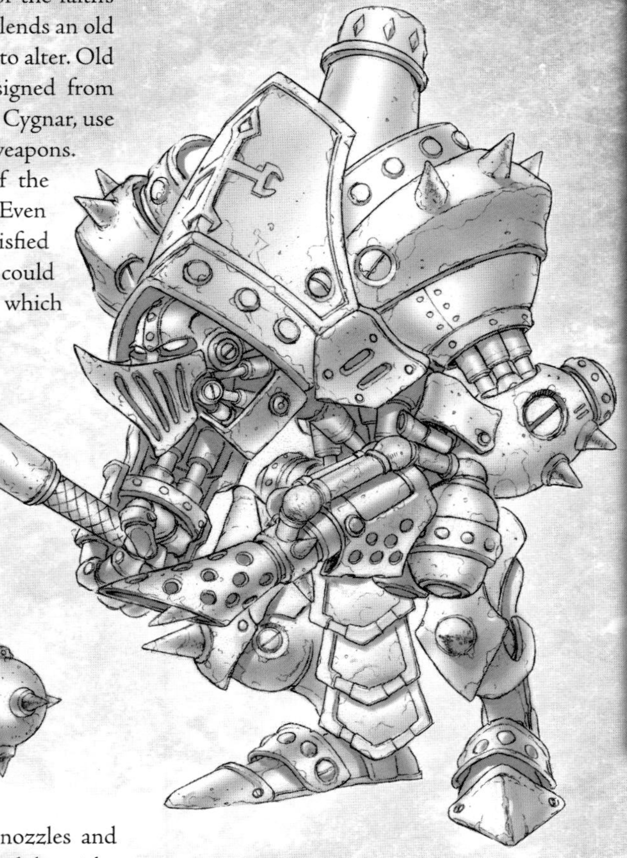

When they designed the Repenter ages ago, the Temple of Menoth armed the light warjack with the very symbols of the god itself. In one fist, it carries a three-headed flail. It is a simple weapon with simple results: swing flail, smash targets. The other hand was replaced with the first projection system for Menoth's Fury, the flamethrower. The first model was little more than a tube attached to a reservoir, while newer versions have fanning spray nozzles and mechanikal pumping mechanisms that propel the sticky fluid away from the 'jack (a problem of earlier models often saw the Repenters catching themselves aflame and exploding). The original flamethrower ignited the oil with an outside sparking mechanism, while the latest weapon vents superheated heartfire into the fuel.

Simple and effective, the Repenter is an ever-evolving icon of 'jack warfare. While it may undergo revisions from generation-to-generation, it is doubtful it will ever truly die out.

SPD	STR	MAT	RAT	DEF	ARM
5	9	5	4	12	17

	FLAME THROWER			
	RNG	ROF	AOE	POW
LEFT	SP	1	–	12

	WAR FLAIL		
	Special	POW	P+S
RIGHT	–	4	13

DAMAGE GRID	1	2	3	4	5	6
		L			R	
	L	L	M	C	R	R
		M	M	C	C	

SYSTEMS: Left Arm (L), Rght Arm (R), Cortex (C), Movement (M)

Point Cost	76
Field Allowance	U
Victory Points	2

Base Size: Medium

Height /Weight	9'10" / 4.25 tons
Armament	War Flail (right arm), Flamethrower (left arm)
Fuel Load/Burn Usage	75 Kgs/ 6 hrs general, 1.5 hrs combat
Initial Service Date	533 AR
Cortex Manufacturer	Fraternal Order of Wizardry (stolen)
Orig. Chassis Design	Cygnaran Armory//Khadoran Mechaniks Assembly

"T'was a sad thing. It just swatted our troops away like a horse shooing flies from its rump, but this horse also carried a very large axe!"

—Vior Konvadir, Vicar of the Khadoran Ragemen Brigade, recounting his first memory of the Menite Revenger

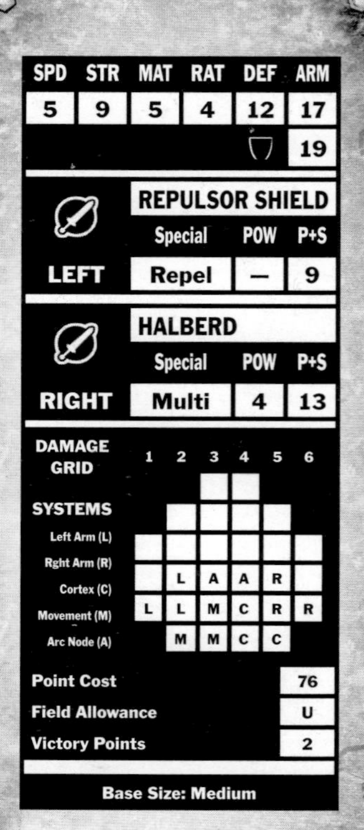

SPD	STR	MAT	RAT	DEF	ARM
5	9	5	4	12	17
					19

	REPULSOR SHIELD		
	Special	POW	P+S
LEFT	Repel	—	9

	HALBERD		
	Special	POW	P+S
RIGHT	Multi	4	13

DAMAGE GRID	1	2	3	4	5	6
		L	A	A	R	
	L	L	M	C	R	R
		M	M	C	C	

SYSTEMS: Left Arm (L), Rght Arm (R), Cortex (C), Movement (M), Arc Node (A)

Point Cost	76
Field Allowance	U
Victory Points	2

Base Size: Medium

SPECIAL RULES

ARC NODE

REPULSOR SHIELD
- •Repel

HALBERD
- •Powerful Charge
- •Reach

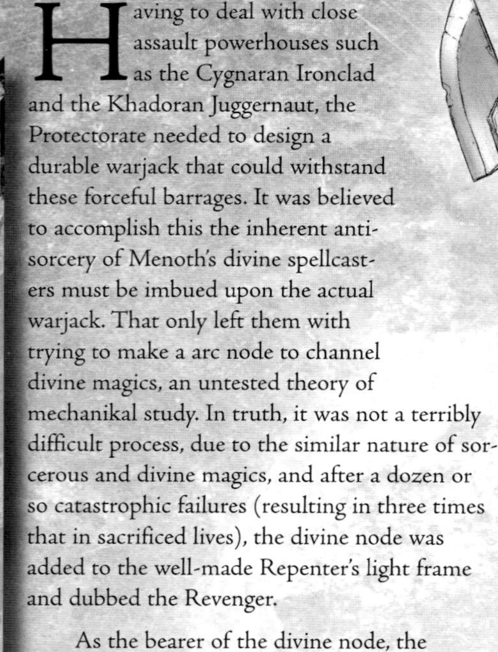

Having to deal with close assault powerhouses such as the Cygnaran Ironclad and the Khadoran Juggernaut, the Protectorate needed to design a durable warjack that could withstand these forceful barrages. It was believed to accomplish this the inherent anti-sorcery of Menoth's divine spellcasters must be imbued upon the actual warjack. That only left them with trying to make a arc node to channel divine magics, an untested theory of mechanikal study. In truth, it was not a terribly difficult process, due to the similar nature of sorcerous and divine magics, and after a dozen or so catastrophic failures (resulting in three times that in sacrificed lives), the divine node was added to the well-made Repenter's light frame and dubbed the Revenger.

As the bearer of the divine node, the Revenger would need to be very protected. The amount of armor could not over-encumber the speedy frame, so the Menite artificers crafted the rare and powerful repulsar shield. Using a parallel divine enchantment process, the artificers inlaid various runes of protection on the warjack's shield. If the powerful runes came into contact with a target all at once, it would be hurled away from the warjack immediately. This gave the Revenger the ability to distance itself from superior combatants like Cygnar and Khador's heavier 'jacks.

To take full advantage of this newfound "breathing room," the engineers designed an enormous halberd with a massive ax-like blade at the end, which allowed the Revenger to hack at the same enemies they had just repulsed. With the halberd's lengthy reach, the 'jack could use its warcaster's spells and the repulsar shield to keep opponents at bay and yet be able to cleave rifts in armor. The Revenger may be classed as a light warjack, but it has been the downfall of more than a few Cygnaran heavies in its day.

REVENGER SPECIAL RULES

ARC NODE

The Revenger may channel spells.

REPULSOR SHIELD

•Repel—If the Revenger hits with the Repulsor Shield, or if the Revenger is hit with a melee weapon, its opponent is pushed back 1".

HALBERD

•Powerful Charge—A Revenger making a Charge attack with the Halberd gains a +2 bonus to its attack roll.

•Reach—2" melee range

Height /Weight	9'8" / 4.45 tons
Armament	Halberd (right arm), Repulsar Shield (right arm), Mark II Divinity Arc Node
Fuel Load/Burn Usage	75 Kgs/ 5.5 hrs general, 1.2 hrs combat
Initial Service Date	546 AR
Cortex Manufacturer	Vassals of Menoth
Orig. Chassis Design	Sul-Menite Artificers

HEAVY WARJACK–CRUSADER

"To wage war, one must know his enemy. These fools have not seen the likes of this."

—Visgoth Ark Razek, about the Crusader in regards to the Cygnarans

In its peace terms, Cygnar decreed that the Protectorate could not keep a standing army. Visgoth Ozeall acquiesced, but soon after commanded his engineers to build warjacks from parts smuggled from Khador down the Black River. They realized the need to mass-produce these 'jacks, but if they were armed, Leto would find out quickly and take steps against the Protectorate. So the construct was designed with open hands in order to pass as a labor 'jack. The engineers incorporated the articulated hands from Cygnar's warjack schematics, and secretly forged weaponry for the warjacks to wield as Menoth commanded. They created the inferno mace, inspired by the flaming maces of the Reclaimers. Between the immensely durable frame of the Ironclad and the powerful arms of a labor 'jack, a strike with an inferno mace rends most armor into scrap. The inferno mace is also capable of unleashing a burst of Menoth's Fury, often incinerating their targets with a single strike.

These warjacks were dubbed Crusaders, and a large amount of the open-handed "labor 'jacks" have recently permeated the Protectorate workforce. When the call-to-arms sounds, the Crusaders will assemble at the front line, ready to hammer and burn the foes of Menoth to dust and ashes.

CRUSADER SPECIAL RULES

INFERNO MACE

•Critical Fire—On a Critical Hit, target model suffers Fire. Fire is a continuous effect that sets the target ablaze. A model on fire takes a POW 12 damage roll each turn during its maintenance until the Fire expires on a d6 roll of 1 or 2. Fire effects are alchemical substances or magical in nature and are not affected by water.

SPD	STR	MAT	RAT	DEF	ARM
4	11	5	4	10	19

	OPEN FIST		
	Special	POW	P+S
LEFT	–	–	11

	INFERNO MACE		
	Special	POW	P+S
RIGHT	Critical	7	18

DAMAGE GRID

1	2	3	4	5	6
	☐	☐	☐	☐	
☐	☐	☐	☐	☐	☐
☐	☐	☐	☐	☐	☐
☐	L	☐	☐	R	☐
L	L	M	C	R	R
	M	M	C	C	

SYSTEMS
Left Arm (L)
Rght Arm (R)
Cortex (C)
Movement (M)
Arc Node (A)

Point Cost	93
Field Allowance	U
Victory Points	3

Base Size: Large

SPECIAL RULES

INFERNO MACE
•Critical Fire

Height /Weight	12' / 8 tons
Armament	Inferno Mace (right arm)
Fuel Load/Burn Usage	115 Kgs/6 hrs general, 1 hr combat
Initial Service Date	513 AR
Cortex Manufacturer	Vassals of Menoth
Orig. Chassis Design	Engines East/Steamwerks Union

HEAVY WARJACK–VANQUISHER

"The Canon states that His children will walk as giants among men. Perhaps this Vanquisher is the means to a Great Truth."

—High Exemplar Mikael Kreoss

SPD	STR	MAT	RAT	DEF	ARM
4	11	5	4	10	19

FLAME BELCHER	RNG	ROF	AOE	POW
LEFT	9	1	4	13

BLAZING STAR	Special	POW	P+S
RIGHT	Circular Strike	5	16

DAMAGE GRID

SYSTEMS: Left Arm (L), Rght Arm (R), Cortex (C), Movement (M)

1	2	3	4	5	6
	L			R	
L	L	M	C	R	R
	M	M	C	C	

Point Cost	112
Field Allowance	U
Victory Points	3

Base Size: Large

SPECIAL RULES

BLAZING STAR
•Circular Strike

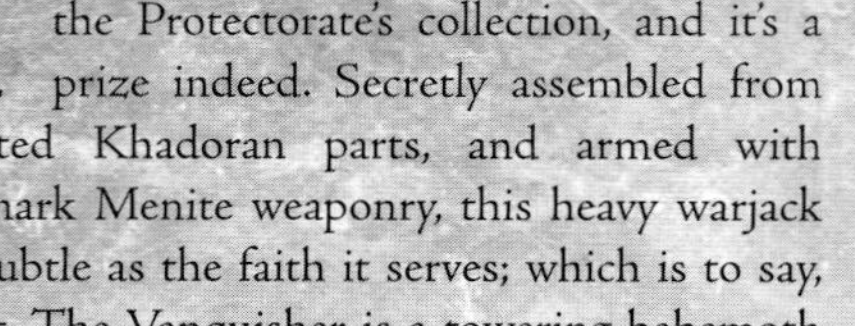

The Vanquisher is the latest warjack in the Protectorate's collection, and it's a prize indeed. Secretly assembled from imported Khadoran parts, and armed with trademark Menite weaponry, this heavy warjack is as subtle as the faith it serves; which is to say, it's not. The Vanquisher is a towering behemoth of armor, a mechanikal genius, and a harbinger of fiery death.

One arm of this 'jack wields a length of chain nearly as long as a man is tall, the end of it capped with the dangerous "blazing star," a viciously spiked sphere that is swung in a windmill motion, visiting swift justice to infidels, often severing limbs, heads, and torsos in twain.

And the blazing star is not the Vanquisher's only weapon. This model is the ultimate instrument of death. The permanent attachment of its other arm is called a flame belcher. It lobs carefully designed cannonballs filled with the vicious Menoth's Fury deep within the ranks of its adversaries. When a shell from a flame belcher impacts with any surface—Menoth willing, another warjack—the shell explodes as a fireball, reminiscent of the volcanic eruptions common to the Bloodstone mountain chains so close to the Protectorate. This bestows the same result as to any living thing caught in the wake of those eruptions—a painful and fiery demise.

VANQUISHER SPECIAL RULES

BLAZING STAR

•Circular Strike (★Attack)—Vanquisher may make a separate melee attack roll against every opponent in melee range of its front and back arcs. Determine damage normally.

Height /Weight	12' / 9.75 tons
Armament	Blazing Star Flail (right arm), Flame Belcher(left arm)
Fuel Load/Burn Usage	125 Kgs/5 hrs general, 1 hr combat
Initial Service Date	598 AR
Cortex Manufacturer	Vassals of Menoth
Orig. Chassis Design	Engines East/Khadoran Mechaniks Assembly

CRYX

BIRTH OF SHADOWS

A BRIEF HISTORY OF CRYX

"Thou who art dead, hear the beckon call of thy master. Up! Throw off thy shrouds, crawl thee from thy tombs, slither from thy graves, break free from thy sepulchral wombs, and take thy revenge upon the quick. I shalt reveal the way to thee!"

—Lord Toruk, Father of All Dragons

Asphyxious, Cryxian general and iron lich, addresses his newly promoted Warwitch, Deneghra:

Thou ask from whence I hail? Dost thou wish to know? The answer I would give thee is not as simple as so many years, or so many lives. I would say that I did not truly exist afore my Lord Toruk came to these pirate kingdoms. Or rather, I have forgotten the weak thing I was once afore his blessing. The Dragonfather came to the Schardes for refuge from his misbegotten children; this is when the first and clearest thoughts stirred in mine skull. I am of the Cryx, just as thou shalt become forthwith. To know even a shadow of mine story, thou first must know thine.

It begins with Lord Toruk. He came millennia ago to the Schardes, claiming them for his own, and the Pirate Kings yielded to him. They surrendered their crowns to the dragon, giving up their seats of authority over the living, and Lord Toruk bestowed them much power for their fealty. He granted them a living death, and with it great powers and dark magics fused within their bodies. These special few turned into the initial Lich Lords of Cryx. It was they, the twelve Pirate Kings, who became Toruk's first generals, and some of them sail to this day in their black galleons, bringing the dark tide of the Dragonlord's will to every coast in Immoren. Over the centuries, these Lich Lords have been granted the task of creating a kingdom of the dead, and whenever one of them falls, another is not far behind to pick up the pieces. The Dragonfather always keeps twelve lords at his command, to inhabit the palaces of the original Pirate Kings.

Tis to this very day that the Dragonfather speaks to us through his Lich Lords, save only a rare few have ever heard his terrible voice. May it be one eve that you may stand in his shadow and quake at the splendor of our lord. I have witnessed the power of the Dragonlord, and should thee earn a sliver of his boon there shant be a mortal on all of Caen more blessed than thee. Such is his unholy glories.

Centuries ago, whilst the fools of the mainland were under the yoke of the Orgoth, Lord Toruk protected this budding nation. Betimes the invaders did test the Broken Coast, only to earn a watery grave 'neath the talons of our lord, their ships burnt to ash with a pass of the Dragonfather's fiery breath. Without him, Cryx might have been fated to give way just as the weak mainlanders did, but we were Toruk's and he was ours.

This did not come without its price. The lands and its people changed over time due to the dragon's blight. The "natives" of Cryx had always been pariahs—exiles, pirates, renegades—but the blight truly hardened them and made their hearts darker. To this day, a thrall bearing a load through the streets of Skell or Blackwater to some unknown destination for its necromancer master has became so commonplace as to almost be ignored, for in Cryx, death is nigh as common as life.

To live in Cryx, one must not fear death but embrace it, for living or undead, Cryxians understand the predator-prey relationship all too well. And they also understand the ultimate predator is their lord and master. This is accepted willingly or no, but it makes no matter. We are all his. We are all Toruk's. We are the Dragonborne Empire, and we doth not fail—not in life nor in death. Through the powers of the Lich Lords, unto all of us, ours is a unique path. We have the power to shatter the manacles of death, to rise again and take our vengeance on those yet living, those who murdered us or failed and let us pass.

From this very ship did I witness as the mainlanders pushed the Orgoth hence. T'was many lifetimes ago. I recall the Dragonfather was pleased. In fact, we were all rather proud, for it takes great courage to throw off the chains of oppression, especially for mere mortals such as they. Our lord issued a mighty laugh as the last of the dark longboats vanished in the west. The mainlanders stood confused and silent in the wake of his roar.

Thereon the Orgoth's leave-taking of these lands, our empire was strongest of all, but we daren't strike. This should not have been so, but Toruk's accursed offspring, the dragons of Immoren, lay in wait. Cryx could have washed over every shore, but alas we could not do withal for the risk was too much. He sensed them, his spawn, out there, biding time in hopes their father became engrossed with distraction, so our lord decreed the mortals were free of threat, free to reign, for now.

Forsooth, it was our lord's one impropriety, giving life to the dragons. Even he admits as such, lamenting the mistake with great ire. The world was young, and he was alone, with no thing alive that could be counted as a peer or a worthy minion. In his lonesomeness he formed the other dragons and gave them each a piece of himself, so they could serve their father, as a devoted brood should.

But it was not to be so. In their resentment of his greatness, the dragons of Immoren conversed and then fell upon their creator. They tried for his life, to steal his power, and had any mortal existed in the world, they would have witnessed the greatest war ever waged in all the heavens, a battle so furious the sky itself rained death upon the lands. The children were mighty, but the father was too terrible for them, even with having given them much of himself. Toruk's sons and daughters fled into the earth to lick their wounds, and some centuries later Lord Toruk came to our islands, and still he doth reside within the volcano at Dragon's Roost.

Nevertheless a pact had been made, one that the dragons of Immoren yet honor—to fight their father when the time arises, to try again for his life. Whilst they fight amongst themselves in sibling rivalry, they maintain their wretched plot to consume our lord's heart. Lord Toruk knows this. He awaits them. With us alongside him, his spawn will fail. 'Tis our chance to partake in his ultimate victory when that day doth come.

Withal the dragons art far from fools. Hence, their blighted lairs art deep within the mainland. Generations of mortals have unknowingly built their cities and citadels about them, like insignificant anthills nigh the anteater's den. They struggle 'gainst the blighted fields and withered mountains, trying so very hard to survive in a land that will never cease to bear ill fruit. Betimes, Toruk's broodlings slink from their lairs and mete out havoc upon the mortals, and 'tis manifest the mortals want them as dead as we do. Many thousands of their soldiers have bled out on the steps of a broodling's den. Even so, foolishly they doth refuse to submit. They would rather quarrel over who wears the tin crowns of mortal kings rather than serve a godly one. Thus, we—the Cryxian Empire—and those we recruit, must overtake the petty fools that claim the so-called "Kingdoms of Iron," not simply to claim their lands, but to destroy our master's broodlings once and forever.

In this age, the dragons art older and more powerful. If they gathered to strike at our lord again—whilst there is little doubt we would overcome them—it would be a hard-pressed struggle at great cost to our empire. Thus, we must first carefully pick apart the persistent Iron Kingdoms. Once this is finished, we shalt sift through the detritus and unearth Toruk's disloyal children. The misbegotten children will feel the vengeance of his true family. One by one our undying armies will claim their black hearts—and hence their power—and after we have harvested what Lord Toruk planted so long ago, he will be whole again. Nothing shalt stand in our path! The Dragonfather will divide his power among us, his loyal children. Vast kingdoms of the damned—fields upon fields of the undying—will be but a sliver of our just reward. The kings of men mayst pay in gold and silver, but our Lich Lords and the mighty Dragonfather trades in bone and soul!

This task set to the Cryx is not a simple one. For long centuries we have prepared. Our fleets and our agents have poked and prodded the mainland, finding the easiest routes to the dragon's lairs, all the while taking great pains not to give the broodlings cause to suspect us. The dragons have yet to know why we wage such petty wars. When they do, it will be far too late. Nor can we give away our true strength to the mainlanders, for they would unite 'gainst us as they did 'gainst the Orgoth. Soon, we will remove them all, and the Father of Dragons will be free to spread his wings over all of Caen!

But first we must tear back the shriveled skin of the mortal world. They deserve nothing more than servitude, and we must rip the bones from their festering corpses to make it thus. At present, they art unworthy of even his shadow, but they shalt earn his blight before we art finished. Whilst they have squabbled for centuries over roads and borders,

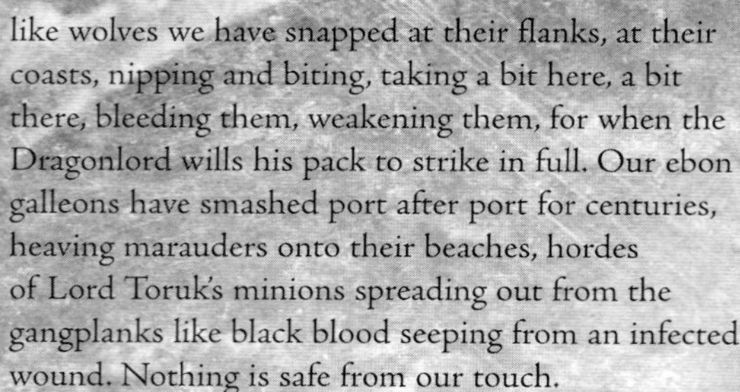

like wolves we have snapped at their flanks, at their coasts, nipping and biting, taking a bit here, a bit there, bleeding them, weakening them, for when the Dragonlord wills his pack to strike in full. Our ebon galleons have smashed port after port for centuries, heaving marauders onto their beaches, hordes of Lord Toruk's minions spreading out from the gangplanks like black blood seeping from an infected wound. Nothing is safe from our touch.

We must lie in wait, the serpent coiled for each strike, to snatch those who are foolish enough to cross our paths. Many have met their end in our seas and straits within the Schardes, and low, they have been dredged up from the depths by our lord's will to serve him. The mortal coil that restrains our foe, once shed or torn free, becomes the very leash in which the dogs are bound. Every battle they fight, these petty mortal kings, add to the Dragonfather's unholy congregation. These mortals walk blindly into the night, unknowing of our true goals.

Yes indeed, we have the power to strike them down. But our plans must be executed very assiduously. We must know where every broodling lurks before going full-scale 'gainst the mainland. There is no knowing how the dragons would react to our undying armies if we were too hasty or careless. Whether they be threatened or curious, we must not risk their arousal until the exact moment Toruk wishes it. To give such beasts even the slightest hint of our lord's plans—nay, such a foolhardy mistake be given sound to assault thine ears.

But our power is great. Greater than ever, for years ago we stole knowledge of the machine sciences from the mainland. Our necromancers took this knowledge and discovered the path of dark mechanika. They unearthed ways to harness a great, untapped resource—the final gasp!—that superb, delicious, wonderful, magical energy all things release 'pon their death. Only we, the Cryx, can siphon that energy. We take it and put it into "soul furnaces," and place these into our own brand of mechanika. The furnaces galvanize brilliant new forms of unlife. They art the very burning hearts of our mighty helljacks and their cousins, the bonejacks. Our most gifted necromancers became necro-techs and followed this new path of dark mechanika. They located a strange, shining stone to feed these furnaces, precious necrotite. To liken it to anything mundane, 'tis a kind of coal mined from those places that have seen tortuous or mass death, where life energy once bled into the mud and ash of the earth to saturate the stones beneath the soil. Battlegrounds, ruined fortresses, sunken vessels—much of the Scharde Islands—art ideal sites, and hosts of thrall gather large amounts of this wicked fuel from the earth in places such as these. 'Tis a convenient resource; a few chunks animate a bonejack for hours, although there is another even more convenient resource—the souls of the living.

But mortal life is not always as disposable as we should like, hence the discovery of necrotite has been a great boon, especially in how we art able to wage our war. Indeed, the original helljacks were not constructs at all, but huge, demonic, and mostly vacant shells that the Lich Lords animated through demanding rituals and taxing spells to be their eyes, ears, and fists on and off the battlefield. Each Lich Lord could only control a few at a time. In truth, the ancient hellslayer constructs required great willpower to keep these dark berserkers from lashing out at their own instinctual targets—targets that sometimes included the necromancers who had created them. But the advent of dark mechanika and the soul furnace ushered new methods to eternalize these hellish servants. Forthwith the necrotech's constructs replaced the Lich Lords' arcane automatons and the numbers increase with every passing night.

And so it has dawned on the Lich Lords that this new type of warfare has invaribly slipped past the broodlings, as our Dragonfather himself is vastly uncaring of what must be like toys to him. It is these new machines, these dark mechanika, that may very well be our greatest weapon against the ancient foes of our lord. Every moment of every day the necrotechs instruct their never-resting thralls to hammer out and assemble more and more of the brazen behemoths. Beasts of bone and iron, borne on the souls of the once living, they hold the key to our final victories—I know it.

Our empire has grown to an epic size, but unlike the mortals who crowd their cities and starve, we prosper day and night. I move through the fields of eternal laborers, I feel them through the ether of undeath, and I know they can feel my presence as well. With nary a gesture, they obey my commands. The Dragonlord has promised us greatness, and I have yet to see a shade of untruth in his words. We will serve in order to one day sit as kings and queens of an eternal kingdom of the undead. A kingdom that fears no coups, that knows no poverty, and that bows to a true, living god.

So the mainland will soon suffer our force in full, and they shalt fall. We will spread the blight to the farthest reaches and back again if he so requests it. If it takes us another millennia, so be it. With every sword stroke or rending claw, we will add another to our ranks. Death is the only promise of this coming war, and that we have already overpowered. Crush us, we return. Burn us, we rise again. Hide from us, we shalt find thee. Through oceans of blood we shalt sail on our black ships to bring death to the living, and unlife to the dead. Mortals have but two options: slavery in life, or servitude in death, and Lord Toruk will not be denied. Every village that falls will be another legion, every city a fortress. There is no more loyal army in all of Caen.

Thou asked, my warwitch, from whence I have come. As Toruk saved thee from thine own weakness, wherefore he, too, saved me. I do not feel the weakness of mortality. It is unknown to me, and unknown to thee, as well. We art Cryx, thee and I. We art eternal. And that shalt suffice as thine answer—for now.

WARCASTER-IRON LICH, ASPHYXIOUS

"How delicious, this sacrifice. You were less than nothing—a festering leech—but you gave your life for me, thus I will give you a new life, a new form to avail a god. You shall be a fang in the maw of the Dragonfather…mayhap one day you shall become a talon…"

—Lord Toruk to the wracked body of the lich soon to be called Asphyxious

Although only twelve entities hold the position of Lord Toruk's mighty Lich Lords, one among the Dragonlord's forces considers himself the closest thing to the thirteenth. As the most active Iron Lich on the mainland of western Immoren, Asphyxious has become the dark dragon's prodigal son. His campaigns have wreaked havoc along the Khadoran and Cygnaran shores, and carved out a small bastion for the Cryx forces just a few miles upstream of Point Bourne. Where a city called Rivercleft once stood, now exists a pit of evil and despair that spawns countless horrors to stalk the night.

Asphyxious, long a powerful member of the druidic Black Circle, lived near the very site where Toruk came to rest after giving birth to his draconic, misbegotten children. Seeing the Dragonlord's arrival as divine providence, the mortal druid set aside his nature worship and looked to Toruk as his new symbol of greatness. The druid sacrificed countless animals to gain the dragon's favor. When the mere blood of swine and goats no longer drew Toruk's attention, he moved on to sentient sacrifices stolen from local villages. Still the dark dragon did not look his way.

When the twelve Lich Lords came down from the volcano that serves as Toruk's roost, the druid realized what he must do. He climbed to the volcano's lip and performed the last sacrifice he could—himself. At the height of this elaborate ritual, the druid cast himself into the molten mountain, finally drawing Toruk's attention. Magma devoured Asphyxious voraciously, the druid's resilience to natural elements barely dulling the pain, and when his body had been stripped to little more than bones, his screams finally fell silent. At that, with his soul still near, Toruk scooped him from the caldera with one massive talon and blew a spark of unlife into the smoldering skeleton. The druid's dark soul, thus ripped from the clutches of Urcaen, now found eternal shelter within this molten skeleton.

Having gained the Dragonlord's favor, Asphyxious assumed his new form. Soon, the Lich Lords crafted him into a powerfully forged Iron Lich, powered by the lives this new form consumed. A thousand years later, Asphyxious still promises dark glory

for the Cryxian army, and now looks to create a new roost for his Dragonlord.

The Iron Lich wields powerful necromantic and entropic energies fueled by his own magical furnace, hot with smoldering necrotite, and by the dead souls trapped in the soul cages that dangle from every necromancer's waist. His magic is destructive, relentless, and without mercy. Asphyxious often leaves behind ashen fields of lifeless grasses and withered trees where once there had been fertile fields and lush woodlands, while blackened corpse husks and bubbling pools of gore are all that remain of his victims.

Death energy fuels Asphyxious, but such are the demands of his iron body that his vital soulfire stores sometimes grow thin. In these weaker moments, the Iron Lich opens his furnace's riveted doors and unleashes a storm of necromantic energy that devours life energies for fuel. In addition to his foul magics, the powerful iron carapace housing him grants great physical strength and his iron talons wield the ensorcelled Soul Splitter, a twin-pronged spear bathed in entropy that consumes metal and flesh. A single scratch from the staff can vaporize a man in seconds.

Asphyxious is a terrible foe in all senses of the word, crafty beyond belief, and capable of any act in Lord Toruk's name. A prime source of the cancer feeding upon western Immoren, he gleefully spreads the shadow of the Dragonlord's wings to the Iron Kingdoms' every corner. If the Iron Lich has any say, that shadow will extend one day to all of Caen itself.

FOCUS	7	CMD	7		
SPD	STR	MAT	RAT	DEF	ARM
6	7	6	3	15	16

SOULSPLITTER		
Special	POW	P+S
Multi	8	15

Damage	18
Point Cost	78
Field Allowance	C
Victory Points	5

Base Size: Medium

Feat: CONSUMING BLIGHT

Constant death follows in the wake of the Iron Lich, and it is on this death that Asphyxious feeds. In a horrific display of necromancy, this terrible undead warcaster may leech the life from the earth itself and all who stand on it.

All living models within the Lich's control area suffer a POW 5 damage roll which cannot be boosted. As well, Asphyxious regains all of his focus points. Consuming Blight cannot be used while casting a spell.

SPECIAL RULES

ASPHYXIOUS

•Soul Cages—Gain a Soul Token for every living model destroyed within 2". Next control phase, replace each soul token with a focus point.

•Terror—Enemy model/units within melee range must pass a command check or flee.

•Undead—Asphyxious is not a living model and never flees.

SOUL SPLITTER

•Reach—2" melee range

•Sustained Attack—Once Asphyxious hits a target with Soul Splitter, additional attacks with it against the same target this turn automatically hit. No additional attack rolls are necessary.

Spells	Cost	RNG	AOE	POW	UP	OFF
BREATH OF CORRUPTION	3	8	3	12	✓	✓
All models in AOE suffer POW 12 damage roll. Corruption is a cloud effect that stays on table as long as Upkeep is paid, and all models moving into or ending their turn in the cloud suffer one point of automatic damage.						
HELLFIRE	3	10	–	14		✓
Target model/unit hit by Hellfire must pass a command check or flee.						
IRON BLIGHT	2	8	–	Spec		✓
Target Warjack takes d6 damage points to its Hull only, in a random location.						
PARASITE	3	8	–	–	✓	✓
Target model/unit suffers -3 ARM, Asphyxious gains +1 ARM. Asphyxious regains one damage point every Upkeep.						
SCYTHING TOUCH	2	6	–	–	✓	
Target model/unit gains +2 STR.						
SHADOW WINGS	3	Caster	–	–		
Asphyxious moves up to 10", ignoring free strikes and terrain penalties and effects, then ends his activation.						
SPECTRAL LEECH	3+	8	–	–		✓
Target Warcaster loses 1 focus point on next turn, plus one for every additional focus point Asphyxious spends when casting this spell.						

WARCASTER-PIRATE QUEEN, SKARRE

"Orgoth works depict horned women assaulting their coastal towns, but we are no more enlightened than they were. Who are these devils that drink blood and tear our men to shreds?"

—Deidra Roanov, Khadoran Winter Guard Kapitan

The horned warrior-women of the lost island Satyx have been part of the Cryxian Empire for centuries untold, having sprung forth from their warrens and glens twisted and changed from years of living in Toruk's blighted shadow. The Satyxis boast a long bloodline of capable swordswomen and vicious combatants. Dragonblight runs thick in their veins, and magic comes to them easily. Many among them have risen through the pirate fleets' ranks, and some captain great black galleons of their own. Captaining one of these dark and deadly barkentines, the gifted "reaver witch," Skarre Ravenmane, has dared to dub herself the "Pirate Queen."

Skarre combines awesome fighting skills with a profound talent for the arcane. Her ship, the *Widower*, seems to sail randomly, routinely disgorging her forces without warning. She strikes and withdraws with equal speed, leaving behind ruin and confusion, and never staking a single claim for her dark lord. Like her sisters, she wields terrible weapons blighted by years of contact with the dragon's minions. Her magic is different in subtle ways from that of her peers; a powerful reminder that long ago even the Orgoth feared the reaver witches. Unlike the necromancers that share her allegiance, her spells follow the dark druidic path of her forebearers—acidic, bloody rain, flesh-consuming swarms, and pillars of flame crackle from Skarre's fingertips.

Like the black druids of ancient times, sacrifice is a powerful component of dark magic. Skarre carries with her a millennia-old ritual dagger that she uses to drain her comrades' energies, willingly or not, to fuel its enchantments. Dark with blood or ichor and pulsing with stolen essence, the blade unleashes a powerful curse upon Skarre's foes. She is swift to cast and swift to act, her dagger often wracking her victim's with gut-wrenching pain, leaving behind twisted, broken corpses.

Unlike the brutal barbed chains of her sisters, Skarre's other weapon is called Takkaryx—loosely translated as "Death Merchant." It is a black-bladed sword, carved from one of Toruk's scales and tempered in a forge of necrotite. The blade is fueled by her malice, and though wielding it drains her, the glee with which she dispatches her victims does much to replenish what strength the sword demands.

Skarre owes a great deal to the dark Dragonlord for her role as the highest Satyxis Witch in the Cryxian fleet. His presence created the Satyxis, and Skarre herself dedicates her powerful sorcery to his unholy faith. She reads portents and auguries in every kill, and claims that the dragon speaks to her through her victims. Through these signs, she steers *Widower* to her private ports of call, trading in blood and selling depravity in bushels. Many women cling tightly to their husbands when the fog thickens along the Broken Coast, for the dreaded Pirate Queen may well be hiding within.

Feat: BLOOD MAGIC

As the dark Queen of the Broken Coast, Skarre is naturally one of the greatest practitioners of the ancient, island born black magic. By sacrificing her own blood, she imbues her followers with dark power, enhancing their own abilities.

Give Skarre 1-5 points of damage. For each point of damage point she takes, all friendly models in her control area gain +1 STR and +1 ARM for one round.

FOCUS	6	CMD	8		
SPD	STR	MAT	RAT	DEF	ARM
7	6	7	4	16	15

TAKKARYX	Special	POW	P+S
	Life Trader	7	13
BLOODWYRM	**Special**	**POW**	**P+S**
	Multi	3	9
GREAT RACK	**Special**	**POW**	**P+S**
	Knockdown	4	10

Damage	16
Point Cost	66
Field Allowance	C
Victory Points	5

Base Size: Small

SPECIAL RULES

TAKKARYX (DEATH MERCHANT)

• Life Trader—On a hit, give Skarre one damage point to add an additional die to Takkaryx's damage roll.

BLOODWYRM

• Life Drinker—Skarre regains one damage point each time she removes a living enemy model from play with Bloodwyrm.

• Sacrificial Strike(★Action)—Remove a friendly warrior model within 1" of Skarre from play. A target model within Skarre's control area then takes a damage roll with POW equal to the ARM of the model sacrificed. This damage roll may be boosted.

GREAT RACK

• Knockdown—On a hit, target model is knocked down.

Spells	Cost	RNG	AOE	POW	UP	OFF
BACKLASH	3	8	–	–	✓	✓
Whenever the target warjack is damaged, its controlling warcaster takes a point of damage.						
BLOOD RAIN	3	8	3	12		✓
All models in the AOE suffer Corrosion.						
DARK GUIDANCE	5	Caster	CTRL	–		
All friendly models within Skarre's control area add an additional die to all melee attack rolls for one round.						
FLY'S KISS	2	8	–	10		✓
Target living model destroyed by Fly's Kiss explodes in a 3" AOE. All models in the area take POW 10 damage.						
HELLFIRE	3	10	–	14		✓
Target model/unit hit by Hellfire must pass a command check or flee.						
SACRIFICIAL LAMB	2	6	–	–		
Remove a target friendly warrior model from play. Skarre gains d6 additional focus during her next control phase. This spell can only be cast once per turn.						

WARCASTER-WARWITCH, DENEGHRA

"It, no…she…she was like a dark dream, a grymkin tale made flesh. One minute a shadowy speck, and when I blinked…there she was…there…next to me…whispering and screaming and commanding… asking and wanting…caressing…loving…."

—Captain Berle Winwort, awaiting execution for high treason

The Cryxian war witches are harbingers of Lord Toruk's rule, each a small piece of the dark Dragonlord himself. Cruel beyond comparison, they commit any and all acts in their lord's name. Their necromantic prowess is second only to the terrible Lich Lords. Indeed, the witches have been so warped by Toruk's influence that some suspect they've been drained of all humanity.

Yet Deneghra would have raised no such doubts in her youth. She and her twin—both beautiful—began life in a small fishing village on the coast of King Leto's kingdom. Simple folk, her parents knew nothing of their daughters' untapped magical potential. Lord Toruk, however, did know, and sent raiders to retrieve them for his dark uses. The pirates, made reckless by their own bloodlust, left the town in ruins after finding but one of the girls.

When they returned to Scharde with their lone captive, Toruk punished their incompetence by having the entire raiding party drawn, quartered, and staked out for the gulls. Their deaths took almost two days and all the while thralls held fast their frightened prize and forced the little girl to watch the bloody ordeal. An evil alchemy was at work here, powered by the torturers' grisly work. Slowly, the girl's wailing subsided. Well into the second day, a faint smile touched her lips, and then broadened as—glazed eyes unblinking—she leaned forward and took in the horrors before her. The girl began to clap delightedly each time a raider died. Toruk's goal had been somewhat achieved.

In the following two decades, the Liches reshaped the maturing young woman's body, mind, and soul into the phantasmal temptress called Deneghra. In time, she so excelled at the arcane arts that most Cryxians bowed to her unbidden—even the terrifying Helljacks bowed to her will. When Lord Toruk judged her ready, he whispered seductively about the debt she owed him for saving her from a weak and mortal life, and unveiled her darkest secret: she had a twin sister who possessed the other half of her powers. The Dragonlord spoke of a Cygnaran sorceress who, while sharing a womb with Deneghra, had stolen part of her inherent power. Deneghra raged. Ranted. Slaughtered a dozen slaves with her bare hands just to clear her head, but could not banish the image of this pathetic twin—identical yet opposite—with power that should have been hers. Still gore-splattered from her murderous rampage, arcane energies dancing around her wicked witch-barbs, Deneghra petitioned Toruk for an army of her own to strike at Cygnar. Pleased with the precision of his machinations, Toruk granted her request. Deneghra embarked with murder in her heart.

WARCASTER-WARWITCH, DENEGHRA

Since launching her dark crusade, Deneghra has scorched a path of devastation. On the battlefield she is a beautiful terror, single-mindedly stalking each victim as if the battle raging around her would not dare cause her harm. Perversely angelic in her wicked beauty, Deneghra drifts along like a phantom, passing through tree, wall, and rock whenever she wills it. She need but whisper and men claw at their skulls in vain pursuit of silence. Yet those same wretches who fall prey to such sweet torture are fully under her spell and would slit a familiar throat—be they comrade, brother, or beloved wife—at her command. Those few who succeed in staving off her seductions become reluctant partners in Deneghra's waltz of blades. She twirls, leaps, glides, and shakes with mocking laughter while enemy soldiers weep as their blades slash air or strike harmlessly off her bladed armor. Once she tires of her playthings, she ends the game with a single sweep of her ancient spear, Sliver. In Deneghra's hand this weapon turns her foe's own shadow against him, entwining her opponent in a writhing mass of black, reptilian coils, and death, rather than being a release, traps her victim's soul in the Cryxian soul cages dangling from her belt.

Some scream in horror at her approach, others beg her for salvation from their asylum cells, but Deneghra yearns for one sound alone—the throttled gurgle of her sister's death rattle. That, and that alone, would be the sweet music of victory to her black soul.

Feat: THE WITHERING

Darkness and death obey the beck and call of the Warwitch. With mere spoken words and an arcane gesture, Deneghra blankets an area with a web of debilitating despair.

All enemy models within Deneghra's control area suffer-2 to all their stats for one round. Affected models cannot run, charge, or make special attacks or power attacks.

FOCUS	7	CMD	8		
SPD	STR	MAT	RAT	DEF	ARM
7	5	5	4	16	14

SLIVER	Special	POW	P+S
	Multi	7	12

Damage	16
Point Cost	76
Field Allowance	C
Victory Points	5
Base Size: Small	

SPECIAL RULES

DENEGHRA

•Soul Cages—Gain a Soul Token for every living model destroyed within 2". Next control phase, replace each soul token with a focus point.

•Stealth—All attacks against Deneghra from greater than 5" away automatically miss. If Denegrha is greater than 5" away from an attacker, she does not block line of sight or count as an intervening model.

•Witch Barbs—Prevents free strikes and negates backstrike bonus against Deneghra.

SLIVER

•Reach—2" melee range

•Shadow Bind—Model hit suffers -3 DEF and canot move, other that to change facing, for one round. A previously bound model is released when a new target is hit.

Spells	Cost	RNG	AOE	POW	UP	OFF
CRIPPLING GRASP	3	8	–	–	✓	✓
Target model/unit suffers -2 to SPD, STR, DEF, and ARM. May not run, charge, slam or make special attacks.						
DARK SEDUCTION	4	6	–	–	✓	✓
Target living model/unit must make a command check. If failed, you take control of the target. Pay Upkeep of one focus point per model, or spell expires. Cannot be cast on Characters or Solos.						
DEATH RAGE	4	6	–	–	✓	
Target Warrior model remains in play for one round after being destroyed.						
GHOST WALK	3	6	–	–		
This turn, target model/unit may move through any terrain, obstacles, or obstructions without penalty. While Ghost Walking, a model cannot charge or slam and ignores free strikes.						
PARASITE	3	8	–	–	✓	✓
Target model/unit suffers -3 ARM, Deneghra gains +1 ARM. Deneghra regains one damage point every Upkeep.						
SCOURGE	4	8	3	13		✓
All models hit by Scourge are knocked down.						
VENOM	2	SP	–	10		✓
A stream of venomous acid spews forth, causing Corrosion to every model hit.						

UNIT–BANE THRALL

"Our scout's torch and lantern went black, and we heard him scream. A moment later, a horrible chill washed over us. We could feel them before we could see them...."

—Tyrell Forlaine, traveling merchant

LIEUTENANT				CMD	8
SPD	STR	MAT	RAT	DEF	ARM
5	7	7	4	12	15
WAR AXE					
	Special			POW	P+S
	–			4	11
Base Size: Small					

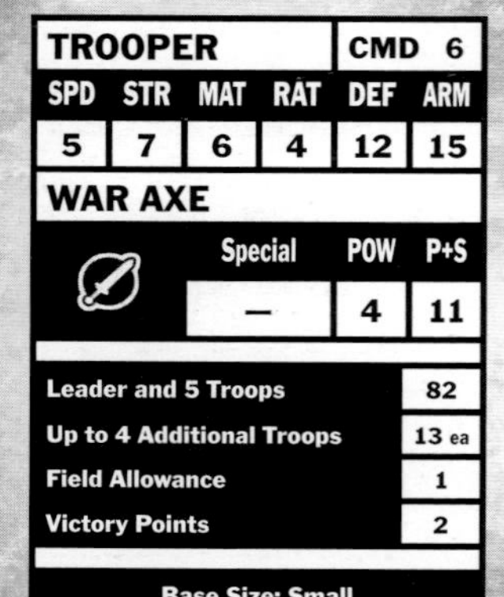

TROOPER				CMD	6
SPD	STR	MAT	RAT	DEF	ARM
5	7	6	4	12	15
WAR AXE					
	Special			POW	P+S
	–			4	11
Leader and 5 Troops					82
Up to 4 Additional Troops					13 ea
Field Allowance					1
Victory Points					2
Base Size: Small					

SPECIAL RULES

LIEUTENANT

- Leader

UNIT

- Dark Shroud
- Stealth
- Undead
- Weapon Master

Bane thralls—undead warriors decorated with countless runes and sigils of their dark rebirth—possess great influence among the ranks of the undying. They often receive the best arms and armor a from whatever battlefield marks their rebirth. Bane thralls are wickedly proficient, and host to a darkness that not only permeates their being, but seeps into the world of the living. So saturated with the cold, dark magic that raised them, they can no longer contain the evil sorcery within. This macabre seepage creates a shroud of mist and fog that emanates from each bane thrall, reaching out with freezing tendrils to caress and choke the living. This dark shroud makes the thralls difficult to discern, hazing their image in daylight, and at night snuffing out most light sources. Bane Thralls thrive on close combat, enjoying greatly the act of cutting down a foe confounded by the shroud they exude.

Tales exist of dark monsters clad in black armor that roam the world. Normally, some goodly hero bests these monsters just as the sun creeps over the horizon, extinguishing their darkness forever. Unfortunately for the folk of Immoren, not all monsters know of these stories, and even if they did, would be less than willing to play their part. The reality is, some darkness never goes away, no matter what the stories might say, and the bane thrall is a testament to such things.

BANE THRALL SPECIAL RULES

LIEUTENANT

- Leader

UNIT

- Dark Shroud—Enemy models within melee range of a Bane Thrall suffer -2 ARM.
- Stealth—All attacks against a Bane Thrall from greater than 5" away automatically miss. A Bane Thrall greater than 5" away from an attacker does not block line of sight or count as an intervening model.
- Undead—A Bane Thrall is not a living model and never flees.
- Weapon Master—A Bane Thrall adds an additional die to its melee damage rolls.

UNIT–BILE THRALL

"Being dead has its advantages. Take the bile thrall, who exploit the senses. Aye, the living call them wretched, but are they not the ones that wretch?"

—Asphyxious, the Iron Lich

The vile nature of the Cryx knows no bounds. Some of the risen dead that the minions of Lord Toruk drag from their graves arise too damaged for normal battlefield use. Some simply lack the strength or skill to be warriors. A few of these unlucky cadavers find new purpose under the knife of a particularly nasty necrotech engineer. They disgorge from their hellish workshops as bile thralls—undead with huge, bloated bodies gurgling with unspeakable pumps and siphons.

These vile mechanika store and amplify the volume and amount of corrosive digestion and decomposition agents created by the undying corpse. Hoses and tubes lead from their distended mouths and other natural or surgically opened orifices, to a firing mechanism similar to the Defiler 'jack's acid cannon. With a lurching spasm accompanied by a deep rumbling gurgle, each bile thrall can force disgusting amounts of their stored fluids out of the nozzle. If a bile thrall faced with multiple targets forces too great a volume of fluid through the hoses, the cannon overloads and the system sometimes breaks down. The black mechanika inside of them gives out, and in a grisly shower of fluid, flesh, and metal the bile thrall ruptures like a blister in a massive purge of over-pressurized intestines. Anything given a good splashing by the exploding bile thrall quickly succumbs to the potent dissolving agents, either melting away to slag or eaten into a bloody unrecognizable mass.

Teams of bile thralls sluggishly waddle across the battlefield, their internal mechanisms sloshing and throbbing, a team of fleshy balloons filled with acidic death. The bile thralls serve as much to attack the enemy's morale as to destroy its troops with their overly disgusting attacks. Little wonder that opposing forces often give them a wide berth. Those who have seen bile thralls in action have been known to go days without eating, and most who can stomach going toe-to-toe with them never forget their putrid stink.

BILE THRALL SPECIAL RULES

LIEUTENANT

•Leader

UNIT

•Undead—A Bile Thrall is not a living models and never flees.

BILE CANNON

•Corrosion—Any model hit by the Bile Cannon suffers Corrosion, a continuous effect that slowly erodes its target. Corrosion does one point of damage each turn during the model's maintenance phase until it expires on a d6 roll 1 or 2. Corrosion is not affected by water.

•Purge (★Attack)—The Bile Thrall sprays out the entire contents of its guts, deflating and automatically hitting all models within 8" of the Bile Thrall's front arc, unless line of sight is blocked by an obstruction. All models hit take a POW 12 damage roll and suffer Corrosion, then remove the Bile Thrall from play.

LIEUTENANT				CMD	7
SPD	STR	MAT	RAT	DEF	ARM
5	4	2	4	11	13
BILE CANNON					
		RNG	ROF	AOE	POW
		SP	1	—	12
Base Size: Small					

TROOPER				CMD	5
SPD	STR	MAT	RAT	DEF	ARM
5	4	2	3	11	13
BILE CANNON					
		RNG	ROF	AOE	POW
		SP	1	—	12
Leader and 5 Troops					41
Up to 4 Additional Troops					6 ea
Field Allowance					3
Victory Points					2
Base Size: Small					

SPECIAL RULES

LIEUTENANT
•Leader

UNIT
•Undead

BILE CANNON
•Corrosion
•Purge (★Attack)

UNIT–MECHANITHRALL

"At the rate we keep killing each other, the Dragon will never want for new recruits..."

—King Leto Raelthorne, at peace talks in Five Fingers

LIEUTENANT				CMD	6
SPD	STR	MAT	RAT	DEF	ARM
6	7	6	4	12	12

STEAM-FIST	Special	POW	P+S
	Combo	4	11

STEAM-FIST	Special	POW	P+S
	Combo	4	11

Base Size: Small

TROOPER				CMD	4
SPD	STR	MAT	RAT	DEF	ARM
6	7	5	4	12	12

STEAM-FIST	Special	POW	P+S
	Combo	4	11

STEAM-FIST	Special	POW	P+S
	Combo	4	11

Leader and 5 Troops	39
Up to 4 Additional Troops	6 ea
Field Allowance	3
Victory Points	2

Base Size: Small

SPECIAL RULES

LIEUTENANT
•Leader

UNIT
•Undead

STEAM-FIST
•Combo Strike (★Attack)

The staple soldier of the Cryxian Empire is the thrall. They comprise much of the workforce, some designed specifically for labor, others for combat. The Lich Lords have seen such success with their use, it was a given to sooner or later coalesce thralls with necro-mechanika. Hence, the most common mechanika-enhanced Cryxian soldier, the Mechanithrall, a frightful combination of necrotech and undead rebirth. This risen warrior is augmented with two steamwork gauntlets, powered by dark energies coursing through conduits and pipes weaving in and out of their cadaverous bodies. The gauntlets greatly enhance their strength—a buffet from a Mechanithrall is nearly as powerful as the swinging fist of a steamjack.

Being among the undead, Mechanithralls know no fear. They selflessly charge into destruction, climbing over the bodies of their comrades to strike at the enemy. Still, a strange cunning permeates their limited sentience, for they have been known to use cover and ambush points to their advantage, despite no fear of death. Mechanithralls are a favopred tool of the Cryxian warcasters, who are always eager to release packs of these necro-mechanikal terrors upon their foes with but a simple command—"kill them that live, pulverize those who do not!"

MECHANITHRALL SPECIAL RULES

LIEUTENANT

•Leader

UNIT

•Undead—A Mechanithrall is not a living model and never flees.

STEAM-FIST

•Combo Strike (★Attack)—A Mechanithrall has a pair of Steam-Fists that can be used simultaneously for a devastating attack. It can make a normal attack with each fist individually, or it may make a special attack with both Steam-Fists at the same time. Make one attack roll for the Combo Strike. Add the model's STR once and the POW of both fists to its damage roll.

SOLO–NECROTECH & INDEPENDENTS–SCRAP THRALL

"Ye see that? That thing just stuffed two other things into that bigger thing! What in Morrow's name is going on?"

—Victor Terrell, Cygnaran long gunner

Part necromancer, part mechanik, part evil genius, spiced with a dash of deranged lunatic—this is what comprises Lord Toruk's necrotechs. While the Lich Lords often spawn many of the nightmares that stalk Cryx, the task of making these perversities walk, slither, or crawl falls to the capable necrotechs. These sadistic engineers are not against self-experimentation, and are rarely less modified with necro-mechanikal augmentation than the thralls and 'jacks they father. Far less than human, necro-techs see the world through evil-tinted goggles, and they renounced the "ways of meat" long ago.

When not designing or assembling the next wave of horrors, necrotechs skitter into battle with their "pretty little children," in search of how to better their creations by witnessing them at work. No idle observers, however, they alone wield the skills to repair their infernal constructs. Even the highly altered techs find it difficult to haul hundreds of pounds of raw material into battle, so they do what they can with what fate and carnage provides. Like the necromancers who raise thralls from fallen meat, necrotechs drag shambling "scrap thralls" from the heaps of metal and bone.

Yet dubbing the necrotechs' hasty creations thralls is a misnomer. Scrap thralls are little more than spare parts of a fallen 'jack slapped together and animated as a shambling delivery vehicle for necrotite-powered bombs. These ramshackle undead are just as likely to detonate when a wayward bullet or arrow strikes them as when they accomplish their last embrace—for their only real goal is to clutch an opponent long enough for the bomb to explode in a shower of bone, metal, and flesh.

NECROTECH & SCRAP THRALL SPECIAL RULES

NECROTECH

- Create Scrap Thrall [8] (★Action)—Necrotech must be in base to base contact with a disabled or totaled wreck marker. With a successful skill check, d3 Scrap Thralls are created from a light warjack wreck or d6 from a heavy Warjack wreck. Remove the wreck marker from play and place the scrap thralls within 3" of their creator. The scrap thralls may not activate this turn. The number of Thrall that can be created is not limited by Field Allowance.
- Undead—A Necrotech is not a living model and never flees.

VISE CLAW (NECROTECH ONLY)

- Immobilize—If the Vise Claw hits, it can either do damage as normal or Immobilize its target without damaging it. An immobilized model may activate normally, but it suffers -3 DEF and cannot move until it is released or its attacker is destroyed. The immobilized model is released if the Necrotech moves or makes another attack with this weapon.
- Reach—2" melee range

SCRAP THRALL

- Independent Model—This model is not part of a unit and cannot run or charge. An army must include a Necrotech at the beginning of the game to field Scrap Thralls.
- Thrall Bomb—If the Scrap Thrall is destroyed or removed from play in any way, it immediately causes a 4" AOE blast. All models caught within the blast take a POW 8 damage roll. Scrap Thrall is destroyed after detonation.
- Death Burst(★Action)—Building up tremendous steam pressure, the Scrap Thrall doubles its SPD to rush an opponent. If the Scrap Thrall makes a succesful melee attack, instead of doing melee damage, the Scrap Thrall grabs the target, hanging on as it detonates. The grabbed target takes a direct hit POW 16 damage roll while all other models caught in the 4" AOE take a POW 8 blast damage roll. The scrap thrall detonates at the end of its activation whether it has hit a target or not.
- Undead—A Scrap Thrall is not a living model and never flees.

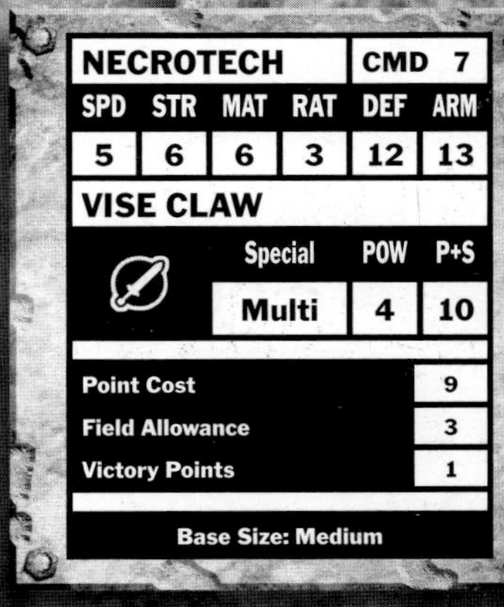

NECROTECH				CMD	7
SPD	STR	MAT	RAT	DEF	ARM
5	6	6	3	12	13

VISE CLAW	Special	POW	P+S
	Multi	4	10

Point Cost	9
Field Allowance	3
Victory Points	1

Base Size: Medium

SCRAP THRALL				CMD	1
SPD	STR	MAT	RAT	DEF	ARM
5	4	5	3	11	12

MECHANO-CLAWS	Special	POW	P+S
	–	4	8

Point Cost	5
Field Allowance	10
Victory Points	0

Base Size: Small

SPECIAL RULES

NECROTECH
- Create Scrap Thrall [8] (★Action)
- Undead

VISE CLAW
- Immobilize
- Reach

SCRAP THRALL
- Independent Model
- Thrall Bomb
- Death Burst (★Action)
- Undead

UNIT–SATYXIS RAIDERS

"As beautiful as the bloom on the Iosan tiger vine, and just as deadly. Steer clear, lads, no matter what yer loins tell ye. There's only death ta be found 'tween those thighs."

—Captain Halford Bray of the *Palaxis*, to his crew after seeing a Satyxis raider on board a passing Cryxian vessel

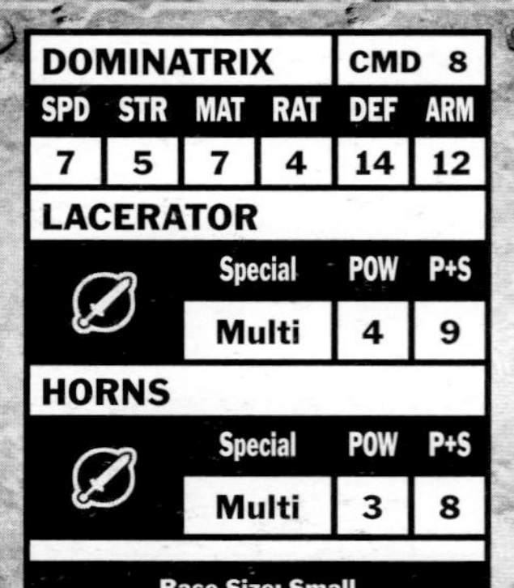

DOMINATRIX				CMD	8
SPD	STR	MAT	RAT	DEF	ARM
7	5	7	4	14	12
LACERATOR					
	Special	POW	P+S		
	Multi	4	9		
HORNS					
	Special	POW	P+S		
	Multi	3	8		
Base Size: Small					

TROOPER				CMD	6
SPD	STR	MAT	RAT	DEF	ARM
7	5	6	4	14	12
LACERATOR					
	Special	POW	P+S		
	Multi	4	9		
HORNS					
	Special	POW	P+S		
	Multi	3	8		
Leader and 5 Troops					64
Up to 4 Additional Troops					10 ea
Field Allowance					2
Victory Points					2
Base Size: Small					

SPECIAL RULES

DOMINATRIX
- Leader

UNIT
- Combined Melee Attack

LACERATOR
- Critical Knockdown
- Feedback
- Reach

HORNS
- Critical Knockdown (small-based models only)
- No Combined Melee Attack

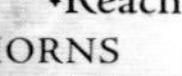

The island of Satyx is a lost, legendary place to the sailors of Immoren. The only evidence of its existence are savage women called Satyxis. These cruel females came unto the waters of The Broken Coast with a will to enslave and kill. When they arrived upon the shores of Cryx, they were surprised to find that a dragon ruled the isle. Rather than wreak havoc, they decided to make this their new home, and before long had allied themselves with the forces of the Cryxian Empire as Toruk's "dark daughters."

Like everything else, they were not immune to the Dragonfather's blight. Over time, they changed, becoming more—or some might say—less than human. Their eyes darkened, their lips became pale, and long horns of twisted bone sprouted from their heads. They found these horns beautiful and took to adorning them with jewelry or tokens to their draconic god. Their personas and movements became more bestial, as they took to crouching, perching, and leaping. But their beauty remained, in some dark and twisted fashion, exuding an aura that draws men's lust. Mythically beautiful, males of every race fall prey to the Satyxis. Their appetite for man-flesh is insatiable.

In combat, a Satyxis raider's womanly frame belies her inhuman strength. She is an efficient killer with a pack mentality. One or two of them charge, using their horns to deliver a blow to knock their victim prone, then the others circle the downed prey and use their chain scourges to hook flesh, each one tearing and pulling from different directions. It is a gruesome fate. They also employ this technique against warmachines, if need be, and are known to use their chains to topple a warjack.

Chain whips are their favored weapons, made from links of black steel, etched with sigils, and topped with vicious hooks. They also favor melee weapons over ranged weapons, preferring to get personal and intimate with their adversaries. In combat, Satyxis stick together in packs, even when alongside other horrors within the Dragonfather's army. Standouts sometimes occupy positions of authority in the pirate fleets, and it is believed a select few have direct access to a Lich Lord or two.

SATYXIS SPECIAL RULES

DOMINATRIX
- Leader

UNIT
- Combined Melee Attack—Instead of making melee attacks seperately, Raiders in melee range of the same target may combine their attacks. The Raider with the highest MAT in the attacking group makes one melee attack roll for the group, adding +1 to the attack and damage rolls for each Raider, including itself, participating in the attack.

HORNS
- Critical Knockdown—On a critical Hit, target model is knocked down. (small-based models only)
- No Combined Attacks—Raiders may not make combined attacks with their horns. Each makes a seperate attack with their horns in addition to other attacks.

LACERATOR
- Critical Knockdown—On a critical Hit, target model is knocked down.
- Feedback—Anytime Lacerator damages a warjack, its controlling warcaster takes a point of damage. Combined attacks only cause 1 point of feedback damage regardless of the number of Raiders combining their attack.
- Reach—2" melee range

SOLO–SKARLOCK

"Witchcraft begets witchcraft."

—Scrutator Severius, upon the condemnation of a cult of Thamar

Even Cryx's powerful necromancers sometimes require assistance. Not just anyone or anything can be useful to the dark magicians on the field of battle. Some of these proficient warcasters have tapped into a new resource—skarlock thralls.

Skarlocks are rare, created only by the most proficient necromancers. Each is quite unique, and many skarlocks have extensive personalities and agendas of their own—sometimes apart from those for which they were raised. Each one is blackened by the dark sigils of its creation, and only small bits of exposed bone actually show between the numerous sigils. The sheer amount of necromantic power used in a skarlock's creation fuses the new thrall with its own sorcerous abilities. While they have little knowledge of spellcraft on their own, they learn rapidly from their masters.

The skarlock has been endowed with the ability to cast a few of its warcaster's spells and can tap into the very magics used in its creation to unleash spells themselves. Any spell a skarlock throws directly mimics that which its master can manifest—making for a spectacular one-two arcane punch. Skarlocks must stay within close proximity to the warcaster, however, in order to maintain this magic channeling link.

The minions of the Dragonlord ever devise new and improved ways to snatch victory after victory from his foes, and with the power of so many channeling 'jacks, and the added benefit of the skarlock thralls, the Cryxian warcasters are truly a relentless force. Mainlanders, be afraid.

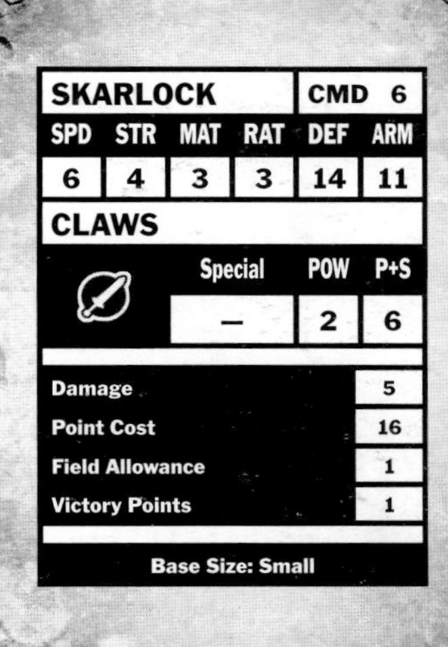

SKARLOCK				CMD	6
SPD	STR	MAT	RAT	DEF	ARM
6	4	3	3	14	11
CLAWS					
		Special		POW	P+S
		–		2	6
Damage					5
Point Cost					16
Field Allowance					1
Victory Points					1
Base Size: Small					

SKARLOCK SPECIAL RULES

•Bound—Each Skarlock Thrall is bound to a single warcaster. The warcaster is considered to control the Skarlock Thrall.

•Soul Cages—Gain a Soul Token for every living model destroyed within 2". During the warcaster's next control phase, remove the Skarlock's soul tokens. If the Skarlock Thrall is within 2" of its controlling warcaster, give the warcaster a focus point for each soul.

•Spell Slave (★Action)—A Skarlock Thrall may cast one of its controlling warcaster's spells with a focus cost of 3 or less without spending any focus points. The Skarlock uses the FOC stat of its controlling warcaster to resolve all effects of the spell including attack rolls. Rolls may not be boosted since the Skarlock has no focus. The Skarlock cannot channel spells or cast spells with a range of 'caster'. Warcaster may allocate focus points to upkeep spells cast by the Skarlock and all spells cast by the Skarlock are considered to have been cast by the warcaster. The Skarlock Thrall cannot act as a Spell Vessel if it moves outside of its warcaster's control area or if that caster is removed from play.

•Undead—ASkarlock is not a living model and never flees.

SPECIAL RULES

SKARLOCK
•Bound
•Soul Cages
•Spell Slave
•Undead

BONEJACK–DEATHRIPPER

"'Tis something primal in us that fears the jaws of untamed beasts. The necromancers capitalize on that with their Deathrippers."

—Professor Viktor Pendrake, Royal Cygnaran University

SPD	STR	MAT	RAT	DEF	ARM
7	7	5	4	15	14

	MANDIBLE		
	Special	POW	P+S
HEAD	Sustained	5	12

DAMAGE GRID	1	2	3	4	5	6
Head (H)			☐	☐		
Cortex (C)	☐	☐	☐	☐	☐	☐
Movement (M)	H	H	C	A	A	M
Arc Node (A)	H	C	C	M	M	M

Point Cost	38
Field Allowance	U
Victory Points	1

Base Size: Medium

SPECIAL RULES

ARC NODE

MANDIBLE
•Sustained Attack

The Deathripper. Cryx's quintessential bonejack. It is the staple of the Lich Lords' forces, and often the herald for large forces. These 'jacks scurry across the battlefield with surprising speed, vents wailing. The high-pitched keen of the Deathripper has been written about in fevered war journals for quite some time, and if many of them are active at once, this fearsome sound becomes the harbinger of the Cryx's approach. It is a sound rarely forgotten.

The Deathripper is the most basic of all Cryx's constructs. It is built mostly from the bones of fallen beasts and arranged to encase a soul furnace that glows bright green. It is light and fast, and often travel in packs. With little armor to protect it as it darts and streaks across the field, Deathrippers are the most disposable 'jacks, easily replaced between conflicts.

It has the simplest of weapons: its powerful jaws. Their mandibles are tipped with alchemically hardened steel, and are known to cleanly rip chunks of metal or flesh from their victims with frightening speed. Within mere minutes, in a blur of billowing smoke, wailing metal, and bleeding hydraulics, a few Deathrippers can strip a light warjack down to its components.

But frenzied attacks are not their only tricks. The ancient masters of necromancy, have mastered the art of creating arc nodes for channeling spells through these 'jacks. Each Deathripper remains in constant contact with the mind of its controlling warcaster. This connection is mutual, allowing the warcasters a further release point for their destructive spells. The Deathripper is as likely to unleash a wave of arcane doom as it is to leap into the attack with jaws gaping. Little wonder that so many in the kingdoms quake before its telltale scream and terrible hunger.

DEATHRIPPER SPECIAL RULES

ARC NODE

The Deathripper may channel spells.

MANDIBLE

•Sustained Attack—Once the Deathripper hits a target with the Mandible, additional attacks with it against the same target this turn will automatically hit. No additional attack rolls are necessary.

Height /Weight	6'4" / 2.5 tons
Armament	Mandibles (head), Necrotech Arc Node
Fuel Load/Burn Usage	20 Kgs (necrotite) or 40 Kgs (coal)/18 hrs general, 3 hr combat
Initial Service Date	UNKNOWN, first seen in 502 AR
Cortex Manufacturer	UNKNOWN
Orig. Chassis Design	UNKNOWN, credited to be the first true Necrotech constructs

BONEJACK–DEFILER

"'Tis a shame they are so effective…they leave so little for us to use."
—War Witch Deneghra, commenting on the Defiler's sludge cannon

One variation of the common bonejack is the Defiler. It serves as the Cryxian light assault bonejack. Fast and mobile, it can cross the battlefield in a few long strides and fix its controller's chosen target in its sights before the fight has scarcely begun.

The Defiler avoids close combat altogether, and instead hoses down the enemy with the wide nozzle of its sludge cannon. This device sprays acidic bursts with great precision, pumping out a thick, viscous corrosive that eats through metal and stone as easily as flame consumes wood. Mundane mechanik experts have yet to discover where the Defiler stores this acid, as it seems impossible to house the sheer volume of the stuff that each bonejack vomits forth.

Like all bonejack variants, the Defiler is equipped with a necro-tech arc node. Some engineers and dark theorists believe that the arc node itself somehow channels the ammunition in from some netherworldly region, and that it is only a matter of time before the Cryx can channel entire armies of the undying through these specially crafted arc nodes. Whatever the source of its ammunition, the Defiler is a horribly efficient machine capable of getting behind enemy lines quickly and delivering terrible acids spewed from its mouth or sorcerous destruction from its arc node.

DEFILER SPECIAL RULES

ARC NODE

The Defiler may channel spells.

SLUDGE CANNON

•Corrosion—Any model hit by the Sludge Cannon suffers Corrosion, a continuous effect that slowly erodes its target. Corrosion does one point of damage each turn during the model's maintenance phase until it expires on a d6 roll of 1 or 2. Corrosion is not affected by water.

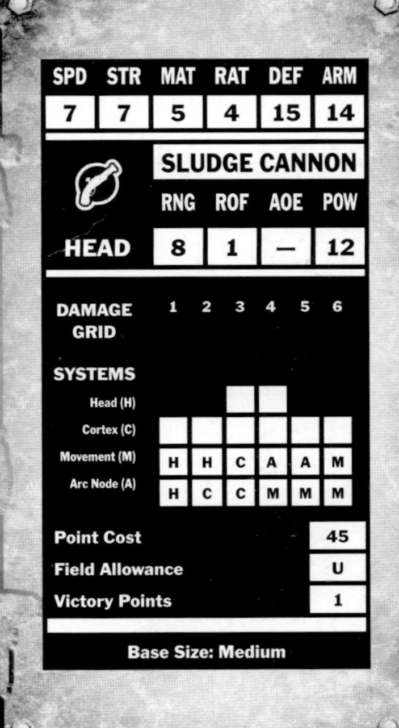

SPD	STR	MAT	RAT	DEF	ARM
7	7	5	4	15	14

	SLUDGE CANNON			
	RNG	ROF	AOE	POW
HEAD	8	1	–	12

DAMAGE GRID	1	2	3	4	5	6
SYSTEMS						
Head (H)			☐	☐		
Cortex (C)	☐	☐	☐	☐	☐	☐
Movement (M)	H	H	C	A	A	M
Arc Node (A)	H	C	C	M	M	M

Point Cost	45
Field Allowance	U
Victory Points	1

Base Size: Medium

SPECIAL RULES

ARC NODE

SLUDGE CANNON
•Corrosion

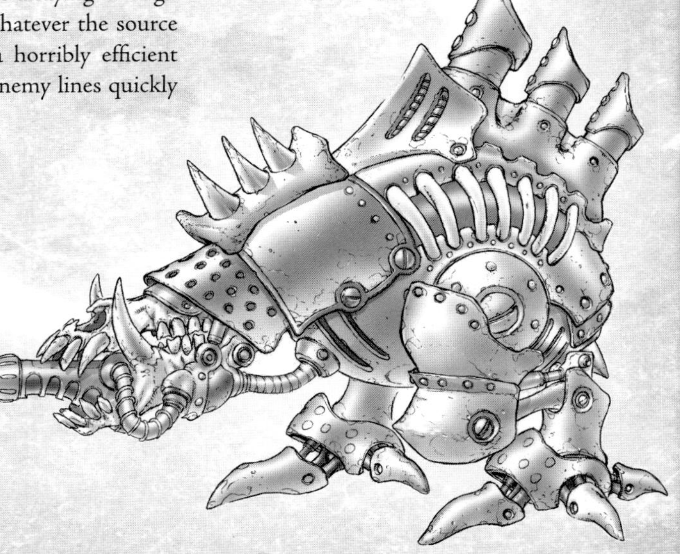

Height /Weight	6'4" / 2.6 tons
Armament	Sludge Cannon (head), Necro-tech Arc Node
Fuel Load/Burn Usage	20 Kgs (necrotite) or 40 Kgs (coal)/ 17 hrs general, 2.75 hrs combat
Initial Service Date	UNKNOWN, first seen in 512 AR
Cortex Manufacturer	UNKNOWN
Orig. Chassis Design	UNKNOWN

BONEJACK–NIGHTWRETCH

"I wish I could say I'm happy to see them using something that doesn't burn, dissolve, or chew on us…but I'm not."

—Captain Aleksandr Radu, Skrovenberg militia

SPD	STR	MAT	RAT	DEF	ARM
7	7	5	4	15	14

DOOMSPITTER	RNG	ROF	AOE	POW
HEAD	6	1	3	14

DAMAGE GRID	1	2	3	4	5	6
Head (H)			☐	☐		
Cortex (C)	☐	☐	☐	☐	☐	☐
Movement (M)	H	H	C	A	A	M
Arc Node (A)	H	C	C	M	M	M

Point Cost	44
Field Allowance	U
Victory Points	1

Base Size: Medium

SPECIAL RULES

ARC NODE

Height /Weight	**6'4" / 2.75 tons**
Armament	**Doomspitter Launchers (head)**
Fuel Load/Burn Usage	**20 Kgs (necrotite) or 40 Kgs (coal)/ 17 hrs general, 2.5 hrs combat**
Initial Service Date	**UNKNOWN, first seen in 590 AR**
Cortex Manufacturer	**UNKNOWN**
Orig. Chassis Design	**Cadre of Necro-Techs under instruction by the War-Witch Deneghra**

For centuries, Cygnar has had the undesirable fate of being the testing ground for Cryxian developments. With their proximity to the dark isles and the wide range of open coastline, it is a small matter to beach a craft on a quiet shore and unload a pack of the latest necrotech monstrosities. In favor of Cygnarans however, is an adaptable spirit, and the fact that Cryxian innovations are historically few and far between. They also seldom vary from certain traditional themes; this one with snapping jaws, that one with corrosive spray—the Cygnaran military eventually learned to deal with most of the horrors.

But Cygnar's familiarity with Cryx's arsenal was shattered a few years ago when the necrotechs began thinking more creatively. From New Larkholm came a dispatch that a Cryxian landing party of bonejacks had been sighted two leagues south of the city. The coastal fort of Westwatch, less than 10 leagues away, immediately sent out a division of long gunners. Confident the city could defend itself until their arrival, the long gunners prepared for another routine cleanup.

On their arrival, they found the walls of New Larkholm shattered, as if by cannon fire. Many buildings had been reduced to smoking heaps, and the inhabitants had taken refuge in cellars or fled into the open countryside. A pack of a dozen bonejacks stirred outside the walls, lead by a single, unknown warcaster. The 'jacks charged and the long gunners took position, closing ranks to minimize their flanks—appearing almost like a giant porcupine covered in rifles instead of quills. Deathrippers would never reach them before the guns shredded their skulls, Defilers might get a few spurts off, but Cygnar's long gunners would suffer but a few wounded at worst. As the bonejacks grew nearer, the gunners noted the smooth, unfamiliar, beak-like skull of this unknown warjack, and they were wholly unprepared for what would come next.

The pack split, fanning out, just out of range of the guns—a tactic seen often, and one they had positioned themselves for. Next would come the ploy of darting in and out of range of their sludge cannons, or moving in for close combat—or so they thought. Instead, the bonejacks simultaneously closed their circle. Guns blazed and a few of the 'jacks fell, but as the rifles cycled their next round, the bonejacks suddenly returned fire with a devastating effect. Clusters of small projectile bombs exploded all around the tight groups of long gunners. In seconds, the entire division of gunners had been reduced to a smoldering heap of flesh flayed from bone, and the blood coursed to the metal talons of the bonejacks, which had not moved after their single volley.

Silently, the 'jacks turned and followed their master back to the landing skiff on the rocky beach. Their mission was a success, and the necrotechs would soon begin mass production of the newly tested Nightwretch.

NIGHTWRETCH SPECIAL RULES

ARC NODE

The Nightwretch may channel spells.

HELLJACK–REAPER

"We had a proper defense line, as planned—Ironclads surrounding the Chargers to protect our last channeling 'jack. Then it all went wrong. Two of those things burst up from the beach and opened fire. Before the Ironclads could move, the helljacks reeled in the Chargers like dragonfish on an angler's line. Our defense had been ruined..."

—Commander Coleman Stryker, regarding a rare defeat at Blue Sands

When battling the Iron Kingdoms' metal giants, a Cryxian commander has one goal: get close and rend metal. Although Toruk's generals found various ways to speed their necrotech constructs across the battlefield to accomplish this goal, it was not enough. Challenged to lure smaller targets, the Cryxian pirates assembled the Reaper helljack to bring the cowards to them. The first of these horrible machines blooded its weapons at the next landing, and word of its capabilities spread among the Lich Lords. Soon after, every Cryx commander had a Reaper at his beck and call.

Made originally from the workings of a Slayer, the two models share many similarities in body and internal construction. The faceplate has larger eye ports, the Reaper needing much greater vision and accuracy to make use of its unique weaponry. The Reaper also lacks the powerful deathclaws of its sister chassis, and one entire arm has been replaced by a viciously long mechanika spike. This necromantically-tempered piston of sharpened steel—the helldriver—can punch deep holes in the thickest of iron skins, driving repeatedly into the target like the stinger of an assassin wasp.

The original helldrivers still had a major limitation, that of being less versatile than the Slayer's bladed fists, its rapid strikes make aiming rather difficult unless a target was pinned or immobile. Inspired by the Uldenfrost coast's whalers, the techs installed an augmented harpoon launcher, and added a necrotite-forged barb to its tip. Thus enhanced, the Reaper's harpoon could puncture and grip the toughest of armors. Since warjacks tend to be unwilling dance partners, the chains used to reel the thrashing catches in have been alchemically hardened and strengthened to withstand vast amounts of pull and drag. Even so, truly enormous warjacks such as the Juggernaut or Ironclad, are far too heavy for the Reaper to pull, which makes smaller targets—even living ones—its chosen prey.

Height /Weight	**11'10" / 6.5 tons**
Armament	**Helldriver (right arm), Impaling Harpoon (left arm)**
Fuel Load/Burn Usage	**40 Kgs (necrotite) or 100 Kgs (coal)/ 10 hrs general, 1.5 hrs combat**
Initial Service Date	**UNKNOWN, first seen in 557 AR**
Cortex Manufacturer	**UNKNOWN**
Orig. Chassis Design	**Lich Lords of Lord Toruk**

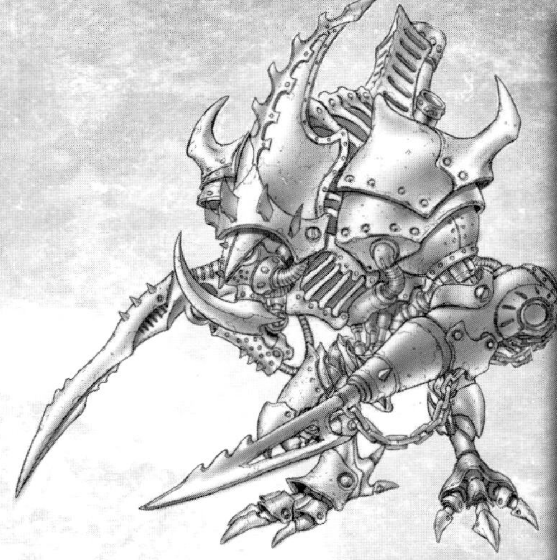

The Reaper is a symbol of the ever-evolving ingenuity of the Dragonlord's servants. It shows that the undying minds of the Lich Lords and their minions are not without craft. Like a stallion trapped in the claws of a Bloodstone scorpion, a Reaper's victim often writhes and wriggles in pain as the helljack gouges mercilessly into them over and over.

REAPER SPECIAL RULES

REAPER

•Tusks—In addition to providing an extra weapon for attacks, the Reaper's Tusks give it POW 2 for Head-butt attacks.

HARPOON

•Drag—If the Harpoon causes damage, its target is reeled into base-to-base contact with the Reaper, stopping short only if it contacts another model or a terrain feature. The Reaper may only drag models with smaller bases than its own. After a successful drag, the Reaper may immediately make one melee attack with any melee weapon. Focus points may be used for additional melee attacks.

HELLDRIVER

•Sustained Attack—Once the Helldriver hits a target, additional attacks with it against the same target this turn will automatically hit. No additional attack rolls are necessary.

SPD	STR	MAT	RAT	DEF	ARM
6	10	6	4	13	17

HARPOON	RNG	ROF	AOE	POW
LEFT	8	1	–	12

HELLDRIVER	Special	POW	P+S
RIGHT	Sustained	6	16

TUSKS	Special	POW	P+S
–	–	2	12

DAMAGE GRID	1	2	3	4	5	6
SYSTEMS						
Left Arm (L)						
Rght Arm (R)		L			R	
Cortex (C)	L	L	M	C	R	R
Movement (M)		M	M	C	C	

Point Cost	113
Field Allowance	U
Victory Points	3

Base Size: Large

SPECIAL RULES

REAPER
•Tusks
HARPOON
•Drag
HELLDRIVER
•Sustained Attack

HELLJACK-SLAYER

"Part a'me wants ta know how dey work, buts da rest a'me tells dat part not ta be so bluddy nutty!"

—Reinholdt, Gobber Speculator and Self-Proclaimed World Traveler

SPD	STR	MAT	RAT	DEF	ARM
6	10	6	4	13	17

	DEATH CLAW		
	Special	POW	P+S
LEFT	Multi	5	15

	DEATH CLAW		
	Special	POW	P+S
RIGHT	Multi	5	15

	TUSKS		
	Special	POW	P+S
—	—	2	12

DAMAGE GRID

SYSTEMS
Left Arm (L)
Rght Arm (R)
Cortex (C)
Movement (M)

1	2	3	4	5	6
	L			R	
L	L	M	C	R	R
	M	M	C	C	

Point Cost	110
Field Allowance	U
Victory Points	3

Base Size: Large

SPECIAL RULES

SLAYER
•Tusks

DEATH CLAWS
•Combo Strike (★Attack)
•Critical Corrosion
•Fist

Massive hulks of metal, magic, and undying soul, the helljacks are necro-mechanikal nightmares that stalk the battlefields in search of prey. Their soulfire furnaces burn hot with savage energy, pushing the mechanika to perform great feats of destruction. The first helljack ever to curse western Immoren with its vile presence, the simple and effective Slayer, exists only to crush and tear the enemy apart with its deathclaws.

The helljack fits well with the more bloodthirsty warcasters, as Cryxian commanders think rarely of tactics when commanding the heavy-handed Slayer. It taps into the remnants of life forces within its necrotite furnace, and the pain and suffering found therein pushes the Slayer to great heights of destruction. The corrosive acids and withering enchantments on its claws rend metal and armor apart, leaving behind wounds that are to metal as infection is to skin. Two long tusks wrenched from some unknown beast adorn the Slayer's armored skull, vicious additions reinforced with sorcery and able to deliver shattering gore attacks.

An eerie green glow pulsates from the Slayer's soulfire furnaces, between the cracks and folds of the helljack's armor, and up through the ever-searching eyes of the iron and bone beast. These two sickly green sockets glow frightfully, a horrid sight that has fathered ancient tales of these emerald orbs. Thus are any greenish lights, like those found floating in the bogs and fens of Immoren, often called "Cryxlight" by superstitious travelers. Stories of these glowing lights leading men to their deaths on the bony claws of Toruk's minions date before the records of human steamjacks, which deepens the mystery of just how long helljacks have emerged from Lord Toruk's black shadow.

SLAYER SPECIAL RULES

SLAYER

•Tusks—In addition to providing an extra weapon for attacks, the Slayers's Tusks give it POW 2 for Head-butt attacks.

DEATH CLAWS

•Combo Strike (★Attack)—The Slayer has a pair of claws that can be used simultaneously for a devastating attack. It can make a normal attack with each claw individually, or it may make a special attack with both Death Claws at the same time. Both claws must be operational to make the Combo Strike. Make one attack roll for the Combo Strike. Add the model's STR once and the POW of both claws to its damage roll.

•Critical Corrosion—On a Critical Hit, target model suffers Corrosion, a continuous effect that slowly erodes its target. Corrosion does one point of damage each turn during the target model's maintenance phase until it expires on a d6 roll of 1 or 2. Corrosion is not affected by water.

•Fist—Both of the Slayer's Death Claws have the abilities of a Warjack fist.

Height /Weight	11'10" / 6.25 tons
Armament	Twin Death Claws (right and left arms), Tusks (head)
Fuel Load/Burn Usage	45 Kgs (necrotite) or 100 Kgs (coal)/ 12 hrs general, 2 hrs combat
Initial Service Date	UNKNOWN, first seen in 531 AR
Cortex Manufacturer	UNKNOWN
Orig. Chassis Design	UNKNOWN

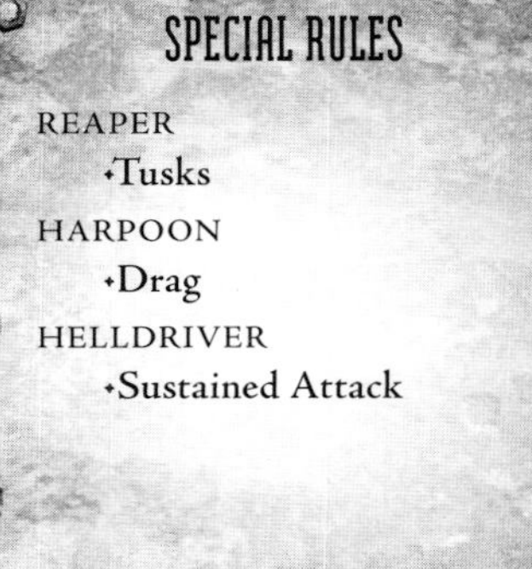

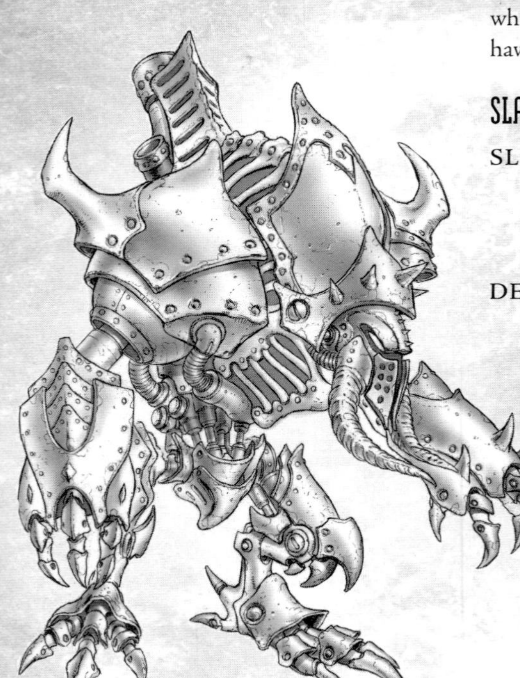

KHADOR

BEARING THE WEIGHT OF THE AGES

A BRIEF HISTORY OF KHADOR

"With all that our people have endured since the Thousand Cities, it is no small wonder we have turned out as strong as we have."

—Queen Ayn Vanar XI

Vendarl the second, Ashtoven, 602 A.R., Chamberlain Fedor Ushkaya speaks to hundreds of Khadoran Winter Guard recruits at their initiation in Korsk before the Queen Ayn Vanar XI:

> Strength! Our oldest tradition. Strength. It runs in our blood. *We* are the Iron Kingdoms. We, Khador. Without us, there would be no Iron Kingdoms. And this is the way of it…
>
> …Generations ago, our forebears watched as the Orgoth longboats furrowed the western shore. They did not bow their heads lightly, but over time their southern neighbors fell and could offer no aid. When that yoke did come, they were the last to bow under it…though they did so silently, wordlessly cursing their new masters. If only the south were as strong as the north, history might have been re-written. But as it were, Khador could not stand by herself against the resources of an entire empire.
>
> So the Orgoth came and ruled for generations from their sprawling cities—cities that once sullied the Motherland's fair skin—cities long since razed to the ground by Khadoran flame. 'Twas our fathers who suffered greatest under Orgoth oppression. These lands…where you stand today, where you walk, where you live…they were all populous with vile, baneful, invaders. They forced your kin of times past to turn the dirt for their food, to mine the earth for their precious gems, to please them by sport, or toil, or death. They were treated as dogs…and the fire in their once mighty hearts faded to barely an ember. Theirs was a simple but all too painful choice: submit or die.

Some lived. Many died. But the Khardic horse tribes of the west—theirs was once an empire that spanned these lands from the peaks of Rhul to the Khardic Sea—and they refused to submit. Most of them died fighting, but some tribes withdrew, migrating into the wild places of the Kovosk and throughout the Thundercliffs. Centuries of quiet were followed by centuries of infighting, as the Khards warred with barbarian tribes of Skirov and Umbreans for dominance of the region. Even the dwarves became involved, for they also populated those mountains, which mark the borders of Rhul. The Orgoth never managed to conquer this savage region and, in time, the tribes launched sporadic raids at the fringes of the empire. The savage east was an untamed, ever-constant menace.

Cygnar claims they should be credited with the first victory over the Orgoth because of their Colossals, while Llael claims it was their so-called "Army of Thunder" that inspired the Immorese to throw off their chains. Fools. Nearly 500 years ago, hordes of Khadorans descended from the west, the horselords leading them. They surrounded and engulfed the first Orgoth city—some nameless hole now swallowed up by the earth—and razed it to the ground. This was years before the rise of the south; Khadorans were dividing the spoils when the first speck of courage struck the mild hearts of the Cygnarans. In less than a full turn of the seasons, Korsk and Rorschik were released from Orgoth control, not with the subterfuge and wizardry of the southerners, but with the very weapons the invaders had used against us—with hatred, and blades dipped in blood.

The great city of Korsk had been liberated, but was still under threat. The Orgoth did not want to give it up easily. They regrouped and beset the city, incensed, and avidly wanting to recapture it. They sent infernal evils, men made of metal and flesh, and fiery engines of mass destruction against her walls, but the city stood strong—as strong as she does this very day, never shaking, never allowing raiders entry into her beloved walls again.

But the Orgoth were yet very powerful. Their forces gathered en masse. It was a matter of time before the odds were deeply stacked against the Khadoran rebels. So our forefathers made pacts with the south through the Iron Alliance. The Cygnaran engineers were doubtless the ones who did most of the convincing, illustrating the designs for the greatest weaponry in all of history, the Colossals. Surely, these gigantic constructs were a wonder to behold. To just see one of these massive machines clench its mighty fists and peer with burning eyes toward the

Orgoth horizon must have been enough to sway our forefathers. This was what they needed to drive the enemies of Immoren away forever. The Cygnarans convinced the Khadorans that with their help, the Colossals could be a reality, and in 160 A.R. the Iron Alliance was born.

In those days, we were forced to use underground factories in Cygnar. The fighting in the Motherland was too thick—our valiant warriors were endlessly keeping the Orgoth at bay. When the bandylegs joined the cause and opened their borders to the Cygnarans and the Llaelese, the old enmities wouldn't die, and Khador was refused a Rhulic welcome. The dwarfs convinced the Cygnarans to cloak the creation processes of the Colossals and to bar the Khadorans from the factories. In spite of this, we had learned what we needed to know. Perhaps we did not have Cygnaran mechaniks or Rhulic insights, but our engineers conjured up our own mighty Colossals just the same. We are not known for our "ingenuity" and this surprised everyone. Always, they underestimate us. Always, the Cygnarans look down on us, as if we are beneath them. These things have not changed for millennia, and I say, so be it. We do not require the approval of the south.

But we must ever be on guard against their ploys. In 188 A.R., information leaked to the Orgoth about our secret factories in the northern mountains. It was believed that these were agents of the southern kingdoms, many believe it was the Rhulfolk who made this known to the enemy. Because of this, the Orgoth—who had been fighting on every front—re-focused on Khador. They brought an immense army of their infernal warriors and undead dreads—larger than any in all Immoren—to bear against our ancestors, to wipe them out forever. It has never been proven whether one or all of our former allies conspired against us in those days, but it mattered not. Our Motherland has ever been our greatest ally. She awoke, having enough of the festering fleas biting her skin, and conjured a winter to meet the armies of the great enemy. It was the fiercest winter of all time. Razor-sharp winds and tower-deep snows immobilized the armies, trapping them in the valleys and the plains, a freezing cold that stole the breath form their very lungs, forcing them to turn away from their mission of doom. Khador herself had saved her people—a sign in the purest sense of the need to forever protect our borders from outside invasion.

Times changed then. The war turned after that hard winter. We could not bear out any southern treachery, so our chieftains were forced to be prudent. They cooperated with the other members of the Council of Ten, the leaders of the Iron Alliance. In spite of their weaknesses, their treacheries, and their greed, the southerners were what our forefathers had for help. This alliance could not fail. It must be as strong as iron, like the skin of our mighty warjacks. If one must sleep with his foe to stave off a greater one, so be it. The Iron Alliance had to suffice.

And so it did. Slowly but surely, the vile Orgoth were pushed back. For two years, the Alliance forced the invaders from Immoren. Like a swarm of locusts, they fell back, slaying innocents, ruining cities, burning fields...the old enemy left behind a swath of ashen destruction, sorely wounding the Motherland in their flight. It was a hard fought, two-year retreat called the Scourge, but the day came when the last of them boarded their black boats and pushed off from our shores, sailing into vast Meredius, back to whatever hell that had spawned them. The Iron Alliance had won. Immoren was once again ours. All that remains of the Orgoth are some scant ruins and scars in the earth from the gashes of their Scourge. None of you should ever forget the harshness our ancestors endured for our freedom.

We watched and watched for the Orgoth to return, but they never did, and the time soon came for rebuilding. In 202 A.R., the Council of Ten convened in Cygnar, in Corvis, the sinking city, to establish a new age for all of our kingdoms. For weeks, the plans were argued and outlined, put down on parchment, then shredded and put down again. The Cygnarans and their Ordic lackeys maintained it was easiest to use the lines drawn by our former captors. Preposterous as it sounds, the council agreed! What had become of heritage? Where were the lands of kith and kin in this great plan? Indeed, many things influenced our ambassadors; wine being the least of them, for assuredly it was treachery that had reared up once more.

When the final maps were laid down, Khador's original borders in the south and east were non-existent. Instead, they gave us the north "as far as we wished it." So generous of them. Inheritors of waste, that's what we were! Much of it simply dreck. Hinterlands. Wastelands. Tundra comprised of jagged, frost-rimed mountains, fallow, rock-strewn hills, endless, barren, plains of ice…snow-filled ravines to swallow us up! Yes, the Cygnarans would like that, would they not? Oh, and in their typical fashion, they did not hesitate to snatch the largest and most fertile portions, claiming the richest lands of Immoren as their own, while their hegemonies made the fools of Ord all too happy to inherit the coastlands of their Tordoran birth, never realizing Cygnar's main interest was for them to buffer the dragon god and his Cryxian spawn. The Llaelese—how shameful it is to think we share bloodlines with some of them—set themselves up next to the ancestral homes of the elves and dwarves, thinking that the non-humans would make "worthy friends." Khador had been duped, fooled by mind-numbing garrulity and ample stores of drugged wines, and likely foul magics were also involved. Forthright men who are not world-wise easily fall prey to the devious doublespeak of the south, that language of greed and treachery, especially when coupled with magical trickery, and that is our state even today.

But we are proud and we are strong. We are men and women of iron resolve. And so we came from those treaties with a will to abide, in spite of the poor choices of our ensorcelled councilors. Men who swore to honor it for the duration of their lineage had signed those contracts, and Khador would make the best of it. In less than one hundred years, our elders brought it to our attention that the families of those councilors had, for whatever reason, no sons. The poorly worded Corvis Treaties no longer had sway in Khador; the lands refused us by those deceitful papers were our lands, and should be again. Cygnar's leaders and diplomats tell of how our queen's hand was dipped in the blood of her own councilor's families. Lies. Typical southern muckraking meant only to incite those who would hear them.

The Corvis Treaties were void. We began the process of reclamation. Our leaders called for support and Khadorans from every corner of life came back to the Motherland—even those among the Fraternal Order of Wizardry severed their ties, returning home, and forming a new order in 243 A.R. called the Greylords Covenant. These men brought magic in great tides back to our cities, renovating our war-torn Colossals and crafting new forms of mechanika to strengthen our expanding borders. We clashed with Cygnar, with Ord, and with Llael in the great Colossal War, and for seven years the massive constructs wreaked havoc upon the land and its people. It ended with our compromise at the Disarmament Conferences that in return for land we would dismantle our Colossals. Truth be told, the constructs had proven too much for the royal coffers to maintain.

There was peace for the duration of Cygnar's Colossal Guard, but eventually our new sovereign, the Queen Cherize, recommenced the Khadoran stance against Cygnar, its hegemonic habits and partisan politics. Around 293 or so, hostilities had resumed. All Colossals had fallen into ruin by that time, having been formally retired roughly a decade earlier. This new campaign—the Border Wars of 297 A.R.—was fought with steel and cannon, and with the latest and greatest wartime innovation, the warjack, making its debut en masse at Ravensgard in 299 A.R and The Ironfield near Corvis in 300.

It is said the barbarians that stormed Midfast in 305 numbered a hundred thousand. There was little hope of the city surviving such a vast horde, but something divine took place. An Ascendant of Morrow called Markus saved the day. It was a turning point. The gods had deemed to join the fray. Over the next seven or eight years, Immoren was in turmoil. Battles were often fought where it was difficult to tell sides, and on occasion three and four armies would clash at a time. When young Queen Vanar V came of age, she sounded the recall, calling for new negotiations rather than risk any more bloodshed. It is known she was a gentle queen.

In 313 A.R., treaties were signed that yielded the sea town of Radahvo to us—since then we have re-named it Port Vladovar. As expected, Cygnar spoke against this, but the Ordic king claimed he had not the resources to maintain the city and it became ours and remains so. Years of negotiations eventually yielded the city of Laedry entirely to Llael. It was their claim that at the place called the Sea of Graves they had held their ground and, by rights, Laedry should be fully theirs. We had already used every resource from within its walls, having grudgingly shared it with the Ryn for a generation. There wasn't a secret uncovered that was not recorded for our use. With this cessation, a rigid peace of sorts blanketed the kingdoms for 200 years.

Until the Cygnaran Civil War. While we Khadorans have managed to allow the two religions of Menoth and Morrow to exist side by side without rancor, paying homage to both gods, Cygnar was unable to accomplish this, the state heavily favoring one religion over the other, resulting in division and much bloodshed. In its eternal hubris, Cygnar exiled their Menites, dictating where the very gods should rest. What arrogance to think that they could simply turn Menoth away from their lands!

Ruslan Vygor was a whelp when the Protectorate of Menoth was founded, but he was raised a devoted Menite, and he was sorely vexed with Cygnar from an early age. Be he mad or inspired, Vygor claimed to be Khardovic reborn when he took the crown. He decreed he would carve a new future for our people, and he gathered hundreds of Khadoran patriots, scores of mechanikal giants from the Greylords, and dozens of tacticians. With Juggernauts and Destroyers, Vygor's forces carved a path through the perilous Thornwood to the very site of Cygnar's first transgression, to the sinking city itself, to Corvis. With the aid of the Greylords and their magics, they made it all the way to the Dragon's Tongue before the Cygnaran armies met them.

In their usual recreant behavior, they bombarded Vygor's army from the other side of the river rather than take the field in open combat. So determined were they not to fight, they broke some of the finest stonework bridges in all the lands, just so they could hide across the turbulent waters. Hundreds of soldiers died, and two score warjacks were scrapped. The Cygnaran cannons did their damage, but what justly turned the tide was a betrayal by mercenary troops, who treacherously turned against the Khadorans. They were trapped between the river and a fresh army—yet another show of Cygnaran treachery, and the last time Khador will be duped by the dogs of the south! King Vygor fell in battle during the Thornwood War in 513 A.R., and only a handful of Khadorans survived the Battle of the Tongue.

In spite of such turmoil and loss in recent times, I believe our finest hour awaits us. For almost a century since the Thornwood War, we have rebuilt. Our warjacks are strong and our people, stronger than ever. We are loyal to the Crown, and to the Motherland, who has delivered unto us many of the lost Orgoth secrets, allowing access to mysteries older than your grandfathers' grandfathers. Khador's heart is her people. Strength is her tradition. We approach a new age, an age where the past is visited upon the present, and an age where that which once bound us will now be used against those who seek to bind us anew. Beginning today, we forge a new Khador. We were strong enough to cast out the Orgoth and now we are strong enough to harness their relics to serve the Motherland.

Our honorable Queen Vanar XI, ancestor and namesake to that gentle sovereign of long ago, has decreed we should prepare for the next step. Strong men and women like yourselves will be on the forefront, the first to take that step. You are Khador's children! Do not falter. The Motherland that has defended you and kept you safe now calls upon your strength, because it is that strength which will overcome our enemies in the battles in the days ahead. It is our oldest, finest tradition. *Your* strength!

WARCASTER—THE BUTCHER OF KHARDOV

"As wild as Khador itself, Zoktavir is a force of nature that stems from ancient blood. Some say his manners and methods are crude, shortsighted, and utterly repulsive, but I ask you, as Khadorans, would you deny that he is not the very personification of victory at any cost? Has he ever failed us?"

—Queen Ayn Vanar XI, when confronted about the continued assignment of the infamous Butcher of Khardov

The mountain men of Khard are known for their size and fighting spirit, but Orsus Zoktavir is a legend amongst his own people. He hails from the long-since abandoned Orgoth fortress-turned-village called Khardov. Seven and a half feet tall and all but half this in breadth, he is indeed a massive man who developed his arcane skills early on. Orsus' past is wrapped in mystery and none seem to know anything of him until the day he appeared in Korsk with an iron grip on the reins of two old warjacks.

He gained notoriety as "The Butcher of Khardov" during his first command, when a village at Boarsgate Keep announced their withdrawal from Khador to join with Ord. Orsus could not abide such untrustworthy notions and, without orders, he took it upon himself to crush this "traitorous rebellion." He gathered fifty men and marched to Boarsgate. A contingent of militiamen awaited him there with wishes to parley, but Orsus howled at the heavens and charged. Crying betrayal, he and his Khadorans attacked. It was carnage. Halfway through the slaughter, the militiamen surrendered, but Orsus kept hacking away. His men tried to restrain him, but in a wild rage reminiscent of Orgoth berserkers, he accused his own warriors of treachery. With his massive axe, he rendered every living man to pieces. His rage was boundless. Moments later, a total of eighty-eight warriors were simply dismembered parts strewn about Boarsgate. Those who witnessed the aftermath told of blood so thick on the cobblestones that rats leapt from one body part to the next for fear of drowning in the gutters. This day became known as the "Boarsgate Massacre."

Word spread quickly of the bloody act, earning Orsus the title of "Butcher of Khardov." The news ultimately reached the ears of the newly crowned Queen Ayn Vanar XI, and seeing a consummate warrior, she exonerated him and openly

condoned this as the reaction of any true patriot. Most other kommanders guessed at the queen's true intent—to parade a new weapon against inside politics. Now, to speak or act against her may result in a visit from the Butcher.

Orsus Zoktavir is without doubt a powerful warrior. He wields his axe, Lola—it is rumored to be named after a long lost love that fuels his rage—with a vengeance. For the occasion when direct force isn't an option, he carries a mechanika blunderbuss to spray lacerating pellets mixed with rock salts into his enemies, hopefully wounding or maiming them enough to preserve the killing blow for his axe. He wears a modified suit of steam-powered rune armor that was literally taken from a functional warjack. In its protective casing, the Butcher is nigh unstoppable.

Younger warcasters such as Sorscha view the Butcher with disdain, more traditional ones like the Dark Prince of Khador see him as nothing more than a weapon, while troops across all of Immoren cannot remove the vision of this axe-wielding giant from their deepest fears. Orsus Zoktavir fights for a deeper cause than even he knows, for something burns in his blood from the days before the Iron Kingdoms, from a time of mountain savages and bloody sacrifices. The Butcher of Khardov is the personification of warfare and bloodshed, and woe to any fool who stands in his way.

Feat: BLOOD FRENZY

The Butcher's rage runs deep. It is the well from which he draws his power and and the inspiration from which he leads his force into battle. His rage is contagious, and when the Butcher relinquishes what little control he has over it, all who march by his side, man and machine, will succumb to this blood lusting frenzy.

All friendly Khador models within the Butcher's control area add an additional die to their damage rolls this turn.

FOCUS	6	CMD	7		
SPD	STR	MAT	RAT	DEF	ARM
5	8	9	5	14	18

BLUNDERBUSS				
	RNG	ROF	AOE	POW
	8	1	—	12

LOLA			
	Special	POW	P+S
	Multi	8	16

Damage	20
Point Cost	69
Field Allowance	C
Victory Points	5

Base Size: Medium

SPECIAL RULES

THE BUTCHER

- Terror—Enemy models/units within melee range must pass a command check or flee.

LOLA

- Brutal Damage—Add an additional die to Lola's damage rolls.
- Reach—2" melee range

Spells	Cost	RNG	AOE	POW	UP	OFF
AVALANCHE	4	8	3	15		✓
A great stone is ripped from the earth and hurled at the enemy.						
FURY	2	8	—	—	✓	
Target model/unit suffers -1 DEF but gains +3 POW to melee damage rolls.						
HOWL	3	Caster	CTRL	—		
All enemy models/units in AOE must pass a command check or flee.						
IRON FLESH	2	8	—	—	✓	
Target Warrior model/unit gains +3 DEF and suffers -1 SPD.						
KILLING BLOW	3	Caster	—	—	✓	
Double the Butcher's STR for next melee damage roll. Expires after use.						
RETALIATION	3	6	—	—	✓	
Target model may make one melee attack out of turn against any model that hits it in melee combat, before taking damage. The retaliating model still takes any damage rolled by the attacking model after resolving Retaliation. Spell expires after target model makes one retaliatory attack. Retaliation attack and damage rolls cannot be boosted.						

WARCASTER–KOMMANDER SORSCHA

"She is a perfect example of what a woman should be. Pale as the ice that blankets us, beautiful as the starry sky, and as deadly as a winter storm."

—Kapitan Sergei Dalinski, Man-o-War officer, regarding the Warcaster Sorscha

When a teary-eyed Sorscha Kratikoff looked into her father's face at the age of thirteen winters and asked to be a soldier like him, he just smiled, patted her dark black curls, and strode out the door to join his unit. Later that month her mother got word of the massacre at Boarsgate. Sorscha's father was among the dead, executed by Orsus Zoktavir, the Butcher of Khardov. Two years later, Sorscha lied about her age and joined the Khadoran Winter Guard. She fought against all odds and not only survived the rigors and mayhem of war but excelled at it, fueled by the image in her mind of her father's bloody end at the hands of the Butcher.

Sorscha served in three consecutive tours of duty with a prestigious border garrison, often seeing bloody conflict. She was inherently attuned to the tactics of the battlefield, and her role went quickly from frontline grunt to tactical advisor and eventually to kommander. She advised the strategic use of warjacks during combat, assisting and coordinating the efforts of multiple warcasters in the field. Her soldiers think of her as a symbol of the Motherland itself, given form in flesh and bone. They fight for Sorscha because she is as dear to them as the land itself.

Her untapped abilities surfaced during a conflict in the south when an accompanying warcasters was slain in an ambush, his 'jacks suddenly silent and dormant. In desperation, Sorscha charged unescorted into the combat. The battle was taking place in a recently harvested hop plantation, and she snatched up a farming scythe on her way into the fray. She cut men down like stalks of grain, but most of her troops were down and she was outnumbered ten to one. One foe sliced her thigh and she fell, shouting more in shock than pain. Suddenly, the world froze. Around her, everything—including her enemies—was encased in a layer of ice and frost. She stood as the Juggernaut warjacks shattered the layer of quickly melting ice that covered them. They

stepped toward her in answer to her whims. Sorscha leaned on the handle of the scythe and felt a newfound connection to the ether of sorcery.

Days later, Sorscha stood before her queen in Korsk. Her new talents were quickly put to the test, and she began to learn sorcery and proper warcasting from the enigmatic and gifted Vladimir Tzepesci. In her year of study with the nobleman, she became enamored, seeing in him a throwback to the days before Khador's defeat in the Thornwood, before Cygnar's ever-present meddling. They had a brief romance before Queen Ayn Vanar XI called her away to service at the height of their passion. Undoubtedly, there is more to this story than is known, for Sorscha has recently become embittered. But those stories are buried beneath an iron discipline and unfaltering dedication to her first love, Khador.

Sorscha was given a fabulous mechanika weapon her last day in Korsk, to represent her "awakening"—an arcane scythe dubbed Frostfang. In addition to dividing flesh and bone, with expert manipulation, the wicked weapon can magically freeze her enemies through the use of advanced integrated mechanika. This weapon seems to unite Sorscha's resourcefulness with the hard edge of her manner and the icy chill in her heart. Only the presence of the Dark Prince Vladimir, seems to thaw her icy soul, if but for a moment. "Fiery rage and icy hatred," she was once heard to say, "these things a good soldier makes, not the warmth and comfort of love."

Feat: ICY GAZE

Wherever Kommander Sorscha treads, winter appears to follow. The celebrated Khadoran Warcaster manipulates winter itself through the power of sorcery, storing up her power to unleash a massive blanket of ice, freezing her enemies in their tracks.

All enemy models within Sorscha's control area become stationary targets for one round.

FOCUS	6	CMD	9		
SPD	STR	MAT	RAT	DEF	ARM
6	6	6	5	16	14

HAND CANNON	RNG	ROF	AOE	POW
	12	1	—	12

FROSTFANG	Special	POW	P+S
	Multi	7	13

Damage	17
Point Cost	71
Field Allowance	C
Victory Points	5

Base Size: Small

SPECIAL RULES

FROSTFANG

- Critical Freeze—On a Critical Hit, target model becomes a stationary target for one round.
- Reach

Spells	Cost	RNG	AOE	POW	UP	OFF
BOUNDLESS CHARGE	3	6	—	—		
Target model's next activation is a charge at SPD +5 that crosses rough terrain and obstacles without penalty.						
FOG OF WAR	3	Caster	CTRL	—	✓	
A bank of fog is centered on Sorscha, providing concealment to all models within the AOE.						
FREEZING GRIP	4	8	—	—		✓
Target model/unit becomes a stationary target for one round.						
RAZOR WIND	2	10	—	12		✓
A blade of wind slices through the target model.						
TEMPEST	4	8	4	12		✓
All models hit by the Tempest take a POW 12 damage roll and are knocked down.						
WIND RUSH	2	Caster	—	—		
Sorscha may immediately move her SPD and gains +4 DEF for one round. This DEF bonus is not cumulative with additional Wind Rush castings.						

WARCASTER–VLADIMIR, THE DARK PRINCE OF UMBREY

"Let us say I was 'an uninvited guest' in the Tzepesci family manor, located at the peak of the mountain known as Stragoi—which I believe means 'crowned' in ancient Kharde. No matter. It was a strange place—seemingly timeless. I recall crossing the threshold was like taking a step a thousand years into the past, with reliefs of the Khadoran horselords of old along the halls, and then this Umbrean entered the room—a strikingly noble, handsome man who could only be Vladimir himself. And I recall thinking it was as if he had stepped right off that princely wall…"

—The words of Gavyn Kyle, supposedly, if that was indeed Gavyn Kyle…

In times of old, before the Iron Kingdoms, certain lands in Khador were the provinces of barbarians. Chieftains ruled these hordes, and horselords ruled these chieftains. Of noble stock, their families ruled for generations with oppressive strength and calculated cruelty, as well as a will to organize the chaos of the world. Their bloodlines have all but faded into obscurity in the fullness of time, like the shadows of a bygone age. The Tzepesci, who were one of the strongest families to rule the provinces of Old Umbrey, is the last of the great families. Indeed, a millennia ago, the Tzepesci were the governors of Old Korska before it fell into ruin, and during the Iron Kingdoms Era they controlled the throne of all Khador for a time.

It is said that when the Tzepesci line comes to an end, a great doom shall be visited upon all Khador. Vladimir Tzepesci—called the Dark Prince for the shadowy prophecy that he bears—is the last of that line. Steeped in the traditions of old, he is a living relic to past glories and bloody deeds, and his noble bearing is testimony of an ancient lineage. An imposing man with coal black hair, Vladimir refuses to shave his head in the latest fashion. So powerful is the blood in his veins, men shy from his gaze. He is a man of few words, but the Dark Prince is accustomed to being heard when he speaks.

As some men are born to paint or write great works of poetry, Vladimir was born to make war. A brilliant tactician as well as a potent warcaster, he has waged many great campaigns in the service of his queen, from time-to-time orchestrating the whole of Khador's military might. A swordsman without compare, he scythes through the battlefield, visiting swift death upon all that dare cross swords with him. Worthy opponents are treated to longer duels, while most enemies are dispatched with little consideration.

Vladimir takes great pride in his armor. Refusing to abandon his family traditions, he wears the same enchanted, ancient plate of his forefathers. Although it has seen some alchemical and sorcerous repair over the centuries, it is the same suit of crimson mail that his horselord ancestor, Prince Buruvan Tzepesci, wore in battle against the Orgoth.

In his service to Queen Vanar XI, Vladimir has trained other warcasters, and it is no great secret that he became intimately acquainted with the young and promising Sorscha Kratikoff during her mentoring. Little is known of the affair other than it ended quite abruptly, and left Sorscha distinctively changed; this has birthed some speculation that she was rebuffed due to her lowly heritage. Whatever the case, Vladimir is determined to stay true to the legacy of his forefathers, who were always strong and faithful in their duties, even at the expense of their own happiness. There are those who call such notions—and his adherence to ancient tradition—nothing more than exercise in vanity, but for Vladimir Tzepesci it is the only life he knows.

Though respected for his great accomplishments, not all who meet Vladimir love him. It is whispered in secret amongst the courts that the time of the Tzepescis has passed, and Vladimir is but an unpleasant reminder of a crueler time. These conspirators neither believe in the grave prophecy nor in the man they see as a threat to their own designs. Rather, they anticipate the day when the Dark Prince falls and the vast treasures of the Tzepesci family are annexed into the vaults of Khador.

Feat: FORCED MARCH

The strategic and tactical prowess of the Dark Prince of Umbrey is legendary throughout the Motherland as well as any land he has touched. Through careful allocation of resources, Vladimir may conserve the energy of his Warjacks and expunge this reserve in one great battlefield maneuver.

All friendly Khadoran Warjacks within Vladimir's control area double their SPD for this turn.

FOCUS 7			CMD 9		
SPD	STR	MAT	RAT	DEF	ARM
6	6	7	5	15	16

SKIRMISHER	Special	POW	P+S
	Mimic	7	13

RUIN	Special	POW	P+S
	Parry	4	10

Damage	18
Point Cost	76
Field Allowance	C
Victory Points	5

Base Size: Small

SPECIAL RULES

SKIRMISHER

• Mimic—Skirmisher may duplicate one special rule from any melee weapon of any warcaster within his control area. Declare the special rule being mimicked before each attack roll.

RUIN

• Parry—A free strike against Vladimir automatically misses.

Spells	Cost	RNG	AOE	POW	UP	OFF
BLOOD OF KINGS	3	Caster	—	—		
Vladimir gains +3 SPD, STR, MAT, RAT, DEF, ARM for one round.						
BOUNDLESS CHARGE	3	6	—	—		
Target model's next activation is a charge at SPD +5 that crosses rough terrain and obstacles without penalty.						
BRITTLE FROST	2	6	—	—		✓
All damage to target warjack that exceeds ARM is doubled for one round.						
IMPALER	4	8	—	13		✓
A target model damaged by Impaler becomes a stationary target for one round.						
RAZOR WIND	2	10	—	12		✓
A blade of wind slices through the target model.						
SIGNS AND PORTENTS	3	Caster	CTRL	—		
For the remainder of the turn after Vladimir casts Signs and Portents, roll an extra die on all attack and damage rolls for all friendly models in his control area. Discard the low die in each roll.						
WIND WALL	4	Caster	Spec	—		
Any ranged attack against Vladimir or any model completely within 3" of him automatically misses. A model inside the Wind Wall cannot make ranged attacks. Spells are not affected by Wind Wall. This effect last for one round.						

UNIT–BATTLE MECHANIKS

"If you fix in the field, you fight in the field."

—One of the mottos of the Khadoran Mechaniks Guild

CHIEF MECHANIK				CMD	8
SPD	STR	MAT	RAT	DEF	ARM
5	7	6	4	13	10

MONKEY WRENCH		
Special	POW	P+S
–	2	9

Base Size: Small

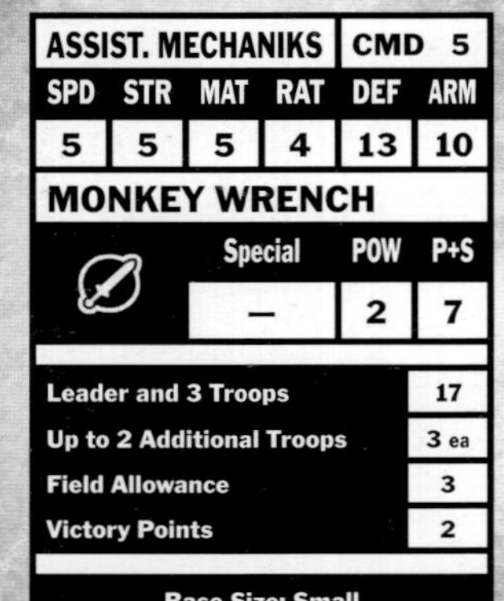

ASSIST. MECHANIKS				CMD	5
SPD	STR	MAT	RAT	DEF	ARM
5	5	5	4	13	10

MONKEY WRENCH		
Special	POW	P+S
–	2	7

Leader and 3 Troops	17
Up to 2 Additional Troops	3 ea
Field Allowance	3
Victory Points	2

Base Size: Small

SPECIAL RULES

MECHANIK CHIEF
- Leader
- Repair [7] (★Action)

ASSISTANT MECHANIKS
- Assist Repair [+1] (★Action)
- Repair [4] (★Action)

In rare instances, Khador's opponents get the better of their warjacks. At these times, skilled individuals are required, often on the battlefield, to make the fixes. Sometimes, a good slapped-together 'jack is the difference between victory and defeat. It is customary that if the Khadoran armies must feed and house these tradesmen, they have to fight like any other soldier, so the "battle mechanik" is also trained as a fighting man. They spend great amounts of time combat training, but remain quite capable of making repairs when called upon.

Unlike some of the other kingdoms, Khador does not see the use in hiring the gobbers to aid their mechaniks, for they are cowardly creatures, unable to heft large pieces of Khadoran warjacks. So, in their stead, Khador employs apprenticed mechaniks to aid their crew chiefs. They are adept combatants, having served in the Winter Guard, and can wield a lug wrench or 'jackdriver with the same efficiency used to swing axes.

The crew chief is the heart of the mechanik team. Sometimes these old vets get hurt on the battlefield, but a Khadoran doesn't let a simple thing such as a shorn-off limb get him down. Injured mechaniks repair their own broken bodies with the same steamwork parts that they fix warjacks. The most common "repair" is to replace a broken or severed arm with a large mechanika version that attaches over the remnant of the former limb. It is a great tool in its own right, imbuing the mechanik with the strength to bend metal or hold armor while his crew rivets and welds it in place. It also grants him an edge in close combat, able to tear and smash opponents. When used as either, the crew chief and his metal additions work in symphonic unison, ever quick to make decisions in the field, even if it means abandoning putting something together in favor of taking something (or someone) apart.

BATTLE MECHANIK SPECIAL RULES

MECHANIK CHIEF

- Leader
- Repair[7] (★Action)—A Mechanik can attempt repairs on any friendly Warjack of the same faction that has been damaged or disabled. To attempt repairs, the mechanik must be in base-to-base contact with the damaged Warjack or disabled wreck marker and make a skill check. If successful, roll a d6 and remove that number of damage points from anywhere on the Warjack's damage grid. The Warjack being repaired must forfeit its activation and cannot channel spells on the turn repairs are attempted.

ASSISTANT MECHANIKS

- Assist Repair[+1] (★Action)—Every Assistant assisting the Chief with a repair adds +1 to the Chief's Repair skill, up to a maximum of 11. An assistant must be in base-to-base contact with the Warjack that is being repaired by the Chief.
- Repair[4] (★Action)—Same as Chief, above.

UNIT–IRON FANG PIKEMEN

"We learned to bring down the powerful mountain bears with long spears over a thousand years ago, but it's quite a different matter to bring down the ones with iron skins."

—Dhurgo Bolaine, Vicar of the decorated Iron Fangs unit of Wolfholme

Since their debut, warjacks have been a cause for concern to every force that has had to oppose them. Only warcasters and their own warjacks were equipped to stop these mechanika constructs, yet spells are often far too short range and the heavy 'jacks can only be deployed so quickly. At first, treachery and ambush was the ideal solution. Digging trenches filled with oil or tar, dropping avalanches onto marching columns, even stampeding enormous herds of animals were tactics applied in the months that followed.

It is said that necessity is the mother of invention, and that war inpires progress. Through volatile experience in trial and error, a miriad of anti-warjack technology and tactics have developed, exploiting the few advantages a man has over a warjack. Speed, skill, and coordination coupled with some good old fashioned ingenuity created the Iron Fangs, elite soldiers trained to effectively bring down warjacks using special blasting pikes to open up thick armor or sever sensitive connections on 'jack limbs.

The blasting pikes' explosives are potent shaped charges, specifically designed to rip into the target instead of showering its wielder with dangerous shrapnel. Although the Iron Fangs are designed to combat heavily armored foes, they're not against using their pikes against lightly armored troops. Needless to say, the results of this can be grisly. In addition, Iron Fangs can form a daunting shield wall. The craftsmen developed each shield to interlock, so the Fangs are able to array shoulder-to-shoulder and form a mobile wall of thick armor.

After 200 years of service, the Iron Fangs have become a heralded tradition of the Khadoran army, and their fraternal bond, legendary. Unofficially, it is said that upon acceptance into the legion of Iron Fangs, a soldier swears a blood oath, casting off the life he lived before and dedicating himself to his fellow soldiers, his country, and the art of war.

SERGEANT				CMD	9
SPD	STR	MAT	RAT	DEF	ARM
6	6	7	4	13	14
BLASTING PIKE					
		Special		POW	P+S
		Multi		7	13
Base Size: Small					

TROOPER				CMD	7
SPD	STR	MAT	RAT	DEF	ARM
6	6	6	4	13	14
BLASTING PIKE					
		Special		POW	P+S
		Multi		7	13
Leader and 5 Troops					59
Up to 4 Additional Troops					9 ea
Field Allowance					2
Victory Points					2
Base Size: Small					

IRONFANG SPECIAL RULES

SERGEANT

•Leader

•Shield Wall (Order)—When this order is given, every Iron Fang Pikeman moves into tight formation and gains +4 ARM for one round. Pikemen who cannot move into tight formation do not benefit from the Shield Wall.

UNIT

•Combined Melee Attack—Instead of making melee attacks seperately, Pikemen in melee range of the same target may combine their attacks. The Pikeman with the highest MAT in the attacking group makes one melee attack roll for the group, adding +1 to the attack and damage rolls for each Pikeman, including itself, participating in the attack.

BLASTING PIKE

•Critical Knockdown—On a critical hit, target model is knocked down.

•Reach—2" melee range

SPECIAL RULES

SERGEANT
•Leader
•Shield Wall (Order)

UNIT
•Combined Melee Attack

BLASTING PIKE
•Critical Knockdown
•Reach

"Blood is the coin of this realm now, and he is the paymaster."

—Kommander Sorscha Kratikoff

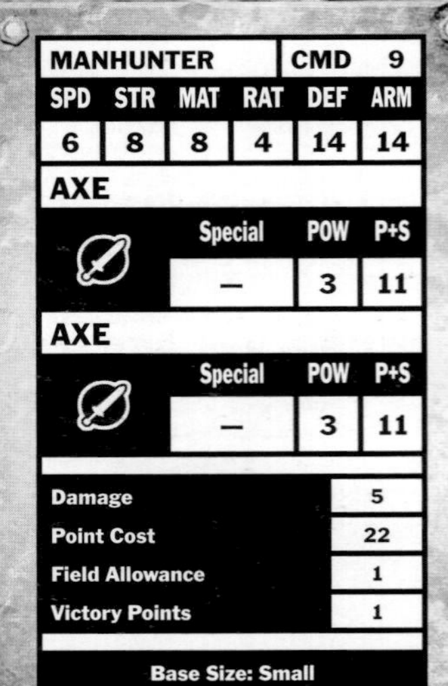

MANHUNTER				CMD	9
SPD	STR	MAT	RAT	DEF	ARM
6	8	8	4	14	14

AXE	Special	POW	P+S
	—	3	11

AXE	Special	POW	P+S
	—	3	11

Damage	5
Point Cost	22
Field Allowance	1
Victory Points	1

Base Size: Small

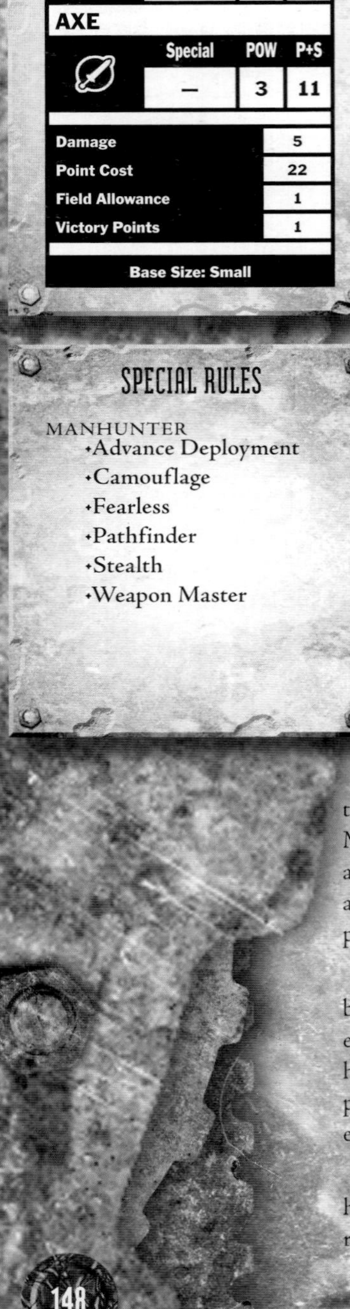

SPECIAL RULES

MANHUNTER
- Advance Deployment
- Camouflage
- Fearless
- Pathfinder
- Stealth
- Weapon Master

Fishing and hunting are the prime sources of food for the Khadoran people, especially considering the harsh taxes on imports. Khadoran hunters tend to be of higher regard than those of other kingdoms. They are experts at tracking and killing some of the most dangerous and cunning prey, such as dire bears and Raevhan buffalo, and some have moved on to the most dangerous and cunning prey of all—man.

First and foremost, manhunters are rangers, able to travel effortlessly in the wilds of Khador. Lowland brush, forests, snow—they are all treated as a well-paved road by a manhunter. They tend to be able bodied and dark skinned from years of working their trade in the wilderness. Their skills are legendary. Manhunters are devoted trackers, serving as scouts and sometimes as assassins, for the right price. They are masters at camouflage, often overlooked while in plain sight.

In exchange for their services, they are well kept by the armies that hire them. Often operating behind enemy lines, they are armed with twin masterwork hand axes for close combat. Whether they are stalking prey in silence or swinging their axes with blinding efficiency, manhunters are frightful killers.

Kommanders and warcasters are sometimes hesitant to call upon a manhunter's services, never really knowing the extent of their loyalties to Khador. Manhunters insist on meeting their employers in person before taking on a job, prompting the hiring officer to sometimes wonder before inviting a hired killer to meet in private, "What if he is hunting me?" There are many whispers of manhunters who enjoy the hunt too much, giving in to their animal urges and the rush of the kill. It is the mere rumor of these "kill mongers" that give pause to officers, but their track records are often good enough to eclipse the possibilities.

MANHUNTER SPECIAL RULES

- Advance Deployment—Place Manhunter after normal deployment, up to 12" beyond established deployment zone.
- Camouflage—A Manhunter gains an additional +2 DEF when benefiting from concealment/ cover.
- Fearless—A Manhunter never flees.
- Pathfinder—The Manhunter ignores movement penalties from rough terrain and obstacles. A Manhunter can charge across rough terrain.
- Stealth—All attacks against a Manhunter from greater than 5" away automatically miss. A Manhunter greater than 5" away from an attacker does not block line of sight or count as an intervening model.
- Weapon Master—A Manhunter adds an additional dieto its melee damage rolls.

UNIT—MAN-O-WAR SHOCKTROOPERS

"We Legion know what it be like to be warjack. Those who retire for whatever reason, they are sad men. They grow old and shrivel to nothing. I no fade like this. When death comes, I die bleeding oil and sparks like metal brothers. When death comes, I die in steam."

—Deidric Harkinos, veteran of the Man-O-War Legion

Warjack cortex materials are hard to come by in Khador. Because of this, their armed forces tend not to create as many of the metal behemoths. Their 'jacks have been historically outnumbered, and the Khadoran Mechaniks Assembly have always focused their theories on ways to get around the issue. After a lot of trial and error, they invented a mechanika suit of enclosed steamwork armor.

The suit was a miraculous creation, imbuing a soldier with nigh warjack-level strength, durability, and protection against the elements. Of course, there are drawbacks to wearing heavy battle armor powered by a steam boiler. Khadorans who spend great deals of time in the Man-O-War suits are susceptible to heat stroke, exhaustion, and the occasional steam leak that cooks them alive.

With the looming possibility of being poached, the Man-O-War requires boundless resolve. Only the most steadfast soldiers are honored with membership. Because of the suit's inherent flaw, this is a tough decision, but nonetheless many soldiers jump at the opportunity; it is not every day that you can feel the world through a warjack's fingers. The original Mechaniks Assembly could never reconcile the massive heat problem, but younger members claim they can fix the dilemma. The shocktroopers are now so respected, feared, and utilized by the armies, it's much too late to amend the process without recalling the entire legion, and the queen's court turns a deaf ear to such jabber.

The Man-O-War shocktroopers wield powerful halberd-like polearms called annihilator blades. One stroke of this weapon is capable of splitting the armor of a light warjack. Against mere men, it leaves them in ruin. For protection, they file into ranks, locking their shields together akin to the formations of the Iron Fangs, but they have powerful cannons mounted into their shields for hurling more than just curses. The shield cannon implanted in each shield is a cycling short ranged weapon. It uses tightly packed powder to propel a thick slug a short distance with surprising force, leveling other unit formations.

The Man-O-War shocktroopers are greatly famed, in spite of the obvious dangers of being bolted into an armored pressure-cooker. No matter the warnings, when a warrior is selected for duty as a Man-O-War, he does not hear them. After all, is it not every soldier's dream to become a clockwork titan?

MAN-O-WAR SPECIAL RULES

KAPITAN

•Leader

•Shield Wall (Order)—When this order is given, every Man-O-War Shocktrooper moves into tight formation and gains +4 ARM for one round. Unit members who cannot move into tight formation do not gain the benefit of the Shield Wall.

UNIT

•Combined Melee Attack—Instead of making melee attacks seperately, Shocktroopers in melee range of the same target may combine their attacks. The Shocktrooper with the highest MAT in the attacking group makes one melee attack roll for the group, adding +1 to the attack and damage rolls for each Shocktrooper, including itself, participating in the attack.

•Fearless— A Man-O-War never flees.

ANNIHILATOR BLADE

•Reach—2" melee range

KAPITAN				CMD	9
SPD	STR	MAT	RAT	DEF	ARM
4	9	8	6	11	17
SHIELD CANNON					
		RNG	ROF	AOE	POW
		6	1	–	14
ANNIHILATOR BLADE					
		Special		POW	P+S
		Reach		4	13
Damage					10
Base Size: Medium					

TROOPER				CMD	7
SPD	STR	MAT	RAT	DEF	ARM
4	9	7	5	11	17
SHIELD CANNON					
		RNG	ROF	AOE	POW
		6	1	–	14
ANNIHILATOR BLADE					
		Special		POW	P+S
		Reach		4	13
Damage					8
Leader and 2 Troops					67
Up to 2 Additional Troops					20ea
Field Allowance					2
Victory Points					3
Base Size: Medium					

SPECIAL RULES

KAPITAN
•Leader
•Shield Wall (order)

UNIT
•Combined Melee Attack
•Fearless

ANNIHILATOR BLADE
•Reach

UNIT–DOOM REAVERS

"Since when did it become our practice to employ such savages and madmen?"

—Vladimir Tzepesci, commenting on the forced deployment of Doom Reaver units into his command

LIEUTENANT				CMD	7
SPD	STR	MAT	RAT	DEF	ARM
6	7	8	4	13	14

FELL BLADE		
Special	POW	P+S
Multi	6	13

Base Size: Small

TROOPER				CMD	5
SPD	STR	MAT	RAT	DEF	ARM
6	7	7	4	13	14

FELL BLADE		
Special	POW	P+S
Multi	6	13

Leader and 5 Troops	100
No Additional Troops	—
Field Allowance	1
Victory Points	2

Base Size: Small

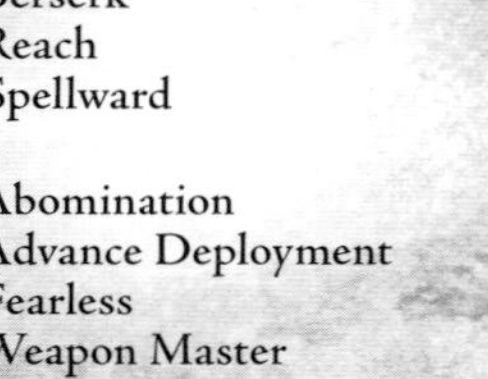

SPECIAL RULES

LIEUTENANT
- •Leader

FELL BLADE
- •Berserk
- •Reach
- •Spellward

UNIT
- •Abomination
- •Advance Deployment
- •Fearless
- •Weapon Master

Khador is dotted with ancient ruins from the Orgoth era—massive stonework temples, fortresses, and deep catacombs. Relic hunters recently unearthed the infamous gibbering Fell Blades. These dark swords are saturated with magic with shifting faces along the blades. Once taken up, the faces whisper dark secrets into the minds of the brandishers.

The first handlers were handpicked swordsmen who found that, over a brief time, they could understand the cryptic whispers. The foreign tongue fueled their rages, transforming them into insatiable killers. Twice as strong, capable of withstanding fatal blows, the wielders went where they willed, killing anything that crossed their paths, and only conversing in the perverse language of the old conquerors. They were the Doom Reavers. Uncontrolled and uncontrollable, they wandered as outlaw swordsmen, engaging in horrid acts. The Khadoran army was ordered to dispose of the Reavers. Hundreds of young soldiers died in the attempt and the Reavers eventually fell, their weapons reclaimed and locked away to be forgotten.

But some years later, Queen Vanar XI had her warmasters procure the dark swords once more. She gave over wayward soldiers to an alternative fate, ordering them chained to a Fell Blade and giving birth to the Doom Reavers once again. These men quickly became savage berserkers, but so far the queen has been able to keep their loyalty. It is said that those who have the hard luck of spending time among them cannot seem to keep the gibbering and the furious cries out of their heads. Truly, the Reavers are a terror to behold.

DOOM REAVER SPECIAL RULES

LIEUTENANT

•Leader

UNIT

•Advance Deployment—Place Reavers after normal deployment, up to 12″ beyond established deployment zone.

•Abomination—Any models/units—friendly or enemy— within 3″ of a Reaver must pass a command check or flee.

•Fearless—A Reaver never flees.

•Weapon Master—A Reaver adds an additional die to its melee damage rolls.

FELL BLADE

•Berserk—Every time a Reaver destroys another model in melee, it must immediately make one melee attack against another model in its melee range, friendly or enemy.

•Reach—2″ melee range

•Spellward—A Reaver cannot be targeted by any spells, friendly or enemy.

UNIT–WIDOWMAKERS

"Is a good patriot who would kill a comrade just to save him from the enemy. Is my kind of patriot!"

—Orsus Zoktavir, The Butcher of Khardov

Widowmakers are the elite sniper division of the Khadoran armed forces. Some regard snipers as little more than cowardly assassins, but Khador has embraced their sniper corps, elevating them to the status of heroes. Those who choose the Widowmakers are not biased, for as long as they are skilled with the rifle and take pride in their work, peasants and hunters may fight alongside the sons and daughters of noblemen. It is scarcely possible to overstate the skill Widowmakers possess with their long barreled hunting rifles. So efficient are they that they can take apart incoming warjacks piece-by-piece with their well-placed shots. Killing a man becomes as automatic as drawing breath.

But rather than take potshots at warjacks, a Widowmaker's primary role is to neutralize officers and unit leaders to facilitate chaos among the enemy. Much like Cygnaran trenchers, they frequently advance ahead of the main battle group, and their arrival is often signaled by the abruptly falling dead before the report of their rifles are discerned.

Widowmakers are also great support during strategic withdrawals.

Part of that order is to ensure their own wounded do not become prisoners. If a downed officer can't be retrieved, Widowmakers make sure they don't fall into the wrong hands. This notion is feared but respected, for a true patriot knows it is better to die by a comrade's hand than to be placed in irons or on an enemy's torture rack.

It is said that Widowmakers are not used in domestic conflicts, but whispers abound that some of the most effective ones have been aimed inward to pick off speakers of dissention, rabble rousing crime leaders, or corrupt politicians suspected of losing their loyalty to the crown. If this is true, these Widowmakers are a lethal solution to such potential problems.

Hated everywhere outside Khador, Widowmakers can expect little charity from their enemies if captured. Indeed, it is common practice among the Cygnarans to hang them without trial, and the Protectorate has been known to brand a sniper's eyes with hot irons and then turn him loose into their own lands. For the Widowmakers, it's understood; hatred and fear comes with the territory.

WIDOWMAKER SPECIAL RULES

KAPITAN

•Leader

UNIT

•Advance Deployment—Place Widowmakers after normal deployment, up to 12" beyond established deployment zone.

•Camouflage—A Widowmakers gains an additional +2 DEF when benefiting from concealment/cover.

•Pathfinder—A Widowmaker ignores movement penalties from rough terrain and obstacles. A Widowmaker may charge across rough terrain.

•Sniper—After a successful ranged attack, a Widowmaker may automatically inflict one damage point instead of making a damage roll. Against a warjack, the attacker chooses which column takes this damage.

KAPITAN				CMD	8
SPD	STR	MAT	RAT	DEF	ARM
6	5	5	8	14	11

HUNTING RIFLE

RNG	ROF	AOE	POW
14	1	—	10

SWORD

Special	POW	P+S
—	3	8

Base Size: Small

TROOPER				CMD	6
SPD	STR	MAT	RAT	DEF	ARM
6	5	4	7	14	11

HUNTING RIFLE

RNG	ROF	AOE	POW
14	1	—	10

SWORD

Special	POW	P+S
—	3	8

Leader and 3 Troops	53
No Additional Troops	—
Field Allowance	1
Victory Points	2

Base Size: Small

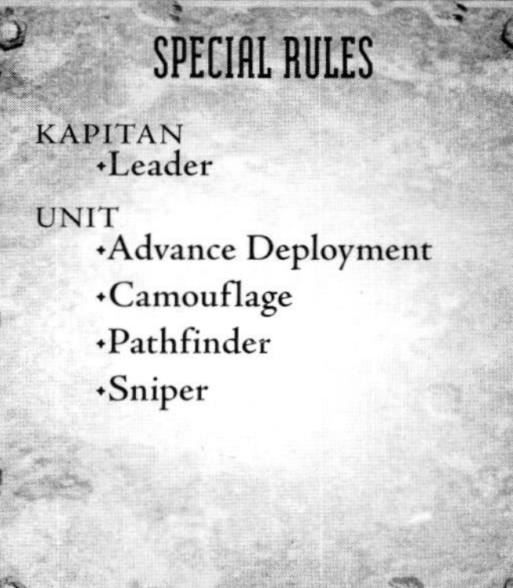

SPECIAL RULES

KAPITAN
•Leader

UNIT
•Advance Deployment
•Camouflage
•Pathfinder
•Sniper

UNIT—WINTER GUARD

"Arrgh! Why the hell don't they use rifles like normal people? It's so much…cleaner…I feel faint…"

—Rodger "the Rake" Digby, Cygnaran long gunner after taking a hit from blunderbuss fire

SERGEANT				CMD	8
SPD	STR	MAT	RAT	DEF	ARM
6	5	6	5	12	13
BLUNDERBUSS					
	RNG	ROF	AOE	POW	
	8	1	—	12	
AXE					
	Special	POW	P+S		
	—	3	8		
Base Size: Small					

TROOPER				CMD	6
SPD	STR	MAT	RAT	DEF	ARM
6	5	5	4	12	13
BLUNDERBUSS					
	RNG	ROF	AOE	POW	
	8	1	—	12	
AXE					
	Special	POW	P+S		
	—	3	8		
Leader and 5 Troops	58				
Up to 4 Additional Troops	9 ea				
Field Allowance	3				
Victory Points	2				
Base Size: Small					

SPECIAL RULES

SERGEANT
•Leader

UNIT
•Combined Ranged Attack

When each Khadoran male reaches 17 winters, he is conscripted into the Winter Guard. Women are not disallowed to volunteer, but this is often discouraged and prohibited if they have children in their keeping. Some conscripts never see real combat, often assigned to police and patrol the towns and cities, yet they remain the staple of the Khadoran infantry.

Each guardsman is armed with a simple axe. It serves as their standard melee weapon, as well as a useful tool for wilderness excursions. For ranged combat, they have few choices. Bows and crossbows are used in the temperate regions but prove difficult to use in the frozen north, Rifles and ammo are far too expensive and hard to attain. But in recent years, northern hunters have employed short-ranged scatterguns called blunderbusses to spray a cloud of projectiles using small amounts of powder. The pellets are generally bits of stone and metal. This effective and ultimately cheap weapon soon enough became the Winter Guard's adopted firearm.

Rapid development on the blunderbuss brought the weapon up to military grade potency. The bite of the blunderbuss is an appropriate transmitter of the harsh, Khadoran winter according to guardsmen, who relish scouring the "soft hides of the southerners" such as the Cygnarans and Llaelese.

WINTER GUARD SPECIAL RULES

SERGEANT
•Leader

UNIT
•Combined Ranged Attack—Instead of making ranged attacks seperately, Winterguards may combine their attacks at the same target, so long as they are in open formation or closer. The Winterguard with the highest RAT in the attacking group makes one ranged attack roll for the group, adding +1 to the attack and damage rolls for each Winterguard, including itself, participating in the attack.

HEAVY WARJACK–DESTROYER

"Now lets see the dogs of Cygnar hide in their trenches and foxholes…we'll blow them out like frightened hares and chop them up like stewmeat!"

-Harisc Vokmir, Khadoran Mechaniks Assembly

When the Cygnaran Mechaniks Guild unveiled their first so-called "light warjack," the Khadorans scoffed at the idea. In Khador, bigger is usually better, and their mechaniks employ this principle to no end. Even larger than Cygnar's Ironclad, the Destroyer is a mammoth of armor viewed as the glorification of the Khadoran temperament.

Its armament is also very Khadoran. Replete with mountains and timber, Khador has seen the heavy use of axes since before the Thousand Cities Era, and when the Juggernaut was fashioned, the Khadorans were inspired by the image of the axe-wielding Khardic berserkers of old. This 'jack hefts the mighty Executioner Axe in one massive arm, a weapon capable of shearing off other warjacks' limbs with a single, mighty stroke, while the other hand is fitted with the potent bombard. This cannon's shells are cast from heavy lead for greater distance and are stored in tanks of frigid water so they shatter easily upon impact. Filled with generous amounts of red and black powder, they explode with great force. The shell fragments are mostly disintegrated by the blast, but shrapnel is sometimes found in the bombard cannon's casualties. The people of Ord have labeled these cannons "Thunder Guns," and with good reason.

Height /Weight	11'7" / 9.5 tons
Armament	Bombard Cannon (left arm), Executioner Axe (right arm)
Fuel Load/Burn Usage	185 Kgs/ 4 hrs general, 45 minutes combat
Initial Service Date	537 AR
Cortex Manufacturer	Greylords Covenent
Orig. Chassis Design	Khadoran Mechaniks Assembly

The Destroyer passed its first trial during the Thornwood War, where they were employed to shell the Cygnaran fortifications on the opposite side of the Dragon's Tongue. Though Khador lost the conflict, the Destroyer had been battle-tested and the mechaniks were satisfied with the results—so satisfied, in fact, that nearly a third of the warjacks ordered to replace the ones lost in the Thornwood were Destroyer models. Indeed, many Khadorans have been heard to say that if there had been more of them at that battle site, the outcome undoubtedly would not have been the same.

DESTROYER SPECIAL RULES

BOMBARD

•Arcing Fire—Bombard ignores normal targeting rules. It can make ranged attacks against any target in line of sight, regardless of intervening models. Targets still benefit from concealment and cover.

EXECUTIONER AXE

•Critical Amputation—On a Critical Hit, every arm and weapon system that takes damage is automatically disabled. After marking regular damage, those systems that took damage have their remaining system boxes marked as well.

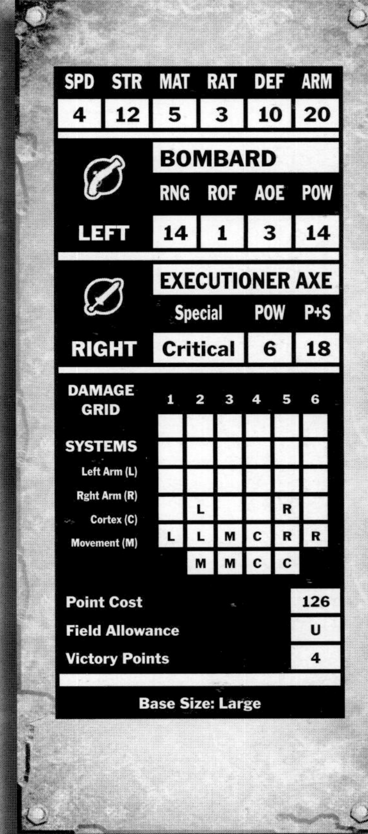

SPD	STR	MAT	RAT	DEF	ARM
4	12	5	3	10	20

	BOMBARD			
	RNG	ROF	AOE	POW
LEFT	14	1	3	14

	EXECUTIONER AXE		
	Special	POW	P+S
RIGHT	Critical	6	18

DAMAGE GRID

1	2	3	4	5	6
	L			R	
L	L	M	C	R	R
	M	M	C	C	

SYSTEMS
Left Arm (L)
Rght Arm (R)
Cortex (C)
Movement (M)

Point Cost	126
Field Allowance	U
Victory Points	4

Base Size: Large

SPECIAL RULES

BOMBARD
•Arcing Fire

EXECUTIONER AXE
•Critical Amputation

HEAVY WARJACK–JUGGERNAUT

"More ice, eh? Well, I reason what they lack in originality, they more than make up for...with ice!"

—Commander Coleman Stryker, upon seeing the Ice Axe used in combat

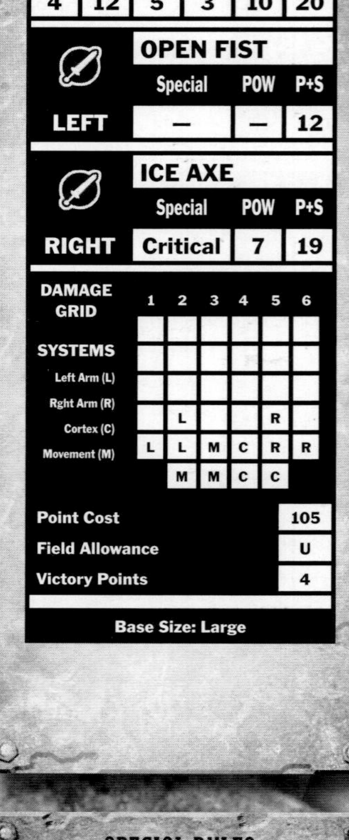

SPD	STR	MAT	RAT	DEF	ARM
4	12	5	3	10	20

	OPEN FIST		
	Special	POW	P+S
LEFT	—	—	12
	ICE AXE		
	Special	POW	P+S
RIGHT	Critical	7	19

DAMAGE GRID	1	2	3	4	5	6
		L			R	
	L	L	M	C	R	R
		M	M	C	C	

SYSTEMS
Left Arm (L)
Rght Arm (R)
Cortex (C)
Movement (M)

Point Cost	105
Field Allowance	U
Victory Points	4

Base Size: Large

SPECIAL RULES

JUGGERNAUT
- Head Spike

ICE AXE
- Critical Freeze

The staple chassis upon which all of Khador's warjacks are based, the formidable Juggernaut is a product of the ingenuity of Khadoran mechaniks. In recent years, this 'jack has been improved upon by determined ice-wizards who, after witnessing Cygnar's 'jacks, wished to bring more arcane might to the mix.

Like the Destroyer, it is durable and tenacious, but the traditional axe has been replaced by a mechanikal version—the Ice Axe. Similar to Kommander Sorscha's scythe, the ice axe mechanikally generates an arcane effect that has the capability to freeze its target, creating a layer of ice and frost. The temperature is so extreme that the target is immediately slowed, any flesh hardens, and any metal becomes brittle—all the easier for the axe to shatter whatever it strikes. Even glancing blows renders stiffened bodies into ghastly, deformed statues of ice. The Juggernaut's other hand is empty and useful for myriad tasks, such as holding an enemy in place while delivering a spike-topped head butt.

Considering the rarity of warjack cortexes in Khador, every square inch of the Juggernaut is layered with thick, overlapping armor. Although this does not allow great mobility or speed, it provides unmatched protection, and in the thick snows of Khador, mobility is a worthy sacrifice in exchange for sturdiness and power. After all, Khadorans respect power, and there is not a soul in all of Khador that doesn't either fear or admire the powerful Juggernaut.

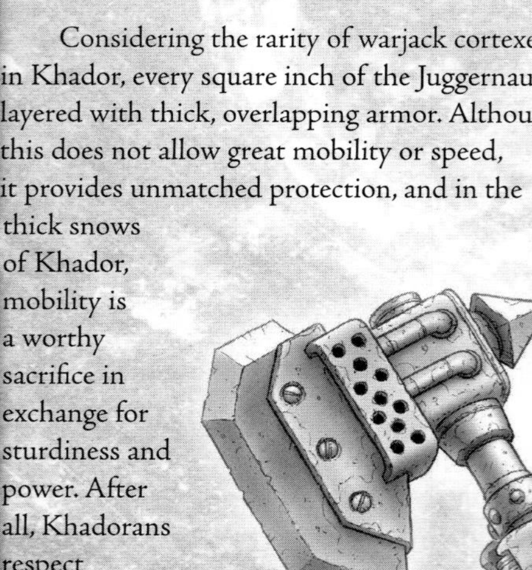

JUGGERNAUT SPECIAL RULES

JUGGERNAUT

- Head Spike—While not a weapon on its own, the Head Spike gives the Juggernaut POW 2 for Head-butt attacks.

ICE AXE

- Crtical Freeze—On a Critical Hit, target model becomes a stationary target for one round.

Height /Weight	11'7" / 9 tons
Armament	Ice Axe (right arm)
Fuel Load/Burn Usage	185 Kgs/ 4 hrs general, 55 minutes combat
Initial Service Date	516 AR
Cortex Manufacturer	Greylords Covenent
Orig. Chassis Design	Khadoran Mechaniks Assembly

HEAVY WARJACK—MARAUDER

"I've never beheld such blasphemy. For Menoth's sake, it is a warjack made to batter down walls. Walls, I say!"

—Visgoth Ruskin Borga, Leader of the Old Faith in Korska

The Marauder is the oldest variant of the classic Juggernaut chassis. The first warjacks rarely had integrated weapons. Instead, they simply employed their fists and massive bulk. The first conflicts ammounted to contests over who could knock over the other side's 'jacks first while the actual troops decided the outcome. The Khadoran warjacks kept getting bigger and slower, whereas Cygnar and Cryx delivered smaller, lighter ones. Khador realized their disadvantage. Their bulky constructs could not move quickly enough to work against the lighter ones.

About that time, an industrial mechanik named Targh Fedro became inspired one day. He observed some stonemasons working in the quarry, chipping and breaking large stones with their rock hammers. He then took an old labor 'jack with broken down arms and replaced them with two attachments resembling battering rams. The idea was simple. Why run after the enemy when you can wait for them to come to you, then deliver one massive, telling blow. He tested the 'jack against the quarry walls. The newly dubbed Marauder brought a hundred tons of stone crashing down on top of it, totally demolishing the quarry wall in a single overcompensated strike from the 'jack rams. Fedro applauded his own success and departed immediately for the Khadoran Engineers Society.

Height /Weight	11'7" /10.25
Armament	Twin Rams (left and right arms)
Fuel Load/Burn Usage	185 Kgs/ 4 hrs general, 55 minutes combat
Initial Service Date	522 AR
Cortex Manufacturer	Greylords Covenent
Orig. Chassis Design	Targh Fedro (credited), Khadoran Mechaniks Assembly

Although Fedro faced legal charges for his radical testing that closed down the entire rock quarry (it is said some masons were killed), his dream lived on. The 'jacks ram-pistons were recreated out of military grade iron and bolted onto the capable bodies of Juggernauts. At first, their enemies scoffed at the warjacks as they lumbered onto the battlefield. But this ceased when a single shocking slam by a Marauder sent a Cygnaran 'jack spinning like a top to land in a crumpled heap.

The Marauders rams are equally effective against walls, as evidenced by the testing of that first prototype. Normally, when enemies holed up in stone castles or keeps, it would take great manpower and often a long siege to batter down their walls. With the Marauder at their disposal, the Khadorans suddenly had an upper hand. In fact, the Llaelese have derived a fear-inspiring alarm that no soldier cares to hear. It is "Marauders at the gates!"

MARAUDER SPECIAL RULES

MARAUDER

•Head Spike—While not a weapon on its own, the Head Spike gives the Marauder POW 2 for Head-butt attacks.

RAM PISTONS

•Batter—Double the number of damage points a structure takes from the Ram Pistons.

•Combo Slam (★Attack)—The Marauder has a pair of Ram Pistons that can be used simultaneously for a devastating attack. It can make a normal attack with each Ram individually, or it may make a special attack with both Rams at the same time. Both Rams must be operational to make the Combo Slam. Make one attack roll for the Combo Slam—a successful hit Slams the target. Resolve this Slam just like the Power Attack of the same name. Add the Marauder's STR once and the POW of both weapons to the slam's damage roll. The Combo Slam is not prevented by any spells or movement penalties that prohibit Charges or Slams.

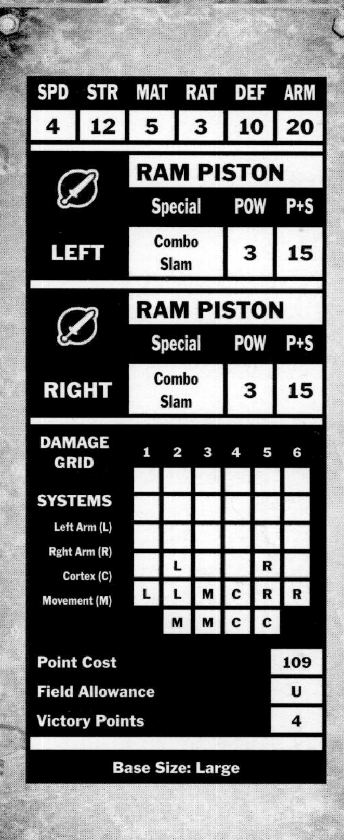

SPD	STR	MAT	RAT	DEF	ARM
4	12	5	3	10	20

	RAM PISTON		
	Special	POW	P+S
LEFT	Combo Slam	3	15

	RAM PISTON		
	Special	POW	P+S
RIGHT	Combo Slam	3	15

DAMAGE GRID	1	2	3	4	5	6
		L			R	
	L	L	M	C	R	R
		M	M	C	C	

SYSTEMS
Left Arm (L)
Rght Arm (R)
Cortex (C)
Movement (M)

Point Cost	109
Field Allowance	U
Victory Points	4

Base Size: Large

SPECIAL RULES

MARAUDER
•Head Spike

RAM PISTONS
•Combo Slam (★Attack)

"Blood and gold, blood and gold! My favorite two colors are blood and gold!"

—Hans "The Mad Wanker" Schrube, Shields of Durant mercenary

Hardin Graves was a Bloodwolf. He was a tall man with a severe scar down one side of his face and wild black hair shot with gray. He wore the bronze broach of the wolf on his bandolier, as well as the black scarf that named him captain. He had 47 men, 2 ogrun, a dwarf mechanik and a gobber bodger under his command, and every one one of them thought they were worth their weight in gold. Sometimes they were, but some days they were more worth their weight in buffalo dung.

Today was such a day. In the last week, his Ironclad—a series five halfjob—had sustained a fair amount of damage. Time and again the dwarf bellowed orders at the gobber while the machine stood inert, shuddering and sputtering sparks and steam.

The day before, they had been camped below the hills just north of Corbhen, headed for a small river community called Mundenberg, a merc-friendly town, when a handful of red-painted barbarians descended on them. The savages had somehow procured some rifles but—thank Morrow—couldn't shoot them worth a damn.

A soldier named Munch had called them 'junkers.' He said apparently they'd seen the Ironclad and thought they'd have themselves a warjack. When they realized they weren't going to be taking 'Madeleine'—that was her name, the Ironclad's—back to the tribe with them, they settled for unloading as much shot into her as they could and melting back into the hills.

So now they were in the small port town, and Graves was sitting dockside and drinking some black grog that tasted like vinegar mixed with wheat grain from a copper mug. The chug and hiss of his warjack rang in his ears as he watched his dwarf and gobber frantically crawl all over the quivering machine, plugging holes and mending tubes. Finally, the dwarf chased the gobber away and worked for a few more minutes before shutting her down and walking over to his captain.

"Cortex is about for shite, captain," the grime-besmirched Decklin Lugro announced, his voice nearly a growl. "There's not much else I can do. Maddy's ill and she ain't goin' ta get much better less'n we get some damps, a harness, and a proper soldering kit."

"That's coin, Lugro." Captain Graves took a draw on his mug, and made a bitter face from either the brackish taste or his mood. It was hard to say. "And who's going to set us up? We're a long ways from Five Fingers. Can't your bodger bodge something? That's what the pug is for, ain't it?"

Lugro's lip twitched before he replied. "Captain, you know and I know that Maddy's been bodged about as much as ye can without junkin' her for scrap."

Graves took a long breath and nodded. His mood had gone from bad to as sour as the black grog. The dwarf was truthful. "Bloody savages," the captain murmured into his mug.

On cue, a woman screamed. The captain's head shot up, and he and the dwarf peered down the docks toward a mêlée that had suddenly erupted. A woman in a half-torn smock was being manhandled by two of his Bloodwolves. Apparently they weren't content with sharing her. Fights often broke out about who gets a woman first, and Captain Graves was usually satisfied to let the men work it out on their own, but this time he noticed a third, older man on his knees, clutching the side of his neck. Even from yards away, Captain Graves could see dark blood spouting from between the man's fingers. People went to grab him as he fell to his side. Another woman screamed, announcing the man's death. It was likely the object-of-affection's father or husband. This was not good.

"Bloody blasted horny idiots!" Graves stood and removed his watchcoat, tossed it on his chair. He drew forth his bludgeon and walked briskly down the docks toward his men. Before entering Mundenburg, he had instructed them to comport themselves. It appears that was asking too much. Now, Captain Graves was going to take out his frustrations on some thoughtless underlings.

He approached them from behind, weaving through the confusion gathering about the dead civilian, and delivered a hard knock to the back of the first soldier's head. The man's knees immediately buckled. He whacked the other soldier three times before the man started to run.

"Never run!" the captain bellowed, leaping after the man as the woman they were tugging collapsed to the ground, wailing. Never run, Graves had told them time and again. For his impudence and cowardice, the captain beat the man bloody and, honestly, during the thrashing be began to feel a little bit better.

MERCENARIES

While many of the sons and daughters of the Iron Kingdoms serve for crown or country, there are those that are not ready to give their lives for a mere soldier's pittance or fleeting patriotism. Some have heard the call of coin and united with other like-minded soldiers to form companies. These warriors of purchased allegiance are known by many names, some more colorful than others but collectively defined as mercenaries.

Mercenary companies have taken part in every major battle in western Immoren since before the days of the Orgoth. Early mercenary companies were almost always filled with swords-for-hire, joining the army that could tip their paymaster's scale the fastest. While things have changed greatly over the centuries, mercenary companies are as diverse as the commanders that hire them. Some follow the ancient Mercenary Code, while some companies are little more than highwaymen. Other mercenaries do not belong to any particular company, preferring to stay independent so that they may freely travel wherever their greed takes them. These mercenary solos tend to be as risky as they are effective—it's not easy to trust a hired gun that can't commit.

Some of the most honorable companies have grown into regular additions to many of the armies across Immoren. Groups such as Draime's Red Raiders and the Khadoran Free Soldiers League have served the Queen of Khador for so many generations that their current kapitans have no knowledge of the original hiring circumstances of their centuries-old charters. In Cygnar, the Bloodwolves, Ironhands, and Thunderhelm Irregulars share Cygnaran fortresses as permanent additions to the king's soldiers. Even Menoth's theocracy understands the need for "expendable" troops, even if their faith is paid for in gold.

Mercenary camps with no morals and cast-iron guts have even been known to seek out employment with the Lich Lords of the Cryx. It takes great resolve to fight side-by-side with undead horrors. Some would say men who choose to join the Dragonfather's armies are worse than the Cryxian abominations alongside them, but no army is exempt from the greedy policy of an unemployed mercenary. Enough gold makes anything seem like a good idea.

There are countless mercenary units in the Iron Kingdoms, and with the rising threat of all-out war, more emerge each day. Some kill for coin, others for land, and some of the more wretched for the sheer thrill of it. Surprisingly, even the stalwart dwarves and a rare rogue elf or two have taken up arms. These elder race rarities are an enigma, but a welcome one, as they bring ancient skills and mysteries to the battlefields of men—often with devastating effects.

Ogrun, trollkin, and other wildlings across Immoren have lately taken on the mercenary's life, some joining units of men, others comprising their own companies. These units—or tribes—often work for far less than their human equivalents, seeing their involvement in the wars of man as a chance to lash out at those who otherwise claim sovereignty over their lands. They relish in the shedding of human blood, no matter the faction.

As long as there is conflict and war in the Iron Kingdoms, there will always be an empty seat reserved at the end of every war room table for the next mercenary captain. War seems to be a constant in western Immoren, and until that changes, the Mercenary Code, and those that follow it, will continue to prosper. Many are her children, and there is no end to her fertility within the war machine that is the Iron Kingdoms.

SOLO—EIRYSS, MAGE HUNTER OF IOS

"Like a ghost, she was. Appeared out of nowhere, turned our new warcaster into a bloody pincushion, then faded away into the shadows. We searched for three days on how that damn elf got in there, and why she even hit us. I thought King Leto made peace with the elves, didn't he?"

—Captain Morris Beaumayne, leader of the Rivercleft patrol

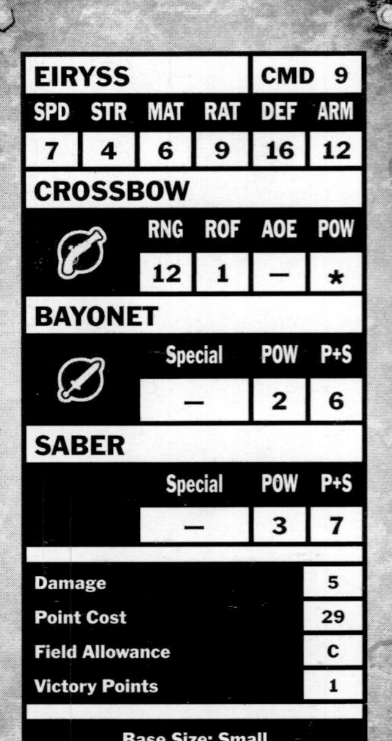

EIRYSS				CMD	9
SPD	STR	MAT	RAT	DEF	ARM
7	4	6	9	16	12

CROSSBOW	RNG	ROF	AOE	POW
	12	1	—	*

BAYONET	Special	POW	P+S
	—	2	6

SABER	Special	POW	P+S
	—	3	7

Damage	5
Point Cost	29
Field Allowance	C
Victory Points	1

Base Size: Small

SPECIAL RULES

EIRYSS
- Advance Deployment
- Bayonet Charge (Order)
- Camouflage
- Invisibility
- Pathfinder
- Technological Intolerance
- Weapon Master

CROSSBOW
- Death Bolt
- Disruptor Bolt
- Phantom Seeker Bolt

Elves have been mysterious and superstitious since far before the time of man, and many seek only the company of their own. They have lost all but one of their gods, and they now seek to cure her ailments before she joins the rest. A few of them have ventured into the lands of man looking for answers to their unending questions. Even fewer of them have ventured out because they believe they have the answer. One in particular believes she has solved the riddle, and that the answer lies with men—more importantly, it lies within the entrails of the sorcerers she hunts.

The Retribution of Scyrah, a sect of clandestine Iosans, blames the surge of human wizardry for the slow deterioration of their goddess. They believe that humans and their mechanikal monstrosities, the steamjacks, are ripping the magical energies of Caen from her. They claim that the continued creation and use of steamjacks causes Scyrah to slip further and further toward her doom. Therefore, the Retribution has deployed their most skilled hunter, Eiryss, to seek out and destroy human spellcasters.

Eiryss is enigmatic and extremely effective, appearing seemingly out of nowhere to offer her services to prospective clients. Her contracts are simple enough: find the enemy warcaster, kill him, and disappear into the shadows. In truth, Eiryss uses her contract as a tool to learn about the army—more specifically their warcasters—making use of her services. She is a consummate assassin of unequaled stealth, fueled by an unending hatred for those she believes are killing her goddess.

Eiryss employs a wide array of gear to aid in her hunts. Skilled with a sword, she is a capable close combat killer, but prefers to deal with prey as any game hunter would—with well-placed shots into unsuspecting targets. After all, why should she sully her hands with the very blood that is poisoning Scyrah? To deliver these shots, Eiryss carries a crossbow carved from the still-green branches of farrowood trees, bound in strips of gold and engraved with runes of marksmanship and vengeance.

The wily and well-protected warcasters she hunts tend to be far more difficult prey than forest boars or yearling deer, so alongside the silver-tipped bolts in her quiver, Eiryss also has several types of mystical ammunition. Crafted from the blackened wood of trees split by lightning and tipped with a copper head bathed in holy oils, the disruptor bolt sparks and burns as it flies at the target. Anyone struck by this brilliant bolt of light and flame is engulfed in an explosion of anti-magic runes, draining precious magical energy the target has stolen from Scyrah. Eiryss' black bolts laced with dark magics are deadly accurate. With these, she is able to find the smallest opening in a target's armor. These black bolts have even been pulled out of an otherwise uninjured warjack's cortex, having been shot through a narrow vent or some other slot. It matters not if the target is walled up or behind closed doors, as her deadly phantom bolts unerringly find their mark. These bolts are sculpted from the bones of a corpse with a restless spirit. They sail through solid matter, piercing the target even if shielded or hidden away. The mage hunter does not even have to see the phantom bolt's quarry, but merely whisper its name in the tongue of the bolt's host spirit.

When hunting with her deadly crossbow, Eiryss will generally camouflage herself. When simple camouflage is not enough, the Mage Hunter can employ ancient elven sorceries to render herself completely invisible. Eiryss can remain hidden like this until the first *thwang* of her crossbow is perceived.

The mage hunter will work for anyone whom the Retribution feels furthers their goal of reclaiming the lost energies being ripped from their goddess. They sometimes do not even require payment for her services, satisfied with the knowledge they have gained. As a rule, armies employing Eiryss do not trust her, though there is no evidence that she has ever turned on an employer. Whether or not her actions are condoned or are actually aiding Scyrah, she will continue hunting until one of two things occurs—either Scyrah fades, or all human spellcasters are dead.

SOLO—EIRYSS, MAGE HUNTER OF IOS

EIRYSS SPECIAL RULES

Mercenary—Eiryss will not work for Cryx.

EIRYSS

•Advance Deployment—Place Eiryss after normal deployment, up to 12" beyond established deployment zone.

•Bayonet Charge (Order)—As part of a Charge, after moving, make a ranged attack followed by a charge attack with the bayonet. Eiryss cannot attack with her other melee weapons after a Bayonet Charge.

•Camouflage—Eiryss gains an additional +2 DEF when benefiting from concealment/cover.

•Invisibility—Eriyss's can forfeit her activation to become invisible. While invisible, Eiryss cannot be targeted by ranged or magic attacks, cannot be charged, and gains +4 DEF against melee attacks for one round. Eiryss cannot become invisible if engaged at the start of her activation.

•Pathfinder—Eiryss ignores movement penalties from rough terrain and obstacles. Eiryss can charge across rough terrain.

•Technological Intolerance—Eiryss may not end her movement within 5" of a friendly Warjack.

•Weapon Master—Eiryss adds an additional die to her melee damage rolls.

CROSSBOW

Eiryss may fire one of the following bolts per attack:

Death Bolt—Target model automatically takes 3 damage points. Against Warjacks, the attacker chooses which column takes the damage.

Disruptor Bolt—Target model takes a POW 8 damage roll and loses all focus points. A hit Warcaster does not replenish focus points next turn and a hit Warjack cannot be allocated focus points or channel spells for one round.

Phantom Seeker Bolt—With this ethereal bolt, Eiryss may attack any model in range regardless of line of sight. Phantom Bolt ignores cover, concealment, obstructions, and intervening models. If hit, the target takes a POW 10 damage roll.

UNIT—GREYGORE BOOMHOWLER & CO., TROLLKIN MERCS

"That sound! Like a lion riding a church bell in the middle of a landslide. I covered me bloody ears in time, but not all me mates were fast enough. Some of 'em ain't heard a sound since..."

—Reid Markus, Cygnaran long gunner

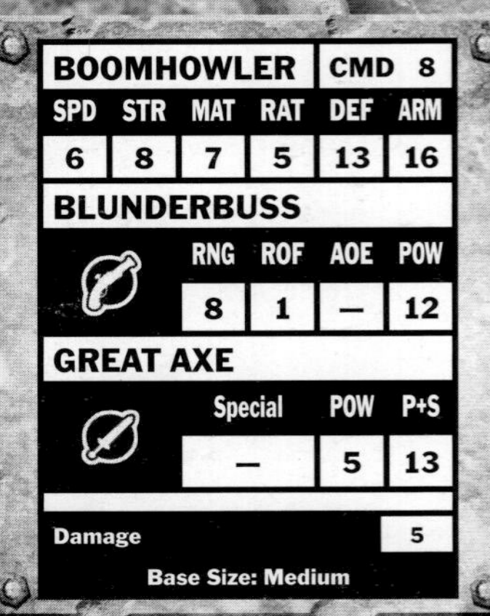

BOOMHOWLER				CMD	8
SPD	STR	MAT	RAT	DEF	ARM
6	8	7	5	13	16
BLUNDERBUSS					
		RNG	ROF	AOE	POW
		8	1	—	12
GREAT AXE					
		Special		POW	P+S
		—		5	13
Damage					5
Base Size: Medium					

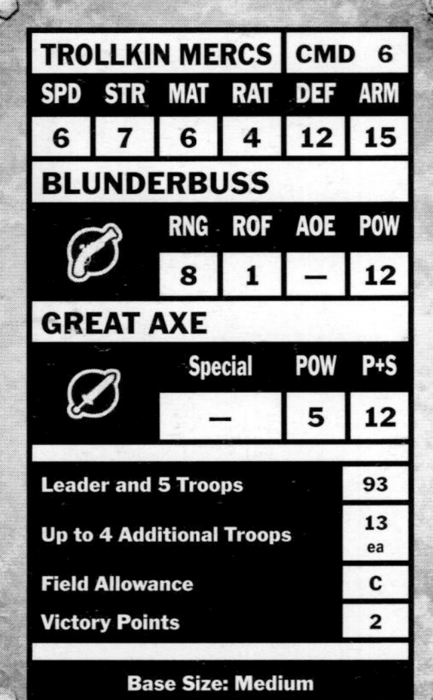

TROLLKIN MERCS				CMD	6
SPD	STR	MAT	RAT	DEF	ARM
6	7	6	4	12	15
BLUNDERBUSS					
		RNG	ROF	AOE	POW
		8	1	—	12
GREAT AXE					
		Special		POW	P+S
		—		5	12
Leader and 5 Troops					93
Up to 4 Additional Troops					13 ea
Field Allowance					C
Victory Points					2
Base Size: Medium					

SPECIAL RULES

BOOMHOWLER
- Fell Call (★Action)
- Leader

UNIT
- Combined Melee Attack
- Tough
- Stink Bombs (★Action)

It's said that Bragg, the legendary trollkin Fell Caller, was quite promiscuous in his day, and thus his peculiar talents have sprouted all across Immoren. These special folk command a power of voice that belies the imagination. Over the past six years, few of these Fell Callers have mastered their preternatural inheritances. Possibly the most noted is Greygore Boomhowler, a crass and nigh intolerable axe-for-hire with a great command over the Gift of Bragg. Many have heard tales of his vocal prowess, yet those who have heard it personally can't recount the experience without emotion.

Greygore hails himself as the reincarnation of Bragg. He wears garish strips of cloth in gaudy colors, and refuses to be quiet, even in an ambush. Indeed, some commanders have paid him and his mercs double-fees to stop singing and gibbering at all hours of the day and night. When Greygore isn't singing, drinking, or fighting, he is performing Bragg's historically favorite duty—wenching. Womenfolk of all races throughout the kingdoms have been entranced by Greygore's legendary voice. Indeed, he is quite the handful off the battlefield, but his antics are well worth it once the battle has been joined.

Greygore is proficient with both blunderbuss and axe, but his true worth lies in his rumbling voice. With a single breath he can release a rolling croon across the battlefield, palpable supernaturally over the clash of swordplay and the crack of gunfire, and heard more from within the body, like a feeling more than a sound. His vocal range is incredible, from subtle tunes in order to calm panicked comrades to shrill screeches that turn a man's hair white. There are soldiers who claim the trollkin's voice was key in winning battles before the first drop of blood was ever spilled. Indeed, more than once, Greygore alone has caused entire hordes to flee.

Blood, of course, must be spilled at times when fear and terror cannot win the day. Then, Greygore calls upon the full force of his power. With a deep breath, he sends forth a heavens-shaking cry, his maw erupting with a wave of sound that shatters glass and splinters wood like some mighty, oceanic wave, even ripping gashes in the metal skins of warjacks. In fact, the sensitive inner workings of the mechanikal giants are susceptible to the swell of sound, rattling cogs loose and unbalancing essential fluids. Truth be told, Greygore's wail taxes him a great deal, and he cannot sustain it for extended amounts of time. This is a sometimes a good thing. Though the force of his blasts are meant for his enemies, the ear-splitting sounds can be heard for miles, and many of the trollkin's allies are as prone to incapacitation as his foes.

Over his travels, the Fell Caller has become a sort of status symbol among his people, and many have tried to emulate him. Should the "descendant of Bragg" happen upon a trollkin settlement, it is not uncommon for many of their young warriors to take up their axes and join him. These volunteers swell and wane in number from time to time, but Greygore cannot be found without at least a few loyal followers. With the respect they give him, it is no wonder why many believe Greygore's claim to be Bragg reincarnated. In battle, they fight with a combination of axe and blunderbuss, and use their trademark stink bombs, which Greygore has had developed by trollkin alchemists. This glass globe shatters on impact, releasing a cloud of noxious vapor that is highly debilitating to those who inhale it—anyone, that is, save the trollkin themselves, who with their legendary immunity to poisons and contaminants battle on, completely unphased.

Whether or not Greygore is the reincarnation of the legendary Bragg or just a self-important bard with a bloated ego, it matters little to his employers. He and his trollkin followers are an impressive addition to any army, and between bouts of drunken revelry he has a wealth of talents to spread among the troops. Still, commanders are often wary of where to assign Greygore and company, for just like at the Caspian amphitheatre, if one instrument is out of tune during the symphony, the results can be disastrous—especially if that instrument can turn men into jelly with but a single, sour note.

BOOMHOWLER & CO. SPECIAL RULES

Mercenary—Boomhowler & Co. will not work for the Protectorate.

BOOMHOWLER

- Fell Call (★Action)—Enemy models within 8" of Boomhowler must make a command check or flee. All warjacks within 8" suffer -2 MAT and -2 RAT for one round.
- Leader

UNIT

- Combined Melee Attack—Instead of making melee attacks seperately, Trollkin Mercs in melee range of the same target may combine their attacks. The Trollkin with the highest MAT in the attacking group makes one melee attack roll for the group, adding +1 to the attack and damage rolls for each Trollkin, including itself, participating in the attack.
- Tough— Whenever a Trollkin takes sufficient damage to remove him from play, the controlling player rolls a d6. On a 5 or 6, the Trollkin is knocked down instead of being removed from play.
- Stink Bombs —(RNG 5, AOE 3") A Trollkin may throw a Stink Bomb as a ranged attack. Living models in a Stink Bomb's AOE suffer -2 to their SPD, STR, MAT, RAT, CMD, and DEF for one round. A Stink Bomb's AOE is not a cloud effect, but it remains in play for one round. Trollkin are immune to the effects of the Stink Bombs.

UNIT–HERNE STONEGROUND & ARQUEBUS JONNE

"Eighteen degrees left! Seven degrees skyward! Three degrees for wind, fire at will!"

"On it. This one's really going to kick them in the shorts."

—Herne Stoneground to Arquebus Jonne, and Jonne's response while trying to attain the perfect angle of fire

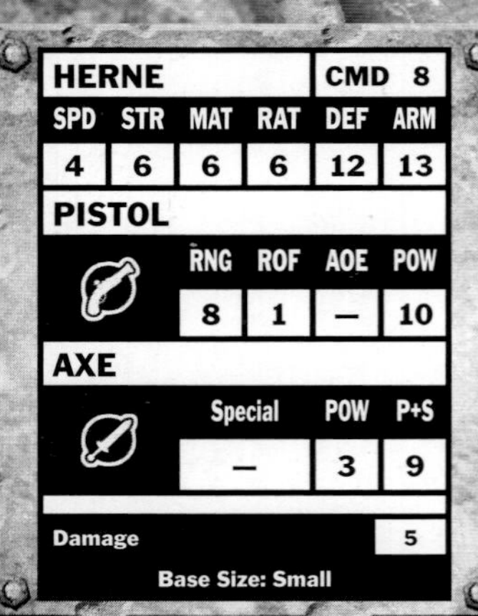

HERNE				CMD	8
SPD	STR	MAT	RAT	DEF	ARM
4	6	6	6	12	13

PISTOL	RNG	ROF	AOE	POW
	8	1	–	10

AXE	Special	POW	P+S
	–	3	9

Damage	5
Base Size: Small	

JONNE				CMD	9
SPD	STR	MAT	RAT	DEF	ARM
6	8	6	4	12	15

BARRAGE ARQUEBUS	RNG	ROF	AOE	POW
	12	1	3"	14

GREAT AXE	Special	POW	P+S
	–	5	13

Damage	10
Point Cost	42
Field Allowance	C
Victory Points	2
Base Size: Medium	

SPECIAL RULES

HERNE STONEGROUND
- Gunner
- Leader
- Loader

BARRAGE ARQUEBUS
- Scatter Shot (★Attack)

When one thinks of dwarves, one rarely thinks of subtlety. Herne Stoneground is a prime example why. Herne served as a traveling alchemist's assistant in his younger days, roaming from stronghold to stronghold learning much in the way of his mentor's trade. More as a hobby than a craft, Herne became very curious about the sciences surrounding gunsmithing. By his second decade he had already mastered the alignment of rare double-barreled firearms, and his wares earned him a great reputation amongst traders and military merchants alike—in some parts, the Stoneground escutcheon is hailed as a sign of cutting edge quality. A Stoneground original fetches many hundred if not thousand Cygnaran crowns on the open market, and some came at a much higher price behind closed doors. Herne could never trust a messenger to deliver his wares, so he always did so personally, although rarely ever seen without a bodyguard or three. Eventually, Herne ran across a well-respected ogrun named Jonne.

Jonne was born and raised in Rhul, where most of his tribe has served as guards and smith hands to the Rhulfolk for hundreds of years. Growing up quickly on the trade-rich border of Llael, Jonne was accustomed to the flash and pomp of the Llaelese merchants. It didn't take long for the adolescent ogrun to make a name for himself on the Black River loading docks, and often merchants asked for him by name. The slightest taste of fame went right to Jonne's head, and he soon signed on with a Rhulic mercenary group called the Emberhold. While in the company he trained his martial skills, and worked as a sword-for-hire (or axe, or mace, or even large rocks!) for any who might be in need of his muscle.

One day, during a delivery of a pair of Stoneground originals, Jonne met Herne Stoneground himself. A pair of ill-fated brigands picked that time to interrupt the sale and thieve the precious mastercrafts. Jonne moved instinctively. He snatched up the two bandits and restrained them until the watch arrived. So fast was his reaction and effective his skill, the surrounding folk broke into applause as the ogrun handed over the brigands. Herne offered Jonne a solid handshake in thanks, and from that day forth the two were fated to become one of the most famous mercenary teams in all the Iron Kingdoms.

After the incident, Herne hired Jonne as his personal guard, to protect him and his products through thick and thin. That was nearly fourteen years ago, and Jonne is to this day bound to Herne. Over the years and through many adventures, the two have become great friends. Jonne has gone far beyond the call of duty for his charge, saving Herne time and again. The dwarf feels safe under Jonne's watchful eye, and while some less scrupulous employers might allow their hired muscle to perish in order to save their own skin, Herne wouldn't think of it. Without a second thought of his own safety, his axe and pistol leap to the aid of any who seek to harm his ogrun friend.

Some years ago, after months of Jonne's grumbling, the duo agreed that small arms manufacturing was not the lucrative business it once was. They determined that true wealth would be found only in large ordnance, so Herne put his mind—and his gunwerks skills—to the task. Before long, the Stoneground Barrage Arquebus was unveiled. In an effort to market the new creation, Herne and Jonne took to the road, hiring themselves out to any would-be customers so that they might get a first hand experience of the gun's effectiveness.

The arquebus, a triple barreled contraption that launches three cannonballs at once, is a beautifully crafted weapon, so massive that only the bulging muscles of Jonne—or "Arquebus Jonne" as he came to be called—can possibly hold it aloft (indeed, the ogrun relies on his dwarven companion for reloading the massive weapon). The heavy clouds of smoke emitted by the powder charges force Jonne to goggle his eyes with thick black glass. Obviously, this impairs the ogrun's vision, but Herne, who after years of powder burns and stinging smoke is immune to these effects, uses his shrewd judgment and mathematical skills to help Jonne aim. Contrary to the opinion of its creator, the barrage arquebus is quite inaccurate, but luckily its ammunition is designed for fragmentation. While the arquebus is devastating at a fair range, Jonne is just as deadly in close combat with his mighty great axe; foes who survive the shelling, Herne's cleaving axe and pistol, often find themselves battered into pulp by the arquebus' heavy iron barrels.

Herne Stoneground and Arquebus Jonne have dined in the victory halls of Cygnar, argued payment options with the kommanders of Khador, and witnessed the pre-battle prayers of Menoth's scrutators. The two friends have only one rule: no elves and no walking dead. Once asked about the possibility of continuing if the other should fall in combat, both Jonne and Herne say something to the effect, "How would that be possible? If he's dead, then I must be, too."

HERNE & JONNE SPECIAL RULES

Mercenary— Herne & Jonne will not work for Cryx.

HERNE

•Gunner—Jonne gains +2 RAT as long Herne and Jonne are in base-to-base contact and not engaged in melee combat.

•Leader

•Loader—When Herne and Jonne are in base-to-base contact, Jonne may use the Barrage Arquebus to make a Scatter Shot special attack.

BARRAGE ARQUEBUS

•Scatter Shot (★Attack)—The Barrage Arquebus can make a Scatter Shot special attack when Herne and Jonne are in base to base contact. When fired in this manner, all three barrels of the Barrage Arquebus discharge at once. After determining the initial shot's point of impact, roll deviation for two additional shots from that point. All models within the AOE of the additional shots take blast damage.

SOLO—REINHOLDT, GOBBER SPECULATOR

"What d'ye mean ye don' know who I am? I'm famous, I am! Bloody famous!"

—Reinholdt, Gobber Speculator and Self-Proclaimed World Traveler

REINHOLDT				CMD 4	
SPD	STR	MAT	RAT	DEF	ARM
6	2	2	2	16	9

Point Cost	15
Field Allowance	C
Victory Points	1
Base Size: Small	

SPECIAL RULES

REINHOLDT
- Assistant
- Coward

WARCASTER BENEFITS
- Lucky Charm
- Reload
- Spyglass

Very few men can claim that they have ventured from one end of the Iron Kingdoms to the other and back, and even fewer gobbers can make such a bold statement. One of these diminutive creatures does more than just suggest however, he downright guarantees he's been everywhere at least twice, and seen it all at least once. Reinbaggerinzenholdt, or Reinholdt for short, claims to have seen many wondrous sights, from Lord Toruk's inner sanctum to the grand banquet halls of the elven courts of Ios. He sports strange trinkets and baubles from all over Immoren, and his accent is nearly indistinguishable from the natives to whichever area he happens to be in at the time. Whatever the cause or source, Reinholdt is a bottomless font of skills and knowledge that would be difficult for a dozen of his kind to learn in a lifetime. Not an expert at anything special (although Reinholdt would argue otherwise), he seems at least partially versed in whatever comes up at the moment. Reinholdt is truly a jack-of-all-trades.

Even with the unsettling doubt of the veracity of his claims, it seems warcasters and commanders the kingdom over have shelled out coin to hire Reinholdt for his myriad of half-masteries. Although he claims to have been a legendary bodger in his earlier days, Reinholdt claims to have "surpassed such petty talents." Too often did he feel that he was doing "all the work" for the mechaniks, and now he refuses to soil his hands with the repair of warjacks. While he still enjoys tinkering with mechanika and toying with theories that often baffle some of the artificers at the Khadoran Mechaniks Assembly, his true joy is the adventure of roaming the kingdoms.

It may seem odd that a gobber with the reputation of a braggadocio could make a difference to the powerful commanders of iron behemoths—but he does, and happily so. While Reinholdt would tell his employers his very presence is a boon and his advice on tactics is without peer, he is indeed a true aid to most warcasters. The gobber claims a great savvy with the alchemy of firearms, and is useful as a speedy reloader for riflemen and pistoleers; sometimes he loads one of his "famous" home-brewed powder charges—leading to spectacular pyrotechnics at various levels of intensity—but he is still quite the handy assistant. Armed with a host of trinkets and artifacts from the lands over, Reinholdt makes great use of his "tools." His crystal Ordic spyglass—which he says he received for helping sway a Cryxian pirate invasion from the shores near Berck—is one of his favorites. Using the glass, he can spy out potential dangers and estimate just how long it will take for that peril to cause him personal harm; gobbers often use "getaway chronology" as a mode of measuring distance. While it may take an employer a while to find the seconds-to-impact method useful, this knack of Reinholdt's is rarely off by much, and if so, usually on the positive side (in favor of the gobber's escape time). When all else fails, some warcasters rub the little guy for luck.

Though he's seen many a battlefield across Immoren, Reinholdt himself is lucky to have not suffered a scratch. This fact, of course, is not from his skill as a combatant, but rather this uncanny luck. He once sneezed himself out of a moving carriage into a patch of thornbriar bushes just before the carriage burst into flames upon hitting a powder trap set by brigands. And once, a bullet reflected harmlessly off of a silver soupspoon in his pocket that he had "acquired" earlier that same day.

Despite his good fortune, Reinholdt is not what one would call a hero. He is far more likely to run and hide than stick around if a situation gets too hairy. Indeed, he's been known to vanish from sight in typical gobber fashion if *any* enemy comes too close. If left with little option, the resourceful chap will search his pockets and pouches for anything that might aid his escape; these tricks range from powerful smoke bombs to distracting contraptions, but have all resulted somehow in his safe exit. Though he may not be a hero, Reinholdt the World Traveler is an interesting bloke with no lack of usable talents and skills. Many commanders utter a deep sigh when the little bodger comes sauntering into their camps from who-knows-where, and whether that sigh is an expression of relief or one of exasperation is often determined by their current state of affairs.

SOLO–REINHOLDT, GOBBER SPECULATOR

REINHOLDT SPECIAL RULES

Mercenary—Reinholdt will not work with Cryx or Protectorate Warcasters.

REINHOLDT

- Assistant—Assign Reinholdt to a single Warcaster; he cannot be reassigned during a game. If Renholdt's Warcaster is removed from play, remove Reinholdt from play as well.
- Coward—If Reinholdt begins his activation more than 3" from his Warcaster, he must pass a command check or flee. Reinholdt must also pass a command check or flee anytime he or his Warcaster is engaged in melee combat. Reinholdt automatically fails any command check if he is outside his Warcaster's command range.

WARCASTER BENEFITS

As long as Reinholdt is in base-to-base contact with his Warcaster, the Warcaster may use one of the following abilities during his activation.

- Lucky Charm—Warcaster may roll an additional die with one attack or damage roll. Discard the lowest die from the roll before totalling the score.
- Reload—Warcaster may make an additional ranged attack without spending a focus point and regardless of the weapon's ROF.
- Spyglass—Warcaster may premeasure up to a distance of 12" between himself and one other model within his line of sight.

TACTICS—BRAIN AMMO

HOW TO GIVE ANYONE WHO DIDN'T READ THIS SECTION A THOROUGH BEAT DOWN

GENERAL TACTICS

There are a number of tactics that are worth keeping in mind as you play WARMACHINE. These will become second nature as you play more games, but are worth thinking about early on. A lot of these are common sense; others take a bit of play to figure out. This is a simple overview of some of the finer points of play, and these tactics are intended as a jumping off point for new players.

You should consider tactics as you begin to build an army. You want to make sure that you know how each element fits into your roster. Think about whether you want to charge into melee combat or let your enemy come to you, or whether you need certain models to accomplish scenario objectives. If possible, you'll want to consider the composition of the faction you're playing against. Make sure your forces are adaptable in case your opponent might have a surprise in store.

Before play, thoroughly familiarize yourself with the models you intend to field. Make certain you have a good idea of the relative strengths and weakness of your force, check the ranges of your weapons, and re-read all the spells possessed by your warcasters. Familiarizing yourself with the rules will not only allow you to play better, but also keep the game moving along.

Another good rule of thumb is to combine fire to remove larger models out of play. Do not spread your fire among too many targets. Drop one enemy before moving on to the next, since even a damaged warjack is a viable threat. Of course, once a model has been crippled to the point of uselessness you may wish to target a more threatening model.

Use infantry to screen warjacks and warcasters. Units can easily block enemy charges. The relatively high defense of some models can also drag out conflicts between infantry troops and warjacks.

Choose your fights carefully. Try to avoid fights that are stacked too far in your opponent's favor or skirmishes that tie up forces for too long, thus using up valuable resources that could be better used elsewhere. Remember that the fastest way to take apart your opponent's force is to knock out their warcasters. Keep your forces ready and mobile and keep your eye on the prize.

Pay careful attention to your control areas. It's easy to overextend your battelgroup and suddenly find your warjacks out of range at a critical moment. Feel free to measure your warcasters' control areas at anytime, but remember this is the only form of pre-measuring allowed in WARMACHINE.

Use your arc nodes to extend the range of your spells. Move your arc nodes into enemy range only when you're ready to use them. Careful deployment of your arc nodes keeps your enemy on the run and second-guessing your attacks.

Use focus points wisely. There is no need to use all your focus points. When allocating points, be careful not to give your warjacks more than they need. Plan out your movement and attacks in advance to best conserve focus points.

Boost attack rolls for weapons with powerful critical effects. The extra die vastly increases the likelihood of scoring a critical hit against the target.

Conserve your feats. Use them only at times when you absolutely need them. They are a great threat when kept in reserve and can easily keep your enemy at arm's length.

Know your enemy. Be prepared for your enemy's spells and feats, they can easily change the tide of war. Do not assume infantry troops are harmless. In the proper circumstances, infantry can hit every bit as hard as warjacks.

Do not be afraid to ask to see your opponent's record sheets. Even the best of us occasionally make mistakes.

Target enemy arc nodes. Losing arc nodes greatly restricts your opponent's ability to target you with unforeseen attacks.

CRYX

Cryx specializes in speed and dirty tricks. Very fast and maneuverable, Cryx is capable of laying waste to their opponents wherever and whenever they choose, always keeping their enemies guessing. The key is speed, pure and simple. Comprised of large numbers of light, extremely fast models, Cryxian armies tend to race forward at breakneck speeds, scything into their opponent's front ranks. A player of the Cryxian faction should not be afraid to hit hard and fast, and never let up. As long as you bear down on your enemy quickly, you should be able to absorb the rate of attrition your forces are sure to sustain.

As much as speed is a great advantage for Cryx, it also has some pitfalls. Players should avoid spreading their forces out or clumping them in places where they cannot reach the enemy. Forces get spread out when fast models are allowed to outpace slower models, or when the controlling player attempts to keep some models in reserve. Whatever the case, the effect is always the same. The first models arrive without support and are decimated. Your opponent then has time to close any gaps in their line and prepare for your second wave. Be unrelenting, but be measured.

Choose your fights carefully. Cryx has the speed and maneuverability to engage the enemy at will. Look for the soft spots. Do not just mindlessly move your units forward without a plan. Make sure the first models to engage the enemy are supported by additional models, and take care not to position slower models in front of faster ones.

Cryxian models tend to be very fast and hard to hit, but they are also lightly armored. Watch out for the withering effect of your enemy's ranged attacks, which reduce numbers before your models ever arrive in melee, especially area-of-effect weapons that cause severe damage even if they fail to hit directly.

Play dirty...but don't cheat! In addition to speed, Cryx has potent magical abilities designed to lay waste to all who stand against them. Use combinations to your advantage. Cryx has a wide variety of spells, abilities, and weapons that play off one another. Nail hard targets with spells that lower their resistances and then gang up to bring them down quickly.

Arc nodes, arc nodes, arc nodes! In addition to some of the most devastating spells in the game, Cryx has a wealth of arc nodes and large control areas. By carefully using your arc nodes, your opponent will have no idea where you're going to strike next.

Target enemy warcasters to keep them on the run. Most of your opponent's army can be easily ignored as long as you go after their warcasters early and often. All that's required to kill off an enemy warcaster is careful deployment of a couple bonejacks and plenty of focus points.

Cryx also has access to many weapons and spells that cause *corrosion*. Most effective against units, corrosion is a death sentence for ordinary troops with a single wound. It is also a potent weapon when used against enemy warcasters, damaging them round after round. But spread out your corrosion attacks. Once a model is affected by corrosion, there's no benefit from repeated corrosion attacks.

Warcasters

Cryx has some of the most powerful warcasters in the game. They're fast, skilled, well armed, and know the foul secrets of all manner of arcane power. Cryxian warcasters are never to be taken lightly. Each one has a specific set of powers and specializations, making them amazing to play with, and a nightmare to play against.

Not only are warcasters of the Cryxian Empire powerful magicians, they are deadly combatants capable of leveling even the most powerful war machines. Some carry soul cages, which allow them to harvest the spirits of their victims and convert this into more magical power.

The dreaded Iron Lich Asphyxious is best used at a distance, channeling damage spells through his bonejacks. Tear apart heavy warjack defenses with repeated castings of *iron blight*, and then go in for the kill with a blast of *hellfire*. If the Iron Lich manages to get into melee combat, he can shred most opponents with little trouble, but keep enough focus points in reserve in case he needs to beat a fast retreat with his *wings of shadow*.

The stealthy Warwitch Deneghra is an obvious choice for quick and dirty missions. Her ability to sneak up on enemy models without being hit by ranged attacks makes her an invaluable resource among the rapidly moving forces. Use her debilitating spells to strip hard targets of their defenses or send her into melee combat supported by a helljack. The warwitch's potent abilities allow her to dance through combat, paralyzing the enemy in their tracks.

Skarre the Pirate Queen is most effective when supported by troops that can fuel and play off her abilities. Keep her surrounded by inexpensive mechanithrall and sacrifice them surgically to remove threats as they arise. Only use her feat when victory is within your grasp.

Warjacks

Cryx fields two terrifying varieties of war machines in its army—brutal helljacks and sleek, arc node-bearing bonejacks. Helljacks are ferocious combatants that tear through enemy units, rend iron, and generally make a mess of anything that stands in their way. Though fast and hard to hit, helljacks are also lightly armored and easily damaged.

Slayers provide the muscle behind Cryx's army. With a staggering number of attacks, the Slayer's ferociousness is without equal. The Reaper has only slightly more finesse with its *harpoon* and *helldriver*. Use harpoons carefully. At times, they are incredibly powerful; at other times, they are nearly useless, but nothing is better than getting in and harpooning an enemy warcaster, dragging them into the waiting embrace of a Reaper, and then turning them into paste with a helldriver.

The real workhorse of the Cryxian army, bonejacks are the lightest war machines fielded in the Iron Kingdoms. They are fast, nearly impossible to hit, and provide their masters with amazing spell targeting capabilities. Though armed with a number of small yet powerful weapons, the true role of a bonejack is to get its arc node in place. Always take a couple more of them than you think you need; they're hard to hit, but a single well placed blow can take one down. Nevertheless, no price can be put on the ability to blast your enemies with *hellfire* at will.

Solos and Units

Cryx has a large number of viscious and dirty units to choose from. Each one has its advantages, but by no stretch of the imagination are any of them considered elite troops. Cryxian units tend to be both fast and cheap or powerful specialists designed to lay waste to anything in their path.

Though relatively slow, bane thralls are potent troops that can be amazingly useful at the right time and place. Their *stealth* ability allows them to shamble ever closer to the enemy, suffering few losses from ranged attacks. Once they make it to the front lines, maneuver them toward hard targets that might be softened up by their *dark shroud* ability. To magnify the effect, cast *crippling grasp* or *parasite* spells on your target to really get the beat-down underway. If anything's left after that, blast away with *hellfire* or *venom* spells to finish them off.

Mechanithrall are a cheap and plentiful unit. Buy them up to a full squad of ten models and set them loose on your opponents. They are effective against units and warjacks alike. Though they have a low melee attack stat, they can make two attacks per combat action that are more than powerful enough to kill most infantry troops with a single hit. Save their combo strike for larger models, where the high POW can punch through heavy warjack armor.

Use bile thrall sparingly for best effect. They can often damage each other with their spray and purge attacks. Deploy them against enemy unit concentrations and avoid getting them too close to units of your enemy's ranged troops.

Skarlock thralls can add significant firepower to your forces. Avoid the temptation to move them too far forward, though, as they can be an all too tempting target for ranged attacks. Use them to take out petty nuisances that are beneath your warcasters, and it is best to always screen them with a unit for protection.

CYGNAR

Cygnar may be the most flexible of all the faction armies. Its forces are fast, skilled, and suited to a variety of roles in the field. Properly supported, Cygnar's infantry has little trouble tearing through enemy warjacks.

Though light and fast, Cygnar's forces tend to lack some of the destructive force of other factions. Cygnar stries for a balance between strength and maneuverability. Having the most advanced weapons in the game doesn't hurt either.

Cygnar's greatest strength is the effectiveness of its ranged attacks. With powerful warjacks, enhanced spells, and a variety of ranged attack units to choose from, Cygnar can lay down a sea of lead. Spells can be used to boost already long ranges and high RAT stats for a truly devastating effect. Imagine a unit of long gunners blasting away from a fixed position with a Defender firing over their heads, all with *deadeye* and *snipe* cast on them, sinking shots into enemy models at what was presumed to have been lurking at a safe distance.

In addition to its ranged attack ability, Cygnar also excels at improving the natural advantages of the army and taking those same abilities away from their opponents. It is easy to stall the advance of incoming enemy models by extending range to pick them off as they muddle their way through an advance, and Cygnar has a wealth of *knockdown* and *disruption* attacks for paralyzing the enemy where they stand.

When constructing your army, try to keep a balance between infantry units and warjacks. Units may be as powerful as warjacks—and less costly at the same time—but they lack the 'jack's staying power. As the battle rages, you might eventually see your long gunner units wither away under enemy fire, but your Defenders will stay strong.

Warcasters

Cygnaran warcasters are versatile and well balanced. Each has an array of weapons, spells, and abilities that suit a variety of battlefield roles. Just keep them from being pinned down in melee combat, for Cygnar has better leaders than melee fighters.

Commander Coleman Stryker is a good all-around warcaster. He is fairly quick and hard to hit, possessing an assortment of disruption weapons, and can usually hold his own until assistance arrives. His spells are balanced between augmentation, attack, and defense. Stryker is a good and solid core for any force.

Captain Victoria Haley is the most powerful Cygnaran warcaster. She's not only focus-rich, but possesses a good number of spells designed to slow the enemy's advance. Save some of her focus points each turn to take advantage of her spear's *arcane vortext*. With her high focus, Haley can support larger battle groups than other Cygnaran warcasters.

The gunfighter, Lieutenant Allister Caine, is a tricky warcaster to field. He's a specialist that can cripple advancing enemies with ease, but a fairly weak warcaster in melee. Send him into combat and blast away with his *spellstorm pistols*, and then have him *flash* away to nearby safety. Controlling players also have to struggle between spending his focus on devastating attacks or to fuel his warjacks. He works best when deployed with a tight battle group consisting of some Lancers that are able to channel his powerful *thunder strike* spell.

Warjacks

Cygnar's warjacks are the trademark of modern battlefield technology. They are quick, mobile, and pack a wallop. Cygnar relies on its heavy warjacks to deliver the big blows as the light 'jacks move swiftly in to deliver more firepower where needed.

Fast and tough, Cygnar's heavy warjacks are potent. The Ironclad easily crushes enemy warjacks with its *quake hammer*, slamming them to the ground and setting them up for volleys of ranged attacks. The Defender is invaluable for softening up enemy hard targets from a distance. Used in a one-two combination with long gunners, enemy warjacks often sustain crippling damage before they ever reach charging range.

The Charger and the Sentinel are fast weapon platforms that lay waste to units and soft targets alike. Remember to fuel them with focus points to boost their damage rolls against harder targets. The Lancer is a solid channeler that can greatly extend the range of Cygnar's offensive spells. It is best to keep your Lancers in cover when possible, since most enemies prefer to shoot at them from afar rather than risking their warjacks in melee against the Lancer's *shock shield*.

Solos and Units

Cygnar is blessed with a large number of trained personnel suited to a variety of battlefield roles. These elite units can hold their own against anything the other factions have to offer.

Long gunners are among the most dangerous units in the game. With their long-ranged dual-shooting rifles and combined ranged attacks, they certainly slow the advance of enemy models. For best effect, position them in places where they can overlook the battlefield, moving as little as possible. Keep in mind they may only fire twice if they don't move, but they'll gain the aiming for both shots!

Gun mages are notoriously dangerous and hard to kill. One of the hardest units to hit, gun mages excel at slowing enemy advances with their *thunder bolt* and *shocker* attacks.

Trenchers are the most versatile unit in the game, invaluable for holding back enemy advances or in scenario play. Position your trenchers where they cause the most havoc and dig in, but don't be afraid to pull them back if their positions are overrun.

Stormblades are powerful units that can bring down the heaviest opponents. Remember to keep them together to protect their captain so they can gain the benefit of his *storm rod*.

Field mechaniks can be of great value in keeping your warjacks in top condition. Use your firepower to hold your opponents at bay as you pull back your heavily damaged warjacks for repairs. In a pinch, fast moving gobber bodgers can be deployed to screen your warcasters from charges or ranged attacks.

To cause a great deal of unexpected havoc, take a journeyman warcaster and assign him a Defender, freeing up focus points for one of your other warcasters. Lone journeymen can also be used to collect inert warjacks that formerly belonged to fallen warcasters.

KHADOR

The backbone of Khador's army is the huge warjacks that easily decimate anything in their path, often with a single blow. These brutes lack the refinement of the warjacks of the other factions, requiring Khadoran warcasters to constantly fuel them with focus points to keep them battle ready. Adapting to the inherent weaknesses in their war machines, the Khadoran army has developed a number of fast moving and hard hitting special forces units, blending them with its lumbering monstrosities into a potent combination.

On the surface, Khador seems to have a simplistic play style—go forth and crush everything that gets near you! With the largest warjacks and an awesome array of spells and powers, Khador justifiably seems unstoppable. Their warjacks easily shrug off attacks that cripple lesser machines, and at the same time delivering crushing blows that drop even heavy jacks with a single strike.

Beneath the surface, Khador has some hidden weaknesses to overcome. First of all, their huge warjacks have sacrificed speed and grace for raw power and defense. With relatively low attack scores, their warjacks seldom hit without boosting their attack rolls. Of course, when they hit, the results are spectacular.

The apparent slow progress of the Khadoran army may also be an advantage. Just when your opponent is lulled into a false sense of security, bust out with *boundless charge* spells or the Dark Prince's *forced march* feat. Your opponent will never know what hit 'em.

Khador also lacks light warjacks. That may not seem like much of a setback until you consider that light warjacks generally cost fewer points and move faster than heavy warjacks. Without light warjacks, Khador also lacks arc nodes. Without the added spell range, focus points are usually spent to overcome the weaknesses in war machines rather than on powerful attacks. Good managing of resources is the key to overcoming these weaknesses.

Most of the time, a Khadoran warcasters allocates his focus points to his warjacks in order to boost their attack rolls. Between low attack scores and slow movement, Khadoran warjacks need all the help they can get. Even though the warcasters have powerful spells, they are relatively short range, and without channelers they often have a hard time reaching their intended targets. Plan your focus point distribution carefully. Think about what you want to accomplish. Don't gamble with potential outcomes.

The warcaster must be protected at all costs. It is preferred to let the warjacks bear the burden of the attack and cause the best part of the damage. The loss of a warcaster is crippling to any army, but more so to Khador; there are very few focus points to go around once a warcaster falls. So carefully plan your deployment. Make sure you can protect your warcasters and support your units to maximum effect.

One of the most effective deployment strategies when fielding multiple warcasters is to form a convoy. Put a couple of Destroyers in the front row with a warcaster behind them, and then position a couple more warjacks behind the warcaster, followed by yet another warcaster. These convoys allow warcasters to support one another as they rely upon their warjacks for protection.

Convoy strategies that work well include elements such as designating different warcasters to control the Destroyers in the front so that no one warcaster is fueling all their *bombard* attacks, and positioning ranks of warjacks tightly together so the warcasters don't need to worry about being hit by slam attacks into their front ranks. Careful use of spells and feats also offer maximum benefit to the entire convoy—*wind wall* and *fog of war* can be used to effectively cover most, if not all, of a convoy.

Needless to say, the simplest tactics are often the most effective ones. Punch a hole through your enemy's lines and crush the hardest targets first. Don't worry too much about getting warjacks damaged; just get them up there. They are built to take a lot of abuse, and once your Marauders are in place, there's very little your opponent can do but pick up the pieces of his beloved warjacks.

Warcasters

Khadoran warcasters embody the spirit of their people. They are grim, determined, no-nonsense warriors that hold their own in any fight. They tend to be powerful melee fighters, with some of the most strategic feats in the game.

Keep your warcasters out of the front lines. Since Khador's warjacks are so difficult to take down, many opponents ignore them altogether and focus on attacking the warcaster whenever possible. Though formidable, the warcaster is still physically weaker than his 'jacks. With Khador's relatively small number of warjacks, care must be taken to keep an enemy from flanking the warcaster. Avoid the temptation to get them into melee. Though any one of them, armed with their magics, could stand toe-to-toe with the heaviest warjacks in the game, they are much too important to throw heedlessly at the enemy.

Sorscha is an extremely potent warcaster with great tactical potential. She not only possesses powerful weapons and spells, but also has the dreaded *icy gaze* feat that can change the tide of battle in a single round. Save her feat until the right moment. It is a powerful psychological tool to keep over your opponent's head. Careful use of the *wind rush* spell allows her to take her opponents completely off guard.

The Butcher of Khardov is one of the most dominant warriors to ever walk the Iron Kingdoms. Get the Butcher's warjacks into melee fast. Pile the focus points on them, then let loose with the Butcher's *blood frenzy* feat to begin cleaving your foes into little bitty pieces.

The Dark Prince is a must for larger scale battles. Between careful use of his *wind wall* spell and *forced march* feat, Khador can close in swifter than expected on enemy forces before sustaining too much damage.

Warjacks

No army in all the Iron Kingdoms can compete with the sheer brutality of the Khadoran war machines. If you are playing Khador, odds are it is because you want to beat your opponent to pulp with some serious heavy hitters. Their warjacks are huge, powerful, and tough. Not only can they deal a lot of damage, they can also take it.

It is generally best to boost attack rolls over damage rolls. A lot of weapons have powerful critical effects that come up more often with an additional die. Khador also hits hard enough that an additional die of damage may not make much of a difference if you crush you enemy with a single hit.

Don't engage enemy units with your warjacks. The last thing you want to do is get bogged down fighting rank and file in melee as your opponent positions his warjacks to take out your warcasters.

Destroyers provide ranged attack support for the Khadoran army. Though far from surgical, they can pitch Bombard blasts far ahead of advancing forces. Juggernauts and Marauders are the heavy hitters of the army. Both are terrifying in melee and rip anything they come into contact with into its base components.

Solos and Units

With a potent variety of specialists at its disposal, Khador may be considered a special forces army. They have the greatest number of *advance deploy* troops, which lends some obvious advantages over other factions, even taking into account the slow speed of their 'jacks. Khadoran units are a good blend of effective rank and file troops and well-trained guerilla fighters developed specifically to fill the holes in their army.

The Winter Guard and Iron Fangs are Khador's basic units. Both are highly effective squads that benefit from good maneuverability and combined attacks. Keep the Winter Guard back to support your flanks and to protect lone warcasters. Send Iron Fangs forward to charge your opponent's front lines.

The heavily armored Man-O-War are Khador's answer to light warjacks. They are the immovable object rounding out Khador's unstoppable force. Position them to tie up advancing enemy units.

Widowmakers easily slow down enemy advances. Use them surgically to take out enemy infantry leaders or later in the game to target weakened warjacks with their *sniper* ability. *Advance deploy* makes them a dangerous wildcard.

Reavers are among the most terrifying melee troops in the game. Impossible to target with spells, insanely powerful in melee combat, and advance deployment makes them a brilliant addition to any army. Just be careful to keep them from butchering each other during a frenzied melee!

Battle mechaniks can be of great use in the unlikely event that one of your warjacks actually goes down. Usually mechaniks are used to keep your weapons in prime order, better to hammer away at your opponent's forces.

Manhunters are powerful assassins. Effective across most terrain, the Manhunter can make powerful charges, potentially bringing down even heavy warjacks. Avoid getting them too close before you're prepared to strike, as they're not built to take many direct hits.

PROTECTORATE OF MENOTH

The Protectorate of Menoth is a powerful faction with few weak points, bringing fire and pain to those who dare refute the Creator. There is no place for subtlety with the Menites of the Protectorate, and they are not to be trifled with. This is a well-balanced army consisting of focus-rich warcasters, powerful war machines, and countless numbers of fanatical infantry sporting destructive weapons.

The Menites are a solid fighting force capable of a fair share of surprises. They rival Khador in the brute force of their war machines, their warcasters match Cryx for magical potency, and though they might lack the sophistication of Cygnar's ranged weapon technology, the Protectorate more than makes up for this shortcoming with the sheer brutality of its weaponry. The Menites may not hit their mark every time, but if they launch enough rockets, the effect is the same.

The Protectorate's core strengths are its many prayers and protective spells, as well as the numbers of its infantry. With the proper support, the Menites excel at making passable models into incredible ones. Spells, warpriest chants, and special abilities work in tandem to increase the effectiveness of Menite warjacks and troopers. Select a warpriest and Choir to follow your warjacks around and keep the bulk of your forces within the confines of a *Eye of Menoth* spell. Play defensive until you're close enough to your enemy to unleash battle prayers.

Channelers are a Menite warcaster's best asset. Strategic positioning of Revengers allow warcasters to remain out of harm's way and, at the same time, pound their enemies with a constant barrage of fiery death. A Choir in the right place can also go a long way toward keeping the Revenger safe from enemy reprisals.

The Protectorate has a great supply of low point cost infantry units that pack a powerful punch, especially when properly supported. Their warjacks are also among the least expensive in the game. Be careful to select a well-balanced army between high numbers of expendable troops and a manageable number of warjacks.

The Protectorate has a powerful mix of ranged and melee capabilities at its disposal. Long-range rockets easily lay waste to weaker units as long as you fire enough into a small area. Flame belchers, flamethrowers, and firebombs are all powerful short-range attacks that decimate stronger foes. Warjacks, Knights Exemplars, and Temple Flameguard provide most of the up close and dirty muscle. Remember to select enough melee units to support your ranged attack units when things get ugly.

And finally, keep your warcasters at a safe distance from the front lines! Menite warcasters are pretty tough, but they are no match for most enemy warjacks or warcasters when melee breaks out. It is best to keep them behind a wall of the faithful. Keep plenty of targets between your warcasters and their guns; not only will the High Reclaimer *reclaim* his fill, but he will also last longer. If you have a warcaster take serious damage, pull them away from the battle with an escort to stand between them and the enemy, and use some of that ample focus pool to heal up.

Warcasters

Menite warcasters are limited in their martial prowess, but they more than make up for this with their high focus and powerful spells, geared toward protection and increasing the combat ability of friendly models, as well as reducing the enemy to cinders. Plenty of focus points means you won't even have to choose which spells to cast and which to upkeep—you'll be able to cast spells all day.

High Exemplar Kreoss is the toughest of the Menite warcasters. With a high damage capacity and one of the best feats in the game, Kreoss can go toe-to-toe with just about anyone. Surround him with Crusaders and Vanquishers and punch a wide hole through your enemy's line. Use his feat to knock down enemy models, then position your warjacks to lay waste to them as they scramble for cover.

Kreoss may be the toughest of Menoth's warcasters, but the venerable Grand Scrutator Severius is the most feared. With one of the highest focus stats in the game, a potent feat, and a huge number of spells at his disposal, Severius can really shake up the battlefield. He's no close quarters combatant, however. Use him behind the lines, allocating focu points to a small army of warjacks, commanding masses of troops, and always maintaining a *Eye of Menoth* spell.

The High Reclaimer may seem deceptively underpowered when you first read his stats, but he can raise hell on the battlefield when properly supported. Keep him surrounded by large numbers of zealots to fuel his divine powers as they fall. When he *reclaims* enough souls from their deaths, lay waste to your enemies with repeated *ashes to ashes* spells.

Warjacks

The Protectorate of Menoth is a faction that can field a large number of warjacks. Its reliable 'jacks are solid, no-frills bruisers that hit often and hit hard. Their low costs coupled with the warcasters' high focus points make for a powerful combination.

Crusaders and Vanquishers are the workhorses of the Menite armies. They're a bit on the slow end, but still tough-as-nails fighters with a powerful punch. The Vanquisher's *flame belcher* often reduces whole units to ash with a single blast.

Revengers may be the most important warjacks in Menoth's arsenal. They're tough, solid troops that can channel powerful spell barrages, keeping their warcasters a safe distance from the enemy. Their armored hulls and *repulsor shields* keep them running in even the heaviest fighting.

Repenters and Redeemers offer a choice of maneuverable ranged attack capabilities. Use Repenters in battle groups intended to close with your enemies. Redeemers are best deployed behind the lines where they can hurl salvos into enemy ranks.

Solos and Units

Most Menite troops are fairly inexpensive and best used in large numbers. Expect to suffer wear and tear, so fill out your unit sizes to bolster their ability to carry on the fight, and always keep some of them guarding your warcasters for added protection.

Temple Flameguard and Knights Exemplar are the Protectorate's melee specialists. Flameguard are most effective when they're kept close together to benefit from combined attacks and shield walls. The Knights Exemplar have the peculiar ability to augment their effectiveness as their brethren fall, so cut them loose to charge the enemy at will.

There are a couple of ranged attack units to choose from within the Protectorate's army. Whenever possible, stack any attack modifiers from spells, special abilities, and aiming bonuses to keep the missile troops hitting. Deliverers are inaccurate but powerful troops. Use them in large concentrations so that even if they score only a few direct hits, they can still cause damage with deviating blast templates. Holy zealots are powerful short-range attack troops that have the power to bring down even the heaviest warjack—of course, they're not always terribly accurate and often blow themselves to bits, so it's a good idea to keep the High Reclaimer in proximity to *reclaim* their souls.

The Choir of Menoth are invaluable members of the Menite army. With their powerful battle hymns they turn the tide of battle to the Protectorate's favor. Consider deploying multiple units to extend these effects over several portions of the battlefield.

Paladins of the Order of the Wall are powerful solos that can go head-to-head with most light warjacks and occasionally even bring down a heavy warjack on a charge. Paladins are best used to support Menite units to give them an edge in combat, and they are especially good at bringing down injured warjacks.

MERCENARIES

Mercenaries add a great deal of variation to standard armies. Opponents get used to playing against the various models and units each faction has at their disposal, and mercenaries introduce that unexpected wildcard to the game. In addition to adding unfamiliar models to the ranks of an army, mercenaries also help get around the innate weaknesses of each faction. For instance, the mage hunter adds firepower, magical abilities, and advance deployment that may be unavailable to some factions. It is also worth noting that mercenaries refuse to work for some factions.

When playing with mercenaries there are a couple things to keep in mind. Models removed from play by mercenaries do not count toward the victory point total of their army. It's best to use mercenaries to soften up hard targets and then use your faction forces to bring them down.

Mercenaries have to rely on their own abilities in the field. They're also not considered to be a part of the faction they're fighting alongside. If a Menite player was using Herne and Jonne in a game with the High Reclaimer and they should fall in combat, the High Reclaimer can't use his *reclaim* ability to gain additional focus points because the mercs aren't considered Menites.

Eiryss, Mage Hunter

Eiryss is an extremely versatile solo that can paralyze the advance of a whole army. She also has a staggering number of specialized arcane attacks—she can rob warcasters of their focus points and make extremely effective attacks without putting herself in the line of fire. Save her until she's needed since she's quite an attractive target, and often she'll only get one shot—make sure it counts.

When deploying the elven mage hunter, remember that she cannot end her movement within 5" of a friendly warjack. As your forces advance, she'll be on the move. It's beneficial to keep a unit of troops nearby to soak up most of the firepower directed her way, since she'll not be able to walk up behind them for protection.

Greygore Boomhowler and Trollkin Mercenaries

Greygore Boomhowler and his gang are tenacious fighters. With their *tough* ability they can take a lot of abuse, allowing them time to come in close to their opponents where they can do their damage. Greygore's *fell call* is a powerful tool, sending enemies scurrying away as your forces advance the field. They are most effective when splitting their attacks between stink bombs and blunderbusses to weaken their opponents until they close within melee range. The trollkin are best employed against factions other than Cryx, as the vast majority of Cryxian forces are undead and unhindered by the *fell call* or stink bombs.

Herne and "Arquebus" Jonne

Herne and "Arquebus" Jonne are incredibly effective models with a great deal of firepower. Whether they're fielded with Khador, adding additional ranged firepower to their heavy armor, or with Cygnar, where they can benefit from a number of enhancing spells, the team is always a welcome addition. The *barrage arquebus* is perfect for devastating infantry concentrations, its blasts peppering the battlefield at random and laying waste to large areas. Move them as little as possible; the aiming bonus makes them more effective when they open up, and keep the ogrun in front of the dwarf, where he can suck up the majority of any damage coming their way.

Reinholdt

Reinholdt is a great supplement to Cygnaran or Khadoran warcasters. The ability to make additional ranged attacks or occasionally re-roll a failed throw is a wonderful bonus. Don't underestimate the spyglass, either—the ability to pre-measure a precise attack can make the difference between success and failure. With his low point cost, there are few reasons not to field this gobber in almost any game.

GLOSSARY

GAME TERMS AND DEFINITIONS

Ability(pg. 27): An ability typically gives a benefit or capability that modifies how the standard rules apply to a model. Abilities are always in effect and apply every time a game situation warrants their use.

Action(pg. 38): After moving, a model can perform one action per round, either a combat action or a special action. Some types of movement or special rules require a model to forfeit its action or restrict the type of action it can perform.

Activation Phase(pg. 32): The activation phase is the major portion of a player's turn. A player may activate each model and unit he controls once during this phase, except for models that fled in the maintenance phase.

Active Model(pg. 32): The model currently activated by a player. Typically, an active model first moves, then performs one *action*.

Active Unit(pg. 32): The unit currently activated by a player. Troopers do not activate independently—an entire unit activates at once. Every member of the unit must complete or forfeit its movement before any member uses an action. After completing the entire unit's movement, resolve each trooper's action and attacks in turn.

Advancing(pg. 35): A model moves up to its Speed (SPD) in inches when advancing. An advancing model can perform an action after completing its movement.

Aiming(pg. 45): A model that voluntarily forfeits its movement by not changing its position or facing gains a +2 bonus to every ranged attack roll it makes as part of its combat action. A *magic attack* does not get the aiming bonus.

Arc Node(pg. 56): A passive relay carried by a channeler that effectively extends a warcaster's spell range.

Area of Effect (AOE), (pg.47): The diameter in inches of the template an area-of-effect weapon or spell uses for damage effects. All models covered by the template potentially suffer the attack's effects.

Armlock(pg. 42): A type of power attack. A successful armlock prevents the opposing warjack from moving or using the locked weapon system.

Armor (ARM)(pg. 25): A model's ability to resist being damaged. A model takes one damage point for every point that a damage roll exceeds its ARM stat.

Arm System: Any warjack system with an arm location.

Army Points: Each encounter level gives the maximum number of army points each player can spend when designing an army. An army cannot exceed the maximum number of army points allowed by the selected level.

Automatic Effect(pg. 52): Apply an automatic effect every time it meets the conditions required to function.

Back Arc(pg. 27): The rear 180° of a model's base, opposite its front arc.

Back Strike(pg. 48): An attack against an unaware model's back arc. A back strike gives a +2 bonus to the attack roll.

Base Size(pg. 27): The physical size and mass of a model are reflected by its base size. There are three base sizes: small base (30mm), medium base (40mm), and large base (50mm).

Bash(pg. 40): A less than optimum warjack melee attack option. Also, a warjack attempting a slam power attack instead makes a bash attack if it moved less than 3". A bash attack suffers a −2 penalty to the attack roll and causes a damage roll of 2d6+STR.

Battlegroup(pg. 28): A battlegroup includes a warcaster and the warjacks he controls. A warcaster can allocate focus points to or channel spells through only the warjacks in his battlegroup.

GLOSSARY

Blast Damage: Every model with any part of its base covered by an AOE template is automatically hit by the attack and takes a blast damage roll of 2d6+1/2POW.

Boosting(pg. 54): A warcaster or warjack may spend a focus point to add one additional die to any attack roll or damage roll. The model must spend the focus point and declare it is boosting the roll before rolling any dice.

Channeler(pg. 56): A warjack equipped with an arc node.

Character(pg. 29): A model that represents a unique individual from the Iron Kingdoms. An army may include only one model of each named character. A character follows the rules for its basic model type.

Charge(pg. 35): A type of movement that combines with a model's combat action to make a charge attack.

Charge attack(pg. 35): If a charging model moved at least 3", its first attack is a charge attack. A charge attack roll is made normally and may be *boosted*. If the charge attack hits, add an additional die to the damage roll. This damage roll cannot be boosted.

Cloud Effect(pg. 52): A cloud effect produces an area of dense smoke or gas that remains in play at its *point of impact*. Consider every model with any part of its base covered by the cloud's template to be inside the cloud and susceptible to its effects. A model inside a cloud effect gains +2 DEF against ranged and magic attacks, which is cumulative with *concealment* or *cover*.

Collateral Damage(pg. 42): If a slammed or thrown model collides with another model that has an equal- or smaller-sized base, that model is knocked down and suffers a collateral damage roll of 2d6 plus the STR of the warjack that initiated the slam or throw. Collateral damage cannot be *boosted*. A model that has a larger-sized base than the slammed model does not take collateral damage.

Combat Action(pg. 38): A model can perform a combat action after advancing, charging, or forfeiting its movement. A combat action lets a model make *attacks*. A model performing a combat action can choose one of the following attack combinations:

- A model *in melee* can make one *melee attack* with each of its *melee weapons* in *melee range*.
- A model not in melee can make one *ranged attack* with each of its *ranged weapons*.
- A model can make one *special attack* allowed by its special rules instead of making any other attacks.
- A warjack that did not charge can spend a focus point to make one *power attack* instead of making any other attacks.

Command (CMD), (pg.25): A model's willpower, leadership, and self-discipline. To pass a command check, a model must roll equal to or less than its CMD stat. Command also determines a warcaster's command range. Warjacks do not have a CMD stat.

Command Check(pg. 57): When a situation requires a model or unit to make a command check, roll 2d6—if the result is equal to or less its Command (CMD) stat, it passes the check. In most cases, this means the model or unit continues to function normally or rallies if it was fleeing. If the roll is greater than its CMD, the check fails and the model or unit suffers the consequences.

Command Range(pg. 57): A warcaster has a command range equal to his CMD stat in inches. A model or unit in a warcaster's command range may use the caster's CMD when making a command check, but is not required to do so. A warcaster can rally any model or unit and give orders to any unit in his command range.

Concealment(pg. 46): Some terrain features and special effects grant a model concealment by making it more difficult to be seen, though they are not dense enough to actually block an attack. A model within 1" of a concealing terrain feature that obscures any portion of its base from an attacker gains +2 DEF against ranged and magic attacks from that opponent. Concealment provides no benefit against a *spray attack*.

Continuous Effect(pg. 52): Continuous effects remain on a model and have the potential to damage it on subsequent turns. Resolve continuous effects on models you control during the maintenance phase of your turn. Roll a d6—if the result is a 1 or 2, remove the effect immediately without causing further damage. On a 3 through 6, it remains in play and the model immediately suffers its effects.

Control Area(pg. 53): A warcaster's control area extends out from the caster in all directions for a distance of twice his Focus (FOC) in inches. A warjack must be within its warcaster's control area to receive focus points or *channel* spells, but it does not have to be in line of sight. Some spells and feats use the warcaster's control area as their *area of effect.*

Control Phase(pg. 32): During your control phase, each of your warcasters receives a number of *focus points* equal to his FOC stat. Each warcaster may allocate focus points to eligible warjacks within his *control area* and to his spells that require *upkeep.*

Cortex: The magical brain that gives a steamjack the ability to reason.

Cover(pg. 46): Some terrain features and special effects grant a model cover by being physically solid enough to block an attack against it. A model within 1" of a covering terrain feature that obscures any portion of its base from an attacker gains +4 DEF against ranged and magic attacks from that opponent. Cover provides no benefit against a *spray attack.*

Critical Effect(pg. 52): Apply a critical effect on a critical hit. A weapon with a critical effect has the label "Critical" to distinguish it from an automatic damage effect.

Critical Hit(pg. 52): A critical hit occurs if any two dice in an attack roll show the same number and the attack successfully hits.

Damage Boxes(pg. 27): Mark one damage box for each damage point a model takes. Remove the model from play once all its damage boxes are marked.

Damage Capacity(pg. 27): A model's damage capacity determines how many damage points it can take before being removed from play.

Damage Grids(pg. 27): A warjack has a damage grid consisting of multiple rows and columns of damage boxes. Different warjacks' damage grids may be slightly different in shape and number of damage boxes, but they function the same.

Damage Roll(pg. 50): Determine how much damage a successful attack causes by making a **damage roll.** Roll 2d6 and add the attack's Power (POW). Melee attacks also add the attacker's Strength (STR.) Compare this total against the target's Armor (ARM.) The target takes one *damage point* for every point that the damage roll exceeds its ARM.

Defense (DEF): A model's ability to avoid being hit by an attack. An attack roll must be equal to or greater than the target model's DEF value to score a hit against it.

Deviation(pg. 47): When an AOE attack misses its target, determine its actual point of impact by rolling deviation. Referencing the Deviation Diagram, roll a d6 to determine the direction the attack deviates.

Direct Hit(pg. 47): A successful attack roll by an area-of-effect weapon indicates a direct hit on the intended target. Center the weapon's AOE template directly over the model hit.

Direct Hit Damage(pg. 47): A target directly hit by an area-of effect weapon takes a direct hit damage roll of 2d6+POW.

Disabled(pg. 51): A system becomes disabled and can no longer be used when all its system boxes are marked. Mark the appropriate system status box to show this. A warjack becomes disabled when three of its systems are disabled.

Disabled Arc Node(pg. 51): A warcaster cannot channel spells through a warjack with a disabled arc node.

Disabled Cortex(pg. 51): A warjack with a disabled cortex loses any unused focus points and cannot receive any more focus points.

Disabled Hull(pg. 51): Disabling a warjack's hull has no direct effect. However, a disabled hull counts toward the disabled systems limit for disabling the entire warjack.

Disabled Movement(pg. 51): A warjack with disabled movement has its Speed (SPD) reduced to 1" and its Defense (DEF) reduced to 7. Disabled movement prevents a warjack from charging or making a slam attack.

Disabled Warjack(pg. 51): A warjack becomes disabled when three of its systems are disabled. Replace a disabled warjack model with a disabled wreck marker corresponding to its base size. A disabled warjack may be attacked and *continuous effects* and spells on it remain in play, so it may continue to take damage. A disabled warjack may return to operation if enough of its damage is repaired.

Disabled Weapon System(pg. 51): A disabled weapon system may no longer be used to make attacks. The warjack may no longer use special rules that require the use of this system.

Disabled Wreck Marker(pg. 51): Replace a disabled warjack model with a disabled wreck marker corresponding to its base size. A disabled warjack wreck provides *cover* and counts as *rough terrain* for movement.

Disengage(pg. 39): A model disengages from melee by moving out of its opponent's melee range. A model disengaging from melee combat is subject to a *free strike* by its opponent.

Elevated Attacker(pg. 45,60): A ranged or magic attack by an attacker on elevated terrain can target any model on lower terrain and in line of sight, regardless of intervening models.

Elevated Target: A model on higher ground than its attacker gains a +2 DEF bonus against ranged or magic attacks from that opponent.

Engaged(pg. 39): If a model is within an opponent's melee range, it is engaged in combat and primarily concerned with fighting its nearest threat. An engaged model is in melee and cannot make ranged attacks. An engaged model can move freely as long as it stays inside its opponent's melee range.

Engaging(pg. 39): A model automatically engages every opponent in its melee range. Engaging models are in melee and cannot make ranged attacks.

Facing(pg. 27): A model's facing is the direction indicated by its head's orientation.

Falling(pg. 48): A model slammed, pushed, or that otherwise moves off of an elevated surface greater than 1" tall takes a damage roll and is knocked down. A fall of up to 3" causes a POW 10 damage roll. Add an additional die to the damage roll for every additional increment of 3". Rounded up.

Feats(pg. 53): Each warcaster has a unique feat that he can use once per game. A warcaster can use this feat freely at any time during his activation, in addition to moving and performing an action.

Field allowance(pg. 24): The maximum number of models or units of a given type that may be included for each warcaster in an army.

First player(pg. 32): The player that deploys his army first and takes his turn first every game round.

First team: The team with the first player.

Fleeing(pg. 58): A model or unit that fails a command check against fleeing immediately turns to face directly away from the threat that caused the command check. A fleeing model activates during his controlling player's maintenance phases. A fleeing model automatically runs away from its nearest threat toward its army's deployment edge, using the most direct route that doesn't take it through a damaging effect or let enemies engage it. A fleeing model cannot perform any actions or use any of its special rules.

Focus (FOC), (pg. 53): A warcaster's arcane power. Add the warcaster's FOC value to its *magical attack* rolls. Focus also determines a warcaster's *control area* and *focus points*. Warcasters are the only models that have a FOC stat.

Focus Cost(pg. 54): The number of focus points a warcaster must spend to cast a spell.

Focus Points(pg. 53): The magical energy manipulated by a warcaster. Each of your warcasters receives a number of focus points equal to his Focus (FOC) stat during your control phase. A warcaster may allocate focus points to eligible warjacks in his *control area* and to his spells that require upkeep, or he can keep them to enhance his own abilities and cast spells.

Forest(pg. 60): A terrain feature that hinders movement and makes a model inside it difficult to see. A forest is considered *rough terrain*, but also provides *concealment* to a model with any part of its base inside its perimeter.

Formation(pg. 36): A unit operates as a single body and its members must strive to maintain formation. There are three different formations: skirmish, open, and tight. A trooper not in one of these formations is out of formation

Free Strike(pg. 40): When a model moves out of an enemy's melee range, its opponent may immediately make a free strike. The model makes one melee attack with any melee weapon in melee range and gains a +2 bonus to its melee attack roll. If the attack succeeds, add an additional die to its damage roll. Focus points may not be spent to further *boost* a free strike's attack or damage rolls or to allow any additional attacks.

Front Arc(pg. 27): The 180° arc centered on the direction a model's head faces.

Game Round(pg. 32): A measurement of game time. Each game round, every player takes a turn in the order established during setup. Once the last player in the *turn order* completes his turn, the current game round ends. A new game round then begins, starting again with the first player. Game rounds continue until one side wins the game.

Hazard(pg. 60): A terrain feature that causes adverse effects to a model entering it.

Head-butt(pg. 41): A type of power attack. A successful head-butt causes a damage roll and knocks down its target.

Headlock(pg. 42): A type of power attack. A successful headlock prevents the opposing warjack from moving or using the locked weapon system.

Heavy warjack(pg. 24): A warjack with a large base.

Hill(pg. 60): A terrain feature that represents a gentle rise or drop in elevation. A hill may be open or rough terrain, depending on the ground's nature. Unlike obstacles, hills do not impose any additional movement penalties. A model can charge up or down a hill in open terrain at no penalty.

Hull(pg. 27): A warjack's blank damage boxes represent its hull.

Impassable terrain(pg. 59): Natural terrain that completely prohibits movement. This includes cliff faces, lava, and deep water. A model cannot move across impassable terrain.

In Melee(pg. 39): A model is in melee if it is engaging an opponent or if it is engaged by an opponent. A model in melee cannot make ranged attacks.

Independent Models(pg. 24): An independent model is one that activates individually. Warcasters, warjacks, and solos are independent models.

Inert warjack(pg. 51): When a warcaster is removed from play, the warjacks in his battlegroup become inert and cease to function. An inert warjack may be reactivated by a friendly warcaster of the same faction.

Intervening Model(pg. 33): If any line between two models crosses another model's base, that model is an intervening model. A line of sight cannot be drawn across an intervening model's base to models that have equal- or smaller-sized bases.

Intervening Terrain(pg. 40): A model with any portion of its base obscured from its attacker by an obstacle or an obstruction gains a +2 DEF bonus against melee attacks from that opponent.

Knocked Down(pg. 49): Place a knocked-down model on its back. A knocked-down model is a stationary target until it stands up. To stand up, a model must forfeit either its movement or its action for that turn. Unlike other stationary targets, a knocked-down channeler cannot channel spells.

Large Base(pg. 27): A 50mm base.

Leader(pg. 24): Usually, one trooper in a unit is trained as a leader, a model with a different stat profile—and possibly different weaponry—that can rally and issue orders to his troopers in formation. While its leader is in play, a unit uses his CMD stat for all command checks.

Light warjack(pg. 24): A warjack with a medium base.

Linear Obstacle(pg. 60): An obstacle up to one 1" tall but less than 1" thick. Linear obstacles can be crossed.

Line of sight (LOS), (pg. 33): A model has line of sight to a target if you can draw a straight, unobstructed line from the center of its base at head height through its front arc to any part of the target model, including its base.

Living model(pg. 24): A model is a living model unless stated otherwise. Warjacks and undead are not living models. A living model has a soul.

Magic Attack(pg. 55): An attack made by an offensive spell. A magic attack follows all the rules for ranged attacks, including targeting, concealment and cover, and all other applicable rules. A warcaster can cast spells, including ranged spells, at models he is engaged with.

Magic Attack Roll(pg. 55): Determine a magic attack's success by making a magic attack roll. Roll 2d6 and add the attacking warcaster's Focus (FOC). An attack hits if the attack roll equals or exceeds the target's Defense (DEF).

Maintenance Phase(pg. 32): During the maintenance phase, remove markers and effects that expire this turn and resolve any compulsory effects on your models. Activate *fleeing models* and *units* under your control at the end of this phase.

Massive Casualties(pg. 57): A unit suffers massive casualties when it loses 50% or more of its current numbers in any player's turn. The unit must immediately pass a command check or *flee*.

Medium Base(pg. 27): A 40mm base.

Melee Attack(pg. 39): An attack with a melee weapon. A melee attack can be made against any target in *melee range* of the weapon being used

Melee Attack (MAT), (pg. 25): A model's skill with melee weapons such as swords and hammers, or natural weapons like fists and teeth. Add a model's MAT value to its *melee attack* rolls.

Melee Attack Roll(pg. 40): Determine a melee attack's success by making a melee attack roll. Roll 2d6 and add the attacking model's Melee Attack (MAT). An attack hits if the attack roll equals or exceeds the target's Defense (DEF).

Melee Combat(pg. 39): A model is participating in melee combat if it is making or receiving melee attacks.

Melee Range(pg. 39): A model can make melee attacks against any target in melee range. A model's melee range extends 1/2" beyond its front arc for any type of melee attack. A reach weapon has a melee range of 2".

Melee Weapons(pg. 39): Melee weapons include such implements as swords, hammers, flails, claws, saws, and axes. Some warjacks have an open fist or a shield that can be used as a melee weapon. A warjack can also use its body as a melee weapon for attacks such as a bash, head-butt, or slam. A melee weapon's damage roll is 2d6+POW+STR.

Model(pg. 24): The highly detailed and dramatically posed miniature figurine that represents a WARMACHINE combatant.

Model Statistic (Stat), (pg. 25): One of the numerical representations of a model's basic combat qualities—the higher the value, the better the stat.

Model Type(pg. 24): One of the categories of models that defines its game function. There are several basic model types: warcasters, warjacks, troopers, and solos.

Movement(pg. 34): The first part of a model's activation. A model must use or forfeit its movement before performing any action. There are three types of movement: advancing, charging, and running.

Obstacle(pg. 60): Any terrain feature up to 1" tall. Obstacles can be climbed.

Obstruction(pg. 60): A terrain feature greater than 1" tall. Treat obstructions as *impassable terrain.*

Offensive Spell(pg. 55): An offensive spell requires a successful magic attack roll to take effect. If the attack roll fails, the attack misses. A failed attack roll for a spell with an area of effect deviates according to those rules.

Open Formation(pg. 36): Troopers up to 1" apart are in open formation. Troopers in open formation are close enough to coordinate attacks and provide each other mutual support.

Open fist: Some warjacks have an open fist that can be used to manipulate objects or as a melee weapon. Open fists follow all the normal rules for melee attacks. A warjack's open fist damage roll is 2d6+STR. A warjack with an open fist may use the armlock/headlock and *throw* power attacks.

Open terrain(pg. 54): Smooth, even ground. Examples include grassy plains, barren fields, dirt roads, and paved surfaces. A model moves across open terrain without penalty.

Orders(pg. 49): An order lets a model or unit perform a specialized combat maneuver during its activation. A unit may receive an order from a warcaster prior to its activation, or from its *leader* at the beginning of its activation. A *solo* cannot issue orders to other models.

Out of Formation(pg. 37): A trooper is out of formation if it is further than 3" from the nearest member of its unit that is in formation.

Overboost Power Field(pg. 54): Each of a warcaster's unspent focus points gives him +1 Armor (ARM) against all attacks. This stays in effect until the focus points are spent or until the beginning of your next maintenance phase.

Point Costs(pg. 29): A model's point cost indicates how many *army points* you must spend to include one of these models, or in the case of units, one basic unit, in your army. Some entries also include options to spend additional points for upgrades, typically in the form of adding more troopers to a unit.

Point of Impact(pg. 47): The point over which an area-of effect attack's template is centered. If the target model suffers a direct hit, center the template over that model. If an area-of-effect attack misses, its point of impact deviates.

Power (POW), (pg. 26): The base amount of damage a weapon inflicts. Add a weapon's POW stat to its damage roll.

Power Attack(pg. 41): A type of special attack useable by warjacks. A warjack can use its combat action to make one power attack instead of making any other attacks. A warjack must spend a focus point to make a power attack. Power attacks cannot be made after a charge.

Power Field(pg. 53): Warcaster Armor creates a magical field that surrounds and protects the warcaster from damage that would rend a normal man to pieces. A warcaster's damage capacity actually represents the power field's protection. The warcaster can use focus points to regenerate damage done to the power field. A warcaster's unspent focus points *overboost* his power field, giving him increased protection.

Power plus Strength (P+S), (pg. 26): A melee weapon adds both the weapon's POW stat and the model's STR stat to the damage roll. For quick reference, the P+S value provides the sum of these two stats.

Push(pg. 44): A type of power attack. A successful push forces the target back 1".

Rallying(pg. 48): A fleeing model or unit can make a command check after its mandatory movement if in formation with its leader or in a warcaster's command range. If it passes the command check, the model or unit rallies and turns to face its nearest opponents—

this ends its activation, but it may function normally next turn.

Range (RNG), (pg. 26): The maximum distance in inches a model can make ranged attacks with a specific weapon or spell. Measure range from the nearest edge of the attacking model's base to the nearest edge of the target model's base.

Ranged Attack(pg. 44): An attack with a ranged weapon. A ranged attack can be declared against any target in *line of sight*, subject to the *targeting* rules. A model *in melee*, either engaged or engaging, cannot make ranged attacks.

Ranged Attack (RAT), (pg. 25): A model's accuracy with ranged weapons such as guns and crossbows, or thrown items like grenades and knives. Add a model's RAT value to its ranged attack rolls.

Ranged Attack Roll(pg. 45): Determine a ranged attack's success by making a ranged attack roll. Roll 2d6 and add the attacking model's Ranged Attack (RAT). An attack hits if the attack roll equals or exceeds the target's Defense (DEF).

Ranged Combat(pg. 44): A model is participating in ranged combat if it is making or receiving ranged attacks.

Ranged Weapon(pg. 44): A ranged weapon is one that can make an attack at a distance beyond melee range. Examples include rifles, flamethrowers, crossbows, harpoon guns, and mortars. A warjack's ranged weapons are generally mounted in place of an arm. A ranged weapon's damage roll is 2d6+POW.

Rate of Fire (ROF), (pg. 26, 45): The maximum number of ranged attacks a specific weapon can make in a turn. Reloading time limits most ranged weapons to only one attack per turn.

Reach Weapon(pg. 39): A model with a reach weapon has a melee range of 2" for attacks with that weapon. A model that possesses a reach weapon and another melee weapon can *engage* and attack an opponent up to 2" away with its reach weapon, but its other weapons can only be used to attack models within its normal 1/2" melee range.

Reactivate(pg. 51): A warcaster in base-to-base contact with an inert warjack may reactivate it. To reactivate the jack, the warcaster must forfeit its action this turn, but may still cast spells and use special abilities. The inert warjack reactivates at the beginning of its next turn and can function normally.

Regenerate Power Field(pg. 54): A warcaster can spend a focus point to regenerate his power field. Each focus point spent in this manner removes one damage point.

Rough terrain(pg. 59): Terrain that can be traversed, but at a significantly slower pace than open terrain. Examples include thick brush, rocky areas, murky bogs, shallow water, and deep snow. So long as any part of its base is in rough terrain, a model moves at 1/2 normal movement rate. Therefore, a model in rough terrain actually moves only 1/2" for every 1" of its movement used.

Running(pg. 35): A running model may move up to twice its SPD in inches. A model that runs cannot perform an action, cast spells, or use *feats* this turn. A running model's activation ends at the completion of its movement.

Scenario(pg. 31): A game with specific setup instructions and victory conditions.

Skill Check(pg. 38): A special action may require a skill check to determine its success. Roll 2d6—if the result is equal to or less than the skill value, the special action succeeds and its results are applied immediately. If the roll is greater than the model's skill value, the special action fails.

Skill Value(pg. 39): The number that a model must roll equal to or less than in order to successfully use its skill.

Skirmish Formation(pg. 36): The default and most flexible formation, which lets troopers be up to 3" apart. A unit must begin the game with all of its members in skirmish formation or closer.

Slam(pg. 41): A type of power attack that combines a model's movement and combat action to make a slam attack.

Slam Attack(pg. 41): A warjack that attempts a slam and enters 1/2" melee range with its intended target makes a slam attack if it moved at least 3". A slam attack roll suffers a −2 penalty against a target with an equal- or smaller-sized base, or a −4 penalty against a target with a larger base. If the slam attack hits, the target gets propelled directly away from its attacker, knocked down, and takes damage.

Slam Damage(pg. 42): Determine slam damage after the target's slam movement finishes. A slam's damage roll is 2d6 plus the attacking warjack's STR. Add an additional die to the damage roll if the model collides with a terrain feature or with a model that has an equal- or larger-sized base. Slam damage can be *boosted*. The slammed model is also knocked down.

Small Base(pg. 27): A 30mm base.

Solo(pg. 25): An independent warrior model that operates alone.

Soul(pg. 50): A living model has a soul. Certain models can claim a model's soul, represented by a soul token, when it is removed from play. If more than one model is eligible to claim its soul, the model nearest the destroyed model receives the soul token.

Soul Token(pg. 50): A model that claims a destroyed model's soul receives a soul token. Refer to a model's special rules for how it utilizes soul tokens.

Special Action (★Action), (pg. 38): A special action lets a model perform an *action* normally unavailable to other models. A model can perform a special action instead of its *combat action* if it meets the specific requirements for its use. Some special actions require a *skill check* to determine their success. Unless otherwise noted, a model can perform a special action only after advancing or forfeiting its movement. A special action's description details its requirements and results.

Special Attack (★Attack), (pg. 48): A special attack gives a model an attack option normally unavailable to other models. Warjacks can also make a variety of punishing power attacks. A model may make one special attack instead of making any normal melee or ranged attacks during its combat action if it meets the specific requirements for its use.

Special Effect(pg. 51): Many attacks cause special effects in addition to causing damage. There are four categories of effects: automatic effects, critical effects, continuous effects, and cloud effects.

Special Rules(pg.26): Unique rules pertaining to a model or its weapons which take precedence over the standard rules. Depending on their use, special rules are categorized as abilities, feats, special actions, special attacks, or orders.

Speed (SPD): A model's normal movement rate. A model moves its SPD stat in inches when *advancing*.

Stats(pg. 25): Short for statistic. Used in reference to model or weapon statistics.

Stat Bar(pg. 25): The stat bar presents model and weapon statistics in an easy-to-reference format.

Stat Card(pg. 25): A model or unit's stat card provides a quick in-game reference for its profile and special rules.

Stationary Target(pg. 49): A stationary target is a model that has been *knocked down* or immobilized, or an inanimate object. A stationary target cannot move or perform actions, cast spells, use feats, give orders, engage other models, or make attacks. A stationary warcaster can allocate focus points to his warjacks and upkeep spells. A stationary warjack can receive focus points and a stationary *channeler* can channel spells. A melee attack against a stationary target automatically hits. A stationary target has a base Defense (DEF) of 5 against all ranged and magic attacks.

Steamjack(pg. 24): A mechanikal construct given the ability to reason by a cortex housed within its hull.

Strength (STR), (pg. 25): A model's physical strength. Add a model's STR value to the *damage roll* of its melee weapons.

Structure(pg. 61): Any large terrain feature that can be damaged and destroyed.

GLOSSARY

System Boxes(pg. 51): Warjacks have damage boxes that are also system boxes, labeled with a letter denoting what component of the model they represent.

System Status Box(pg. 51): When all system boxes for a specific system have been marked, mark its system status box to show that it is *disabled*.

Terrain(pg. 59): The type of ground, either open, rough, or impassible.

Terrain feature(pg. 59): A natural or man-made object on the battlefield.

Terrifying Entity(pg. 57): A terrifying entity is one with either the *terror* or *abomination* special ability. A model *in melee* with an enemy that causes terror, or within 3" of an abomination—friendly or enemy—must pass a command check or flee. Make this command check after the active model or unit completes it movement, before it performs any actions.

Throw(pg. 43): A type of power attack. A successful throw attack sends its target flying, causes damage, and knocks it down.

Throw Damage(pg. 43): Determine throw damage after resolving where the thrown model lands. A throw's damage roll is 2d6 plus the STR of the attacking warjack. Add an additional die to the damage roll if the model collides with an obstruction or with a model that has an equal- or larger-sized base. Throw damage can be *boosted*. The thrown model is also knocked down. (pg 33)

Tight Formation(pg. 36): Troopers that form up shoulder-to-shoulder are in tight formation. These troopers must be in base-to-base contact, or as close as the actual models allow, and all must share the same facing. The tight formation must be at least two troopers wide, and can have any number of additional ranks. Troopers that begin their activation in tight formation cannot run or charge.

Totaled Warjack(pg. 51): A warjack is destroyed or totaled when all of its damage boxes are marked. Remove a totaled warjack from play and replace it with a totaled wreck marker corresponding to its base size. Any continuous effects or spells on a warjack instantly expire when it is totaled. A totaled warjack may not be repaired.

Totaled Wreck Marker(pg. 51): Remove a totaled warjack from play and replace it with a totaled wreck marker corresponding to its base size. A totaled wreck provides *cover* and counts as *rough terrain* for movement.

Turn Order(pg.32): The order in which players take their turns each game round, starting with the first player.

Trooper(pg. 24): A warrior model such as a soldier, rifleman, or mechanik that operates in groups called units.

Unaware Model(pg. 48): A model is unaware of any models that begin and end their activation entirely in its back arc. A back strike gives a +2 bonus to the attack roll of any attack made against an unaware model from its *back arc*.

Unit(pg.24): A unit is a group of similarly trained and equipped trooper models that operate together as a single force. A unit usually contains one leader and two or more additional troopers.

Upkeep Spell(pg. 55): An upkeep spell remains in play if the warcaster who cast it allocates a focus point to it during his control phase.

Warcaster(pg. 24): A warcaster is a tremendously powerful sorcerer, warpriest, or battlemage with the ability to telepathically control a group of warjacks.

Warjack(pg. 24): A warjack is a steamjack built expressly to wage war.

Warriors(pg. 24): Warcasters, troops, and solos are collectively referred to as warriors.

Weapon System: Any warjack system capable of being used to make attacks.

Victory Points(pg. 31): Every model and unit is worth a set number of victory points. Award a model's or unit's victory points to the player or team that removes it from play or causes it to flee off the table.

TEMPLATES

PHOTOCOPY THESE TEMPLATES FOR PERSONAL USE

MODELING
WARMACHINE™

The crown jewel of the Iron Kingdoms, Cygnar is the birthplace of warjack technology. They are the progressive leaders of every industry, be it arcane or mundane. Disciplined, inventive, steadfast, unfaltering—these are the core traits of the Cygnaran people, and it is why they have triumphed over every resentful adversary defiling their borders throughout the ages.

The symbol of Cygnar is the golden Cygnus—a regal swan of ancient mythology. Legend tells that the Cygnus led the first king of Cygnar to the site where Caspia stands today—a city that has never been held by any but Caspians, even during the Orgoth rule.

Standard Cygnaran military colors are vivid blue with gold trim, blue representing the sky, the surrounding sea, and the freedom of these elements. Throughout history, the exact tone of blue has ranged from indigo to a light, storm-cloud grey. Under some regimes, uniforms and paint schemes have also been dominated by black or white, but always with the golden trim.

COMMANDER COLEMAN STRYKER AND CAPTAIN VICTORIA HALEY—CYGNAR'S FINEST WARCASTERS.

IRONCLAD (HEAVY WARJACK) SHOWN WITH A CYGNARAN WAR BANNER.

Commander Stryker and a veteran Ironclad from his first battlegroup. Note the darker 'midnight-blue' color scheme, abandoned in favor of the modern primary blue, when King Leto Raelthorne seized control of the Cygnaran throne in 596 AR.

LANCER (LIGHT WARJACK)

the mix. Once you've got a flat base color, the highlights go on easily—just follow the edges of the armor plates.

The next step is to add the deep wine color that contrasts with the white armor. If you were neat with your body color, all of the areas that are going to be red, should still be black from the undercoat. If your brush strays a little (as is inevitable) you should take the time to go back and re-paint in black, as this will create the definition between the white and red areas.

I mix a deep red color from a strong red such as Red Gore or Vallejo Red and a spot of black. I also add a little red ink to give some extra depth. Since this is a fairly deep color, it should cover over the black rather easily—I only require one coat. For the highlight mix, I add a little more red and then a spot of white; this starts to get a little pink, but as long as you keep the highlights small, the overall effect will be deep red.

The warcasters are generally painted in the same colors are the warjacks. I generally paint the robes off-white and use deep red and gold as contrast colors. There are some great opportunities to really go to town on the warcasters and some of the troops; the large flat areas on the robes and cloaks beg for some extra decoration, and it's that sort of richness that fits the ceremonial feel of the miniatures perfectly. The Scrutator is a great example of this—look at how the simple addition of some patterning has given the whole miniature a sumptuous, decorative feel. And while it looks like it to would be difficult to achieve, it's actually easier than you might imagine. The patterns are added in a lighter shade of the base color, mixed as you would for a mid-tone highlight. I use a good quality size 00 brush and ensure my paint is at the right consistency to flow smoothly onto the surface. Then I paint on fairly random swirling, spiraling shapes, trying to be neat but working quickly. You might have to have a few practice tries at it, but you'll be surprised how easy it is. The main thing is to get the paint at just the right consistency and use a good brush with a fine point. Of course, this isn't the type of thing you should do on every miniature in your army, but it's worth spending a little more time on your Menite warcaster.

Useful Paint Colors

Games Workshop: Red Gore, Blood Red, Sunburst Yellow

Vallejo: Red, Carmine Red, Yellow

The largest challenge you're going to face when painting Khadoran troops is achieving a good, bright, flat, red color. At best, it's a difficult color to paint over large areas and achieve an even coat. It doesn't seem to be easier to get an even tone over a white undercoat, so I stay with the black, which makes it easier to apply the metallics and lends strength to the shading.

The base color I use is a mix of Red Gore and Vallejo Red. I thin this with red ink rather than water. It's definitely going to take you two or three coats to achieve a flat, even coverage, but it's worth persevering. With a flat color, you can keep the highlights simple and still end up with a great looking miniature. Just concentrate on keeping the paint application as neat as possible, thick enough to cover well, but sufficiently thin to flow smoothly.

I keep the highlights simple, using Blood Red mixed with yellow and then white. If the overall effect looks too pastel, glaze it over with red and yellow ink to revive some richness and depth. I keep the highlights towards the edges of the armor, leaving the main, flat areas in the basic body color.

Khadoran warcasters use the same red on their armor, coupled with rich, dark leathers and black for a striking color scheme. I prefer to paint their skin in pale tones, especially on the Butcher—I really wanted to give him an unsavory look! I started with a light colored skin tone, with just a spot of blue added to knock some of the warmth out of it, then I highlighted by adding white. I used a thinned down magenta to add some shading and a little blue round the eyes gives a deep sunken look; pure black eyes finish the effect. The head is made to stand out more by painting the fur collar in grey, shaded with black. Sorscha's color scheme is fairly similar, but she has more black details. This makes her pale face stand out even more than the Butcher's, especially when her face is framed with black hair and a fur hat.

Khador

Strong, bright red is the main color of the Khadoran forces. The warjacks are painted almost exclusively in this color and the warcasters frequently use it on their armor. This makes for striking battle groups.

Cryx

The armies of the Cryx are dark and brooding. Black iron armor is coupled with pale metallics, and the warjacks glow an evil green. Pale bone is a striking contrast to the dark metals.

STAGE 6
More white is added to the blue for the highlights

STAGE 7
Details are picked out with Brazen Brass

STAGE 8-9
Brass areas are highlighted with Gold

STAGE 10
Details are picked out with Gunmetal

BASING YOUR MINIATURE, STEP BY STEP

STAGE 1
White glue is painted on base, being careful not to get on the feet.

STAGE 2
The base is dipped in a shallow container of mixed grain sand until an even coverage is obtained.

Useful Paint Colors

Games Workshop: Boltgun Metal, Chainmail, Bleached Bone, Light Green

Vallejo: Black, White, Gold

Cryxian warjacks are slightly different to paint from the other factions, mainly because there is no main color used on the body—just different shades of metal, the main one being dark iron. The are a few different ways to get a really good dark iron color, but I have found the best is to start with a mix of Boltgun and black, then build up a couple of highlight layers with Boltgun and Chainmail. You can apply the highlights as you would when painting the body color of other warjacks, concentrating the lighter tones towards the edges of the armor, or you can apply the lighter shades with dry brushing. You really don't want to lighten the overall color too much—just enough to bring out the shape. When the highlights are dry, I add a slightly thinned wash of Tamiya Smoke—just as you would when painting the metal areas on other steamjacks—being careful to get even coverage with no patchiness. For a really dark effect, try adding black ink to the Smoke.

You don't want to paint the whole miniature in the same dark color. Vary the shade on the edging and some of the different shaped plates. This lends some really interesting effects. Use pale gold for some of the decoration, and sparingly use Smoke to take the warm edge off the color. The only strong color that is commonly used is the green for the glowing insides of the warjacks.

The warcasters use very much the same color palette. Dark iron and pale metallics with black or dirty brown clothing looks very effective when coupled with the pale skin of the war witch and the bleached skull of the Iron Lich.

Basing Your Miniatures

When you have finished painting your miniatures and the paint is thoroughly dry, the last stage is to finish off the base. While this process is pretty straightforward and quick, it's really worth putting a little thought into it. The way you base a particular miniature can make a difference between something that looks adequate and an effect that embodies the miniature's background and depth, substantially adding to the character of the model. Think about it—it's not really appropriate to have your mighty Cryxian force treading on fresh green grass—the ground should be scorched from the curse of the Dragon Lord's blight! Similarly, the bases of your Khadoran Juggernauts should suggest the wastes of the rime-swept Motherland.

Different settings and climates are easy to achieve with some pretty basic materials. The pictures on this page show how to model an effective broken terrain effect that can be altered subtly to suit the miniature. Just follow the stages shown, being mindful of avoiding flue on the painted miniature.

Once you've mastered this basic technique, you can alter the way you apply it for all sorts of different effects. Try painting glue over the surface in patches and sprinkling some baking soda over it and you've achieved a very realistic snow effect. Washing over the finished base with black and dark browns and then dry brushing with grays evokes a tortured landscape for the Cryxian miniatures. More static grass lends a lush finish, while less will make the base look rocky and parched; leaving the grass off completely and painting the base in red-brown tones achieves an even more desert-like finish. Don't be afraid to experiment. You'll be sure to find some great effects to suit the miniatures you're bringing to life!

STAGE 3
The sand is left to dry thoroughly and then given a coat of dark brown ink

STAGE 4
The sand is drybrushed with mid brown and then bone to bring out the texture.

STAGE 5
White glue is painted on in patches and static grass is firmly pressed into place.

STAGE 6
the static grass is drybrushed with bone when dry and the sides of the base are painted black to neaten the finish